"Greydon," she bit out. "This is improper."

Her tongue swiped over her bottom lip, and she felt him tense behind her. Her brow furrowed, but then she realized that he could see her in the reflection of the window...just as she could see him. In the shadowed gloom and the flickering bursts of candlelight, he looked like a dangerously mystical creature behind her—a beast from the myths of old come to claim the virgin on offer. Not that *she* was on offer. *Heavens, Vesper, stop.*

She moistened her lips again, and she could have sworn he growled. His face was so strained, he looked pained or furious, though that could be a distortion of the glass.

"Rules of conduct are in place for a reason," she said, her voice sounding much too breathy for comfort. "I depend on them to act accordingly."

"No one is here to judge."

"*We're* here," she said, her eyes glued to his in the windowpane. "I am unmarried and you are an unwed duke."

Greydon's gaze burned like a brand, and heat swept over her skin. "So?" he rasped.

Fall in love with Amalie Howard!

"Amalie Howard's books sit at the crossroads of history and herstory—Victorian romance, but with a dollop of strong women who take charge of their destinies…and as a result, who rescue the men in their orbit. Refreshing, steamy, and stocked with characters you don't normally get to see in the genre—her books are a must-read for me."

—Jodi Picoult, #1 *New York Times* bestselling author

"Amalie Howard tells a story with self-assured style, wit, and energy…her writing sparkles!"

—Lisa Kleypas, #1 *New York Times* bestselling author

"The fresh voice historical romance needs right now.…I will read every word she writes."

—Kerrigan Byrne, *USA Today* bestselling author

Never Met A Duke Like You

"Howard pairs unconventional aristocrats in this page-turning Victorian romance. Admirable and progressive protagonists and *Clueless*-inspired plot are sure to have readers charmed."

—*Publishers Weekly*

"Howard gives readers main characters with intriguing layers and relatable flaws to cheer for as they navigate the peaks and valleys of their reunion love story, gradually unveiling each character's thoughts, fears, and feelings along the way."

—The Romance Dish

Always Be My Duchess

"A dreamy summer romance designed to sweep you up into a world of ballerinas, hunky dukes, cheeky girl gangs, and delicious sex scenes. Light on angst and heavy on charm, it's a feel-good read of the highest order."

—*Entertainment Weekly*

"The story slayed me from page one." —*Paste Magazine*

"Howard creates great characters and dialogue... A real treat."

—*Library Journal*

"Howard's lyrical writing enlivens her bright, empathetic characters and her sharp eye on their class and cultural disparities only enhances their romance. Readers will be riveted."

—*Publishers Weekly*

"Fabulous writing... such a delicious escape. Utterly delightful!"

—Eloisa James, *New York Times* bestselling author

NEVER
MET A
DUKE
LIKE YOU

Also by Amalie Howard

Always Be My Duchess

NEVER MET A DUKE LIKE YOU

AMALIE HOWARD

A Taming of the Dukes Novel

FOREVER

NEW YORK BOSTON

Cover design by Daniela Medina

Forever
Hachette Book Group
1290 Avenue of the Americas, New York, NY 10104
read-forever.com
@readforeverpub

Originally published in trade paperback and ebook by
Grand Central Publishing in November 2023
First Mass Market Edition: August 2024

ISBN: 9781538737743 (mass market), 9781538737736 (ebook)

Printed in the United States of America

BVGM

10 9 8 7 6 5 4 3 2 1

Content Guidance

The discussion of mental illness, the Lunacy Acts of the second half of the nineteenth century, and treatment within lunatic asylums are part of an underlying plot thread in this novel. There are also some scenes that may be disturbing to some readers, in which the hero's father is physically abused and intentionally drugged by his caretakers in a mental asylum, leading to his eventual death. There is some conversational reference to sex workers in the Victorian era as well as their appearance in a gentleman's club. In keeping with the conventions of this era, words like *jades*, *courtesans*, *light-skirts*, and *Cyprians* are used, and I have tried my best to keep these both authentic and sex positive within context. Intimate scenes are described in chapters 11, 17, 18, and 23, and in the epilogue. Some offensive language is used in the narration as well as in dialogue.

For all who march to their own beat

Chapter One

Lady Vesper Lyndhurst marched through the garden, wrenching the petals from a daisy though she had yet to end up with an answer other than *he loves me not*. She flung the mutilated flower to the ground and crushed it with her bootheel for good measure. It was a silly child's game that had no meaning whatsoever.

Flowers couldn't tell a person if someone loved them.

Look at what happened to poor Marguerite in *Faust*. She'd succumbed to a *he loves me* petal and was seduced by a devilish sinner who left her high and dry with child. Vesper shuddered to imagine where such a scandal would lead her. She would be ruined, and her family would be shamed.

Not that Vesper didn't love the *idea* of love *for other people*—she adored seeing her friends happy and was quite good at playing matchmaker. So good, in fact, that her bosom friend Briar had nicknamed her Cupidella. A smile touched Vesper's lips as she ducked under a twisting bough that snatched the untied bonnet from her hair and tossed it into the wind. She let it fly.

Secretly, she rather liked the name. After all, she'd earned it, with not one, not two, but *three* love matches to her credit.

Three, because she was counting the Duke of Montcroix, who had just married a charming French ballerina after a scandalous arrangement that had been too delicious for words. Vesper hadn't *technically* orchestrated their happy ending, though she had been the one to practically push Nève into the duke's arms and convince him to go after the woman of his dreams. Even if she hadn't had a *direct* hand in it, she still counted them as a win.

Dukes, of course, were a generally easy lot when it came to matchmaking. They might need a good shove in the right direction, and spend their youth frittering away their inheritances, but dukes were expected to marry. And while the shining pinnacle of her matchmaking efforts was certainly Laila and Marsden, her latest coup was an upstairs-downstairs affair between Evans, the Duke of Montcroix's footman, and her own cousin, Georgina.

A small sigh escaped Vesper's lips. She'd seen the two glancing at each other and it had required only a nudge or four to set things in motion. Sometimes a couple needed a helping hand to find their way. A tiny worry gnawed at the edge of her mind—upstairs and downstairs matches weren't de rigueur. Evans might have been pretty, but he was certainly lacking in worldly experience, and her cousin wasn't much wiser either, which meant, unfortunately, they'd had to rush to the altar with a baby on the way.

That had been a small tarnish on her matchmaking reputation.

When Vesper had made the announcement of the wedding during their monthly ladies' afternoon tea, her friends—Laila, Nève, Effie, and Briar, the Hellfire Kitties as Vesper had fondly nicknamed them, much to Laila's dismay—had been shocked and quick to air their concerns about expenses and babies, and whether Georgina and Evans would prevail.

It was the first time her friends had treated her as if she'd done something troublesome by bringing a couple together, and their disapproval had lodged itself deep. She was not accustomed to having her efforts criticized, yet she could see some merit to their argument. Perhaps next time, she would try to keep her efforts within her own circles.

Vesper reached out to pluck another daisy and wrenched the petals from the stem. *He loves her, he loves her not. He loves her... he loves her... not.*

Heavens, even the bloody daisy was judging her!

Paying more attention to the mangled flower in her hand than to where her footsteps led her, Vesper let out a muffled shriek as she nearly tumbled over a low wall of crumbling stone. Her directionless journey had led her to the abandoned neighboring estate. The castle in the distance was limned by the descending sun, giving it an eerie, almost otherworldly glow. She frowned, taking in the neatly tidy grounds. For a property neglected for such a long time by its owners, the gardens seemed well-kept.

A memory of a dark-haired boy roaring from the ramparts arose.

Vesper shoved the thought of *him* away.

Once upon an absurd time, she'd imagined them declaring a grand love for each other, combining their estates, and living happily ever after. But Aspen had scorned her terribly with his cold rejection at her come-out, crushing her heart and every one of her hopes into dust. The affection she'd so carefully treasured crumbled to ash, and she'd locked her fragile, broken heart away forever after.

In moments of silly nostalgic weakness, she had thought of the boy who'd been her first love, but those moments were few and *far* between. Her best friends knew of the heartbreak, of course, but none of them would dream of mentioning him. At least not without *dreadful* consequences!

Vesper hesitated for a moment and then hopped over the wall. A feeling of uncommon daring overtook her as she strolled through the tidy garden paths, not encountering a single soul. Shouldn't there be at least a gardener or a groom about so she could announce her presence? Then again, it wasn't like any of them would care whether the girl from the neighboring estate was wandering through the hedgerows.

You're trespassing.

She ignored that thought, too. Perfect, poised Vesper Lyndhurst never broke the rules and never did anything untoward. But it wasn't as though the family was at home and Greydon certainly wasn't at the estate.

Considering the dwindling number of dukes, most of London remained on constant tenterhooks wondering if and when the esoteric duke would return from his travels, but Greydon remained conspicuously absent from both town and his ancestral seat. His dazzling, influential mother, however, ruled the ton with a diamond-studded fist.

Vesper squashed the twinge in her belly at the notion of running into him after so long. It'd been years since she'd laid eyes on him. He would look different now, no longer the tall, gangly youth with bent spectacles and the crooked grin she remembered. He'd worn his deep brown curls flopped onto his wide brow back then, and his singular brown eyes were always focused on the text of some thick book. His eyes would forever make her think of the tiger's eye gemstone he'd shown her from his father's collection of rarities.

Was Greydon even still alive?

Vesper hadn't seen an obituary, and her father would have said something if the estate had been taken over by a new duke. She had gathered from accounts in the newssheets over the years as well as tidbits from her papa that the duke led archaeological digs and conservationist efforts into areas of the world that no aristocrat would dare enter. She'd read that he had built wells with his bare hands while unearthing monstrous fossils in some obscure part of the west in America.

Although a part of her admired him for his courage to venture off and follow his passion, Vesper thought about his responsibilities here in England.

Not that she was worried about him or *his* marital future. The Duke of Greydon wasn't her problem, even if she could find a lady who would enjoy stepping out with a man who likely embodied the ossified skeletons he so loved. Any man who preferred dead fossils to people had to be a complete bore.

Chuckling under her breath, Vesper hitched her skirts and hopped over the wall, hissing when her ankle caught the ragged edge of a stone. Peering down, she caught a hint of red against her white silk stocking. It seemed to be a small scrape, nothing for her to cry over. Though perhaps that was a sign it was time for her to turn back. The hour was growing late in any case, and she could smell the threat of rain on the evening breeze.

Tilting her face up to the sky, she saw it had shifted into tones of gilded crimson and blushing purple, and a few ominous storm clouds had gathered overhead. She tugged her pelisse around her shoulders, glad she'd worn the thing, and wondered if she'd make it back to Lyndhurst Park before the rain.

Lightning flashed in answer.

Well, that couldn't be good.

She glanced behind her toward her home and squinted, then turned back to the castle that was a dozen lengths away. Rain showers in the country were frequent—the little squalls came hard and fast—and, given how far she'd trespassed, she'd be drenched to the bone if she made for her own residence now. She didn't mind a bit of rain, but those incoming thunderclouds looked very angry.

Mind made up, she hiked her skirts and raced toward the looming turrets of Greydon Abbey. Glancing overhead, she caught sight of the towers of the north wing, a flash of lightning illuminating what looked to be a face in one of the narrow upper windows. A man's face. The *duke's* face. In the next second, it was gone. Vesper blinked. Her imagination was working overtime, considering she'd just been thinking about him.

Feeling the first of several large drops splash onto her bare head—in hindsight, she should have retrieved her bonnet—a feminine shout reached her ears, and she veered in that direction.

"Quickly, my lady!" the woman urged from the kitchen entrance. The minute she crossed the threshold, the deluge began in earnest, coming down in a thick white sheet that obscured her vision.

"Goodness, that storm came out of nowhere," Vesper panted, pleased to see her rescuer was Mrs. Dempsey, the Greydon Abbey housekeeper. The woman had always had a kind word for a younger, much too impulsive, and very talkative Vesper.

"Sweet April showers do spring May flowers, my lady," the housekeeper said with a warm smile. "I seem to recall you dancing in the rain with fairy wreaths in your hair and galoshes on your feet proclaiming the same."

The memory was fleeting but Vesper let out a puff of laughter, staring through the archway at the tempest in the courtyard currently creating quite a pond and tiny rivers on the cobbled stone. That loud, impatient, free-spirited girl was long gone…buried under countless hours of decorum and drilled-in etiquette.

She removed her damp pelisse and shook it out. "Alas, there's nothing sweet about that, Mrs. Dempsey. *That* is a monsoon that will drown any flowers in its path!"

"Let's get you some hot tea while you get dry, shall we, my lady?"

"Is Greydon here?" she asked, remembering the face she thought she'd imagined in the north tower.

"No, my lady. His Grace is not in residence. Hasn't been for some time. Though we have had word that he is in London." Vesper's breath hitched. Since when?

She'd spent most of the little season at Lyndhurst Park in Dorset. Surely her father would have said something, but he'd been busy with his work in Parliament.

The housekeeper let out a small sigh, a slightly doleful expression on her face as if she'd given up hope that the master of the house would ever return to the ducal seat. It had been an age. *Not*, of course, that Vesper was keeping track.

She turned, taking notice of the servants who were standing at attention around a table laden with what was obviously their supper. "Oh, please, do not trouble yourself on my behalf. This storm will pass soon and then I shall be on my way, Mrs. Dempsey."

"It's no trouble, my lady." She flicked a hand and one of the maids disappeared.

After the staff bobbed in unison and resumed their seats, Mrs. Dempsey ushered Vesper into a sitting room where the fallow hearth had been hastily lit. Vesper rubbed her arms as a chill sank into her bones and the rain pelted against the windowpanes in sheets. With the howl of a rabid beast on the prowl, the wind picked up and reminded Vesper her predicament could be much worse.

In moments, Mrs. Dempsey returned with a tea tray, which included a few plain neatly cut sandwiches and sweet tea cakes. With a sigh of happiness, Vesper sipped the hot tea, feeling it warm her insides and then glanced up at the kindly housekeeper.

"Thank you, Mrs. Dempsey. Please don't let me keep you from your supper. I will be fine. This tea is all I need. And besides, I well know my way around this house, and I can let myself out once the rain slows. Do not worry about me."

The woman frowned, as though unsure, but then gave a brisk nod. "If you need anything—"

"I will call for you," Vesper said with a smile. "I promise."

After a second cup of tea and several of the sandwich bits, the rain showed no sign of lessening, and Vesper felt restlessness stir. Sitting here eating alone felt uncomfortable. She wrapped the remainder of the cut cold chicken and egg salad sandwiches along with two of the cakes in a napkin and stood. Her legs were stiff and aching. Perhaps a brisk walk would help. There was no one in the adjacent hallway, although she heard the quiet rumble of other servants from some not-too-distant location.

Munching on a simple but tasty triangle of fresh bread and crushed hard-boiled egg, she walked through the dimly lit foyer, noticing there was only a single candelabra illuminated. Grabbing the candlestick, she ambled into the gallery beyond, the light just enough to see the portraits that hung in their gilded frames. She paused in front of one that showed the duke as a boy with his parents.

Her heart gave an odd lurch. Dressed in a fitted coat with white breeches, Greydon had tied his long hair away from his face in a queue, but those wayward curls could not be tamed and sprang free to dance upon his temples. He was smiling in the portrait, the gleam of mischief visible in those singular brown eyes. Arrogance was stamped on that proud brow, innocence in the curve of his cheek...a boy on the precipice of becoming a man.

Her best friend and first love. Then her sworn, mortal enemy.

How things had changed.

"Hide-and-seek is a game for children, and I am a *man*," he'd told her one summer afternoon when she'd jumped out from her clever hiding place in the garden's hedgerows. "Go play with Judith."

Stung, Vesper had bristled at the mention of his mother's new ward who'd arrived from America six months earlier, not because she didn't like the girl, but because the dolt had had the audacity to lump her in with a *child* five years her junior. Judith was seven, for heaven's sake!

"She's a baby."

"I am not a baby!" Vesper remembered Judith shrieking. She and Aspen had both yelled in unison for Judith to go away. Vesper had felt a pang at the girl's tearful expression as she'd run inside, but she had bigger fish to fry. Namely, her supposed best friend who was suddenly too big for his stupid britches.

"One year at Eton and already you're too good for everyone?"

Brown eyes had flashed with ire behind his new spectacles—fancy wire-rimmed ones that made him seem older. It was the first time Vesper remembered thinking that Aspen had looked unfairly winsome, and the tiniest wing of a butterfly had brushed her untried heart.

Until he'd opened his mouth anyway. "You cannot be traipsing after me willy-nilly, sniffing at my bootheels like a sad little mongrel!"

The butterfly had died an instant, horrible death. "I am *not* a dog! You take that back, you pompous, bloody bird-witted *ass*, you take that back right now!"

"Or what?"

She hadn't given it much thought until her fingers had curled into a fist of their own accord, and she'd punched upward and struck him right in the nose. Her former best friend had toppled head over heels. His new glasses had gone flying and the blood had fountained everywhere, gushing like an old broken pipe.

She had been mortified, as usual acting without thinking, but Aspen had been even more so, especially when his mother—the most perfect duchess in existence—had arrived in the midst of the commotion on the heels of a sniffling Judith. The duchess's soft mellifluous concern had echoed through the courtyard and Vesper had instantly burst into tears at being caught brawling like a hoyden. She hadn't even been able to do much other than bite the inside of her cheek to stop her sobs when Aspen had refused to look at her, his humiliation complete.

To be bloodied by a girl two years younger? Oh, the disgrace of it!

Vesper pinned her lips between her teeth, remembering how devastated and sorry she'd been. She'd written him countless unanswered letters, been turned away at the door by a younger and saddened Mrs. Dempsey, and then Aspen had left for his second year at Eton. Their childhood friendship had taken an irreparable turn after that.

Over the years after his father died, she'd heard gossip from the servants that the young duke was in residence, though he rarely stayed in Dorset for long. And he never called upon her, no matter how much she wished and wished he would. He, Judith, and the duchess seemed to prefer the air at their residence in Brighton.

His return to London coincided with Vesper's first season, and the nineteen-year-old Duke of Greydon, all grown up, serious, and debonair, had set all the debutante hearts aflutter. Hers included.

Vesper had already been declared an Original and the

season's catch, but her sentimental heart had always secretly pined for the boy she'd once adored. However, the solemn duke had been unfailingly polite when they'd finally come face-to-face at her come-out, and after a cool, impersonal inspection of her person, he'd turned away without even requesting a dance.

A ruthless cut direct.

The slight had not gone unnoticed, especially by the other debutantes vying for his attention, and *nothing* could have stung more. Crushed and heartbroken, his callous dismissal had been a declaration of war. In response, Vesper had gone out of her way to ignore him for the entirety of the season.

The scandal sheets had had a field day.

The season's most eligible bachelor shunned. The season's loveliest lady ignored.

Stifling the annoying ache at the still-raw memory, Vesper wandered down another hallway and climbed a set of steps that led to the upper level of the residence where the private library and music room she'd loved were situated. Perhaps it had been the best for everyone that Greydon had left England not long after the whole debacle. For her, especially.

No matter. That was a long time ago and she was no longer an easily wounded girl.

Upstairs, the carpets were plush, the ballroom floor polished and shiny. Although no one knew when the duke would be back from his travels, the servants kept the place spotless as if expecting his return any day. It was common knowledge that the dowager duchess never came to Dorset. She spent her time between London and Brighton while the ancestral seat of the Duke of Greydon sat in melancholy disregard.

Vesper couldn't imagine why. It had so much history. Her fingers trailed over the pianoforte's ivory keys in the music room. She'd played it so many times during her childhood.

She and Greydon used to make up ditties and perform for the servants. Vesper huffed a laugh, playing a chord and hearing the echoes of the categorically terrible shanties in her head. She supposed her memories of the duke weren't *all* bad.

After leaving the music room, her exploration took her to the west wing—and the private ducal apartments—where an odd sound like a thump caught her attention. Perhaps she'd imagined it. But then she heard it again. The hairs on the back of her nape rose.

Goodness, was it a rat?

"Hullo?" she said into the first bedchamber, and then laughed at herself. As if a rat would answer. She breached the threshold and waited, holding her breath as if the lord of the manor would magically appear and demand to know why she was invading his private space. But despite the immaculate nature of the chamber, it was obvious by the slightly musty smell that no one had occupied it for some time. Her shoulders relaxed a smidge.

A distant rumble made her frown. That might have been thunder.

Curious now, she strained her ears, but there was nothing more. Old houses made strange noises all the time, and besides, she should not be in here anyway. This was where the duke slept…when he was in residence, which he was clearly not.

Still, it was untoward of her to trespass. Propriety was everything, after all. And she'd spent years refining herself until she'd learned exactly how to present her face, her body, and her mind so that there would never be any indication of the maelstrom that swirled inside.

Unless she was with her friends—they appreciated the spark and energy that burned within her and loved her as she was.

She left the room, then peered out a window in the corridor overlooking the courtyard and noticed that the sky was lightening. *Finally.* She was retracing her footsteps to the staircase when she heard the strange muffled thump again like something being dragged across a floor. Above. That definitely *wasn't* thunder! She peered upward to the ceiling, a hand to her chest, ears alert.

Surely there wouldn't be any danger in a ducal residence? Besides, the servants were just belowstairs. One scream and they'd come running. Sucking in a breath, she went against her instincts to flee and crept along a tapered corridor with a staircase at the end. The sound, though dulled, was clearer now. There was another floor above. A sprawling old attic in this tower, if she recalled correctly.

She pinned her lips. Perhaps she should call for help rather than venture up there herself. But then it might be nothing but a marauding rodent and she would look the fool. Maybe just a quick looksee then. The candelabra was heavy. If worse came to worst, she would have protection, if indeed the face she'd seen in the window was actually real.

Creeping down the narrow passageway that led to the attic, she huffed a breath before pushing open the absurdly heavy door. Honestly, who still used doors made of iron? Her brain registered three things before a furious roar of *Hold it open!* met her ears and she let go of the massive door in a fright and heard it slam shut behind her.

One, she was not alone.

Two, the face she'd seen had most definitely been real.

And three, the Duke of Greydon was very much in residence.

Chapter Two

"Devil take it!"

Aspen Drake, the Duke of Greydon, palmed his nape and swore a blue streak in frustration. He should have been waiting near the bloody door, but he'd been on the other end of the attic thinking about smashing a window so that he might climb out onto the cracked stone gable beyond. The gargoyle out there seemed solid enough to hold his weight even if the fascia was crumbling in places. Then perhaps someone would finally be able to hear his shouts for rescue.

If he didn't tumble to an ignominious death first.

By the time he'd heard the very welcome squeak of the door hinge and bolted across the width of the attic to secure the door, he'd been much too late and his frantic shout had gone unheeded. Barely an arm's length away, he watched in gut-clenching slow motion as the edge of the heavy door released from the tips of pale, elegant fingers and swung shut almost immediately. Instead of securing his escape, Aspen's fist pounded on hard, unyielding metal. One glimpse of blessed freedom and he was trapped once more. Only now he wasn't alone.

He lifted his glance to take in the shocked features of the woman who had entered in a fragrant waft of spring rain and freshly tilled earth. Her small palm was lifted toward him as if she'd expected him to collide with her. A small crease marred her brow, pink lips parted in stunned surprise. But it was the eyes that pierced him—those blazing lapis lazuli eyes that no amount of distance or time could erase from memory. He sucked in a breath, his chest tightening.

Curse his luck that it had to be her.

One Lady Vesper Lyndhurst…neighbor, beautiful heiress, and insufferable know-it-all with a fearsome uppercut. He resisted putting his fingertips to the slight bump on the bridge of his nose as a phantom ache settled there. It didn't miss his notice that she'd grown even more stunning, though absence—a nearly seven-year one at that—had a way of distorting perception. Lady Vesper had *always* been fetching. He rubbed a balled fist against his spasming chest and exhaled loudly.

"*Greydon?* Is that really you?" she whispered in a hushed voice.

"Yes. I'm not a ghost. It's truly me. In the flesh." Turning, he thumped his head backward on the door and groused at the ache reverberating through his skull. "God damn it!"

"I beg your pardon?" she said to him, blond brows shooting high at the coarse oath.

Aspen groaned as the reality of their predicament returned in full force. It wasn't *her* fault. It was bloody well his. He should have been glued to the deuced wall! "The door. Never mind. It's jammed for some reason and there's no way out from inside."

Blue eyes met his, widened, and swung back to the door without its inside lever. Her lips parted in disbelief. "Jammed?"

She wedged the tips of her free hand into the thin seam, not that he hadn't been doing that for hours, but the sodding thing had refused to budge. "There's no handle," he told her.

"I can see that," she said under her breath. "Where on earth is it?"

"How should I know?"

She spun. "Perhaps because you're *in* here?"

An accusatory gaze slammed into his, and Aspen threw his hands wide. "Don't look at me for answers. I had nothing to do with it going missing, and now you're stuck here just like me. That won't work by the way." He let out a sullen gust of air as she propped the candelabra on a nearby ledge. "Trust me, I've been here much longer than you and I have tried everything possible."

She peered at him over her shoulder, both hands now scrabbling for purchase she would not find, despite his warning. She'd always been stubborn. Aspen rolled his eyes, then glanced down at his own torn fingernails. She'd learn when those delicate fingertips were aching and bleeding. "How long *have* you been in here?" she asked in despair.

"Hours. I lost count when the rain set in and blocked out the sky."

Pausing, she sent him a look. "Did it occur to you to call for help, Your Grace?"

He shot her a glare that rivaled hers in intensity. "No, of course not. I sat here enjoying a spot of tea and crumpets while conversing with the charming dust motes about their hopes and dreams."

"No need to be sarcastic, Greydon."

"Then don't be obtuse."

She hissed through her teeth at him and went back to prodding at the doorjamb.

Her blond hair was coiled in a loose knot, though tendrils escaped all around her flushed face, and her blue walking dress was muddied at the hem. A muscle in his jaw leaped as he took in her face again—the promise of youth had been more than fulfilled, though he knew a spoiled and cold heart lurked beneath. She might be beautiful, but peel away the layers and there was nothing beneath them but vanity. Not that he should fault her for that he supposed, after all, she was just like his mother and most of the aristocracy.

"Lady Vesper," he said, his voice coming out harsher than he'd meant it to. "What are you doing here?"

She paused. "I was caught in the rain, so I sought shelter until it passed."

"Here?"

"Your house was closer than mine," she replied.

Aspen frowned. "Which meant you were on my property."

"On the boundary between our estates," she said with a sniff. "Your residence was closer, as I said. Besides, what does it matter? You were not at home."

"I am clearly at home," he countered.

Her eyes went skyward. "Not supposed to be here then. Even your housekeeper is unaware of your presence. Did you arrive in secret? Skulking around like a shadow who doesn't want to be seen?"

"At least I'm not trespassing."

"Good God, you're as intolerable as ever." She made a dismissive gesture. "Trust me, being soaked through would have been a much better alternative than being stuck here with you."

"You'll get no argument from me," he said.

With a growl of frustration, she aimed a kick at the solid oak door. Aspen saw her gaze sweep the dusty space, looking for something, anything, to break free of this room. It was no use. He'd already scoured every inch, and beyond piles of old books and trunks full of clothing, there was nothing he could use to bludgeon or lever the damn medieval slab of a door open. He'd shouted his voice raw for hours calling for help before realizing that the centuries-old, thick castle stone would deaden any sound.

"How did you know to come up here?" he asked her.

She ducked her head. "I happened to be on the floor below when I heard scratching."

"In my private apartments?" His brows shot high.

"Not exactly," she admitted, flushing. "Barely."

Aspen couldn't help the grin that curved his lips. "Let me guess. On the boundary? Standing on the threshold of decorum? You are renowned for toeing the line of propriety quite closely, Lady Vesper."

She closed her eyes as if struggling for patience. "I was simply lost and heard a noise."

"Greydon Abbey has not changed in three centuries and you've walked these halls many a time before. Yet you were lost?"

"Yes."

"That's reaching even for you, Viper." His old moniker for her made her eyes fly open and satisfaction poured through him, hot and gratifying.

"My name is Vesper."

"That's what I said."

A hint of a scowl marred the perfection of her features. "That is *not* what you said at all, Your Grace."

"Then that makes us both liars, doesn't it? You claimed to be lost in a castle you know as well as your own home and I called you by a name you seem to have conveniently forgotten."

"Goodness, we must find a way out or I will not be responsible for my actions." With a muffled oath, she hastened over to the narrow window, though that would be as discouraging as the door, he knew.

Aspen shoved a hand through the disheveled mess of his

hair. "I told you, my lady, I have tried everything, and you were the only one to hear me in nearly an entire day."

"You said hours," she gasped. "An entire *day*?"

"I arrived just before dawn from London and did not want to wake anyone. I came up here to look for an old document that I needed, only for that sodding block of a door to shut behind me. I've been stuck ever since."

"But the servants, they must tend to the rooms?" she said. "Surely someone will come."

"They weren't expecting me. If they had been, there would have been much more activity on the upper floors. Besides which, there's only a small staff here these days." In his absence, his mother had sacked nearly all the household servants. Funding her social calendar had been more important than paying them. Aspen stared at Vesper and lifted his bruised fists. "You were the only person to venture close."

"And now we're both trapped," she finished on a sigh. "Because of me."

He shrugged. "It wasn't your fault. The door is old and heavy, and I have no idea when or how the handle disappeared. You couldn't have known."

"There has to be a solution." Vesper whirled in a swirl of navy skirts, her pretty face determined. "We only have to find it."

Aspen stared at her. "Have at it."

"You won't help?"

"I have tried every which way to open that door, down to breaking my fingernails to the quick." He waggled them for emphasis. "I have bellowed my voice raw, pounded and kicked the floorboards, thrown things into the walls. I have thought about breaking and squeezing through a window."

She gave him a doubtful look at that. The windows were practically slits and there was a slim-to-none chance that he could fit through the opening. Frowning, she peered through the window beside her. "And if you were successful, fall to your death on the rocks below?"

"I don't enjoy tight spaces."

She laughed. "That's ironic. You go on digs all around the world collecting fossils from underground spaces much smaller than this room. Enlighten me, but isn't that what a bone hunter does?"

"Paleontologist is the official term if you truly wish to be enlightened," he said, his mocking tone matching hers. "The discovery of new things is usually worth the little discomfort I endure. Though up here, a few trunks of clothing and old books aren't exactly a worthy trade-off."

Giving up on the window, she walked back over to him and primly arranged her skirts when she sat on the edge of a nearby trunk. "Why were you even up here in the first place, if you hate attics so much?"

He shrugged. "My father used to keep old bone bed maps up here along with the rest of his things the duchess didn't approve of cluttering up her library. I was in search of them to sell to a colleague in America. They're quite valuable."

"Bone beds," she said and wrinkled her perfect slope of a nose. "That sounds dreadful."

"I study fossils, my lady. Bones are a natural part of that. Bone beds are places where extinct reptiles used to congregate."

A flicker of interest bloomed in her eyes, though she tried to hide it. "Are you back for good then?" she asked. "Or do you plan on leaving again to rejoin your colleague?"

Aspen pondered the question. Learning of his mother's intent to have him declared dead had been enough to put him on a transatlantic liner. But he had far more pressing reasons to return. It was time he saw to his duties as duke; he'd avoided them long enough. Judith had come of age, and it was his responsibility to ensure she was settled with a suitable match. And it was very much *past* time that he avenge the sins of the past.

Rather than dwell on the reasons that had driven him from England—his father's death, his mother's cunning betrayal—he shifted his attention to Vesper. "Marsden mentioned that you're good at arranging matches." Aspen didn't miss the self-satisfied smile that lifted her lips. "Are you?"

"Why do you ask?" she replied coyly.

She practically preened with vainglorious conceit. Clearly, her self-adoration hadn't changed. And from what he'd gleaned from spending time with her father in London these past few months, *everyone* adored her as well. And yet. "Why haven't *you* married?"

Her smile vanished. "I *beg* your pardon, Your Grace? That is rather personal."

Aspen's gaze canvassed her tousled hair, pleasing face, and equally pleasing form. "You're three and twenty. Much past the age of a blushing debutante. Didn't I hear that Huntington and Eldridge offered for you?"

"I didn't realize you had a weakness for gossip."

"Tell me why you rejected them." He narrowed his eyes when those high cheekbones burst into brilliant splotches of crimson. "Or are you still considering them?"

"No," she bit out and tossed her golden head. "But you needn't concern yourself. I hardly lack for offers, I assure you."

"Hmmm... And still you remain unwed. Is it that you're too picky?" Aspen said. "Or too mouthy?"

"You odious bas—" Her face mottled as she clamped her lips together, bottling whatever expletive she'd been about to spout at him. Aspen delighted in her reaction, thrilled at still being able to get a rise out of her.

"Or is it that those poor, poor men couldn't handle your sting, Viper?"

That rigid composure dipped and she bared her teeth. "Snakes don't sting, you bloody ass, they bite."

Aspen smirked. She might have grown into a prim and proper woman who prided herself on her poise and grace, but she still possessed a quick temper and sharpened tongue. He much preferred this version of her. Although he'd do better to remember what provoking her could lead to, he recalled as he rubbed the bridge of his nose.

Vesper stood again and paced the length of the attic, muttering inaudible words under her breath. She fumbled at the door, pounding at the wood before giving up with a bellow of despair. "This is hopeless."

"There's no help for it," Aspen said. "We will simply have to wait until someone comes along to rescue us."

"Isn't that just rich?" she said with a humorless chuckle, resuming her seat on the trunk and dropping her head to her knees. "Every damsel dreams of being rescued from a tower by a handsome knight, only in my case, said knight is in the same snare as the damsel."

He glanced at her, breath faltering on an unexpected hitch. "You think I'm handsome?"

Her chin snapped up. "No, of course not. It was a generalization. Ladies in need of rescue and dashing knights. It's part of the story. Not *our* story." She huffed and shook her head. "Not that we have a story at all. Oh, deuce it, never mind."

Aspen grinned, and once again rubbed the bent bridge of his nose. "Alas, any chance for me to lay claim to beauty was lost to me by an irritable imp intent on my destruction." He made a pained face. "Don't worry. It only hurts when I touch it like so or when it rains."

"It was an accident!" Her face went scarlet again as he chuckled. "You're teasing me."

"Only a little," he murmured, confused himself as to why he was deriving pleasure from such a thing. Perhaps the solitude of his own company had affected him more than he realized.

She peered at him, blue eyes scrutinizing his nose. "Does it truly hurt?"

"No."

"I *am* sorry, you know." Vesper rubbed the knuckles of her right fist as if reliving the impact. "I never meant to hit you."

Aspen let out a disbelieving snort. "Yes, you absolutely did. I know that because I taught you that move, and you executed it with precision and skill. My nose and my pride were in tatters, but if you were a lad, I would have pounded you on the back and congratulated you for an excellent uppercut."

"I wasn't a lad."

He nodded. "Which is why my pride took such a beating."

"I'm sorry nonetheless." She wet her lips and he couldn't help noticing how full they were and how soft they looked. Her mouth—much like the rest of her face—was flawlessly drawn. A perfect Cupid's bow that begged to be kissed and have sinful things done to it. Aspen dragged his eyes away, cursing himself. Hell, he was hungry and tired. And it was making him daft.

"I don't suppose you have anything to eat, do you?"

Blue eyes sparkled with something other than vexation. "What if I did?"

"I will grovel at your feet." The fervent words were ruined by the ferocious rumble of his belly. His eyes perused her person. Whatever she had, if she did have anything, was bound to be small, but he would savor a crumb at this point. "Fawn and genuflect, polish your boots with my tongue, whatever my angel of mercy requires."

"No polishing will be necessary, Duke."

Even at the unintended—he was sure—innuendo, the promise of food was too much. It saturated his brain with hungry need. His stomach roared its displeasure. *Loudly.* Enough for her eyes to widen as she hurriedly withdrew a small wrapped linen square from her skirt pockets and handed it to him without a word.

Aspen's fingers trembled as he opened the packet. Hell, he wasn't going to swoon, was he? But as he beheld the two triangle remnants of a sandwich and two disintegrating tea cakes, he felt his body waver. His eyes nearly rolled back into his head as the smell assaulted him. Without any manners at all, he crammed one of the triangles into his mouth, not even pausing to savor it.

"Christ, it's so fucking good," he mumbled around his mouthful. Aspen didn't even care that he was behaving like an animal. He was starving. This was the first thing he'd eaten in over a day. He pinched the remaining crumbs with his thumb and forefinger, bringing them to his mouth and licking them off his fingers. Vesper's color was high as she watched him with a fascinated expression.

"I don't expect you've anything to drink in those magical pockets of yours?"

Pursing her lips with a look of regret, she shook her head. "I'm sorry, no."

He glanced at her to see if she was being facetious, but her expression was genuinely disheartened, as though she wished she *did* have more. He never knew with Vesper: one minute she was sugar and spice, and the next, she was hellfire and vinegar. At least she had been anyway. He was still navigating this self-restrained version of her.

"This was enough, thank you." Holding the napkin aloft, he shook the last of the bits into his mouth. He wasn't above licking the fabric clean, but that would be going too far. "I suppose I owe you an answer in return. Earlier, you asked whether I was planning to stay in town. I am for now."

"For the season?"

Aspen nodded, an idea taking root as he considered the woman sitting opposite him with a speculative look. Perhaps *she* could help him situate Judith. He tapped at the bridge of his nose again, drawing her eyes to the old injury. "And I've just thought of a way you can make this up to me."

"I just fed you!" she exclaimed.

"That was for the humiliation. This will be for the pain and suffering."

Her pretty mouth fell open, and he had to force himself from grinning at her furious expression. "You just told me that it doesn't hurt, you bloody fibber!"

"It's truly no wonder you haven't wed with that sharp tongue of yours, Viper."

She glared in outrage. "I'd watch *your* tongue, Lord Ass, or it will be following through on promises made on polishing boots, and mine are very, *very* dirty."

Aspen couldn't help it—he laughed at the moniker and raised a brow. "How dirty?"

"I meant muddy, not whatever it is you're thinking in that vile head of yours," she shot back, cheeks on fire. "Honestly, is your mind always in the gutter?" Her voice stuttered on the last and that lovely blush bled down her swanlike neck into her décolletage, even as her eyes flashed daggers of blue flame at him.

"The gutter is fun. You should come off your pedestal one day and see for yourself." His lips curled into a smirk at the parry, and her fists balled as she fought visibly for composure.

"To lie with dogs and catch fleas? I think not," she said, her chin jutting with a healthy dose of disdain.

"I am offended, my lady," he said in false affront. "I'll

have you know I bathe every day and have never seen a single flea."

"You mock me, Your Grace." Tight-faced, she turned her head away with a dismissive sniff, and Aspen forced his erotic fantasies into submission along with his amusement. He was as hot-blooded as the next man, but he was supposed to be charming her into compliance not thinking of seduction. Though he much preferred an impassioned, unraveled Vesper to this cool, counterfeit version of her.

He squeezed his eyes shut. *Seduction?* What was he thinking? He needed her guidance with Judith, that was all. Once he was out of here, he'd find a lovely, willing brunette—he was studiously partial to dark hair for reasons—to slake his needs.

"Jokes aside, I do need your help," he said quickly before he changed his mind.

She narrowed her eyes at him, her mistrust clear. "What kind of help?"

"I'm here in town for as long as it takes to see my estates and my mother's ward settled," he said.

Vesper's eyes widened. "Judith?"

"One and the same," he replied.

"How is she?" Vesper asked haltingly. "It's been an age, and since your family decamped to Brighton, our paths haven't crossed."

Aspen gave a low huff. Decamped was a polite way of putting it, not that Vesper would know that he'd been the one to give his mother the ultimatum: Brighton or New York. He quashed the usual spike of anger that accompanied thoughts of the duchess and focused on Judith. "Eighteen and headstrong. She needs to make her bow this season."

A pair of blond brows lifted. "The season that will start in a fortnight?"

"The very same," he responded, frowning at the aporetic mirth lighting her gaze.

Vesper's husky laughter was low and deep—a surprisingly lush sound that didn't belong in this dark, dusty attic. He was well aware that it was at his expense, but that didn't matter, not when those candid peals filled him like forgotten music. Vesper Lyndhurst was alarmingly lovely at any other time, but when she smiled—and when she laughed like she was lit from within—her beauty was incandescent.

Aspen struck the asinine thought from his brain. What fool used words like *incandescent*? Him, apparently.

"I fail to see the humor in my request," he bit out as her chortles dispersed.

When she'd calmed, she wiped at her eyes and sniffed. "You do realize how insensible that is, don't you, Your Grace?" When he didn't answer, she went on. "A debutante has to be fitted for a wardrobe, invited to events and balls, and she has to be vetted by the denizens of society."

"So? There's time." Brows dipping, he stuffed his hands into his pockets and glowered. Why on earth did she look like he was asking her to perform a miracle? It was the season, not a matter of life and death. A few dresses and trinkets would do, and as far as invitations and being vetted, that was what *she* was for. If indeed she was the matchmaker she was lauded to be.

She sent him an incredulous look. "You have surely left your good sense across the Atlantic, Your Grace. Debutantes have been preparing for their bows at court for *months*, some an entire year. She has to be presented to the queen."

"Presentation at court is merely a formality. A come-out only requires connections and money."

He wasn't certain that he had much of either, considering his prolonged absence from England and how much of his coffers the duchess had emptied.

But he would have money, once he found his father's bone bed maps. Edward Cope and Othniel Marsh, the American paleontologists whom he'd met in Berlin, would buy them in a heartbeat. And their rivalry would drive the price significantly upward. He had fossils, too, a large number collected over the years, that he could sell at auction to Sir Richard Owen here in England.

Blue eyes regarded him. "You ask the impossible, Your Grace."

"You're right. I suppose it's really too much to ask." He exhaled and rubbed a hand over his chin. "But I heard from Marsden that you were the matchmaking queen of London, and if anyone could make such a miracle happen, it would be you." He was laying it on rather thickly, but desperate times and all.

That clever gaze narrowed again. "Are you trying to flatter me?"

"Is it working?" he shot back with a hopeful grin.

Loose curls bounced as she tossed her head, but not before he saw her hide a smile of her own. Was that because of the flattery or something else? "I am hardly *that* oblivious to artifice, Your Grace."

"And if I begged on bended knee?" he teased.

"Promises of genuflection again, Greydon?" she replied. "Your travels seem to have changed you into somewhat of a supplicant."

Aspen licked his lips, noting that her gaze instantly tracked the movement. His eyes narrowed just as hers squeezed shut, a sound of aggravation leaving her. Was that a wisp of desire or disdain? Probably the latter. Grown-up Vesper was impervious to him, as she'd proven before he'd left for America. "I am very good at taking a knee when I need to, my lady," he said softly. "Some things are more easily won when one yields."

Her throat worked and a shuddery exhale left her lips. She turned, pretending to examine a trunk. "You are also full of unwelcome innuendo. It is rather irritating."

He cleared his throat, remembering that he'd catch more flies with honey. "My apologies. What is it you require to take on the task?" he asked bluntly.

"Six months at least," she said, her voice strengthening. "Three months for a *modicum* of preparation, even with your mother's influence."

Aspen weighed his approach. The smugness he'd noted before when he'd mentioned Marsden had been telling. She *prided* herself on that match. He was willing to wager she'd be interested in this challenge. "So you're saying you *can't* do it then?"

Aspen hid his triumphant grin when she straightened that competitive spine of hers. "I didn't say that," she snipped. "It will be expensive and quite possibly bring more harm than good to Judith. At the very least it is unlikely our efforts will bear fruit this season."

"I understand," he said, hiding his satisfaction as cool blue eyes met his.

"Very well then," she said. "If you can find a way to get us out of here, I'll help you."

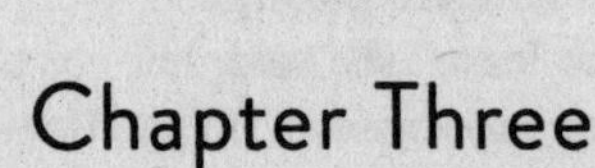

Chapter Three

Vesper was ready to tear her hair out by the roots or collapse from exhaustion, whichever came first. Her legs ached from pacing the floorboards, her fists were bruised from pounding the door, and her voice was strained from yelling. It had long since gone dark, if the inky sky beyond the windows was any signal.

She glared irritably at the man propped up against a trunk with maps and papers spread out all around him. The candles in the candelabra she'd brought had nearly burned down to the stubs, even though they'd used only one at a time to conserve the wax. "Why are you just sitting there staring at those papers? I can hardly see how that's any use at all."

"The servants are abed," he said, glancing up with a patronizing note in his voice that made her bristle. "You'll wear yourself out fretting as you are. Sit, rest, and get some sleep."

Vesper glowered. "*Fretting*? I am trying to get us rescued, you daft lump! Papa will be worried sick if I don't return home."

"Trying, quite futilely might I add, and I'm certain that your father knows you're more than capable of looking after yourself," he grumbled as he peered up at her over the pair of fine, gold-rimmed spectacles he had perched on his nose.

A frown gathered between Vesper's brows as he plucked said spectacles off his face and cleaned them with the edge of his loosened cravat. When had his cravat become unknotted? He hadn't been wearing a coat when she'd arrived, dreadfully untoward in itself, but what was one to do when stuck in a musty, locked attic?

She must have been caught up in her efforts to summon help, because she just now noticed he'd unbuttoned his waistcoat and rolled up his sleeves as well. Good grief. The man's state of undress was bordering on scandalous.

Who will know? a voice mocked. *You could strip bare and not a soul would care.*

Vesper's ears burned as she studied a pretty navy flounce on her walking dress. *She* would care. She would care very much. It simply wasn't proper. A breath slipped out of her as her gaze darted back to the ripple of movement, those long fingers mesmerizing as they deftly polished the glass with the linen.

Her cheeks heated as her eyes inched upward from his hands to take in those strong forearms, roped with veins and dusted in crisp dark hair. Dear God, she couldn't look away if she tried. A man could only get that robust from working with rock and dirt all day, even if he was a duke and not expected to be performing manual labor. She wondered what those thick, muscular arms would feel like wrapped around her and gave an indelicate shiver.

Oh, hell in a handbasket.

Her body went uncomfortably hot and her throat felt like it was coated in sand. She tore her eyes away and focused on the clean glass lenses he was replacing on the bridge of his nose. "I didn't realize you still wore spectacles."

"For reading." He straightened them into place and peered at her over the top of the rim. "The print in research papers is often rather small. A doctor in New York recommended one of his own designs to help ease the head strain."

"Your travels took you to New York?"

He nodded. "To finalize the sale of my mother's home, yes."

Before moving to England, Aspen's mother had been a beautiful American commoner who'd fallen madly in love with a duke. Theirs had been a love story that Vesper had admired from afar but held close to her overly romantic heart. Now, with said heart ruthlessly flattened by the very man in this attic, Vesper was well aware that she might have romanticized the glimpses she'd seen of them as a young, idealistic girl with stars and roses in her eyes, but wasn't that what love was about? Hope and possibility? The late duke and his duchess had been the epitome of a grand love.

Not that *Vesper* would know anything about that personally.

Greydon wasn't wrong about her...fastidious nature. She wasn't wed because she couldn't bear the thought of anyone knowing her secret—that the Vesper beneath all the practiced poise was, in fact, a woman who struggled to keep her thoughts corralled and refrain from speaking out of turn.

She shook her head. Marriage was not in the cards for her. She derived pleasure from the matches she conceived, and that was more than enough. Wasn't it? As if compelled, she peered at Aspen and couldn't help noticing anew how the fine fabric of his shirt clung lovingly to his broad shoulders.

Oh, enough ogling of the duke's musculature. He's Aspen not Atlas!

A wicked voice inside her cackled at that—those sculpted shoulders were more than capable of holding up the Earth. With a growl at her foolishness, she frowned at him. "Can't you put on your coat? You're being unseemly."

"I'm sweating," he replied without looking up from another map he had unrolled.

"It's cold in here," she said and rubbed her arms. The earlier storm and the cooling evening air had brought a chill to the drafty attic.

"Then you wear the coat," he replied carelessly without even glancing up from his maps.

Vesper's mouth fell open as if he'd just commanded her to strip to her drawers. She flushed. "I couldn't possibly!"

"Why not?" He looked up then at the near-shriek in her tone.

Poise. Polish. Perfection.

Striving for restraint, Vesper repeated the chant to herself. She would not let Aspen Drake undo everything she'd become. He was a passing inconvenience, nothing more, and she'd survive him, just as she had before. His appearance was no invitation for the old Vesper to return.

"It's a man's coat, Your Grace. *Your* coat. It wouldn't be proper."

His mouth curled. "So you would rather freeze to death than put on a piece of clothing that belongs to me? For the sake of propriety? That makes a lot of sense. Decorum before death!"

"It's not done," she replied stubbornly.

"Suit yourself," he said. "But don't come crying to me when your teeth start to chatter because some dour-faced patroness of the ton says it's *not done*."

"You're insufferable," she shot back at his droll tone.

He held out the garment. "Take the coat, Vesper."

"Hell will freeze over first."

"It probably already has since you're here," he muttered.

Vesper blinked. Did the deuced rotter just insinuate she was... *Lucifer*? Her temper pricked, but she fisted her hands in her skirts, walked primly over to the narrow window where the clouds hid the moon and the stars from view, and forced herself to stay put. And stay calm.

Why was she even letting him get a rise out of her?

Poise. Polish. Perfection.

She rubbed her hands over her arms, ignoring the rash of goose pimples that had just spread across her skin. She regretted leaving her pelisse in the downstairs salon. Had Mrs. Dempsey found it? Surely the housekeeper would have put two and two together—a lady would not have left without it.

A full-body shiver racked through her body.

"Oh, for fuck's sake," she heard the duke mutter.

A few seconds later he was sliding his coat over her shoulders. "I don't need—" she began, but the duke cut her off with a growl.

"Don't be so stubborn."

He reached his hands around her from the back to tug the lapels together, and his warmth nearly derailed her senses.

"Thank you," she whispered.

"You're welcome." Was it her imagination or had his voice gone more gravelly than usual? And gracious, why were her nipples tightening in her bodice from the sound of it? She gave herself a mental shake—they were tight because she was cold, not because that smoky voice of his did untoward things to her body.

"How is it that you're warm?" she asked.

"I've always run hot," he rumbled, and she squeezed her eyes shut.

Vesper couldn't help her quiver then, though it had nothing to do with the cold and everything to do with the man standing behind her. His arms rose to wrap around her, but she dared not look down at those muscled forearms. This close, those dangerously bare and very masculine arms would be her undoing…

"Greydon," she bit out. "This is improper."

Her tongue swiped over her bottom lip, and she felt him tense behind her. Her brow furrowed, but then she realized that he could see her in the reflection of the window... just as she could see him. In the shadowed gloom and the flickering bursts of candlelight, he looked like a dangerously mystical creature behind her—a beast from the myths of old come to claim the virgin on offer. Not that *she* was on offer. *Heavens, Vesper, stop.*

She moistened her lips again, and she could have sworn he growled. His face was so strained, he looked pained or furious, though that could be a distortion of the glass.

"Rules of conduct are in place for a reason," she said, her voice sounding much too breathy for comfort. "I depend on them to act accordingly."

"No one is here to judge."

"*We're* here," she said, her eyes glued to his in the windowpane. "I am unmarried and you are an unwed duke."

Greydon's gaze burned like a brand, and heat swept over her skin. "So?" he rasped.

Vesper whirled to face him. A dreadful mistake clearly. If she wished, she could reach out to place her palm on the soft lawn of his shirt... bask in the delicious heat of him. Step forward and press her cheek to that broad chest and snuggle into it like a bedraggled kitten next to a toasty hearth.

She dug deep for tranquility before her body did things that her mind did not condone. "Unless you wish to see yourself to the altar, you will mind your distance, Your Grace," she told him, proud that her voice did not quaver. "While you might not respect society's rules, I do not wish to be ruined."

Beyond his spectacles, honey-brown irises striated with amber bored into hers. "Honestly, this prudish and buttoned-up version of you is astonishing. There's no one here to wield the scales of ruination, Vesper."

Why did that sound like the worst kind of insult? And why did she even *care*? "You're here," she said mutinously.

"And I do not wish to be ushered to the altar. Trust me, your precious virtue is quite safe."

"That may be true, Your Grace, but as I am not a duke, I'm afraid there are different rules for me. Highborn ladies are expected to conduct themselves with politesse and decorum." She sniffed, her disdain obvious. "You would know this if you took the time to remain in England longer than a month instead of traipsing around wherever the winds take you like a rootless vagabond. But then again, without your silly adventures, whatever would you have to brag about?"

His eyes widened with affront. "Better a vagabond than a witless spinster with a clockwork heart who fills her hours poring over *The Ladies' Book of Etiquette, and Manual of Politeness*."

Ouch. Vesper flinched as those words hit home, right into the windup heart he'd accused her of having. She let her bristling temper fly. "As opposed to the boy who fills his time with the bones of dead things? And I am *happy* to loan you the copy of my handbook since you seem to suffer from a complete dearth of manners."

"I'm not a boy, Vesper."

The soft snarl of her name on his tongue made her insides liquefy.

No, he wasn't a boy. He was a man—a tall, strong, and riled man currently crowding her personal space and *daring* her to react. Vesper huffed a shallow breath and moved to step away from him, but he shifted to cage her against the windowsill with his arms. Plumes of his scent curled up around her—faint bergamot, tilled earth and crisp mountain air, heated sweat. All male. All *him*.

She refused to react, refused to display even one ounce of alarm. "What are you *doing*, Your Grace?"

He inched closer, eyes smoldering. She swore she could see flames sparking within those eyes, but perhaps that was the refracted candlelight. Still, she gulped.

"Proving something."

"That you've grown up? Cultivated a few hairs on your arms? Sprouted a few muscles? Good for you." Dear God, her bravado and all good sense were fading fast.

Both fled as that mouth of his curled into a wicked smirk and she felt her knees waver like saplings in the wind. His lips hovered a hairsbreadth away, the tip of his nose nearly touching hers. Vesper's throat dried. Heavens, was he going to kiss her? All thoughts of propriety floated away as her eyelashes fluttered down, lips parting in willing invitation.

Because blast the rules, society, respectability, all of it—she'd never wanted anything more.

Fueled by equal jets of vexation and desire, Aspen was a heartbeat away from kissing the brazen harpy senseless. Calling him vainglorious! Insulting his life's work! She'd never held back when they were children, but somehow the insults said in such haughty, prudish tones made him feel like a bull with a red rag. How dare she—a self-centered, spoiled heiress who likely spent her days meddling and casting judgment on the affairs of others—impugn *his* character?

He dragged in a gulp of air and regretted it when the sweet scent of her swamped him. She still smelled like rain and spring flowers. Those beckoning pink lips parted, and he leaned in, heart pounding against his ribs so loudly he could hear it thundering in his ears. *Thump, thump, thump!*

No, wait. That wasn't his heart...that was the door.

Vesper's heavy-lidded blue eyes snapped open. "Is that what I think it is?"

He nodded, both of them turning toward the door in unison. The knock came again, this time accompanied by the stern, very real voice of his butler. "Is anyone in there? Show yourself this instant!"

Dear God, they were rescued! Before answering, Aspen sprinted across the room to station himself beside the blasted door. He'd learned his lesson the last time.

"It's the duke," he said loudly. "The door is jammed and missing its handle on this side, Braxton. Open it, if you please!"

When the door cracked ajar, it was all Aspen could do not to hug the servant who stared at him with wide, disbelieving eyes before drawing a clumsy bow. The man blinked several times as if seeing a ghost. "Your Grace, is that you?"

"Yes, it's me, Braxton," Aspen said, wedging a foot in between the door and the jamb. He wasn't taking any chances. "Not some specter haunting these upper floors. However did you know to come up here?"

"The gardener saw the candlelight from the grounds, and since this is the private family wing, he thought it strange."

Relief flooded Aspen. It was just as well the gardener had noticed or he and the lady would have been spending the night sleeping on a hard wooden floor. They could depend on his servants' discretion for a few hours but even he knew that passing a night together could have been a recipe for disaster.

"After you, Lady Vesper," he said.

Braxton's eyes goggled when Aspen held the door for her to hurry out. She'd removed his coat, he noticed, leaving it folded on the trunk. Though, she had no need to worry. Braxton would sooner cut off his own arm than bring shame to the Greydon household with something as salacious as gossip.

Not one ounce of scandal had ever touched his family, even when there'd been plenty to be had behind closed doors.

"My lady," the butler said, bowing to Vesper. "Mrs. Dempsey thought you had gone when the rain stopped. At least it appeared that way."

"No, but it was fortunate you came, Braxton," she told him kindly. "The door is broken, you see. I heard a noise and came to investigate, and well, found myself in quite a predicament. Much like the duke, I expect." She bit her lip, darting a glance at Aspen who remained stone-faced. "I must be getting home."

"I'll see you to your residence," Aspen said, returning for his coat and shoving his arms into the sleeves.

She shook her head as if she couldn't wait to be rid of him. "It's not necessary. I know the way, Your Grace."

"I insist. It's pitch-dark outside and you cannot cut through the fields. You'll have to take the road and it's much longer. Braxton, my phaeton, please."

"Your Grace," she said again, this time he could not help but notice, through gritted teeth. "I do not require an escort."

God, she was frustratingly contrary. He was tired, hungry, and irritable, and in no mood to be managed. But he knew that insisting would get him nowhere. Aspen unclenched his jaw and calmed his tones. "Lady Vesper, as much as I respect your wishes, will you *kindly* allow me to accompany you home? It is the gentlemanly thing to do, after all." His brow canted. "And you did cast me in quite an unfair light with my supposed dearth of manners, so I must beg you to reconsider."

Her mouth thinned, but she was too well-bred to argue, especially in front of a servant who was pretending not to notice the tense volleying between them. "Of course, Your Grace. That would be *lovely*."

Neither of them brought up the fraught moments before

they'd been rescued, though Vesper's color remained high as they descended to the foyer. Braxton went ahead to see about the carriage. After stopping to retrieve her pelisse from the salon, they left quietly through the front entrance to the courtyard. Besides the butler, no other servants were about, thanks to the lateness of the hour.

The sky had cleared enough for a brilliant full moon to peek out, casting a silvery light over the cobblestones, when his phaeton rolled into the courtyard. Braxton nodded to him, handing over the reins, and once they were both situated in the two-person seat, Aspen signaled to the horse to go.

"You don't have to worry about Braxton," he told his silent companion. "He's steadfast in his loyalty."

She folded her hands in her lap. "That's good."

"When do you plan to travel to town?" he asked as they headed down the road, the noise of the wheels against the road loud in the silence.

"In a few days, once the house in Mayfair is prepared." She wrinkled her nose as if remembering the promise she had made in the attic. "Where is Judith at the moment?"

"She's already in London, I imagine, with the dowager. I wrote to my mother of my arrival, letting her know that I intended to be home for the season." He cleared his throat. "I failed, however, to mention that I would be stopping here in Dorset, which was likely why no one knew to expect me." His sigh was low. "And well, you know the rest."

"No one is ever here," she said. "At Greydon Abbey. That's why I was walking in your gardens earlier."

He shot her a look and directed the horse into the courtyard of her estate. It had been much quicker of a drive than he had recalled, and a part of him felt strangely disappointed that their time together was at an end. Strangely, too, his irritation had dissipated. "Trespassing you mean?"

"To-may-toe, to-mah-toe."

Aspen chuckled, making her stare. "Only Americans say to-may-toe."

She descended without his help, a small answering smile quirking the corner of her lip. "And you're half American."

"It's a weak argument, but the hour is late, so I'll grant you the point." He shook his head and winked. "Pleasant dreams, my lady. May you not be visited by handsome knights and fair damsels trapped in small spaces throwing decorum on its paltry ear." For some inane reason, Aspen wanted to see that blush once more, for posterity. "Or maybe *do*."

There it was, most gratifyingly, like a sunset over a wheat field.

Even her scowl didn't wreck it. "Good *night*, Your Grace."

Chapter Four

Ensconced a week later in the drawing room at her Mayfair home, Vesper stared at her closest friends in turn—Laila, Effie, Briar, and Nève—their faces reflecting the exact same emotion: complete and utter astonishment.

Effie, the shyest of them all, was the first to speak. Pale gold eyelashes fluttered over a too-expressive gaze. "Let me reiterate: you found yourself trapped with the Duke of Greydon in an attic because of a broken door, where he asked you to help launch his ward, Miss Judith Thornton, into society, and then"—her ice-blue eyes widened dramatically—"you nearly shared an *almost* kiss?"

"That's what happened," Vesper muttered, though she hadn't used those exact words. The duke had barely touched her and yet her lips still tingled. In the days following the incident of near-ruination, she'd pressed her fingers there often enough, fantasizing about how an actual kiss from the duke would have felt. Firm? Soft? Wet? And then she'd chastised herself immediately afterward for her nonsense. Proper ladies did not dream of indecent things.

And in any case, she did *not* want to kiss the Duke of Greydon.

The man couldn't even bother to follow up on their agreement in person. Instead, he sent a note to confirm the terms of the arrangement. She was rather livid about that. As though she were some lackey receiving ducal instructions! She'd promptly written a curt message back and sent along her annotated copy of *The Ladies' Book of Etiquette, and Manual of Politeness*, referring him to chapter XVI, Polite Deportment, and Good Habits. He hadn't responded, of course.

"What *I* want to know is what's an almost kiss?" Briar asked, holding a tea cake in midair, freckled nose wrinkling. After taking a bite, she tossed her head, sending a thick spiral of her bronze-brown hair bouncing into her brow. "Did you kiss him or didn't you? How does one *almost* kiss someone? Were you just breathing on each other?"

"No, silly," Laila said, rolling a pair of dark eyes. "She means that he was so close that she could practically taste him. Isn't that right, Vesper?"

She felt her core throb at the memory of his deeply mouthwatering scent and the way her skin had sparked as though grazed by lightning, but she managed to give an airy shrug.

"Quite the scandal," Nève put in with a grin, running a hand over her pregnant abdomen. "Being alone and unchaperoned with a man? A *duke* no less. It's a wonder you're not being rushed to the altar by your father or your brother."

"Lushing doesn't care and Papa knows that I'm not ready to wed," Vesper replied, a hint of heat grazing the tops of her cheeks. "And even if I were, it would never be to His Graceless. Thank God no one saw us. One would think with a mother like his—such a paragon of the ton—that he'd be well versed in how to behave like a duke."

"Tell us how you really feel," Laila said with a too-perceptive glance.

Vesper blushed harder and then scowled. She didn't swoon or simper or carry on. Nothing affected her. Not *usually* anyway.

When Lord Huntington—who *had* offered for her years ago—had scoffed at her succinct refusal of his suit, saying a lady of her bellicose ilk was a danger to high society, she hadn't cared.

What had been her sin? Being too smart? Knowing her own worth? Understanding that a gentleman like Huntington would be akin to a jailer? But since Lord Huntington wasn't alone in his thinking, Vesper had learned to soften her sharper edges, keep her intemperate moods hidden...all in the name of civility. A darling of the ton could do no wrong. A mask of sangfroid and beauty could be a weapon or a benediction in itself.

"Are you well, Vesper dear?" Effie asked. "Your face is quite flushed."

Vesper pressed the backs of her knuckles to her wretched cheeks. "I must be coming down with a fever."

"Lust fever," Briar teased.

"Briar!" Vesper cried.

"She's not wrong. I've never seen you this hot and bothered about anything or anyone," Nève interjected, her face curious. "Montcroix had mentioned that Greydon was back in town and you two might have had history, but I don't understand, who exactly is he to you?"

"Her childhood infatuation," Effie piped up. "And the reason no man in England or elsewhere has ever measured up." She let out a soft gasp and covered her mouth. It was clear her friend hadn't quite meant to add that last part, yet Vesper's lips still thinned. "Though of course, we are forbidden by the lady code of friendship to ever speak of him," Effie added quickly with a sheepish look.

"It was so sad what happened to his parents," Briar added. "They were *the* love match of their time. Such a great tragedy that his father's condition brought an end to their story."

"Condition?" Nève asked.

Briar let out a sad noise. "He was committed to an asylum because he was a danger to his wife and child."

Vesper's heart ached and she wanted to press a hand to her chest, but she kept it busy with her cup and saucer. She'd always been in awe of the affection she'd seen between Greydon's parents, and the pain of losing that kind of love wasn't something Vesper wanted to dwell on.

Before any of the others could chime in, she flicked a hand. "I do not wish to talk about the duke, childhood friend or not, or his family." She straightened her shoulders and grinned. "But I *do* plan to find Judith the most marvelous suitor—she'll be the talk of the season by the time I'm through!"

"It's rather alarming how much matchmaking excites you," Briar teased.

Vesper fixed them with an overbright look and sipped her cup of tea. "I am rather brilliant at it," she boasted. "Look at Laila and Marsden. She couldn't be more well-loved."

"Just this morning in fact," Laila blurted and then went scarlet.

They all giggled then. Even Effie hid her face behind her teacup and stuffed a tea cake into her mouth. Honestly, it gratified Vesper that Laila was so madly in love with her husband. Now if only she could see Effie and Briar as comfortably settled. But they both were dead set against wedlock. Effie loved her animals and Briar her endless causes for women's rights. Neither of them were interested in being encumbered by husbands.

Vesper sighed then turned her attention back to brighter matters. "In addition to finding Judith her perfect match, I'm thinking I shall arrange a rendezvous between Mr. Cross and Mrs. Elway. They've been giving each other longing glances every time they cross paths."

"Your father's man of business?" Laila asked turning serious. "And your housekeeper? Vesper, I agree that you do have a sense for these things, but sometimes, it is also wise to leave well enough alone. Mr. Cross has been in your father's employ for years as has Mrs. Elway. What if it doesn't work out between them? Their livelihoods and comfort would be at stake."

"It will work out," Vesper said with a confident toss of her head. "A nudge here, a nudge there, is all it takes. They'll be happy before they know it."

Effie glanced up, and said softly, "Not all couples are meant to be pushed together."

"She's right, Vesper," Briar interjected, a thoughtful look on her face. "Perhaps you need to keep out of people's business. You got lucky with Laila and Marsden, but Laila's right, it's about their livelihoods. Don't meddle."

Vesper's cheeks went hot with embarrassment at her friends' unexpected chiding. She wasn't *meddling*. "You're wrong. Laila said it herself, I have a knack for it. And they will live happily, marvelously ever after. Just like Evans and Georgina."

Laila's frown deepened. "I think you are obsessed with happy endings. Sometimes, these things have to happen on their own."

"Doesn't everyone want a happy-ever-after?" Vesper glowered at her friends. "I'm just giving them some help, that's all."

"Why not let them find their way on their own?" Effie said so softly, it was nearly inaudible. "If fate wanted them to be together, they would be."

Vesper lifted a supercilious brow and reached for her tea. "If I'd left Evans and Georgina up to fate, they would have pined for each other until the end of time." She stood, brushing the crumbs from her skirts. "Besides, it will do the dour Mr. Cross some good to smile for once in his life. He's been rather stingy of late with my pin money. I've been giving all of my funds to my cousin Georgina for the baby's care and I'm in need of more and he refuses to comply with my requests. I need to do this for the good of everyone."

Dead silence ensued.

"Vesper!" Laila gasped, eyes rounding. "You cannot think to manipulate such a situation to your advantage! This is not like finding Miss Thornton a match during the season. Mr. Cross is your father's man, not a pawn for you to direct at will. Your father dotes on you enough to let you get away with many things, but the duke will not be happy should he find out what you've done. Not to mention the poor housekeeper you intend to embroil in your schemes! What of her?"

"I heard her say she wants to marry!" Vesper was affronted that Laila would make her efforts sound so... selfish or prosaic. And yet a lick of doubt curled through her, but she shoved it away. "And besides, how would Papa find out?" She narrowed her eyes on her best friend and plopped back into her seat. "You wouldn't say anything, would you, Laila dear?"

The marchioness looked affronted. "Of course not, but you go too far, Vesper. I only wish to caution you. Do not let success and grandeur confuse that head of yours."

"Did I steer you wrong with Marsden?"

Laila bit her lip. "Well, no, but..."

"Then leave me be, Laila. Concern yourself with your husband and your infant son instead of whether I am overstepping when it comes to matchmaking. It is the only thing that makes me happy. The only thing that I have and that I am good at, deuce it!"

Another round of looks was exchanged as the tension at the tea table ratcheted skyward. Vesper set her cup and saucer into her lap and bit furiously into a sandwich, feeling the unwelcome sting of tears behind her eyelids.

"That's not true, Vesper," Effie said, reaching a hand out, and then dropping it back into her lap. "You're good at many things."

"Name one." The savory bite turned to ash in her mouth. Goodness, she'd never felt so pitiful and forlorn in all her life. First the incessant blushing, the self-woe, and now the need for validation. She was Lady Vesper Lyndhurst, the paradigm of what all young ladies aspired to be: clever, rich, handsome. And yet, doomed to be forever, and tragically, alone.

A contemptible tear crept out from beneath her lashes. Vesper swallowed and lowered her gaze to the gold-rimmed saucer balanced on her lap, her moods swinging violently between despair and frustration.

"You're an excellent hostess," Nève said gently as the girls stood and crowded around her. "And the most accomplished lady of my acquaintance."

"You have the biggest heart of anyone I know, with what you do for the women I work with," Briar added. Vesper sniffed. "You are unfailingly loyal. You would face an army to protect those you love."

Effie squeezed her shoulder. "Everyone looks up to you, Vesper."

Laila crouched down beside her chair. "I'm so sorry, Ves. I didn't mean to make you feel sad or unworthy. You've been my best friend for years and it's our job to look out for each other, that's all. Marsden and I wouldn't be where we are without you. You *are* rather brilliant at matches."

Mollified, Vesper exhaled with a watery grin, feeling marginally cheered. "I am, aren't I?"

"Yes!" her friends chorused together.

That was the only validation she needed. Thank goodness she had them.

Aspen had forgotten how much he despised London. It was crowded, noisy, and it reeked to high heaven. He tugged on his well-tied cravat, nearly dislodging the stickpin from its folds. He'd be much more comfortable in sturdy tweeds and worn boots rather than this pristine cravat and snowy shirt along with the finely milled coat and trousers that made him feel as if he were wearing a suffocating stage costume.

But needs must, and his usual attire would make him quite the spectacle in the private card room at the Earl of Lushing's new social club in East London. Just then the man himself sauntered toward the table where Aspen sat with the Duke of Montcroix. The earl grinned and spread his arms wide. "So what do you think of my jewel, Greydon?"

"How did you manage to do all this?" Aspen asked. "Surely your father would not approve of you emptying his ducal coffers on a gentleman's club or whatever this new fixation of yours is?"

Lushing laughed and shrugged. "Harwick doesn't give a shit what I do, but it's not his money, thank God. I went into business with Stone's railway and shipping ventures and made a killing." He lifted his glass of whiskey. "To continued adventures in money-making!"

Aspen's gaze shifted to the Duke of Montcroix, informally known to his friends as Stone, who lifted his tumbler in return with a wry twist of his lips. The man was a genius with numbers and had diversified and increased his assets a hundredfold. His knack for business, despite the ton's collective disapproval of a duke doing something as pedestrian as working for money, was unmatched.

"How does one get in on this money-making action?" Aspen asked.

The duke turned a sharp gray gaze to him. "You wish to invest?"

"I'm sure you all are familiar with my mother's extravagances and clever maneuvering. It's a wonder she hasn't driven me to the poorhouse or had me committed like my father to gain further control of my remaining inheritance, reduced as it is." He cleared his throat. "Did you know she planned to have me declared dead and my cousin Eustace, thrice removed, made duke in my stead?"

Lushing's eyes widened in shock. "Devious."

"Indeed," Aspen agreed.

"Is this Cousin Eustace the heir presumptive?" Lushing asked darkly, and when Aspen nodded, he shook his head. "Be careful that she doesn't get rid of you."

Aspen wouldn't put it past his mother. "I'm working on uncovering the doctors who helped falsify my father's records. Once I have the truth from them, I'll deal with her."

"Next thing you know, she'll be wheedling you for heirs. Much easier for her to control." Lushing took another sip of his drink.

Lushing and Montcroix were the only ones who knew what the duchess had done, and how deep her deception went. When he'd been a very young, very green duke, she'd run everything like the scheming master puppeteer she was. Never again.

Aspen grimaced. "I don't intend to wed, so she can forget about heirs."

Stone shot him a curious look. "You're not here for the marriage mart this season?"

A vision of blue irises and plump lips danced through his brain, and Aspen almost cursed, even as his blood heated. "Not interested."

Lushing quirked an eyebrow as he deftly dealt them each a hand of cards. "Or is it that you've lost your edge on how to woo a woman or forgotten the pleasures of a willing pair of feminine thighs, lost in the backwaters as you've been? I wager the only holes you've seen are the ones in the ground."

Stone snorted as he studied his cards. "You're bloody vulgar, Lushing."

"Guilty," he replied with an insouciant wink.

"I was in the Americas, not a nunnery," Aspen said, leaning back in his chair. "I've seen plenty of both kinds, I assure you. And no complaints from the women." He might be a paleontologist with a focused avocation, but that didn't mean he was a monk. Aspen did not make it a habit of ignoring his body's carnal needs, and he'd never had a lack of willing bed partners.

Stone observed him across the table with a circumspect look. "Surely there's a chit who will catch your eye. Don't you plan to stay in England now that you're back?"

Fervently, Aspen shook his head. "No. I would not have returned home for another year at least, considering the successful trajectory of my most recent expedition. I'm only here long enough to prove to the House of Lords that I'm alive and to see Judith settled."

"Judith, hmm," Lushing pondered aloud with a slow smile that never meant anything good. "I can help with the fresh-faced Miss Thornton, if you like."

"No," Aspen shot back. "Stay away, Lushing. I mean it. Unless you've changed your eternal stance on being London's worst libertine." When his friend blanched comically, they all chuckled. "As I thought. Keep your distance then."

Stone cleared his throat. “Now then, back to more serious matters. If you’re truly interested in investing, Greydon, instruct your man of business to contact mine tomorrow,” Stone said.

“Speaking of business,” Lushing chortled, eyeing them over his cards, “play is to you, Stone.”

“I’ll take another,” he replied. “And after this round, I must be going. Can’t keep my duchess waiting or she’ll have my head.”

Lushing snorted before withdrawing from play with a sigh. “Never thought I’d see the day when you were so henpecked, Stone.”

“You’ll understand when you find a wife of your own.” The duke grinned and pocketed his winnings. “Or when you finally grow a pair of ballocks enough to ask Briar to marry you.”

“I’d rather geld myself,” the earl replied with a look of pure horror. “Before that bloodthirsty chit has a chance to do it and you know she’s threatened to many a time.” Lushing and Briar’s opposing views on everything from the weather to women’s rights had been a source of contention for most of their adult lives, and it was obvious they were still at odds. “You’ve only just returned, Greydon, so this is news to you, but the chit is going to get herself in trouble with her racket and propaganda.”

“You just hate that she refuses to listen to you,” Stone told the earl.

Lushing shrugged. “She should pay heed to me.”

“Because you’re a man and know better?” Aspen asked, lifting a brow. “You do realize how belittling that sounds? Women have their own brains.”

“Calm your know-it-all tits. That’s not what I mean,” Lushing ground out before raking his fingers through his hair in frustration. "I value the termagant's intelligence and her passion for her beliefs, but I simply do not wish to see her get hurt."

"Then why not marry her?" Stone suggested. "As her husband, that should give you some sway in her capers or at least offer her protection against those who might wish to do her harm."

Lushing rolled his eyes. "*Sway*... as you have with your duchess?"

"Excellent point. Let's keep it at protection then," the duke said with a resigned but fond smile. "Geneviève's nature is rather forthright, I suppose."

"Good thing you're smitten with her."

"Naturally."

Aspen shook his head in wonder at seeing his old friend so openly and unapologetically in love. The fleeting notion that *he* might one day be so lucky flitted through his brain, along with that haunting pair of brilliant lapis lazuli eyes, and he clenched his jaw. *No, no, no.* He quickly directed his ruminations toward something much less perilous.

Lushing's establishment, that would do.

The club was in a rather dodgy part of town, but as Aspen looked around the space, it was clear that no expense had been spared. From his earlier tour, he'd seen that the building included the public house and boxing club next door.

His childhood friend had been busy in the years that Aspen had been gone, and successful, too, from the looks of it. Vesper would have certainly benefited from her brother's windfall and contribution to the family coffers—which meant she'd be an even richer heiress now. The suitors would be lining up for her in droves. He fought a scowl and banished that thought with more force than necessary. Vesper Lyndhurst, or her many fawning admirers, wasn't his concern.

You need her help, a voice reminded him.

That was true. Since he'd much rather deal with Vesper than the conniving mother he hadn't spoken to in years, he would still have to play nice, for Judith's sake. He'd grown fond of the girl over the years. She'd been the only one to write to him, after all, and he owed it to her to offer his support for the season.

Aspen glanced up at the handful of beautiful women in glittering gowns, twittering behind their fans as they gathered along the railing of the floor above. The vantage point gave them a perfect view of the gentlemen enjoying the games—and the free-flowing drink—below. The women were courtesans, if he had to guess. Any one of them could take the edge off his frustration. Perhaps that was what he needed to clear his head.

"I don't know how you do it, Stone. The five of them are pandemonium incarnate," Lushing muttered.

"Five of what?" Aspen asked, drawn from his musings.

"Not what, *whom*. The ladies of charm and chaos, intent on taming every gentleman in Christendom," he replied. "Led by none other than my exasperating sister, and including Stone's lovely wife, Lady Marsden, Lady Evangeline, and Lady Ballbuster Briar herself."

Aspen's heart kicked in his chest and though he knew he shouldn't, his lips formed the questions before he could stop himself. "How is Vesper not yet married? Didn't Eldridge and Huntington offer for her?"

"Yes, both did," Lushing said. "Huntington, the ignorant toff, made the mistake of humiliating Evangeline and insulting Vesper's intelligence so she wiped the proverbial floor with his ego."

Of course she did. Aspen stifled his smile. "And Lord Eldridge?"

"She said no to him, too. Too boring and too nice." The earl sighed and dealt another round of cards, signaling to the waiting footman to fetch more whiskey. "Since when is *too nice* a problem? My sister has refused every suitor, and my father indulges her to the point that the marauding hellion feels that she isn't obliged to wed at all." He shook his head. "Harwick adores her attention—she dotes on him as much as he dotes on her."

"It's good that she's so close to him," Stone said.

"Yes, but what happens when he passes on and the responsibility of her future falls to me?" Lushing shuddered and took another sip of his swiftly delivered whiskey. "By then, it will take a chisel to remove her from the spinster shelf."

Aspen laughed at his friend's droll expression. "Surely it's not as dire as all that. She understands her duty."

Lushing looked aghast. "Do you *know* my sister?"

Aspen sealed his lips with a snort. He'd known a headstrong girl who did what she wanted when she wanted. And he'd seen for himself that her impassioned nature was well and alive, despite pretty garments and excessive politesse. She'd gifted him her bloody etiquette book, for heaven's sake! It was a clever parry, he had to admit.

"You should know that I've asked for her help with Judith's launch into society," he said to Lushing. "God knows what my mother will do in her search for the best title money can buy."

Stone sent him a sidelong glance. "You do realize that the dowager likely intends for *you* to wed the chit, Greydon."

The thought had crossed his mind. Judith might have grown into a charming and pleasant girl, but she would laugh in his face if he even attempted to suggest such a ludicrous thing. As much as they cared for each other, their feelings were decidedly platonic.

"Judith would take issue with that I assure you," he said calmly. "And you already know wedlock is not for me."

The earl and the duke exchanged an amused look before Lushing chortled and hooked a thumb toward Stone. "That's what he said."

Chapter Five

"Goodness, I have never seen so many people gathered in one place in my life," Vesper muttered as a woman with a large feathered headdress nearly collided with their small group, forcing them to squeeze together to avoid punishment by plumes. Honestly, what was the point of an entire frond of peacock feathers during a masquerade when everyone had to duck to avoid death by impalement? The amount of plucked birds stuck in coiffures in this ballroom was truly astonishing, and half of the guests weren't even birds! Why did a woman dressed as a mouse require *feathers*?

"Lady Eldridge wanted to impress," Laila remarked. "She's trying to attract a wife for her son since you turned him down, but everyone knows he's pining for you, Vesper."

Vesper gave a small snort. "Hardly. Eldridge and I are a terrible match." She ducked as yet another woman with an enormous plumed hat sauntered past. "Goodness, what is with all the feathers in everyone's costumes? Is it the new rage?"

"Yes and it's the first ball of the season so everyone is out to impress," Effie said groaning and scrunching her nose, her creamy complexion paler than usual. "Sadly, Viola wouldn't take no for an answer." Effie hated these crowded and large events, but her younger sister had thrown a fit to attend, which meant that poor Effie was there under duress. "Briar was smart to decline."

"Everyone with a pulse is here," Nève said, fanning herself with a disgruntled swipe. She, too, did not love crowds unless she was dancing for them in her previous life as a ballerina, but Vesper's friends had all agreed to help her champion Greydon's ward at her first official ball. Nève had insisted on being there, despite nearing the end of her pregnancy, arguing that her mother had danced right up until birthing both her and her sister, Vivienne.

Vesper turned to the young woman at her side. "Judith, you must waltz."

In the last fortnight, Vesper's, Laila's, and Nève's modistes had been busy, and Judith was now in possession of a wonderful wardrobe for the season including the gorgeous rose-colored gown she wore tonight. No silly plumes in her hair, thank God, just a few matching roses tucked into her crown. Judith looked incredible, if Vesper might say so herself. The girl was comely with glossy dark curls, pleasant features, and intelligent green eyes. A debutante with her looks and social connections would not be difficult to match, and Vesper was already anticipating the victory.

"Must I?" Judith replied.

A chorus of voices answered "Yes!" and Vesper hid her smile at Judith's dejected look.

Greydon had facilitated their reintroduction over tea at his London residence, and the young woman who'd been but a child when Vesper had seen her last had been refreshingly down-to-earth and amiable.

"Do you remember me?" Vesper had asked Judith after Greydon had taken his leave.

"Yes, you're lovelier than ever," Judith had said with a blush.

Vesper had laughed, lifting an amused brow. "Lovely? Is that so? With dirt on my hems, a penchant for loquacity, and an irascible temper?"

Their shared amusement had broken the ice. "Nonetheless, I remember wanting to be just like you. Brave and unafraid of anything."

"More like foolish and headstrong. It was a miracle that I stayed in one piece with such impetuous proclivities," Vesper had replied, warmth infusing her. "I suffered through quite a bit of polishing over the years, I'll have you know." She'd waved an arm over her person. "This version of me did not come without significant time and effort."

"I see." Judith's expression had been hard to read. "Aspen was never the same, you know, after that summer. I think he always regretted how things ended between you, and I was a sad substitute for a replacement best friend."

Vesper's heart had constricted at Judith's blunt disclosure. She hadn't any idea that Greydon had been affected at all by the end of their friendship. Then or now. Not that it mattered; there was nothing either of them could do about the choices they'd made, and the past was in the past.

It was the future that mattered to Vesper, and that meant finding Judith her perfect match.

Unfortunately, the girl wasn't making that easy. "Honestly, I don't know why Greydon is making such a fuss," Judith murmured as she looked around the crowded ballroom. "I don't want a season or suitors."

Vesper frowned. "The duke wants what's best for you."

"He doesn't *know* what's best for me," she'd muttered, sparking Vesper's tacit umbrage, considering it was the way of English high society—where powerful men made all the rules.

Speaking of the fractious, odious duke... where was the rotter?

A vicious thrill blossomed at the thought of him, though Vesper had no idea if Greydon would attend this evening. If he did, she certainly intended to give him a piece of her mind. As much as she relished the idea of securing an enviable match for Judith, she wasn't his deuced underling!

Lord Eldridge approached and for once Vesper was glad for his distraction. She made quick work of introducing Eldridge and Judith, then watched like a proud mother hen as he escorted the girl to the ballroom floor.

"I think Eldridge hoped to ask *you* to dance, Vesper," Effie remarked with a sniff. "I don't think he's gotten over your refusal to his offer of marriage. He hasn't stopped staring at you all evening."

Vesper blinked and kept her smile firmly fixed. "I turned him down years ago. He knows we are just friends."

"Where's Stone?" Laila asked Nève. "Marsden looks like he's about to drown himself in the punch bowl in sheer misery. He was peeved at having to accompany me until I told him Montcroix would be here."

Nève lifted one shoulder in a shrug. "I assume he'll arrive with Lushing, if they can even find us in this abominable crush. They met at their club earlier. You look marvelous, by the way. I love that costume."

The two-piece gown was threaded in gold and royal blue filigree and set off her friend's umber complexion, gleaming dark eyes, and lustrous hair to stunning effect. Laila was quite a talented modiste, whose penchant for designs of Mughal origin was thanks to her Indian parents.

"Isn't it lovely?" she said with a twirl. "I made the mask myself, too." The gold demi-mask complemented her dress perfectly with its intricate embroidery, seed pearls, blond lace, and frond of bright blue ribbons at one end.

"Gorgeous!"

"Comfortable, too," Laila said proudly.

"Not mine." Huffing under her breath, Vesper adjusted her own mask with an irritable flick, feeling the sweat dampening her hairline beneath the ribbons. "Honestly, what is the point of masquerades anyway? They aren't at all the rage."

"They are in Paris," Laila said.

"We're in England," Vesper shot back. "Must we copy everything the French do?"

Nève grinned. "We French are renowned for our visionary tastes. That color is incredible on you by the way, Vesper."

"Thank you." The deep cobalt-blue gown and the feathered mask that had been dyed to match brought out the violet hints in her eyes, and the dress had been sewn to fit her curves like a glove. She bit back a smothered snort that the gown, ironically, had been designed in Paris.

Effie wore something that at first looked to be a cross between midnight satin shot through with silver thread, but upon further scrutiny, the silver thread appeared to be some animal's shed pelt.

"You have fur all over you," Vesper whispered to her.

"The cats in the shelter were restless," Effie said and passed a futile swipe over her skirts. Her pale ice-blue eyes brightened. "Speaking of, I have a surprise for you. Remind me when we leave this dreadful, soul-destroying place."

"Is it drinkable?" Vesper asked. "Because I am going to faint from thirst."

Effie looked as though she'd just suggested they commit murder. "No! That's barbaric! Who drinks kittens?"

"I beg your pardon?" Vesper frowned in confusion at her friend, but before she could ask Effie to explain, the majordomo announced the latest arrivals and her breath stuck firmly and thickly in her throat. "The Duke of Montcroix, the Duke of Greydon, and the Earl of Lushing."

Vesper's heart started drumming out a frantic beat as she lifted her eyes to the top of the stairs where the three men stood, debonair, powerful, and dashing. Her mouth dried, her gaze finding purchase on the only gentleman who could unsettle her so spectacularly. God, it was positively unfair that such a boorish thorn in her side would be so handsome.

Greydon's broad shoulders were barely contained by the superbly fitted black jacket, the ivory knot at his throat making his suntanned skin glow. Those thick, unruly locks were barely tamed by pomade, brushed away from his crown, and when his eyes locked on her she could feel the intensity of that tiger's gaze from behind the plain black mask he wore.

The men moved down the stairs like a trio of jungle cats and Vesper felt her chest constrict with anticipation as they prowled closer. She stood tall under Greydon's scrutiny, but inside she felt shivery and nervous as though it was her very first ball and she was awaiting her first introduction.

Goodness, what was the *matter* with her?

Greydon wasn't here for her. He was here for his ward.

And he wasn't *prowling*. He was walking. There was no hunt. She wasn't prey. Her hand fluttered to her throat. Vesper had the sudden urge to flee but instead she straightened her shoulders and stiffened her spine. She'd never run from a thing in all her life, and she wasn't about to run from a man...especially one who had *wronged* her!

Silently fuming at her own inconsistency, she dragged her eyes away, watching as Nève reunited with her husband, the stoic duke kissing her knuckles in an intimate way that had eyebrows rising.

"Chérie," Stone said. "Allow me to present the Duke of Greydon. Greydon, my beautiful duchess."

"Your Grace, it is a pleasure to meet you," Nève replied as she dropped into an elegant curtsy.

"The pleasure is mine." Greydon bowed, then gave Nève a genuine smile that had Vesper narrowing her eyes. Perhaps he was only unforthcoming and belligerent with her. She bit her lip hard when he turned her way, flecked brown gaze glossing over her with little if polite interest before moving on to Laila and Effie.

"Lady Vesper, Lady Marsden, Lady Evangeline, it's been an age though you all look quite well."

"Your Grace," Effie and Laila chirped, sinking into curtsies.

Vesper stood tall and glared down her nose at him. "*You.*"

Tawny-brown eyes met hers, one brow arching. "Me."

"I got your note," she said and glowered. Was that a bloody sparkle in his gaze?

"And I received yours." His brow arched higher, lips curling into the slightest of smirks. "Though I must admit, Lady Vesper, you seemed to have missed chapter nineteen."

Vesper recoiled. Chapter nineteen? She ran through the book in her brain. That was the chapter on ballroom etiquette. Was he casting an aspersion on her comportment? Because she hadn't curtsied? Oh, the nerve of him! Noticing the avid interest of her friends, she clenched her jaw and forced her face into serene submission. "I assure you, Your Grace, I have not."

"I've read some of your work on your recent exhibitions," Effie said to him, diffusing the uncomfortable tension and displaying the first sign of animation since they had arrived at the ball.

"You have?" Greydon asked, surprised pleasure coloring his tone.

She *had*? Vesper frowned, startled by the searing bite of…something. Not jealousy. It couldn't be. Effie was more than welcome to His Graceless. Vesper had no claim to the man or interest in him for that matter. Her frown deepened as she caught the rest of their exchange.

"I was impressed by your take on extinct creatures," Effie was saying. "What are they called again?"

"Richard Owen coined the term *Dinosauria*. It means terribly fearsome reptile."

"Fascinating."

Effie giggled, and Vesper ground her teeth. That heated feeling exploded in her belly again when Greydon gave Effie a charmed, effortless smile that held none of the rancor he seemed to save specially for her. Vesper sniffed and tossed her head. "Well, I for one think they are boring. Dead and dusty elephantine reptiles. How tiresome and uninteresting."

"Vesper!" Effie said, eyes rounding.

Greydon turned his stony face to her. "Do you?" he murmured. "Boring, tiresome, *and* uninteresting?"

It rubbed that she was the only one who could take him from charming to churlish in a matter of seconds. Vesper snapped open her fan, cursing how embarrassingly waspish she'd become in the space of a few heartbeats, but she was committed now and she could not back down. On principle.

"Indeed," she said.

His face remained inscrutable. "One could argue that boredom is simply the lack of an interesting opinion."

She exhaled in a rush. Did the cad…just insult her? Before she could summon a scathing retort, he continued.

"You are not in the minority with that opinion, however," he said in a low voice, and she met his intense stare. "Nonetheless, we can learn quite a bit from the past. How creatures lived or why they went extinct." His soft, patronizing tone dug under her skin, and Vesper bristled. "But I suppose an heiress content with"—he slid a cursory glance down her person—"pretty gowns and fancy parties has no need to understand such complex subjects."

Suddenly, Effie let out a suffocated sound, eyes shuttling

between them, but then she spun around to speak to Laila as if she did not want to be caught in the crossfire. And there would be! Vesper's temper boiled at the insinuation that she was incapable of intelligent conversation.

"You misunderstand, Your Grace. I believe quite a lot can be learned from the past. I simply think a gentleman like yourself might be better served directing his time to his estates. You are a duke, not a pedant."

"A pedant, you say?" His voice lowered to a rasp, sparks flashing in that temperamental gaze. "You pass judgment so easily, Lady Vesper? What do you have to recommend you besides your father's name and your family's wealth?"

She sputtered. "I have much to recommend me, you . . . you ass!"

His reply was a mocking lift of one brow that did more to antagonize her than any words could have done. The rest of their group was pretending not to listen to their hushed, heated quarrel, though her brother looked like he was on the verge of exploding with laughter.

"How *dare* you?" she seethed, going hot with embarrassment. "You don't know a thing about me, Your Grace!"

"I suppose not," he said easily. "I'll just have to remedy that, won't I?"

"Not if I have anything to say about it," she shot back. "I'm helping you with Judith because she's lovely and sweet, and can't control the fact that her guardian is an absolute ogre!"

A corner of those stupidly full lips curled. "So rude, Lady Vesper. I expected so much more from a lady of your impeccable, refined, *well-bred* standing."

Vesper's chest heaved, her fan working overtime to cool her burning face at his mocking tones. "Oh, you unspeakable—"

"Easy now, sister," Lushing said and cleared his throat as if to dissipate the murderous strain in the air. "This is my cue to make sure the carpets and polished floors of this beautiful residence remain blood free. Shall we head to the refreshments room for a pinch of naughty punch or display our prowess on the dance floor? I, for one, vote for any demonstration of prowess, since I am rather skilled in that area." Her brother grinned and waggled his eyebrows, but even his antics couldn't bring a smile to Vesper's face. She was much too vexed.

Too bloody *outraged* at Greydon's absolute gall.

Her friends, however, could not disappear fast enough. Vesper bit her lip and stood there as the group paired off, leaving her alone with the man of her foulest nightmares. She'd brought it upon herself, after all. She hadn't been so provoked—so *riled*—in years. Six years to be exact—precisely the amount of time that the infuriating ass had been gone. Cringing slightly, she swallowed hard and strove for equanimity. Perhaps a visit to the retiring room might be in order.

She opened her mouth to excuse herself when her nemesis extended his arm. "May I have this dance, Viper?"

"I beg your pardon?" Brimming with agitation, she stared at the duke and his outstretched hand as if it were a snake meaning to strike. Her head was shaking before her mouth could decline the request. "No, you may not."

"Afraid?" he murmured, closing the distance between them. Vesper brushed against the marble column beside her, precluding any escape.

Poise. Polish. Perfection.

Her mantra flew like a desperate arrow through her thoughts. She moistened suddenly dry lips and tilted her chin up to meet his changeling eyes. They swirled with brown, gold, and tawny flecks, pupils dilated as if she wasn't the only one affected by their impassioned spat and dangerous proximity. "Of you? Never."

"I think you're lying." The cad actually smirked in a way that made her insides quiver...and not in an awful way. Or even in an angry way, which would be much more preferable to this breathless, boneless, *brainless* sort of feeling.

"I'm not," she said with more calm than she actually possessed. "I don't wish to dance."

"But what about your promise to help, Lady Vesper? Poor Judith will be left to the indignity of knowing the ton's most beloved heiress gave her sponsor, the Duke of Greydon, the cut direct. *Again.* And in front of gossiping witnesses no less."

Vesper froze, her eyes scanning the crowd to see Judith deep in conversation with the very loquacious Lady Eldridge, who would no doubt carry the tales to anyone who would listen. The conniving scoundrel was right. She took his fingers and squeezed hard, jaw clenching. "Fine. One deuced dance."

"There's my girl," he teased when they were on the ballroom floor and the strains of a waltz began.

"I'm *not* a girl and I'm most certainly not yours," she ground out and suppressed a scowl.

Why was it always *him* who managed to provoke her? No one ever got under her skin or riled her the way he did...as he *always* had, even as a boy. Her hard-won equanimity was constantly at risk in his presence.

Grimly, she followed him into the first turns, her body rigid.

"At least try to look like you're enjoying my company, Lady Vesper," the duke murmured in a dry tone. "I'd be better off dancing with a wooden marionette."

"Why should I?" she said with false sweetness. "You've insulted me horribly. You're irritating and obnoxious, and I wish I were anywhere else right at this very moment."

"I believe, if we're citing grievances, that you launched the first stone." He whirled her adeptly into the next sequence of steps. "Boring? Tiresome? Uninteresting?"

"If you're truly bothered by my words then perhaps you should have reconsidered that condescending message you had delivered to my residence," she tossed back.

"I apologize," he said, making her stare at him in shock. "You are right."

"Did the Earth just stop spinning on its axis?" she asked. "Because I'm certain I heard you apologize."

With a smile that made her pulse trip, the duke brought her close and then turned them both, his cheek almost grazing hers. "But let's be honest, Viper. You like when I irritate you, don't think I haven't noticed. Red cheeks, glassy eyes, parted lips, shortness of breath. One could easily think you were in the midst of an or—"

"Don't you dare say it!" she nearly shrieked.

His face was the picture of innocence though his eyes glinted with devilry. "In the midst of an *ornery* discussion. What *did* you think I was going to say?"

Oh, she was going to cheerfully murder him. With her bare hands. In private, of course, where no one could see and judge her for it.

"Nothing. What are you getting out of this?" she asked, taking a deep breath in an attempt to get her agitated emotions under control.

"A dance?"

She narrowed her eyes. "This baiting and incessant provocation. Surely a man like you has better things to do."

"Tending to my estates like a proper duke, you mean." Smirking, he shot her a look that didn't have much heat in it.

Vesper felt her cheeks burn with mortification. She hadn't meant to insult him earlier or imply that his estates were in neglect because of his absence. It was awful of her to suggest he was incompetent. "I didn't mean what I said earlier."

"Then what did you mean?" He eyed her. "That I've been

derelict in my duties? Trust me, you won't be the first to say such a thing. Just speak to my mother and she will be happy to inform you of my many shortcomings as duke. In fact I'm such a disappointment to her that she hoped to have me replaced."

"She can't do that. Primogeniture is the cornerstone of the aristocracy."

"By law, a missing peer can be declared dead after seven years," he said. "Thankfully, Judith informed me in time and here I am."

Vesper opened her mouth and closed it. She *wouldn't* feel sorry for him. As if he could read her thoughts, the duke's stare fastened on her through the clasp of their raised hands as they turned, the backs of their knuckles grazing, and she nearly stumbled.

That gaze *scorched.*

Gracious, how could a pair of eyes convey so much feeling?

Vesper felt her breath fizzle, the sound of her heartbeat thundering in her ears. Greydon shifted close for the next step, his hands slipping around her waist in the most innocent of touches... that felt nothing less than iniquitous. Vesper swallowed her gasp, and she could have sworn his irises burned brighter.

Her lips parted on a sigh, and his fingers flexed at her waist. Vesper dragged her stare away from the beguiling trap of those eyes... and made the mistake of looking at his mouth. Everything inside of her hitched at the sinful sight of his tongue peeking from between those two parted arches to moisten his lower lip. No man should have a mouth that lush... so vexingly kissable.

Composure slipped away on wisps of silken desire.

The press of his fingers seared through the layers of her

gown, corset, and undergarments. Her throat felt tight, her heart beating a throbbing cadence she could feel in her veins...in her belly...in between her thighs.

The more she tried to fight it, the more she *felt* it.

A half-desperate Vesper focused on the diamond stickpin in his neckcloth instead, forcing herself not to take in the golden tanned skin above it or imagine whether that warm hue covered his whole chest. She'd read about men in other countries who removed their shirts on excavation digs. Contrary to what she'd said earlier, she kept up on worldwide paleontological discoveries...for informational purposes, of course. Though she hadn't known about the duke's own publication, which was a source of irritation.

She cleared her throat. "After our dance, you must dance with Judith. If it's one thing the gentlemen of the ton love, it's some good stiff competition."

Greydon smirked. "Stiff?"

Exhaling, Vesper spun and shot him the sultriest smile she could manage under the circumstances. "Yes. Considering that's all you men think about, then absolutely. The stiffer the better."

The duke gaped, and Vesper hid her gratification. She wasn't some green miss! She had wiles of her own...clearly ones that only rose to the surface when he was around.

"I beg your pardon, my lady, but I believe I must have misunderstood."

She feigned innocence. "You were talking about competition, weren't you, Your Grace? I've heard that men enjoy it. Indoors, outdoors, in all manner of situations."

"Do they?" he choked out.

"So I've heard."

Vesper wasn't even sure what they were talking about at that point, but it hardly mattered. The duke might irritate her to no end, take her emotions from a standstill to a stampede, and make her blush like a neophyte, but she had been honing her skills on the aristocratic battlefield of the ton for years. Perhaps that was the key to the Duke of Greydon—treat him as she would any annoying suitor—like a vexing nuisance.

A handsome, hot-as-sin nuisance but one nonetheless.

The music came to a stop and he drew her close, his breath gusting over the shell of her ear. "You are a flirt, Lady Vesper."

"I'm certain I have no idea what you mean, Your Grace," she said, ushering him in the direction of Laila who stood in conversation with Judith. "Stop prevaricating. You have a job to do. Introduction, dance, stiff competition."

He narrowed his eyes at her. "You're mocking me, aren't you?"

"*Moi?*" She put a hand to her bodice in mock affront. "I would *never*, Your Grace."

Greydon shot her a dry look. "Yes, Viper, you would."

Chapter Six

Aspen stared at Judith, whose cheeks were red from dancing. Her face was contorted in the most mulish expression known to man as she glowered at the gentleman penciling in his name on one of the few vacant spaces left on her dance card.

Vesper had been right that attention from a duke would spark competition. The minute they had finished their quadrille, Judith had been whisked away by the Earl of Lushing and then the Duke of Montcroix, undoubtedly orchestrated by the tenacious Lady Vesper. Afterward, Judith had been deluged with requests for a spot on her hitherto sparsely filled dance card.

"It cannot be that bad, Judith," he murmured after the young lord took his leave. "You're acting as though each dance is a walk to the gallows."

Her mouth tipped down. "Isn't it?"

"Well, for me, yes. I loathe dancing."

She shot him a sharp-eyed glance. "You didn't look like you loathed it when you were dancing with Lady Vesper. In fact, you seemed rather enthused."

"Not at all. She's a friend, and we're both here for *you*," he said, avoiding Judith's gaze…and also ignoring the reaction that the sound of Vesper's name had sparked inside him. Unwittingly, they both swiveled to where the lady in question was dancing with her brother.

Vesper's face was animated, her eyes sparkling beneath her mask as she and Lushing twirled in a foursome with another couple. The earl said something and a peal of laughter rung out like the sound of wind chimes, making Aspen's stomach clench and jaw slacken.

"You've a bit of drool on your chin," Judith teased.

He snapped his mouth shut and composed himself with a brisk inhale. "We're not talking about me, we're talking about you. Any one of these gentlemen take your fancy?"

Judith's grin vanished. "No."

"Why not?" he asked.

"Aspen, this isn't..." Her cheeks colored as she twisted her fingers around her fan. If he hadn't been watching her, he'd have missed the resigned expression that bled over her face. Frustration and guilt warred there, too. "Never mind."

He followed her stare to where his mother was descending the staircase to hushed excitement. She did love to make an entrance. His belly soured, but he kept his face blank. Her presence had been a necessary evil. His mother's return to London had been understandable, unavoidable even...for Judith's sake.

In truth, the duchess wouldn't *be* so mysterious if he hadn't forbidden her from coming to London in the first place. Though of course, to no one's surprise, she had spun the narrative to paint herself in the most flattering light as though it had been her choice.

Darling, London has lost its luster.

I prefer the country air to the stink of the Thames, don't you?

Brighton is much better for my constitution.

Her purported disdain for town had become quite well-known, and people coveting her far-reaching influence still flocked to the residence in Brighton for her musicales and soirees during the off season. His mother had not suffered despite his decree. As if she could sense him looking, she caught his eye. Aspen stiffened when she sauntered over to where he and Judith stood.

"Duchess," he greeted, barely able to look at the woman who'd given birth to him. No one could survive such a terrible betrayal and not be scarred for it, and hers had cut deep. All he could see was his poor father *dying* in that asylum while she feigned virtuousness. She might be beautiful on the outside, but her beauty hid a rotten, selfish core. "You look well. Clearly Brighton suits you."

She did look well. Her face remained unlined, her pale complexion smooth. Her eyes were as hard as diamonds, astute and as sharp as ever while they roved over him with satisfaction. What *she* had to be satisfied about where he was concerned, Aspen had no idea.

"Greydon," she said in clipped tones. "It's been too long. I despaired of you ever returning and feared for your life."

"So much so you hunted down Cousin Eustace in my stead," he muttered out of the side of his mouth, not loudly enough for anyone close by to hear, but Judith glanced up at him with gathered brows. "Though as you can see, there is no need to call upon Eustace. I'm quite hale, mercifully."

"Mercifully," she echoed, though the set of her mouth was tight. He had no doubt that she was already at work on another scheme now that it was clear she could not control the ducal purse strings through a weak-minded Eustace. In truth, Aspen might not have cared. He could have quite happily stayed on the other side of the Atlantic and assumed a new identity.

And what would have become of Judith?

Your father's murderers?

He forced himself to smile though it felt more like a grimace. A pair of blue eyes caught his from the ballroom floor, and he could see the flash of concern in them. Of course Vesper would see right through the false grin. Despite the nearly seven years of separation, she was still the only one who could sense when he was unsettled. It was how she'd always been able to beat him at cards in their youth—she'd known when he was bluffing every single time.

"I was surprised to receive your summons so late," the duchess said, drawing his attention.

Aspen let out a huff. "And yet, here you are with bells on."

She assessed her ward with a practiced eye. "I suppose you paid a fortune for all this. How did you manage to secure an invitation to this ball so quickly? They went out months ago and Lady Eldridge is exceedingly particular about the guest list."

"With my help, Your Grace." That cool, lilting voice slipped over him like a silken blanket, but Aspen held himself rigid, knowing his every tic would be noted and cataloged for future use by the woman who called herself his mother. "So lovely to see you. It has been an age."

"Lady Vesper," the duchess purred. "How wonderful of you to come to my son's rescue."

His mother's gaze swept briskly over Vesper, taking in the expensive cut of her clothing, the diamonds winking at her fingers and throat. She hadn't changed one whit—people were nothing but social pawns to her, ones meant to be played to advance her own position in society. If they were useless, she shunned them. If they could serve her, she used them without a qualm.

Vesper smiled. "Of course, Your Grace. It is my pleasure to help the duke and the very lovely Miss Thornton."

Good God, was he the only one who could see through his mother's insufferable guile?

"Lady Vesper has been indispensable, Your Grace," Judith chimed in. "I was lucky that His Grace and Lady Vesper had renewed their acquaintance and she so graciously offered to assist."

Offered? More like agreed under duress. He let out a soft snort and sensed Vesper's similar amusement. "Oh, I don't know if indispensable is true, Miss Thornton, but I do believe I can be of assistance."

"While we're grateful, Lady Vesper, I'm here now," the duchess interjected.

Aspen interrupted before Vesper could reply. "Lady Vesper has connections and an unimpeachable reputation amongst her peers, Duchess. If she desires, I'm hopeful she will continue to advocate on Judith's behalf."

The duchess's eyes flashed with ire—she did not like to be challenged—before a practiced and utterly disingenuous smile appeared. "Of course, Greydon. You know best."

It was a win. A small, but deeply gratifying one.

Barely a week after the ball and Judith was now refusing an offer to a completely acceptable viscount. Her truculent behavior was getting on Aspen's last nerve. Finding an appropriate suitor for his ward had to be the most bloody difficult exercise of his life. Why on earth were women so demanding? Or so picky?

He blew out a disheartened breath and palmed his chin. "Viscount Jarvis is master of a solvent estate, is in possession of a pleasant face, and you will be a viscountess, Judith."

She stuck out her tongue, her face pinching. "You say that like I am winning something. Viscount Jarvis is three times my age, Aspen."

"He's not *that* old."

"Old enough to be my father at least," she retorted.

"Judith, please be reasonable." Fighting for calm, he removed his spectacles and cleaned them, the familiar sequence working to settle his ratcheting frustration. How was this so bloody hard? Modern marriages in the aristocracy were made based on strength of alliance. On paper, Jarvis was an acceptable match. She did have a point, however. The viscount *was* old...and the thought of him with Judith was not entirely pleasant.

"I am being reasonable," Judith said. "And besides, I'm simply following your mother's instructions."

He froze. "I beg your pardon?"

She shot him a dour look and perched on the edge of his desk, her legs swinging with no care for respectability. "You do realize that she put the viscount up to this, don't you?" When his brows snapped down, Judith nodded. "I saw them whispering during the ball, their heads together like sneaky little coconspirators."

"She asked for him to offer for you?"

"Yes. And then she told *me* in no uncertain terms to refuse any offers resulting from the ball. That more would come as the season went on." Judith shrugged and leaned back onto her elbows. "Gentlemen like having what other gentlemen have. That's the reason so many of them asked me to dance after I partnered with you, Montcroix, and Lushing."

His eyes narrowed. "What if you had liked Viscount Jarvis?"

"Then I would agree to marry the rotten old codger." She grinned. "But I do have a very proficient brain in my head that is more than capable of choosing the right path for myself. I have plans, you see."

"Plans?" he echoed.

"Yes, Your Grace. I wish to follow in your footsteps and become a studier of relics. I've my own collection of items and fossils already, and if you had the time, I could show you—"

Aspen sighed. "We've had this conversation before. You are a lady and your place is here."

"I'm *not* a lady," she shot back glowering.

"You know what I mean. The duchess intends for you to find a husband this season. And a title."

She threw him a look over her shoulder. "You could marry me. And then that would solve things, wouldn't it? We could go on adventures together all over the world. Can you imagine how brilliant that would be?"

Aspen's mouth dropped open as he removed his spectacles again, cleaned them, and propped them back on the bridge of his nose. Surely the chit wasn't serious? He'd thought she'd laugh in his face if he ever had the audacity to put such a ludicrous proposition to her.

An earnest expression met his, and his stomach dropped. "No, Judith," he ground out. "That's never going to happen."

He had been expecting tears, so it was to his great astonishment that the girl doubled over in laughter, a wheezing sound coming from her mouth as though she were struggling to breathe. "You. Should." More snorting and gasping ensued before she'd sufficiently composed herself to continue. "Have seen your face."

He glared at her. "You were jesting?"

With one last snort, she wrinkled her nose and wiped her streaming eyes. "Of course I was joking, you dolt! You're like family to me. Wedding you would be like wedding my brother and blech!" She pretended to choke and made a gagging face. "Gracious, the thought is enough to give me conniptions."

At one point, Aspen had wondered about them being actual siblings, but his mother had never left his father for any great length of time to have had a secret pregnancy. And truth be told, a woman so obsessed with her social status and influence would never risk such a scandal.

However, it had long remained a mystery as to how Judith had come to be his mother's ward. The girl had just arrived one day, and the duchess had given little explanation when she'd brought the seven-year-old orphan into their lives, though he'd learned years later that her parents had perished at sea. Ever since, Aspen had always thought of her as a little sister.

"You're much too young for such hysterics," he said drily.

"And yet you wish to marry me off to the oldest goat in England. I bet he lives in a mausoleum that smells like mildew and old stockings." She laughed and pulled a disgusted face.

"You are absurd," he said, but he couldn't keep the smile from his face.

She glowered at him. "Besides, you're not the type I fancy anyway."

His brows rose. "Ah, enlighten me then. Who do you fancy?"

Something flicked across her face—an odd expression—as if she had something to say, but then it was gone. "Not the type you have in mind, I can assure you. But let's turn this back to you and your marriage plans."

"I don't intend to wed," he said, standing and scrubbing a palm through his hair.

The little minx stared at him. "Are you certain about that?"

"Speak your piece or begone, brat. I've work to do."

Judith grinned and hopped off the desk, strolling toward the door. "You only ever get this churlish and fractious when you have something to hide. Does it have to do with a certain beautiful blonde with a smile that could launch a hundred thousand ships and eyes like the most perfect forget-me-nots?"

Lapis lazuli, he corrected absently before frowning. "You are mistaken."

"Am I?" she teased. "Don't worry, Aspen dear, I shall ferret out your secrets as I always do and take them to the grave. But I wouldn't rule a wedding out of your future just yet. If I am forced to brave the marriage mart, then you must be as well."

He shook his head. "This isn't about me."

"Perhaps I, too, can be as brilliant at matchmaking as the vivacious Lady Vesper," she said, skipping backward with a smile full of mischief on her face.

His brow furrowed even as his pulse leaped at the sound of her name. "Judith..."

"She's prettier than when she was a girl, no?" she said from the study door. "Don't think I haven't spied you staring at her and pining like a sad, smitten poet when you think no one can see you."

"There's no...pining," he sputtered. "It's called polite observation. You're my ward. I must make sure she's doing right by you."

"Polite *obsession* rather." She giggled, and he recognized that sly look all too well. "You can't fool me, Aspen! Measures will need to be taken."

Feeling his face burn, he schooled his expression into something grim. "Judith, whatever you're thinking, I forbid it. Do not interfere."

But she was gone before he'd finished uttering the command.

"What am I to do with this, Effie?" Vesper demanded, staring in horror at the *gift* her friend had delivered. She'd been hoping for a nice bottle of wine, maybe even a bottle of expensive whiskey. But no, said present was white, furry, and in possession of the biggest, bluest eyes she'd ever seen.

And it was also alive. Very much alive and very squirmy.

"Have you never seen a cat, Vesper?" Effie replied with no small amount of amusement. "They're commonly used to catch mice and rats in barns and stables on estates, but occasionally, they make for rather lovely companions."

"I *know* what a cat is, thank you!" Vesper scowled as the small white ball of fluff settled itself into her lap, shedding white fur all over her skirts. She could feel the tiny pinpricks of sharp nails kneading into her legs. Now this gown would be ruined. She sent a hapless look over to her lady's maid, Lizzie, who instantly busied herself near the wardrobe, the traitor.

"You should name her." Effie grinned, pleased with herself. Vesper wanted to throw both creature and friend out on their presumptuous rear ends.

"It's a girl?" Vesper asked, staring down at the fur ball.

"Yes, I checked myself," she replied. "Considering you already have Lushing, you did not need another obnoxious male in your life so a female it is."

Effie's silvery-blue eyes were full of excitement. Vesper didn't have the heart to tell her that cats had always made her sneeze dreadfully or that she couldn't keep a plant alive, much less a small animal that would depend on her for food, water, and affection.

"Why would you give me such a gift, Effie? I cannot take care of it."

Effie leaned in, stroking the animal down her spine and the kitten let out a sweet mew that made Vesper want to stroke her, too. No, no, she couldn't. Touching it spelled disaster. She'd read somewhere that some animals tended to imprint on their owners.

"You can learn," she crooned while making a ridiculous

face at the fur ball. "And you need a distraction and something to love. I've read that pets have a positive effect on their persons and are a great outlet for excess energy. Lord knows you have plenty of that."

Vesper sniffed. "Everyone knows cats don't truly love anyone. They love themselves."

"Then you shall be a match made in heaven," Effie said firmly with a dogged expression. "You can pretend *not* to love each other."

"Take her back. I mean it, Effie."

She shook her head. "No exchanges, no returns."

"We're not at the local haberdasher's, Effie," Vesper snapped, making the poor cat arch her tiny spine as she graced them with a long hiss. "See? She hates me already."

"You startled her," Effie said, lifting the kitten in one hand and lulling it back to sleep against her neck. "She's so soft, Vesper, and so good natured. Here, you try." She hoisted the bundle toward her and tucked the small animal into the crook of Vesper's neck and shoulder before she could protest. The kitten *was* soft, her fur sleek and smooth, like the fluffiest gossamer. Vesper fought the urge to snuggle into it as the tiny feline let out a loud purr.

"Pets provide unconditional love, even cats," Effie explained with a gentle smile. "They raise our sense of well-being and self-esteem. You'll see."

"You're wrong," Vesper replied, even as she rubbed her face against the kitten's fur, feeling something like ease slide through her veins. Odd, but comforting.

"See?" Effie said. "It's like the children you pretend are a burden, but you visit at the orphanage every week with food, clothes, and books. Don't think we don't know of your escapades to St. Giles, which would give your papa apoplexy, by the way. Lushing, too."

Vesper's heart gave a little lurch. It wasn't that she hadn't expected her friends to find out about her secret excursions. What she hadn't expected was how much she loved reading to the children and spending time with them. It made her feel liked for who she was, not *what* she was... a rich, pretty heiress valued for her impeccable connections. What did that say about her? That deep down she preferred the company of orphans to being in a sea of strangers?

She had her friends, and she loved them, but they all had their own pursuits.

The Hellfire Kitties weren't indolent types. They were all intrepid women who blazed through life... whereas she simply feigned her way through it.

"You have to give her a name," Effie said, interrupting Vesper's thoughts.

Vesper's fingers stilled over the creature's velvety ears, which she'd been stroking ever so softly. "Her name is Cat."

Effie frowned. "That's terribly uninspiring."

"If it's mine as you say, then that's her name. Cat," Vesper replied and then made a sour face. She was supposed to be resigned to the gift, not petting it or enthusiastically naming it, even if her choice was as *uninspiring* as Effie said. "Don't expect to come back here and not find out the thing has run off and gotten lost or something equally tragic. That will be on you."

"I think you underestimate yourself, Vesper."

"Lizzie, come here and take it," she said sourly.

With a groan, Vesper handed off the purring bundle to the lady's maid, accompanied by a reluctant request to get a saucer of cream or a bit of chicken from Cook in the kitchens.

It was a cute little thing, but she had no place in her life for a pet. She had enough trouble taking care of herself. With her luck, she'd forget to feed it and the poor creature would starve. Then that would be forever on her conscience. No, she'd find a way to give the kitten away to a good home without hurting Effie's feelings. Her friend was quite peculiar when it came to her animals.

Effie sat back in her chair and reached for a sandwich from the tea tray. "So any more news on your latest adventures in matchmaking?"

"Which one?"

Her friend shook her head. "Mr. Cross and Mrs. Elway—" Effie cut off abruptly so she wouldn't be overheard by the lady's maid who had just returned from dropping the kitten off in the kitchens. She didn't have to worry, however. In this specific instance, Lizzie was a treasure trove of information about both the man of business and the housekeeper.

"Don't worry about being quiet. Lizzie won't say a word, and as to how things are going, not well by any stretch," Vesper admitted. "He's immune to my methods."

To Vesper's dismay, the reticent and inflexible Mr. Cross had proven to be rather difficult. He would not entertain any of her discussions about how wonderful Mrs. Elway was at her job or how efficiently she ran the household. Vesper had even dropped hints that the woman spoke favorably about him but they had gone completely over the man's head.

But every setback had a solution... she just had to find it.

Effie leaned forward and propped her chin into her hands. "What are his interests?"

"Numbers," Vesper said. The man was as boring as a man of affairs could be.

"And pie," Lizzie added from where she was putting away clean laundry in the armoire.

Come to think of it, Vesper had never seen him out of the study, except for one time in the kitchen when he'd been enjoying a slice of hot strawberry and rhubarb pie. She still remembered the look of bliss on his face as he'd savored each bite.

"Lizzie, you're bloody brilliant. Pie, he loves pie!"

"Excellent," Effie said with a smile. "What about Mrs. Elway? What does she like?"

"She loves romance," Vesper said, thinking hard. "I've seen her collection of novels. She's addicted to the things. Perhaps a letter with some poetry might do nicely."

Lizzie moved closer to where they sat. "Don't forget flowers. When the weather is nice, she takes her luncheon in the rose gardens."

Vesper's mind whirled happily. She could work with that. A posy of flowers here, a slice of pie there. She grinned as a plan took shape.

"What about Judith? Any luck with that?" Effie asked, after pouring herself some more tea. "She seems lovely. We spoke for some time about birds. She has two rescued parakeets in her care. They'd gotten loose and flown away, and she found them in her garden, can you believe? I always say that most creatures have an innate good sense about people."

Vesper wanted to roll her eyes. Clearly Cat already had a *good sense* about her because she hadn't returned with Lizzie. No, she'd stayed in the kitchen where she would undoubtedly be fed and fawned over. The thought was inexplicably disheartening...even the dratted cat was smart enough to stay away from her.

"Hopefully, it will be easy to find her a match," Vesper replied.

Effie nodded over her cup. "What about Greydon? He's unattached and seems pleasant enough, don't you think? He's rather intelligent, too. They'd make a brilliant match."

The thought of Greydon with Judith made something hot clench inside of her. They would make an attractive couple, and they had history as well as shared interests. If she looked at them objectively, they made sense. There was only one problem. She was *not* objective when it came to that man; she was the furthest from it.

Vesper stiffened, only just realizing that Effie was staring at her with a knowing grin.

"What?"

Effie narrowed her eyes. "I knew it! You like him."

"You're being absurd."

"Am I?" her friend asked with a much too astute expression. "Your face went hard and you looked like you were going to tear into someone. And the other night at the ball when I brought up his publication, I almost thought you meant to tear into *me*." Eyes brightening, her grin widened. "For the record, I've no interest in pursuing the Duke of Greydon."

"Nor do I!" Vesper griped, but Effie only laughed.

"I might not be as popular as you and Laila or as worldly as Nève and Briar, but I know attraction when I see it. And you, my friend, are tumbling faster than a coin in a wishing well, even if you refuse to believe it."

"You're wrong, Effie. Greydon inspires nothing but frustration in me." But even as Vesper made the denial, something wild and untoward inside of her fluttered to life.

Chapter Seven

Aspen tugged on his neckcloth, cursing his valet for his truly exceptional cravat skills. The man knew how to tie a knot tighter than a garrote. Add in the overwarm temperatures, unnatural for this time of the year, and he was miserable… and that was *before* mingling with the cream of society.

"Explain to me why we are here again?" he said to Lushing.

"To see and be seen," the earl replied.

"Garden parties are the absolute worst invention. It's much too hot, I nearly stepped in dog shit over there, and there are mosquitos galore."

Lushing sent him an amused glance. "You sound like a crotchety old goose. Outdoors is so much better than being stuck inside a ballroom ripe with perspiration and avarice," he said. "This is not so bad. There's fresh air, lots of open space, plenty of trees for an afternoon tryst." He grinned. "If you sit on the grass near the lake, I guarantee you'll even spot an ankle or two."

Aspen grumbled under his breath. "I would much rather be in a dust bowl somewhere, digging up bones. At least that is a practical and worthwhile endeavor with measurable results. This feels like entering a Roman coliseum. To the victor go the spoils!"

His friend chortled and flung an arm over his shoulders. "Now you're getting it, but the marriage mart can be so much more interesting than naming a pile of cracked fossils, my friend." He pointed at a pink-cheeked woman who wore so many frills, it was impossible to determine where she ended and the fabric began. "That's Lady Gertrude. She's in her second season with a dowry that matches the overabundance of silk in her dress. I have nicknamed her Lady Trifle."

"That's rather insulting," Aspen said.

"Why? She looks like a delicious dessert." He waggled his brows. "I wouldn't mind a taste, to be sure. If I wasn't certain I'd be roped into marriage like a wild buck on those American plains you love so much, I'd ask for an introduction."

Idly, Aspen wondered if the women cataloged gentlemen in much the same way. Earl with terrible humor. Duke with a questionable pastime. Viscount in his dotage...

Lushing interrupted his grim musings as he pointed again, this time across the verdant gardens toward the refreshments tent. A sharp-faced woman he vaguely recognized stood in conversation with his mother.

"You might recall Lady Charlotte, Montcroix's stepmother and former fiancée."

Aspen nodded—he'd heard of the scandal that had rocked the ton when the lady in question had left Montcroix at the altar for his father, the duke.

"I call *her* Lady Mantis." Lushing gave a mock shudder. "Did you know the female praying mantis eats the male after mating? Barbaric. You'd think Lady Mantis would be satisfied being a duke's widow with an allowance that any lady would envy, but she's ever on the prowl." Brow raised, Lushing glanced at him. "She even made a play for Montcroix, believe it or not. You were lucky you were gone—she'd have picked her teeth clean with your bones—and made you a pauper."

Aspen barked a derisive laugh. "And my mother? What have you named her?"

Lushing looked mildly discomfited for a second before he shrugged. "Lady Bedlam."

That was rather apt, given her actions. Aspen pushed past the usual knot of pain that throbbed behind his ribs and buried the old feelings of futility. He'd been a boy. There hadn't been much he could have done, and by the time he'd been old enough to say anything or go against his mother's false claims, his father's health had been well in decline. He was back now, and that was all that mattered.

"Fitting," he murmured. "What about Judith?" he asked, eyes falling to the girl at the dowager's side.

"The fetching Miss Thornton? I haven't decided yet." Lushing moved to prop himself against a tree. "Though she is rather lovely, isn't she? It wouldn't surprise me if she were married off by the end of season."

"Jarvis has already offered for her," Aspen said with a slight tone of distaste. The more he thought about it, the worse he felt. Perhaps he *was* being too hasty.

The earl made a scoffing noise. "That old toad is looking for another wife? Good God but he goes through them like stockings. What would this be? Wife number four?"

"Three." Aspen cleared his throat, guilt filling him even as he attempted to defend the offer. "He's solvent and sane. Despite his age or his bad luck with spouses, he's not a terrible choice."

Lushing favored him with an incredulous stare. "Tell me that you did not try to marry off that sweet, charming girl to that relic of a viscount. I'm surprised he hasn't cocked up his toes by now."

"She refused him," he said and grimaced.

"Good for her," Lushing said, looking relieved. "At least

she has a working head on those pretty shoulders. I shall have to call her Miss Sensibility."

But Aspen was distracted as the single most vexing woman in all London arrived in a smartly drawn carriage. "Lady Viper," he murmured.

"That's harsh, even for you, Greydon. Being tasked with marrying her off can't be much fun but the poor chit's hardly a serpent."

He blinked. "No. Not Judith. Never mind."

Lushing followed his stare. "Oh yes, your favorite foe." He sent Aspen a sidelong glance. "You know she isn't the same girl you left behind all those years ago, don't you?"

"What do you mean by that?" he asked abruptly.

"The performance she puts on for the ton isn't real," the earl said. "She might seem indomitable, but on the inside my sister is fragile."

Aspen nearly snorted. The Vesper he'd known was as fragile as rock. From his most recent interactions with her, it seemed she was still indolent, proud to a fault, stubborn, and felt she could do no wrong. "What performance?"

"The one of the perfect, jejune society princess." Lushing blew out a breath. "In fact, she would be shunned if some of these nobs knew what she was up to. I bet you didn't know she volunteers with orphans every week. In the squalid streets of St. Giles, no less. Or that she helps Briar with women who find themselves in dire situations."

Aspen's eyebrows hit his hairline. That could not be true. Lushing was simply ribbing him as usual. The Vesper he knew was hardly the sort to pursue anything of real substance, much less *volunteering* with the needy. He hesitated, recalling how genuinely kind she'd been with Judith, then shook his head. The frivolous society darling may not be mean-spirited, but he could not fathom Lushing's words as truth.

His gaze lifted to Vesper and every muscle went tight.

By God, she took his breath.

In a swirl of pale lemon-colored skirts, she descended from the Duke of Harwick's carriage. Fresh-faced and rosy-cheeked in that appealing color, she looked good enough to eat. Would she taste like lemon and fresh cream? Abruptly, Aspen's mouth flooded with water.

"My sister seems to favor our father as her companion to these events," Lushing muttered. "Lord knows why."

Because it's safe. The duke was enough of a deterrent for her not to be forced to entertain unwelcome suitors. He'd noticed at the last ball that she'd danced with only her brother and her friends' husbands. With the exception of himself, she had politely refused all others. What was she so afraid of?

He cleared his throat. "Perhaps the duke enjoys these things. I'm relieved Vesper is here, at least, for Judith's sake."

"If my sister has anything to do with it, Miss Sensibility will be wedlocked in no time and not to an old goat of a viscount either." The earl actually shot him a baleful glare. "Lord knows after the success of matching Marsden and his marchioness, which if you ask me was more a fluke than Vesper's influence, there'll be no dissuading her now." He shook his head. "She's always been a hopeless romantic, that one."

Aspen's eyes went wide with surprise. "A romantic? I wouldn't have pegged her as such. She seemed quite resistant to marriage the last time we spoke."

"Not for herself. She seems to find meaning in everyone else's happy-ever-after. What can I say? My sister has always marched to the beat of her own drum, even if she's succeeded in compartmentalizing her entire nature into neat, decorous little boxes." Lushing pushed off the tree, tugged on his jacket, and winked. "Come on, I have to greet the duke, and then we can mingle and stir up the pot."

"I'd rather not," Aspen said, but his objections were ignored.

Following the earl as he headed in the direction of his father, Aspen kept his eyes averted from where they truly wanted to land, but the closer he got, the more impossible it became. Resisting her *ached.*

He bowed to the duke. "Your Grace," he greeted the Duke of Harwick.

"Greydon," the duke said. "Good to see you outside of Parliament. It was a frenetic session this week, was it not?"

"It was indeed," he said. His friend sent him an inquisitive look and Aspen rolled his eyes in response. If Lushing actually cared about what happened in the House of Lords, he would be more informed about politics.

As it was, Harwick seemed to be in agreement with Aspen that the Lunatic Asylums Act of 1853, currently over a decade old, was in dire need of amendment. He hoped to speak with the duke more about existing regulations and basic welfare in asylums and what they might propose to improve the treatment patients received while in their "care."

Aspen glanced at the woman standing serenely beside her father. "Lady Vesper," he said. Christ, she even *smelled* like fresh lemons.

She curtsied, eyelashes fanning down in a modest display. Ever the picture of decorum and elegance, Aspen was well aware of the sharp tongue and claws that lurked beneath that sedate exterior, even if she didn't bring them out with anyone other than him.

"Your Grace," she murmured, and Aspen wasn't sure the husky whisper was meant to bolt straight to his groin, though it did, uncaring for present company.

"Care for a stroll down to the water, my lady?"

He needed the walk to cool off, but he also needed to discuss her plans for Judith. Yes, that was it, nothing to do with wanting to keep her close at all. She took his arm, and they walked down to the edge of the Serpentine where a few small children were feeding the swans.

"Viscount Jarvis offered for Judith," he said.

A pair of bright blue eyes met his. "Viscount *Jarvis*? He's still alive?"

Aspen couldn't help his chuckle. "What is it that everyone seems to have against old age? First Lushing and now you."

"Pardon my boldness, Your Grace, but the man is positively ancient," she replied. "And besides, there's the unfounded rumor that he marries his wives for their dowries, gambles their money away, and then does away with them to start afresh."

Horrified, he stared at her. "Is that true?"

The grin that lit her face was dazzling. "No, Greydon, I am teasing. But we can do much better than Jarvis for dear Judith."

Something about the way she said *we* made him feel warm inside. She glanced over her shoulder at where Judith stood near his mother, a small frown marring her brow. She was fetching in a violet-embroidered ivory dress, but Aspen couldn't help noticing that she looked unhappy to be there.

"I should have thought there would be more interest by now, especially after the ball," Vesper said. "She seemed to have had a lot of potential suitors."

Aspen nodded. He'd had the same feeling. Even now, the gentlemen shied away, almost as if they'd been warned to keep their distance. His gaze narrowed on his mother. He'd be naive to think that she didn't have some angle when it came to Judith making an acceptable match, at least according to what served her best. He wouldn't have been surprised if she'd hoped to tie Eustace and Judith together, had she been successful in her succession scheme. So what was she up to?

His glance slid to Vesper who stood watching the lake with a small smile on her lips. The memory of her supple, lithe body in his arms when they'd danced at the masquerade ball made his skin prickle with awareness. But it wasn't physical attraction that drew him back to her again and again. He trusted her. Despite their past and what had happened between them...he undeniably knew he was safe to be himself with her.

Did she feel the same way?

Aspen closed his eyes and mentally berated himself. What was he thinking? What did it matter how she felt? Nostalgia was a devil of a thing. Vesper Lyndhurst was simply a means to an end—once Judith was well matched he could return to his life. But that didn't mean he could erase their shared past or ignore the press of so many shared memories.

Turning his attention back to Vesper, he pointed to one of the empty rowboats. "Fancy a spot of adventure, Lady Vesper?"

Those blue eyes lit with amusement. "If I recall correctly, the last time you manned a rowboat, Greydon, the skiff tipped and you and Lushing both fell in."

"We were thirteen and you were eleven," he said, his lips twitching. "And if *I* recall, you threw rocks at us because I wouldn't let you join us and be the captain."

"You're right, I did," she replied, a blush blooming. "But in my defense you did say, quite erroneously might I add, that captains were male."

"I stand corrected." He arched a teasing brow. "So should I be afraid of retaliation?"

The perfect Lady Vesper gave him a grin so full of mischief that he nearly burst out laughing. "I suppose you'll have to take your chances, won't you?"

Vesper peeked at the man who steadied her in such a thoughtful manner while she stepped into the small watercraft and her fingers flexed convulsively on his arm. She wasn't afraid. It had been years since she'd conquered her fear of the water but she wasn't going to turn down the aid of a strong, muscled arm to support her.

Shaking her head to rid it of images of the male physique, Vesper reminded herself that he was an ogre who liked nothing better than to argue with her. And yet, the ogre had occupied her every thought for the better part of a week. Well, he and the dratted cat that seemed fond of curling up on her head to sleep.

She'd woken three nights in a row to find her mouth full of fur, overcome with fits of sneezing, and her eyes streaming, thanks to her new extra-fluffy bedfellow. No matter how many times she banished the creature to the carpet, Cat would find a way to scale the counterpane and commandeer the bedsheets . . . along with Vesper's head.

"You are frowning quite fiercely," Greydon remarked. "Are you nervous? We don't have to go."

She shook her head. "No, of course not. I am fine."

"Are you certain?" he asked gently, still holding the boat in its position on the shore, and she stiffened. "Lushing told me that you fell through the ice as a child and nearly drowned."

She hissed a shattered breath through her teeth. "He told you that?"

"He did." Striated brown eyes in the sunlight met hers. "That's why I said what I did about captains being boys back then. I knew you'd be mad enough to forget about being scared." He canted his head. "We can stay on the bank if you prefer."

Something in her chest loosened and warmed. "No, Your Grace, I'm not afraid of the water. Not anymore." She grinned up at him from her perch. "A few years ago, I made Papa pay for sailing and swimming lessons." His jaw slackened, eyes on her, and she shifted in discomfort. "Why are you staring at me?"

"Because I've never known anyone like you, Vesper."

A smile tilted her lips. "Stubborn?"

"Fearless."

Her gaze flew to his to see if he was mocking her, but there was only sincerity in his expression. Her stomach dipped at the open esteem on his face. "My father would probably not agree with that designation. I'm rather reckless and I'm certain he bemoans my skewed sense of personal safety. Still, it was important for me to conquer my fear."

Greydon seamlessly pushed the boat off from the shore and hopped in, settling himself in the seat opposite and grasping hold of the oars. Now that he had her attention, she couldn't help noticing how effortlessly he rowed, drawing them away from shore toward the middle of the lake. She tried desperately not to notice, but every bunch of his muscles beneath his sleeves had her pulse fluttering. Thanks to their time locked in the attic, she *knew* what those naked forearms looked like, too, ripped and corded with muscle.

Enough! Stop drooling over his dratted arms.

"Why were you frowning earlier?" he asked.

"I was thinking of my cat." She gave an irritated sniff, though thankful for the conversation. "Effie's cat. She saddled me with the thing."

Dark eyebrows rose. "Why?"

"I suppose she thought I needed a friend or something to care for," she replied. "I've already warned her that it won't be my fault if the creature runs off in search of better pastures and an owner who actually likes cats."

"You don't like them?" he asked with a curious expression.

She lifted one shoulder and let it drop. "They're adorable, but they look like they're plotting murder half the time.

I'm never sure if I'm going to find a half-eaten mouse in my bedchamber or cat's piss in one of my boots. Each day it's a surprise."

"I've heard that it's a sign of affection when they bring you dead animals," he said, pulling hard on the oars in mesmerizing rhythm. "At least that's what my papa told me when I was a boy and we found a carcass of a squirrel in the scullery from one of the barn cats."

Vesper wrinkled her nose. "That's disgusting."

"It really was. What's the cat's name?"

"Cat."

He frowned. "Yes, the cat. What's it called?"

"Oh, her name *is* Cat," she said with an airy wave and then felt her cheeks heat. "Short for...er...Catalina."

His lips curved into a wicked grin. "You just made that up, didn't you? Who names their cat *Cat*?"

Vesper sent him a defensive look. "A person who has no intention of being a cat owner and was forced to accept the deuced thing under duress. And besides plenty of people do the same." He'd stopped rowing once they were out in the middle of the lake. Other boats with laughing occupants glided past them. "If I recall, you once had a canary you called Birdie."

"I was six," he said, propping the oars inside the boat. "And at least I did not name him Canary. Birdie is somewhat imaginative."

She tilted her face up to the late afternoon sun and wished she didn't have to wear her bonnet. "To-may-toe, to-mah-toe."

"You are unnaturally fond of that riposte." He grinned, the expression making his face soften. "I forgot how much you adore having the last word in arguments, even if they aren't really words but made-up gibberish."

Heat unraveled through her at his light teasing. The duke

leaned back and crossed one booted foot over his knee. Vesper fought not to notice the pull of the fabric, but it was impossible in such close confines.

"Speaking of when we were younger, this reminds me of our adventures on the River Jordan in Dorset." When both boys had realized that there was no possible way to stop her from sneaking after them and following them into the woods, they had taken her under their wings. "Remember that time that you and Lushing capsized the boat we built?" She laughed at the memory of two bedraggled boys climbing up the bank—one dark-haired, one redheaded—arguing about who was the captain and who was the first mate. "The SS *Pirate* I believe that one was called. At least we were both more creative in our naming then."

"I'm surprised we didn't just go with *Boat*."

Vesper laughed. "I don't think any of them could even be considered an actual boat. They were more of a let's-hope-it-floats-and-not-kill-us kind of vessel."

Greydon tapped his heel into the worn floorboards. "At least this one feels sturdy enough." He glanced at her. "I miss racing our horses along the coastline, too. Do you still go hell-for-leather like you used to?"

"Not in a sidesaddle," she said with a low laugh. In truth, she missed those adventures as well. She used to love the thrill of giving the horse its head, crouching low over its neck, and feeling the wind tangle through her hair. It'd been a long while since she'd felt so free to do as she pleased without being judged by all and sundry. "It's not really the done thing in town."

He canted his head. "Do you always do what's required of you?"

"Usually," she said, stiffening at the slight tone of mockery.

He stared at her for such a prolonged moment that Vesper felt the back of her neck start to sweat. "I see you, Viper," he said softly. "The real you underneath all those rules and regulations."

Her breath snagged. "What do you see, Lord Ass?"

"A firebrand hiding behind layers of expensive silk. A woman who lives on the surface because she's afraid of what's deeper."

"So?" Her skin felt too tight, her lungs squeezing.

His eyes, burning now, observed her. "She shouldn't have to apologize at all for who she is."

"Sometimes, evolution is a necessity," she replied tersely, and changed the subject. "What did you mean before about working with my father in the Lords?"

If he was bothered by her abrupt about-turn, he didn't remark on it. "He has made remarkable inroads in education and schooling for the poor."

"He has," she agreed proudly. "Papa might wear his coat inside out or forget his hat, but his heart is made of gold." She glanced back to the people milling around in their finery on the shore. "The same cannot be said for so many of the ton who care only to advance their own fortunes and serve their own wants, instead of something for the good of all."

The duke nodded as if surprised at the sentiment, and she squirmed in slight discomfort, belatedly remembering the rules of being a society heiress. Most gentlemen did not welcome women speaking out of turn. She'd taught herself restraint in conversation...though this was *Greydon*. He'd never curbed her chatter or her opinions.

"He's a good man," Greydon continued. "I've always looked up to him."

Her father *was* a good man, the best of men, in fact. And Vesper was proud that he used his power in the House of Lords to better society as a whole. "He hopes to pass a bill that grants schooling to all children. Papa has always believed that every child, no matter their circumstances of birth, deserves the chance to better themselves. He and the Earl of Shaftesbury, who has been instrumental with the Ragged School Union, are good friends and have met weekly for years. They knew each other as boys at Harrow. He told me they always dreamed of making the world a better place for all. Shaftesbury is certainly driven to do so."

"The earl is sharp," Greydon said. "I've gotten to know him in recent months while I've been in London, thanks to your father's introduction." He exhaled with a wry grin. "I'm very grateful to the duke and hope to show my appreciation for all he's done to catch me up on matters that occurred while I was away."

Vesper blinked, an idea occurring to her. Greydon and her father were not her usual fare of star-crossed lovers, but a helpful meeting of compatible minds, nonetheless.

"Perhaps I can arrange a spot of tea at Harwick House." Her face went hot. The spontaneous invitation sounded much too bold and she rushed to soften it. "With my father. That is, if you wanted to. It would be much less formal than Parliament and perhaps you can get to know one another better."

The stark surprise in his eyes was genuine. "I…thank you, I would enjoy that."

"Are you interested in the Ragged School Union then?" she asked, curious.

He shook his head, a dark cloud passing over his expression for the briefest of moments. "I certainly support your father and Shaftesbury in those efforts within Parliament, but my interests lie elsewhere. In the treatment of lunatics specifically."

Vesper waited, but he didn't continue with an explanation.

"Is this because of your father?" she asked hesitantly, considering the late Duke of Greydon had been committed to an institution.

His lips flattened, gaze darkening as it fastened to someone behind her on shore. A moment passed, the tension in his shoulders so great she could feel it, and then he gave a short shake of his head. "No. It's because of my mother."

"Your mother?" she echoed, confusion filling her at his harsh tone and the unguarded loathing in his voice. "But she loved her husband."

Vesper had never seen a pair of eyes frost over so quickly, those long fingers of his clenching the sides of the boat, knuckles going white. "Certainly enough to have him committed."

She'd heard rumored rumblings, of course, but had never believed them. People in the aristocracy loved to tear down things when they were envious. The Duke and Duchess of Greydon had been devoted to each other, to the point that the duchess's heart had been broken when her precious, beloved duke had been taken from her.

Her brows pleated. "I don't understand. What are you saying?"

"The duchess condemned my father to his death."

Vesper's mouth fell open, but she refused to believe it, not even coming from Aspen himself. "She wouldn't. She *loved* him."

The duke gathered the oars and turned the boat around to head back to land. His laugh was cold and hollow, a far cry from his earlier warmth. "One day, Vesper darling, you'll learn that love is the sweetest and most sinister of lies."

Chapter Eight

Hiding in a small alcove off the teeming ballroom, Vesper closed her eyes for a moment. God knew why her brother Lushing had taken it upon himself to host a ball, one that had been wildly anticipated, even with its short notice. Hasty but tasteful invitations had been delivered by hand barely a week ago, and even while competing with other events that had been advertised for weeks in the papers, their ballroom was nearly at capacity.

Vesper had the most peculiar urge to flee.

It was barely the start of the season and she was already resenting the absurd number of parties, even the one hosted in her own home. This wasn't like her at all. Considering she loathed sitting still, normally she enjoyed the excitement of a grand ball, the fashions, and the countless social intrigues. For some unknown reason, however, those things seemed to have lost their charm and she couldn't help but feel something integral was missing.

Perhaps not something but *someone*.

A vision of a face framed in dark waves with honey-flecked brown eyes and lips a Cyprian would kill for formed in her mind's eye, and she shoved it away as fast as the vision had come. No, Aspen Drake did not belong in her thoughts and had no bearing upon her enjoyment of the season. She required no escort or suitor, and especially not him. He might be in possession of a fascinating intellect and a unique charm she'd never found in anyone else, but letting him in—*again*—would be a disaster.

Vesper exhaled, and put her mind to the work at hand, namely finding Judith the perfect suitor. She should not be complaining. A packed crowd like this was ideal for her to uncover a host of potential matches and that was the whole point of the exercise, wasn't it? But as she observed her friends dancing, the hollowness in her chest swelled.

Laila was scandalously close in Marsden's arms, gazing through half-closed eyes at the man who clearly worshipped her, body, heart, and soul. Nève wore a similarly smitten look as she waltzed with her mercurial duke, who no one thought would ever fall for something as quixotic as love. An odd sensation gnawed at her and Vesper rubbed at her middle. The ache throbbing there was faint but constant. Was she ill? Had she eaten something untoward at supper?

She quelled the edginess riding her nerves. Shifting from her hiding place, she moved to where Judith was standing like a lonely wallflower, sipping on some punch. "You don't feel like dancing, Miss Thornton?"

Despite their childhood connection, they had agreed to use the formal addresses in public. The dowagers in the ton were quite finicky about rules and politesse, and considering her late entry to the marriage mart, Judith had to make an excellent impression.

"No partners yet." The girl lifted her dance card that had two names scribbled in. She did not look too put out by that, however. "Are you enjoying the ball, my lady?"

Vesper nodded, despite her earlier thoughts that she'd

rather be anywhere else but here, and inhaled a deep breath, a practiced smile on her lips. "I am. So what do you think of the season thus far?"

"Underwhelming," the young lady said with a peeved expression that she instantly tried to hide.

"Please, speak your mind," Vesper encouraged. "I am all ears."

"It's just that if I have to listen to another gentleman speak about himself *ad nauseum*—in the third person no less—about what a marvelous husband he shall make, I will be ill. Honestly, is it always this bad? Like a parade of spoiled desserts where one has to choose the pudding that will make one the least sick?" She made a foul face and gagged as though she'd tasted something quite disagreeable.

Vesper burst out laughing, the girl's irreverent observations making her brighten up for the first time all evening. "You're not wrong."

"I'm a dreadful ingrate, aren't I?" Judith said with a put-out expression. "I should be happy—it's so beautiful, all the dresses and the dancing and the luxury. But I'm not happy. All of this fanfare, it's not for me."

"How so?"

"These men have nothing to offer, at least nothing I want." She gestured at herself. "They want a pretty face for showing off, a pair of sturdy hips to bear them an heir, and a dowry to settle their not-so-secret gambling debts. Thanks to my parents, God rest their souls, I am passably in possession of the first two, and thanks to Greydon, I have the last, though in truth, a part of me wishes I did not."

Vesper stared at the girl, her heart lurching at the sound of the duke's name. She focused her thoughts instead on Judith's American parents, whose ship had sunk during a transatlantic crossing. That was how she'd ended up in England at Greydon Abbey. It was true that she was pleasing on all fronts, and as the duchess's ward, she had enviable connections. So why the reluctance?

"You don't wish to make a match this season?" Vesper asked.

"What I want doesn't matter," the girl replied.

Vesper turned to face her, lowering her voice. "If you could have anything at all right this moment, what would it be? What is your deepest wish?"

She didn't hesitate. "I want to travel as Greydon does, find ancient artifacts, and make a name for myself."

"You don't wish for companionship? For love?" Vesper asked quietly, knowing that most young ladies Judith's age had roses in their eyes when it came to matters of the heart. She, too, had suffered from the same affliction until it had been pared from her like the poison it was. Vesper shook her head. Fate had a delirious sense of irony if it had given her gifts to matchmake and yet her own outlook on love was so poor.

"I didn't say that, but if I met someone on my travels, that would be different." Judith shrugged. "At least I would know that we shared similar interests and that they loved me for me." Her eyes sparked with emotion. "I don't know about you, my lady, but in the end, it's not just about love, it's about being valued for the whole of who we are. None of these gentlemen know me or wish to know me. How could such a future portend anything other than disappointment?"

Vesper blinked, Judith's words—wise beyond her years—sinking in. Maybe that was why no gentleman had ever been able to capture Vesper's heart ever since her awful first season. Because deep down, she felt a similar contradiction. The ton idolized perfection, not someone who bucked tradition.

Perfection was a myth. A myth she'd dedicated her entire

adult life to…because it meant she didn't have to worry about making a misstep. She'd been too peculiar, too outspoken. Too brash. The mask was less risky than any possibility of mistake. She only had to follow the rules. Every answer was planned, every step choreographed. It was *safe*, even if the burden was at times tedious. But it was a burden Vesper had willingly carried, because more than anything she did not want to be shunned…or rejected.

"So you wish to be an archaeologist?" Vesper asked, discomfort twisting within.

"Yes. I'm fascinated by artifacts from the past that shed light on the modern-day experience. How those things shaped humanity and culture throughout history. Cups, jewelry, books, those kinds of things. I want to be like Aspen." She brightened, warming to the subject. "The duke's rather brilliant, you know. He found one of those ancient reptiles and some other wretched bone hunter took the credit for it. He told me that he didn't care to be famous—he just loved the science of it."

Vesper felt curiosity bloom at that. Since they'd become so close, surely Judith would know more about Greydon's parents. It was perhaps intrusive, but curiosity overrode propriety. "May I ask you a somewhat personal question, Miss Thornton?"

"Of course, my lady." Genuine interest lit her face. "Anything to offset this tedium."

Vesper felt the smallest flicker of guilt at being so nosy, but it wasn't as though *he* hadn't broached the subject himself. "Did you know if the late duke and duchess were close?" Vesper asked, and was taken aback by the shuttered expression that instantly clouded Judith's face.

"I'm not gossiping," Vesper prevaricated hastily. "I just meant that growing up, I always looked to their marriage as the epitome of a love match, and Greydon mentioned something the other day that things weren't as rosy as I'd interpreted them to be."

"He said that?" Judith asked in a soft voice.

"He did." Vesper nodded, without adding that Greydon might be less than amused by her following up on his cryptic mention of such. But what could she do? He clearly hadn't wanted to elaborate and put a close to her questions.

Judith didn't speak for a few minutes, though a thoughtful frown settled between her brows. "There was gossip among the servants over the years. They said the duke had been quite close with his son and the duchess apparently resented that." Judith bit her lip, eyes falling away. "When I arrived, I was something—a novelty of sorts—that she could distract herself with after she came out of mourning, but eventually the newness of me faded. I was a child in need of care, much like her own son, but left to a governess and my own devices. I suppose Greydon and I bonded over that." Judith sucked in a breath and lifted her shoulders. "If what you're asking is whether the duke and duchess got along, then the answer is no. Behind closed doors, she and the duke were strangers to each other. They slept in separate wings, were at constant odds, and yet, put on a false front to the outside world."

Vesper blinked. "They were estranged?"

"That's putting it kindly, according to the servants." Judith blushed a deep crimson with a discomfited look and wrung her hands. "But none of that matters. It's water under the bridge. Greydon is duke now, and I owe the duchess so much for taking me in."

A frown pleated Vesper's brow. It didn't sound like it was water under the bridge for Greydon...his feelings for his mother and what she'd done were quite clear.

Just then, the music shifted into a rousing polka and a

gentleman approached them and bowed. "Miss Thornton, I believe this is my dance."

Vesper gave an unenthusiastic Judith an encouraging nod, watching as they joined the other dancers. Sir George Weatherby was a solid candidate and exactly the sort of suitor who would make a good husband. While he was obsessed with his foxhounds and rarely ventured to London, he was fit and in good health, and well-off. In that, he was not a fortune hunter, which was one less thing to worry about. He was also in town to find a wife.

Too bad Judith seemed so apathetic.

Vesper's gaze drifted to a couple talking in the entryway to the servants' stairs at the other end of the ballroom and she nearly goggled after recognizing that it was Mr. Cross and Mrs. Elway who were locked in cozy conversation. She brightened.

One thing was coming along, obviously.

She wanted to move closer so she could hear, to ensure that her instincts were correct, but she settled for attempting to read their lips. Their body language wasn't contentious, but neither was it intimate. Had the scroll of flowery poetry she'd conspired with Lizzie to leave in the kitchen for Mrs. Elway with a pretty nosegay worked? She'd been remiss in not following up with her lady's maid on the housekeeper's reaction.

Watching them more carefully now, she frowned. They weren't arguing, but they were involved in a spirited discussion that didn't look pleasant from where she stood. The fact that they were speaking was good, but the fact that the interaction seemed to be more quarrelsome than charmed was not.

Drat. There should at least be some sighs and swooning by this point. Vesper had not written a name on the note, though she'd instructed Lizzie to mention casually that

Mr. Cross had been seen in the kitchens to at least plant the seed that *he* could be Mrs. Elway's secret admirer. The poem and the posy would have done the rest. Everyone loved a spot of Browning—"How Do I Love Thee" could melt the most truculent of hearts.

"*How do I love thee?*" she whispered. "*Let me count the ways. I love thee to the depth and breadth and height / My soul can reach, when feeling out of sight / For the ends of being and ideal Grace.*"

The hairs on her nape rose as the energy of the room shifted, siphoning the oxygen from her lungs in a way that only one person had the ability to do. Her heart leaped a fraction of a beat as someone moved to stand behind her.

"*I love thee to the level of every day's / Most quiet need, but sun and candlelight.*" The low baritone in her ear was warm, masculine, and deeply recognizable, but Vesper did not dare turn around even as every muscle in her body locked. "Browning, if I am not mistaken."

"I did not know you liked poetry, Your Grace," she said, her heart skipping another fraction of a beat as her reply emerged on a mortifying half sigh.

"I enjoy reading of any kind," he replied in a tone that felt like roughened velvet. God, his *voice*. The sultry graze of it was a shocking caress against her rioting senses, arrowing to her breasts, her stomach, and lower.

There was something profoundly sensual about having a man at one's back without seeing his face, feeling the deep rumble of his speech and the warmth of his breath on bare skin. As if the absence of sight sharpened all other senses. If she closed her eyes, it wasn't too hard to pretend that they were alone and he was a lover about to unhook the buttons at the back of her gown and peel it from her body.

At the utterly indecent idea, she had to press her knees

together to suppress the tremor between her legs. Her body was acutely aware of him—the breadth of his sinewy frame, that bergamot and crisp mountain air scent, the heat that she could feel radiating against her back. One step in reverse and they would touch.

Like they'd been in the attic in front of the window...his muscled form crowding hers in a way that secretly thrilled. Unconsciously, she leaned into him, her head tilting slightly and baring her neck to him.

"I see Judith is having a wonderful time, thanks to you," he whispered, making her shiver with pleasure at his praise... and *not* the nearness of his body. It was unconscionable what this man's presence could do—unravel so many years of practiced politesse, so much so that she longed to turn, throw decorum to the dratted wind, and beg him to praise her more.

Goodness, what was wrong with her?

It was as though she'd become a different woman in the space of a few scattered heartbeats. She hardly recognized who she was when he was near—perhaps because she'd buried the wilder parts of herself that had always bloomed around him. She needed to keep her wits together and do what she'd promised with Judith, not become distracted by a man who would be off to distant shores the minute his ward was engaged.

The Duke of Greydon was, and would always be, her Achilles' heel.

Vesper swallowed hard and cleared her dry throat. "Yes, she is," she said, her voice quite steady, thank heavens. "However, it seems that Miss Thornton wants to travel instead of settling down in marriage."

She could hear the surprise in his sudden intake of breath. "Did she tell you that?"

"She did. She wants to hunt down lost artifacts."

"She must truly like you," he said after a long beat, delivered with faint skepticism.

Vesper felt her brows furrow at that. Honestly, was it so bizarre that someone would confide their innermost thoughts to her? His reaction made it seem like Judith's dreams were some well-kept secret only given to the worthy. "Is that so hard to believe?" she retorted without thinking, a trait she'd thought she had exorcised.

A low chuckle made warm, mint-scented breath feather across her nape. "I'm the only one she's ever shared that with. If the duchess knew, she would never approve."

"I'm aware," Vesper said and then frowned, nearly giving in to the urge to whirl around to face him. "Why would you say that as though I'm exceptionally unlikeable?"

Unlikeable enough to reject in spectacular fashion as he had once before.

Her stomach rolled at the awful reminder.

"On the contrary, you're not." The two emphatic words were not the balm she hoped they would be. They were seven years too late.

"You don't know me, Greydon," she said softly, though a tiny part of her chafed as if it resented the choice she was making. The part that *craved* more validation and praise from him.

"I think what scares you is that I might know you better than anyone here," came his rumbling reply. "And you like it."

His lips grazed the shell of her ear in the measliest of caresses. A full-body shiver rushed through her. The kiss, if it could even be called that, was followed by the faintest of chills, as though a breeze was left in its wake.

She spun, heart pounding, but the Duke of Greydon was gone.

Aspen slipped through the balcony doors and dragged in a heaving gulp of air. Why on God's green earth would he touch her thus? The temptation had been too much to bear when she was *right* there, a radiant goddess in green silk, the sweet scent of her clouding his senses along with any ounce of sound judgment! Every time, he was drawn into her orbit.

His half vow to stay away had been tossed aside the moment he'd seen her at the pillar, keeping a keen eye on Judith as she'd promised instead of enjoying the ball herself. And when her soft voice had whispered the lines of poetry in that tone of unguarded yearning, he'd been compelled to reply in kind like a besotted sap.

He rolled his shoulders, trying to release the tension.

And his inconvenient arousal.

One inhale of her intoxicating fragrance, the slightest brush of his lips against her skin, and he'd almost been lost to a desire so primal he'd never felt its like. Every muscle in his frame ached—from his jaw to his throat to his limbs, not to mention the mallet in his trousers that was finally going back to normal. He sucked in another full inhalation of warm evening air...anything that didn't smell like Vesper was welcome. He'd dunk himself in the Thames, if he thought it would help.

His shaking fingers gripped the stone guardrail so hard it felt as though it would crumble beneath him.

How do I love thee? Let me count the ways...

The recollection of her wistful dulcet voice wrapped around him like a ribbon of handspun silk. Lushing was right—she was a romantic.

Which begged the question as to why she wasn't interested in love for herself, just for other people. Before he'd approached, he'd seen Vesper refuse several requests to dance. It was obvious she genuinely cared about Judith making an acceptable match, her attention firmly focused on his ward. She wasn't the disingenuous, self-centered girl she'd been at her come-out. Discomfort itched along his skin like nettles. Aspen's brow furrowed. Or had that been part of the persona she'd perfected over the years?

Had he been so very wrong about her all along?

"I didn't expect you to remain in town," a voice said, its familiar, proscriptive tones making his spine snap straight. He turned to face his mother.

It was like looking into an eerie female version of himself. Dark curls, twined at the crown with ropes of pearls—despite their diminished circumstances, nothing would stop her from being richly turned out—brown eyes, and the full mouth he'd inherited from her. He resented that he looked like her at all.

"You seem quite irate about something," she said, observing him from the doorway. "And you look tired."

He lifted a cool brow. "I'm not a child, Duchess, and it's been years since you had any right to comment upon my state of mind or appearance."

"You must dance with Judith." Her painted mouth twisted in disapproval. "That man she's dancing with is much too common. He doesn't possess a title and is a step away from being gentry. I want better for her."

"Shouldn't Judith decide what she wants?"

The duchess's eyes narrowed as she approached, closing the distance between them, the lilac scent of her perfume filling his nostrils. It shot him back a decade into the past, to the memory of shouting and the sound of crashing vases, his mother in a violent temper and his father red-faced, panting, and heartsore. As far as Aspen knew, his father had never lifted a finger against her, but the physical evidence of her cold rages in the mountain of broken porcelain was plentiful enough.

His father had been the misfit duke who preferred books over people. The duke's interest in history—and learning about the wonders of the world—was the first of many things Aspen found he shared with his father. As a young man, whenever he was home from school, Aspen would comb the library and read every book in his father's private collection.

During his father's internment in the asylum, Aspen's love of fossils had developed when he'd found a journal on the subject with the duke's annotations in the margins. Pursuing the same hobby had made him feel closer to the father he missed so much. It had irritated the duchess, but there was nothing she could have done to dissuade him.

"Judith will do as she's told," the dowager went on. "Which is more than I can say for you, running away from your duty as you have. It's more than time for you to cease your nomadic ways and choose a wife."

"One of your selection?" he returned coolly. "So that you may exert your influence as you'd planned to do by installing Eustace in my stead?"

Her mouth flattened. "Eustace was a precaution and you know it. How would I have known you were still alive when you refused to answer my letters." She lifted a shoulder. "If you cannot do so for yourself, I'm more than happy to choose for you." The duchess joined him at the banister, and every hair on his body rose to attention as if in the presence of peril. Not that she could hurt him, but she was capable of terrible things.

"That will not be necessary," he said, jaw clenched.

"Judith will make an excellent duchess." There it was—the seed of her plot—marrying him off to a bride under her control. She glanced up at him, but he kept his expression blank. "I've made sure she's had an impeccable education and understands what the role of being a duchess requires."

He glowered. "I'm not in the market for a duchess, Mother."

"Nonsense. You're healthy and it's time for you to give the dukedom an heir." She turned to face him then, her haughty face cold, but Aspen made sure to give none of his true thoughts away. His efforts must have failed, however, because she let out a disappointed huff. "You know, Greydon, I've read recent accounts of mental perversions being a hereditary condition. I'd hate to think your father's moral failings did not end with him."

Her words were light, but the intent was not. It was meant to harm . . . to decimate.

Aspen froze. "Are you threatening me?"

Her eyes glittered with ill-concealed malice. "Why would I do such a thing? You're my son. I simply want you to consider all paths for your future." She stared out into the lamplit gardens. "We wouldn't want you to follow in your father's reprehensible footsteps and end up locked in a padded room."

"You sent him there," he growled below his breath.

"For his own good. He would have harmed himself, or worse, his family, in his delusions. I couldn't let my only child suffer at his hands. Who knew what he would have done to either of us, if left to his own devices?"

Aspen gawked at her, mouth agape and his heart hammering behind his ribs. She would never not surprise him. Did she honestly think he would believe that *she* was the innocent party? That she was afraid for *his* life? Or for *hers*? She was truly sick to suggest the duke would have hurt one hair on anyone's head.

"Father would never have put a finger on any of us and that's the fucking truth."

Her lips turned down. "I am still your mother, Greydon, and you will address me with respect."

"You stopped being my mother the day you decided social stature was more important than family." He turned to her, heart pounding with powerless wrath, even as she glared daggers at him. "One day, for your sake, I hope you will face the reckoning of your past."

She stared at him like the hornet she was, nothing hinting at her thoughts but the hard line of her mouth and the diamond-bright purpose in that unblinking gaze. The duchess was a woman accustomed to getting her own way, no matter the price.

"Dance with Judith, Greydon," she said, dismissing him as if he'd said nothing at all. "Do not start a fight you cannot win. As for Lady Vesper, I saw you in the ballroom standing much closer than was appropriate. She is the least of your priorities."

He scowled. "How dare you? You are out of—"

The duchess raised an arm, cutting him off. "I'm certain you would not want her flawless reputation to be ruined, would you?" Her eyes glinted with malice. "Gossip is so unpredictable, after all." Aspen stilled, his blood roaring between his ears. Dear God, would she truly besmirch Vesper's good name? Her face hardened. "Do your duty."

The unspoken *or else* could not have been clearer.

Chapter Nine

A frustrated Aspen sat in the Duke of Harwick's study and stared down at the notes he'd written at yesterday's assembly in Parliament. He removed his spectacles from the bridge of his nose, cleaned them, and placed them in his pocket with a tired sigh. Vesper had come through on her word once again and arranged an informal tea with the duke. An impassioned conversation on what had befallen his father and the Lunacy Act had led to an impromptu session in the duke's study where they discussed what steps might be taken to champion changes to the bill.

"What's the matter?" Harwick asked, peering up at him from the other side of the desk.

"This Lunacy Act and its amendments are archaic," he said with ill-concealed rancor. "It does nothing besides give asylums more autonomy over their own regulation and patient care. People like my father died because of their excuse for treatment. And to make matters worse, there's no mention of unlawful admission."

Harwick nodded. "Which is why we are striving for a new amendment to address those concerns. I know this is close to you, Greydon, as you have confided to me." His white eyebrows drew together in a concerned look. "Perhaps it might behoove you to take a step back. Separate your emotions from the actions."

"I suppose you're right," he said, scrubbing a hand through his hair and then tugging on his cravat. "I couldn't help my father as a boy, but I can be damn sure no one else goes through what he did. And I still intend to find those doctors the duchess employed."

The change Aspen intended to make was important. The health of one's mind was an overlooked thing and his father had paid the ultimate price when he'd been deemed mentally unsound. The memory of the duke being carried from his bedchamber by three burly men, his head lolling from the effects of sedation had never left Aspen. He'd been only nine and small for his age. The duchess was to blame, of course, but there should have been some measures in place to provide a check and balance of sentencing a perfectly sane man to an asylum.

"Your father isn't well, my son," his mother had cooed when he'd tried to stop the men from leaving with his father. "He needs help."

Aspen remembered arguing, "Why can't he be helped here at home?"

Convincing tears had trickled down her cheek, more for the servants who were watching and sniffling behind their own handkerchiefs than for him. "It's for his own safety and ours. Don't worry, he will be well taken care of, my sweet boy."

"Can we visit him?" he had begged.

"Of course we can."

That had been a nightmare in itself. Aspen had been horrified by the spartan nature of the room his father had been given and the plain, homespun nature of his clothing. The duke had aged decades in weeks, his hair unkempt and his face unshaved. He'd lost weight, too. What had bothered Aspen the most had been the haunted look in his father's eyes as he'd struggled to remember his own son, his stare glassy and vacant. Drool had leaked from the corner of his mouth, even as he'd mumbled in less than coherent sentences.

"What's wrong with him?" Aspen had whispered to his mother.

The duchess had dabbed at her eyes. "He's ill, my boy."

"Will he get better?"

"I hope so," she'd replied in earnest.

Fists curling at his sides, Aspen gnashed his teeth together. It had all been a lie, of course. From time to time, he'd heard rumblings in the household—the servants always knew the truth of everything—and he'd made it his business to sneak around and listen.

The rumors had been shocking...that his father's illness had all been a ploy of the duchess with falsified doctor's records to gain financial control of the ducal estates. But it wasn't until he'd heard from his mother's own mouth that she would be glad to be rid of the tight-fisted old codger once and for all that the truth of her duplicity had sunk in. Back then, he'd thought about confronting her with the gossip, but he had no proof.

The handful of times Aspen had visited his father over the next three years, he'd barely spoken, only stared at Aspen with that haunted, hollow look.

Until the very last time when Aspen had gone alone.

The duke had been covered in bruises, which the orderlies claimed were from him losing his balance. Aspen had his doubts—one such bruise on his arm was shaped like a handprint. Anger had poured through him like molten lava.

"Father," he'd whispered. "I'm going to get you out of here."

A thin hand had reached for his, shocking Aspen into

stillness. His father's blue eyes had been surprisingly lucid for the first time in years, his voice rough with disuse. "You. Live. Son."

"Yes, we can live together," he'd replied, throat clogged with emotion. "We're going. I don't care who I have to bribe or fight."

"No," his father had mumbled, before a hacking, wet cough overtook him. "Too. Late."

"I can..."

"Proud. You." He'd squeezed as much as his frailty would allow. "Work hard. Respect...earned."

That had been the last conversation Aspen had with his father, and it had broken him. He'd poured everything into his studies. Aspen had returned to London for one season after university, and couldn't bear a single second of the pretense, of all the lies and intrigues that drove the ton. He'd seen Vesper, once his constant childhood companion, now grown into a beautiful young woman destined to take her place among the ton.

She'd been all smiles and haughty perfection, and all he could see had been a younger version of his mother—a spoiled, selfish darling who'd ruin the life of any gentleman foolish enough to fall at her feet. Nothing of the girl he'd known remained. And there had been so many suitors fawning and begging for her favor.

The spike of jealousy he'd felt had made him ashamed. And angry that she could make him feel so untethered. Unwilling to be reduced to just another pathetic suitor—or a weak reflection of his father—he'd snubbed her quite deliberately.

Before she had the chance to reject him.

Before *she* could hurt *him*.

In hindsight, he'd been much too broken and wrecked

after the duke's death and his mother's deception to make much sense of anything. Including the beautiful heiress he might have judged unfairly all these years. For no good reason at all, his former best friend had become the nucleus of all his frustration and pain. Directing his anger at her had meant he didn't have to be angry at himself. He realized that now. And perhaps he'd done Vesper an enormous disservice by painting her in such an unflattering, unforgiving light.

She'd agreed to help him. She'd been kind to Judith. She'd kept her word.

All traits that were the opposite of what he'd convinced himself to believe of her.

In the end, leaving London had been as much for his sanity as it'd been to find some version of truth and meaning in his own life. Even Judith hadn't been enough to keep him on English shores. He felt immense guilt for that, too, for abandoning her, but his dark desolation would have also drowned her. Examining fossils and bones had taken enough of his focus and attention, allowing no room for emotions and ruminations.

Fossils didn't lie. Bones were dependable.

His life abroad had been full, and busy, but now that he was back in London, he was forced to admit it had been a lonely life as well. Bones were dependable, but they were also dead.

Aspen shook his head. Now wasn't the time for self-pity or regret for any of his choices. He turned back to the duke and cleared his mind of memory.

"I'm fine," he said to Harwick, who was still watching him with a look of concern. "The fact that my father, a duke no less, could have been judged via inquisition to be of unsound mind to govern his affairs, with little more than an accusation and a medical opinion, is astounding to me." He scrubbed at his jaw. "How was she able to do it? I know there were doctors involved—she couldn't have admitted him without them."

Harwick gave a thoughtful nod. "It happens more often than you know, though it is usually the opposite—it's the wife who is declared a lunatic so found."

"It's reprehensible," Aspen said, anger filling him anew.

"You should get some air," the duke said. "A walk will settle your mind. The gardens are lovely this time of the afternoon."

Aspen let out a tight breath. Perhaps a walk would do him good. "Thank you, Harwick," he said. "I know the way. I shall rejoin you shortly."

"Take your time," the duke replied. "The work will be here."

Nodding at the man, Aspen strode from the study and made his way toward the small gardens at the back of the residence. Shrill voices arguing from behind an open door slowed his pace. When he recognized one of them, his pace slid to a pause. It wasn't in him to eavesdrop, but Vesper sounded agitated...which wasn't like her, unless of course, it was because of him.

With anyone else, she was usually the epitome of restraint.

Not now, however.

Curious considering his earlier thoughts about lumping her unfairly into the same ilk as his mother, he cocked his ear toward the conversation. It wasn't as though he was snooping. The door was ajar and they were speaking loudly enough for anyone passing by to hear.

"I need more money," Vesper was saying. "This is the way to get it."

"Didn't your scheme with your father's solicitor and the housekeeper to make him love-drunk enough to be less grouchy and loosen the ducal purse strings work out?" another voice asked. It sounded like Lady Briar though Aspen couldn't be sure. He frowned as the meaning sank in. Good God, Vesper hadn't, had she? Such a thing irked—that she would go to such lengths to manipulate someone just to get more pin money.

Didn't she have enough already?

"Not yet," Vesper replied, her arrogant lilt making Aspen cringe and banish his earlier opinions. "Which is why I needed your help, and this"—the sound of crumpling paper reached him—"is the way to do it."

A sigh. "Vesper, these things take time and planning."

"Both of which we don't have, Briar. The new clothing alone will need to be paid for. I cannot afford to wait or ask Mr. Cross for more funds. He might be on the cusp of falling foolishly in love with a bit more elbow grease on my part, but he's not stupid. I can't risk him getting suspicious."

Irritation filled Aspen at her plotting. Of course it had to be about new gowns. Hearing the sound of scraping chairs and rustling dresses, he veered briskly down the corridor to head out into the garden before he was discovered. He'd barely made it a handful of steps when a frantic shriek made him spin, only to catch a flailing mess of silk-encased limbs as a woman tumbled into his arms.

Vesper was in such a froth that she'd tripped over the threshold of her own parlor. In the next second, she was resigned to the bruised bones she was sure to get out of it and threw her arms up to protect her face. But it wasn't wainscoting she hit, it was a wall of a different nature.

A wall of a duke.

"I beg your pardon," she gasped against his broad chest,

the force of him no less hard than an actual wall panel, but the arms that cradled her were more than gentle. The appealing feel of him blanketed her senses and all Vesper wanted to do was curl her fingers into his ribs, tuck her head into the curve of his shoulder, and sigh with pleasure. But of course she could do no such thing.

A distant memory of him hugging her when her mama had died from consumption filled her head. Much smaller then, he'd held her near the sea cliffs while she'd wept into his shirt, his own tears falling into her hair. At the aching sense of familiarity, a small part of her buried deep mourned the loss of their friendship. Though that hadn't been *her* fault.

He'd been the one who had spurned her in front of the entire ton and left.

Peering up, she caught sight of the embittered, furious scowl on his face, and then frowned herself. She hadn't meant to crash into him. Why was he looking so aggravated? It wasn't as though she'd thrown herself into his arms on purpose. "Apologies, Your Grace. I wasn't watching where I was going, and I tripped."

"You need to be more careful." His tone dripped disdain, catching her off guard.

"I said I was sorry," she snapped in bewildered affront. Why was he so angry? Had something happened with her father? But before she could ask him, he cleared his throat.

"Are you hurt?" The terse rasp cut to the quick, and she blinked, using her hands to push off his chest. That would require his own arms to loosen, which they did not. Vesper couldn't deny that she liked being held by him, though anger simmered at his curt, confusing manner.

"No." She spoke to a fold in his neckcloth, unwilling to lift her eyes. "You can release me now."

"Can I?" he drawled.

Something in his voice dug at her. It elicited a strange feeling, as though there was more layered in between those two words. She didn't like it. His tone felt flinty... well, flintier than usual. The last time she'd been facing him this closely, he'd almost kissed her and she had wanted him to. Now his embrace, while helpful, felt slightly pernicious. She couldn't keep up with the man's mercurial moods!

"What do you mean, *can you*?" She wriggled in his implacable hold and scowled, eyes lifting to his. He was irritated. At her, clearly, for no reason at all. "I didn't give you leave to catch me in the first place."

"So you wished for me to let you fall?" A slight smirk appeared, though his eyes still flashed with vexation.

"Would you have?"

She felt his shoulder lift in a shrug. "If I'd known it was you, perhaps."

"God, how are you this insufferable! And why are you still here? Teatime ended hours ago."

A sardonic smile lifted his lips. "Regretting your invitation already? Do I require Her Highness's permission to stay longer?"

Heavens, had he always been so caustic? Why on earth had she offered to invite him here at all if he was going to be this obnoxious? She flushed, mouth flattening as she lost the wafer-thin grip on her emotions as she always seemed to do in his presence. "Perhaps *you* should have moved out of the way since *you* cannot suffer to be a gentleman for one infernal second." She shoved futilely against his brick slab of a chest. "I'm sorry to have caused you such inconvenience, you... you... shag-bagging slubberdegullion."

One of the women at a shelter house in Shepherd's Bush had screamed the insult at a man who had come to find her and it meant a slovenly, shabby dastard. At least, that was what she thought it meant. Aspen was being an arrogant cad and deserved it.

Dark eyebrows rose, the slightest huff of amusement leaving his mouth. "That's new."

"What?"

"Such filthy sentiments falling from such pretty lips."

How dare he judge her? She blinked. He thought her lips were pretty?

Oh, wise up, won't you!

Vesper scowled, more at herself than him—she'd kick her own arse in privacy later. She wriggled again and then froze when his arms tightened, bringing her breasts close enough to brush his coat. She didn't dare breathe. As it was, her nipples were already at horrifyingly taut attention—didn't they know that the rest of her was furious with him?

Vesper swallowed a hysterical giggle at her half-feverish, patently absurd thoughts. Goodness, *why* was he so muscled? It was like being plastered against a rock. A warm, sinfully hard rock that her breasts worshipped and the rest of her was quickly warming up to... Vesper clenched her knees together to stop from squirming and *felt* that intense gaze land on her. Her cheeks heated as his fingers flexed reflexively on her waist, his gaze going dark with...something almost feral. Was it possible he felt the same?

Warmth sparked and built at the thought.

She breathed out. "Aspen..."

"Why do you need money?" he asked abruptly.

Vesper froze, desire draining away at the strange, blunt question. "What are you talking about?"

"Your conversation earlier with Lady Briar. Arranging a match between your father's man and the housekeeper."

She balked in horror. "You were spying on me?"

"I'm certain everyone in the vicinity was privy to your sad

little woes about not having enough pin money to buy your insignificant trinkets, my lady. Hence your sly machinations to get your way."

Vesper stared up at him, seeing the hint of distaste in his gaze. It bloody stung that he would still think so poorly and the very worst of her, even after all she was doing for him with Judith. "You know nothing, and my plans are none of your business."

Her throat worked even as her eyes burned from the prick of sudden tears. Why *should* she care what he thought of her?

She glared at him. "Why are you still holding me?"

"I'm not," he said.

Blast him, he was right. His arms were no longer banded tight around her, but hanging loosely at his sides, and yet here she was like a snuggly kitten, shoring up against him as if her misbegotten legs had forgotten how to do their job. Burning with mortification, she stumbled backward out of his sphere, a piece of paper floating to the ground between them.

Before she could retrieve it herself, he'd bent and grabbed the crumpled parchment in his hand. Vesper squinted at it, recognizing the message she'd written to Briar that she had brought over to discuss. It must have dropped from her grasp and gotten caught in her dress when she'd collided with him, and in the heat of the moment, she'd forgotten about it until now.

Damnation!

"Give that back!" she demanded, snatching for it as he quickly sidestepped her and strode toward the steps that led into the garden. She raced after him in outrage at his audacity and yanked at his coat just as they reached the bottom of the stone steps, but the wretch held the paper above their heads easily out of her reach. Vesper bit back a curse. She hopped up to the step behind her, putting her at eye level with him, and grabbed for it again.

"What is it?" he said, avoiding her reach and holding it aloft.

"None of your concern," she snapped. "Give it back."

Vesper was so close she could see the swirling glints of gold and topaz flecking the inner rim of his irises... so much so that she could lean in and seal her mouth to his, if she so chose. Gracious, why should she want to kiss him? He was a vexing, meddling tyrant! Inhaling sharply, Vesper licked her top lip and watched his pupils flare as his gaze dropped to her mouth. Her earlier resistance fizzled as something hot and fierce unraveled in her core at the intensity of that stare while warning bells went off in her brain.

This wild attraction between them was like a perilous sea.

Powerful, consuming, and ever so deadly.

Reason renewed—*somewhat*—Vesper moved up to the next step, which put her above him in height, and reached for the parchment again. When her fingers were a hairsbreadth away from victory, he sidestepped her again and headed into the garden. In a state of indignation, she gaped at his disappearing back before hurrying after him. What game was he playing?

He unfolded the letter as he marched away. " 'My dearest friend,' " he read aloud. " 'The situation is dire. I have come to the opinion that a charity ball is the only way to raise the funds I need. As such, here is a proposed guest list for this endeavor.' "

Vesper's heart pounded. That note and list was between her and Briar, but what she was most worried about was that farther down next to his mother's name, she mentioned him in less than gleaming terms. Her cheeks burned with mortification.

Don't read more, don't read more, don't read more, she chanted in her head as she hurried to match his pace. She could see the glaring lines: *His Graceless, however, is the most insufferable, arrogant man on the planet who thinks he's better than everyone. He will not be invited.*

"What's this money for?" he asked over his shoulder.

"I told you—none of your deuced business!"

He rounded a tall elm, and she was rushing to catch up with him when she crashed directly into his side. Breath left her in a whoosh, her feet skidding on the graveled path and arms whirling like a windmill as she lost her balance. The duke swiveled to catch her after a panicked shriek left her lips, only to lose his own footing—*dratted gravel!*—and they went toppling together...right into the shallow fountain at the bottom of her garden.

Soaked through, Vesper gasped, spluttering and eyes blinking. She shoved clumps of sodden hair out of her eyes, only to start laughing hysterically at the sight of the equally waterlogged Duke of Greydon looking like a drowned, spitting kitten. Well, more like a drowned, spitting tiger. A pair of glowering brown eyes met hers and she snorted from trying to stifle her giggles. It was no use! She burst out laughing.

"I'm happy to see you find this amusing," he muttered, glaring down in disgust at his ruined clothes. He scowled at her. "And this is the second time you've crashed into me today. I'm beginning to think it's a condition with you."

"And I'm beginning to think that contrary to your previous claim, you would not choose to let me fall after all."

Seeing the parchment he'd stolen floating on the water, she snatched it up, but the ink had long smeared. She wondered if he'd read more of it before it'd been damaged. She hoped not for her sake! Vesper shoved it into her pockets, but not before his eyes had narrowed on the movement. She bit her lip.

"We're going to talk about that," he said.

Greydon moved toward her and then paused, with a quick

flicker toward her wet bosom. He shook his head as Vesper shot him an unreadable look and then hiked her skirts to dart past him. He was still staring at the scandalous glimpse of her wet stockings glued to her legs when she tossed her reply over her shoulder.

"It has nothing to do with you, Your Grace," she lied. "So no, we won't."

Chapter Ten

He was truly a glutton for punishment.

A dinner at Harwick House this soon was not ideal, barely after Aspen's last unfortunate run-in with the lady of the manor two days ago. The chemistry bubbling between them was a dangerous thing, one he needed to be mindful about, especially now that his opinions about her seemed to be on shaky ground. She was different, yes, but he wasn't convinced that his instincts were wrong.

The vision of her in that fountain—blond hair dripping down in wet curls around her face, droplets coating her thick eyelashes like diamonds, those blue eyes sparkling with laughter and mischief—had hit him like a fist to the gut. He'd never wanted to kiss her more.

Aspen ground his jaw and stared straight ahead while his valet straightened his fresh suit of clothing. The evening ahead was going to require forbearance on his part, but it was necessary. Harwick had invited him and it was an offer Aspen had not been able to refuse, at least not without causing offense to the man supporting him in the House of Lords. The invitation to tea had led to a fruitful discussion and action steps that Aspen had been more than grateful for. He supposed he had Vesper to thank for that.

He hoped that she might not be in attendance. Perhaps she would have other plans. An heiress like her was always in great demand. However, to his great despair, when he arrived at Harwick House that evening, he quickly realized that it was not to be a quiet dinner. In fact, it was a dinner *party.* Aspen almost turned on his heel and left.

"There you are!" The duke's elated expression wasn't nearly enough to make him change his mind. "I confess, Greydon," Harwick said, "I was glad you accepted. Tonight would have been rather intolerable on my own. It's my daughter's circle, you see." He squinted at him. "Though your circle, too, before you took off for destinations unknown. You won't be bored to tears with the conversation of an old man, never you worry."

"It's not *that* I'm worried about," he muttered as his eyes collided with a pair so vibrantly blue he became mute for a moment. Vesper's mouth parted in silent surprise when he entered the dining salon with her father, her gaze going wide as if seeing him was as much a shock to her as the reverse was to him.

He didn't even notice the other guests in the room, most of whom he already knew. Lushing, the duke's heir, was there of course, chatting with Lady Evangeline and Lady Briar in the corner. The Marquess of Marsden stood with his wife next to the Duke of Montcroix and his duchess. There was another young couple he did not recognize at the far end of the room in conversation with Judith, whom he was surprised to see. She'd not told him she'd be venturing out tonight.

Harwick clapped him on the back, drawing his attention. "We can continue our discussion about who else we need to bring to our side in the House of Lords to have the best position. We didn't get to finish the other day and I'm eager to put a plan in place."

Aspen nodded. "As am I."

"Vesper, I hope you don't mind that I invited Greydon," Harwick said.

"Of course not, Papa." Her mellifluous voice rushed over Aspen's senses like tinder to flint. Desire flickered and roared into being when he turned to face her. She looked exceptionally lovely in a coral-colored gown that made her creamy complexion glow with rosy health.

Lushing handed him a glass of whiskey. "Glad you're here, Greydon. Didn't realize that Vesper had invited you or I would have mentioned it earlier. She took away my invitation privileges when I invited a woman I was courting."

"You brought your *mistress*, Brother, and I did not invite the duke," Vesper shot back without inflection, though the slight downturn of her lips hinted at her frustration. "Papa did, and now the whole table will have to be rearranged."

Lushing laughed. "Come now, Sis, there's always room for one more! Isn't that what you always say? No man left behind, food and wine for everyone... at least anyone with a fortune, a title, or a pretty face."

Vesper's cheeks went scarlet. "You make me sound like a conceited half-wit. I don't say anything of the sort." Her gaze slid to Aspen even as she said her defense. "*Everyone* is welcome to our table, though I do draw the line at women my brother generously compensates to warm his bed."

"What do you have against jades? They do honest work," Lushing shot back with an admonishing look though his mouth curled with glee at antagonizing his sister.

Her eyes narrowed to a glint. "You know very well I have nothing against anyone making a living, Jasper. In fact, I probably spend more time with such women than you."

Aspen frowned. Lushing had been having him on when he'd said she frequented places like St. Giles, hadn't he? A society heiress of her ilk would be hard-pressed to leave Mayfair, much less fraternize with light-skirts. Lushing's eyes widened and he started backing away. "Gads, she called me by my Christian name. We're done for! Run for your lives!"

"Enough, boy," Harwick chastised, but there was no heat in his tone as if the squabbling between the siblings was a usual thing. He shook his head at his son. "I don't know why you bother riling your sister. She'll only get her revenge some way or another, and you know it."

Aspen watched as Vesper spoke with a nearby footman, instructing him to add another place setting to the dinner table. The duke cleared his throat. "Seat him near me," Harwick ordered. "We have some business to discuss."

Vesper's body stilled, but she nodded to the waiting footman. The reason for her reaction became apparent when they were all seated and he found himself situated opposite her. Aspen was certain that having to stare at him for the duration of several courses had not been part of her plan. If she'd had her way, he'd probably be sitting at the other end of the table or out on the terrace.

By himself.

"Thank you for making a place for me, Lady Vesper," he said as the servants brought in the first course.

"Of course, Your Grace," she replied like the perfect hostess she was. "You are always welcome at Harwick House. I believe you are already acquainted with everyone here."

Nods and smiles were exchanged, Aspen's gaze passing down the table to stop on the couple he couldn't place. The man was very handsome and the girl seemed quite shy. If Aspen had met them previously, their names eluded him. He had been gone from England for a long time, however.

"Not everyone. I fear I am not acquainted with the couple at the end."

Vesper let out a small hum of surprise. "Oh, but you have, I'm certain of it. You must recall Mr. Robert Evans, though you will know him as the former footman of the Duke of Montcroix, and his fetching wife is my own cousin, Georgina. They've only recently married."

He blinked and then offered a polite nod.

"Your Grace," the couple greeted him with shy but friendly deference.

A smug smile quirked Vesper's lips, and Aspen realized that she must have had something to do with their union. Not that he was anyone to judge, but marriages between aristocrats and commoners were rare. More often than not, that usually meant it was a love match... where the loss of one's station and reputation was worth the reward of the relationship, at least in Georgina's case.

The young lady kept peeking at her husband as if he were a vision that might disappear and the man himself seemed a bit bemused by everything. He was an ex-footman seated for dinner at a duke's table after all, though Harwick seemed more enraptured at the presentation of the second course—fillet of sole in beurre blanc—than anyone present in his dining room.

Aspen smothered a laugh. His own mother would have sooner cut off her nose than welcome a former servant to hers. It was one of the things he admired about the Duke of Harwick—that encompassing sense of fairness. His work in the House of Lords sought to better society for all, which was why Aspen looked up to him.

His gaze flicked to Vesper for a split second. She certainly used to have staunch opinions of justice and equality. Or was that something she'd buried as well? Had he been right about her all along? The conversation he'd overheard about her matchmaking the duke's man of business with the housekeeper came back to mind. That whole plot reeked of pure selfishness instead of altruism. If she could be that opportunistic for a matter of pin money and new gowns, what did that mean for this couple? Or Judith, for that matter?

"That was your doing, I assume?" he asked Vesper, not deigning to hide the hint of scorn. "The pair of them."

A proud grin touched her lips. "It was."

Lady Evangeline who was sitting to his right chimed in, "She has a gift, Your Grace. What is it now, Vesper? Four couples?"

"I suppose it's much easier than putting one's own heart on the line, isn't it?" he replied to Lady Evangeline, though he didn't miss Vesper stiffen across from him. Out of the corner of his eye, he saw her stab viciously into her fish. Perhaps she was imagining that the flaked carcass was him. He hid his smile behind a polite cough.

"How so, Your Grace?" Evangeline asked.

"When one has no risk to themselves, it is much easier to play. Setting up a match costs the arranger nothing but a misguided sense of cleverness."

"I beg your pardon," Vesper said, eyes flashing, though her tone remained scrupulously polite. "*Misguided?*"

He lifted a brow as if he hadn't realized she was listening. "Inflated, then?"

She smiled sweetly, all teeth. "The only thing inflated here is your ego, Your Grace." The only outward expression of her anger was the tightening of her fingers upon her fork, and oh, how the sight of that gratified him.

"What are we talking about?" Harwick inquired.

"Lady Vesper's success at matchmaking," Aspen replied. "I've just learned that she's rather... clever at it. Case in point, the newlyweds here, Mr. and Mrs. Evans." He lifted his wineglass. "I toast their continued happiness, and of course Lady Vesper's extraordinary powers of blissful persuasion."

"Hear, hear!" Lushing crowed.

Aspen wasn't finished, however. A perverse sense of devilry filled him, mostly because Vesper was glaring daggers at him from across the table. He had the sudden urge to see how far he could provoke her into breaking from that composed mien. Inasmuch as they used to be able to read each other, they'd also had an innate ability to rile the other. "And now I hear she's on to her next match." Her face blanched, eyes darting to her father for a scant second before going blank. "This time even closer to home. Mr. Cross and Mrs. Elway are in your own employ I understand, Your Grace? She truly does have a gift."

The duke blinked, a frown forming between his salt-and-pepper brows. "My man of business? And the...housekeeper?"

"The very same," Aspen replied with an innocent look. "Love blooms everywhere the lady treads, it appears, except in front of her."

Vesper's expression was so sugary he could taste it. "Perhaps because what is *in front of me* is nothing I want."

"Are you certain?"

"Quite," she said, and signaled for the course to be cleared.

Poor Lady Evangeline looked as though she'd prefer to duck beneath the table to join Lushing's hound, which had been resting its head in her lap. The Duchess of Montcroix shot him a fascinated look, an intrigued smile playing upon her lips. Stone whispered something into her ear and his duchess blushed.

Conversation continued at the other end of the table where Lady Briar was speaking with Evans and his bride while Marsden was in conversation with Lushing and Judith. Aspen briefly wondered if that was Vesper's new game—a match between her brother and Judith. Given Lushing's tendencies to sow his oats across England and Europe, Aspen wasn't sure that his friend was the best option for a husband. He was certainly titled and an eligible bachelor, but Judith deserved someone she at least shared interests with.

Wasn't that what made a marriage sustainable? Common passions? He couldn't help glancing at Vesper. They used to have so much in common.

"I beg your pardon, *my* Mr. Cross and *my* Mrs. Elway?" Harwick repeated with a concerned look as though the revelation had finally hit. "Surely not? Vesper, why would you arrange such a thing?"

Vesper glared at him, and Aspen lifted a brow in challenge. He wanted to dig at her, to chip away at that polished exterior and see if anything of the old Vesper remained. The hothead with the big heart who didn't care about getting her dress dirty or saying what she felt in the moment without guarding every single one of her words. An odd pang of nostalgia hit him unexpectedly.

"It's nothing to worry about, Papa," she said with a forced grin. "They've been making calf eyes at each other in secret for weeks. I'm simply facilitating the process."

Aspen nodded sagely. "Bringing people together requires a delicate and skillful touch. I'm rather in awe of her," he said. What he was truly in awe of was how valiantly she was holding on to her infamous sangfroid.

"Are you, Your Grace?" she bit out with a sweetness that bordered on ferocity. "You have a poor way of showing it by insulting my intelligence at every turn."

"How so, Lady Vesper? I've just praised your brilliance to everyone here." He leaned back in his chair, steepled his fingers, and smirked, appreciating the darkening flush on her cheeks the longer he stared. Her mouth was pinched, but the look in her eyes wasn't quite anger. If he didn't know better, Aspen would think she was also secretly enjoying the word-play. Perhaps even getting aroused by it. His own blood fired at the idea.

"Compliments couched in condescension is hardly praise," she said. "But perhaps you think me lacking in wit to notice."

"On the contrary, Vesper darling."

As soon as it bypassed his lips, Aspen wished he could take the sobriquet back. He saw the precise moment anger overtook the desire when she flinched as if the endearment in current company was more than she could bear. Throat working, she set down her fork, her voice low. "Your eyes betray your ridicule, Greydon. Admit it. You think my efforts to facilitate a love match a joke, don't you?"

It was a wonder that the lacy tablecloth between them didn't go up in a tower of flames. Her eyes sparked with fury, that trembling mouth parted in rage, and all he wanted to do was drag her onto the table and make her his next course. Make those flashing eyes brighten anew with lust instead of anger.

He lifted a brow, toying with his glass. "I think you love the idea of love, but if you have not experienced it for yourself, how can you be sure your efforts will last?"

"Marsden and Laila withstood the test," she said and peered down the table. "Montcroix and Nève are a match made in heaven. Evans and Georgina will last as well. Perhaps it is you who has no idea of true love and wish to darken everyone else's doorsteps with your dour shadow because no one in their right mind will ever have you."

Her teeth were gnashed so tightly he could hear them grinding. Aspen sipped his wine, even as the barb landed. "Goodness, my lady, don't hold back."

"Vesper, what has gotten into you?" her father interrupted with a sharp frown.

She flinched at the reprimand, and for a moment, Aspen suddenly regretted pushing things so far. He enjoyed sparring with her, but not at the expense of being chastised by anyone but him.

"Apologies, Your Grace," he said. "I was the one out of line. The fault is mine."

An astonished gaze lifted to his, but he pretended not to notice it, or wonder why that small, unvarnished expression made his heart give a thump.

During the next course, he directed the conversation to the duke and their plans for getting the amendment to the Lunacy Act they'd been working on together in front of the House, but Aspen couldn't help but register Vesper's every move. Even when he wasn't looking directly at her, he was aware of the rise and fall of her silverware, the undulation of her throat, the elegant heft of a wineglass, the pursing of that perfect mouth. When she chuckled at something the Duchess of Montcroix said, the pleasant sound filled him to bursting.

After a while, the duke's voice faded away, and Aspen found himself mesmerized by the faint freckles above her nose. They'd been more prevalent as a child, but perhaps now, she hid them. Everything about her seemed flawless. *Fake.* Where was that dauntless girl she used to be, who made no excuses for who she was?

The memory of the note he'd read days before rose. Perhaps she was still in there. The note had been written on the back of a pamphlet outlining a collective effort to provide clothes, shoes, books, and food to the poor. He had glanced at it, wondering why *she*, of all people, had had something like that in her possession. He knew why she'd wanted to hide the note—her opinions about him were no great surprise.

Perhaps the pamphlet had been Briar's. Unlike Vesper, she was known for her militancy when it came to women's causes, which he knew nettled Lushing to no end. This version of Vesper was much too . . . priggish to flout propriety.

"Your Grace?"

He broke out of his thoughts with a start. Lady Vesper was the one who had spoken, though Montcroix was staring at him with no small amount of amusement. "I beg your pardon?"

Unreadable blue eyes met his. "You appeared to be frowning quite intensely in my direction, Greydon."

"I beg your pardon. I was thinking."

Vesper didn't reply, only nodded politely and then excused herself to visit the retiring room. Lushing snorted from his end of the table. "That's a dangerous pastime, Greydon, ask anyone. Leave that to the ladies, I always say."

"Smartest words I've ever heard come out of your mouth, my lord," Lady Briar said with a melodramatic sigh.

"I am known for my good sense on occasion." The earl gave his signature grin. "Among other things, of course. What I lack in intelligence, I make up for in pure brawn." Aspen smirked at the theatrics. It was all a front. The Earl of Lushing had a very sharp brain, one that he refused to use, however, depending on charm and wit in its stead. Lushing grinned and made a muscle with his arm. "You are welcome to come inspect at your leisure, Sweetbriar."

The lady glowered. "For the last time, that is *not* my name, you brainless oaf!"

"Children, please," Harwick said, though it was a half-hearted protest as if this sort of bickering at the dinner table wasn't uncommon. Aspen wondered if it was an everyday occurrence. Dinners at his home had never been this boisterous . . . or amusing. In truth, he was having a rather agreeable time.

Chuckling, Aspen shook his head—those two had always been like cats and dogs. It was a wonder that Vesper hadn't yet made a match out of them, but that would likely take a miracle. They were either going to marry or murder each other. All odds favored the latter.

"Are these soirees always like this?" he asked Evangeline.

"Yes," she replied. A smile lit her pretty face. She reminded him of a winter creature, with her pale blond hair and icy eyes. They were the wrong shade of blue, however. He preferred blue eyes full of banked fire instead of arctic quartz. "Sometimes, things get thrown."

He blinked. Surely he'd misheard. "As in insults, food, or utensils?"

Evangeline let out a giggle. "All three."

"You're joking," he said.

She shook her head. "Discussions can get *quite* enthusiastic. Vesper only has one rule—that no one is unnecessarily cruel—but everyone is encouraged to speak their minds. Or throw items to make one's point, if required. I cracked a plate once," she went on. "And then we all cracked plates. It was rather exhilarating. Did you know the ancient Greeks practiced kefi in the spirit of joy and passion, and to ward off bad energy?"

In Greece, perhaps. Such a thing happening in a very pristine English dining room was quite unheard of, however. If anyone had even dreamed of lifting their voices at the dinner table in his house, his mother would have had apoplexy. Dinner parties were quiet and sedate affairs with excessive formality and dignified conversation.

Not arguments, insults, and smashing dishes.

"Kefi was her idea?" he asked. "Vesper's?"

Lady Evangeline stared at him in amusement. "Why does that shock you, Your Grace? You knew her growing up—she hasn't changed that much. She might show an exceedingly proper face to the ton, but if you know anything about Vesper, you know she's never quite who she seems."

Aspen snorted. "Trust me, I'm aware."

He'd been trying to rattle Vesper's relentless composure, and here was an undeniable sign that maybe some part of the old Vesper was in there after all. She was open with her family and trusted friends, but kept him at a distance. So why was she so intent on keeping up pretenses with him? Like he was nothing more than a stranger? He rubbed a fist over his chest.

Why did that inexplicably bother him?

Chapter Eleven

The dinner was an absolute disaster.

And the interminable evening was not over yet. The gentlemen had retired to the library for cigars and brandy, and the ladies were diverted by a rousing game of whist. Vesper had hidden in the privacy of the retiring room for five minutes of quiet to compose her rapidly fraying poise.

God, the nerve of Greydon, baiting her like that! Bringing her integrity into question! Calling her clever while she knew he thought the opposite! The man made her want to pull her hair out by the roots. And the way he'd looked at her during the endless goading…those heated brown eyes smoldering with all kinds of indecent promises beneath that fringe of thick, sooty lashes. He had always been an intense sort of person, but the way he looked at her made everyone else disappear.

Vesper stared at her reflection before smoothing any loose strands of hair. She looked as though she'd been thoroughly pleasured. Her eyes were overbright, her lips red from pinning them between her teeth, and her color was higher than usual, but for all that, she looked and felt…more alive than she had in months.

She didn't dare dwell on what such an inconvenient epiphany meant.

Vesper had been torn between wanting to kick him and kiss him. The undercurrent between them only served to raise the ante, making passions run hot, both the argumentative kind and the take-it-to-the-bedsheets kind. With a frustrated groan, she bit back a scream as her silly, traitorous pulse skipped a beat.

Would he be as intense in bed? Her core clenched on nothing even as her brain fought for control. Splashing some water onto her cheeks, she willed them to cool. But images of the Duke of Greydon taking control in the bedchamber, that heated gaze burning through her as he undressed her, were practically impossible to ignore.

Suddenly, she was burning up everywhere!

Her face, her chest, between her thighs.

"Enough," she growled.

Did he think those penetrating stares would not cause a reaction? Or maybe he *had* known and was doing it on purpose. Gracious, had she been that transparent?

Oh, the absolute horror of it if he knew!

"Damn that salt-butter rogue!" she groused at the mirror, pressing cold knuckles to her cheeks in an attempt to cool them. Cursing was liberating. It was her small, private way of breaking the rules. Perfection came with a cost, after all. "Sodding cockle-brained whoreson." A giggle escaped her lips...if only she could say that to his stupidly handsome face.

She would do well to remember that she didn't even *like* the man.

But that was the problem, wasn't it? She didn't have to like him to remember all those soft, adolescent yearnings that had plagued her for years. One never truly forgot one's first love. *Or a broken heart*, Vesper reminded herself. Surely she wasn't angling for another?

Taking a deep breath, she straightened her shoulders and left the water closet, slowly making her way back toward the salon.

Halfway there, a strange noise caught her attention and she ducked her head into the nearby billiards room. A roaring fire was burning on the grate, but there was no one in sight. Vesper walked inside and ran her palm over the soft green felted covering of the billiard table, reaching for one of the colorful balls on the surface and realizing that that was what the sound had been—the balls hitting each other. She dragged her fingers over the red ball's polished circumference and nearly jumped out of her skin when a throat cleared.

"Do you play?" the Duke of Greydon asked.

Deuce it! She hadn't seen him standing on the other side of the room near the bookcases that lined the wall. "I do not make a habit of it, no," she replied.

He ambled toward her, and she tensed. "Would you like to learn?"

"Are you offering to teach me?" He nodded, stopping a few feet away from her to grab one of the polished pool cues, and her eyes narrowed. "Why?"

"The pleasure of your company."

She gave a nervous laugh, the husky rumble of his voice igniting those embers she'd struggled to cool moments before. "Come now, Your Grace. You must be desperate for diversion to find any pleasure in *my* company. After all, you've made your opinions of me quite clear."

Was that a hint of regret crossing his features?

He cleared his throat. "Forgive me for pushing things too far. It's been a long week." She gaped at him as he went on. "And you're right. I'm quite desperate." His gaze was hooded, but the light tone and teasing capitulation made her eyes narrow. She didn't quite trust him. "Lushing has disappeared to retrieve some fantastic bottle of wine from your father's cellar and now I'm bored. Please distract me."

"Why should I?" she countered, wandering the perimeter of the table so that it stood firmly between them. The smirk on his lips told her he knew exactly what she was doing. "If you're bored, then that makes you the issue. It should not fall to me to provide amusement for you to escape your nature." She exhaled, daring a peek at him. This game between them was dangerous though it did not stop her from continuing. "You were abominable at dinner. Goading me horribly and giving away my secrets without any consideration for those involved."

"Was it a secret? If I recall, you were quite vocal about your plans the other day with Lady Briar."

Vesper opened her mouth, thought for a second, and closed it. He wasn't wrong. "Still, you were beyond provocative."

"I can't help it. You're easy to rouse, and frankly, I enjoy it."

"Why?" she asked, casting a glance at him. Did he take perverse pleasure in seeing her squirm? That kind of playground behavior was childish in the extreme.

He studied the placement of the balls on the table with such concentration she feared he might not answer. But finally, he lifted his gaze toward her. "Perhaps because I wish to see the fire of passion burning in your eyes again, even if anger toward me is the cause."

Perplexed, she stared at him. What an odd thing to say. Why would it bother him whether she displayed emotion or not?

"Sometimes you confuse me, Your Grace," she murmured.

"Do I?" he asked. When she nodded, he held out a second cue stick. "I'll tell you what. Let's make this interesting and put some incentive in it for you. The game is usually to a set number of points but if you get within two points of my score at any time, I'll owe you a favor of your choosing."

Gracious, was he that confident in his ability to stay ahead of her? Perhaps he intended to draw this game out for as long as he could. Vesper's breath caught at what that might mean and ignored the thrill it elicited. "Only two points? That's hardly fair, considering our vastly different skill levels."

An eyebrow rose. "Three points then?"

"I suggest we make it four to be fair, since I am only a novice and I am certain you are a master." A wave of exhilarated energy coursed through her body, a heady sense of competition fueling her, but then she frowned. "What happens if I don't get the points?"

"Then nothing," he said with a lopsided grin. "I would already have benefited from the aforementioned pleasure of your company. And trouncing you soundly, of course."

She narrowed her eyes at him, ignoring the way that the raspy emphasis of *pleasure* on his tongue suddenly made a waterfall of it flood through her. Dragging her eyes away from that devious curve of his mouth, she shook her head. "This feels like a trap."

"Are you always this suspicious?" he shot back, arranging the balls into the starting position.

"It's called being wary of treacherous men," Vesper shot back. "And you, sir, are quite possibly the most treacherous of them all."

"How so?" he asked in sudden seriousness.

As if she would ever confess that he had broken her heart so irreparably that she'd had to build an entire persona made of ice and politesse just to survive him. Hearts were such fragile things, whereas willpower was as impervious as one needed it to be. "Is it your intention to play or do you plan on interrogating me all night long, Your Grace?"

He smiled at the prevarication. "Two more questions then. Are you familiar with the rules?" When she nodded, he canted his head. "White ball or spotted?"

"Spotted," she replied.

Then play began in earnest. The duke chose to go first, despite it being a disadvantage, but his skill was evident. Watching the way he handled the stick and the dexterity with which he lined up his shots was mesmerizing. Vesper could have watched him in action all day, but she had a wager to win and a favor to lord over his head.

When his turn was over and he'd accumulated six points, she let out the breath she'd been holding during his last shot. He was good... better than good, but she was a quick study. After removing her gloves for a better grip, Vesper lined up the cue stick, and feeling his eyes on her, fumbled the shot completely. Her poor little spotted ball hit nothing but air and then rolled to a dejected stop. Heavens, she wasn't normally this clumsy or full of nerves.

"Here," Greydon said, coming to stand behind her and repositioning the ball back to where it was. "Lesson number one. You're gripping the stick too tightly. Loosen your grasp. It has to slide through your fingers."

His deep voice rasped against her ear, making her lower body tighten in explicit, immediate want. Vesper closed her eyes, striving for composure, even as his bare hand slid over hers. She couldn't quite hide the quiver that tore through her at the scandalous touch of skin on skin. Where were his gloves? Where were *her* gloves?

Heavens, why am I thinking about bloody gloves?

"Steady," he whispered when she tensed.

"I can't help it," she whispered back. "I feel like a fox trapped beneath a hound."

Dark laughter rumbled over her, warming her in places

that needed cooling, not heating. "Put your left palm flat on the table, line up the tip over your knuckles, and hold the base with your right." The words should not be as provocative as they were, but her brain was exploding with images that had nothing to do with billiards and everything to do with something wickedly carnal.

On this very table.

Good God, she was beyond shameless!

"And then?" she whispered in a breathy exhale that sounded nothing like her.

"Patience, little fox." Vesper held her breath. His body bracketed hers in a way that couldn't possibly be decent, his left palm mirroring hers and his right closed over the knuckles of her other hand. "Once everything is in place, like so, then you line the shot up, exhale, and then thrust forward."

On the word *thrust*, Vesper swore she'd felt an infinitesimal roll of his hips, and every covetous cell inside of her toppled to his delicious dominance. She wanted...she wanted him to do it again! If she had a lick of good sense in her brain, she would stand up, push him away, and give him the blistering set-down he deserved. But her common sense had long since mutinied and all she could feel was need dragging along her nerve endings like wildfire.

"Ready?" he whispered.

She wasn't at all ready for anything he proposed. Swallowing hard, she nodded once.

Letting him lead, Vesper followed his motion and watched as the spotted white ball collided with his ball, then cannoned into the red ball, and spun toward the corner pocket where it dropped in. "Wait! Isn't that four points? I'm within *two* points. That means I've won the wager and you, sir, owe me a favor!"

Vesper squealed in victory and spun in his arms, only to

find herself sandwiched between a very firm male and the unyielding edge of the billiards table. She gulped. Goodness, he was hard *everywhere*! Pressed scandalously against him as she was, all she could feel was his thickened staff against her belly, hot, steely, and proud. The stark evidence of his arousal drove any hope of breath from her lungs, her pulse thundering with instant, ravenous need.

Heavens.

"Aspen," she began, searching his eyes. "I want..."

He loomed over her, those striated irises of his nearly swallowed up by his pupils as she trailed off and moistened her dry lips. His nostrils flared with something all too primal. "Is this the favor you're claiming then?" he whispered huskily, that hooded stare dropping to her mouth. "Do you want me to kiss you, Viper?"

Her cheeks burned, the urge to deny it eclipsed by the sheer lust raging through her veins. It was *her* favor. Her wish. And she wanted that sculpted mouth on hers more than anything. Desperate to touch him, she raised her palms and braced them against his wide chest, feeling his muscles flex. She should push him away if she had any sense at all.

Instead, her fingers curled into the fabric of his coat. "Yes."

In a moment of perfect synchronicity, Vesper drew on his lapels as his head descended, his lips meeting hers in a satisfying, hungry collision. The first press of the kiss was explosive, a culmination of weeks of exquisite temptation and stars above, it was divine.

His taste—brandy and something deeply and distinctly *him*—filled her mouth as he coaxed her lips to part. His tongue met hers in a sleek thrust, and she nearly died at the sublime feel of it. How could someone else's tongue in her mouth feel so bloody *good*? Or even better, hers in his? Vesper's legs went weak at the sensual assault as Greydon devoured her, one palm cupping her head and the other kneading her hip. Her spine was curved back over the table and she relished every second of it...relished giving in.

Relished being at his breath-stealing mercy.

It felt like they'd been kissing for hours, though it was only a handful of fraught seconds at the most. Greydon pulled away panting, eyes gleaming with bronze fire, and reason sifted into the impassioned fog that had clouded Vesper's brain.

It took only a moment for her to register the unlocked door to the game room and the fact that she—an unmarried lady—was bowed backward over a billiards table in an incriminating and most definitely ruinous display. Anyone could walk in and discover them. They were in the privacy of her own house with trusted guests, but still...they were treading a hazardous line. God, she was so sick of lines and rules and respectability. For once, she wanted to surrender to her impulses.

"Do you want me to stop?" he rasped. Her eyes slid back to the man whose lips hovered over hers, that hot, searching gaze scouring her face for answers to questions she could not answer. There were no whys or hows. There was only *now*.

Vesper forgot about the door. "Devil take it, no."

Aspen stared down at the virago in his arms in surprise. The urgent capitulation on her lips stunned him, *incited* him, because there she was—that wild creature he'd glimpsed before, the one she kept on strict rein and hidden from the world. As if someone like her—a bit different—should ever have to hide how unique and precious she was.

Her eyes shone like polished lapis lazuli, the fires in them at full flame. They were even more beautiful fueled by passion as they were by anger. And her lips...full, pink, and swollen from his kiss. Vesper Lyndhurst had always been beautiful, but in this moment, so uninhibited and deeply provocative, she transfixed him.

Aspen was aware of how many rules they were both breaking and the fact that they were in a compromising position that anyone could trespass upon. Lushing was due to return at any moment. There were footmen standing in the corridor just outside the door. Vesper's father, who had retired after one glass of brandy, could decide to play a late-night game of billiards or chess. The other gentlemen who had joined their wives could wander down the hallway.

Anything could happen.

But he didn't care, and clearly, neither did she.

Aspen had felt her brief hesitation, followed her cautious glance to the door. If she'd told him to stop, he would have without question, but a part of him had desperately hoped she wouldn't. That she would agree to see where this *thing* between them led for a few more scalding minutes, even if it meant a chance of discovery.

And the risk was great for both of them...

Aspen hadn't intended to kiss her, but she'd looked so damned delicious that his body had acted before his brain could catch up. And when she'd pulled him down toward her, claiming the favor she'd won, he was already half lost to the fantasy of how she would taste before his lips met hers. Her mouth had been soft, the perfect counterpoint to his, and the first sip of her had been his downfall, a sampling of sweet dessert wine that had gone straight to his head...and his cock.

"Are you certain?" he asked.

Her eyelashes dipped. "Are *you*?"

With a groan, Aspen slid both hands down each side of her

rib cage to her hips and hefted her easily onto the edge of the billiards table. There were sufficient petticoats in the way to prevent the position from being truly erotic, but it was enough to run his blood to lava. He wedged his way in between her knees, his hips at the perfect position to mimic an act his body was beginning to crave with a throbbing intensity.

Vesper gasped at the intimacy, and without another moment's hesitation he pressed his lips to hers again. He licked deep, exploring every part of her mouth, and delighted when she returned the act with as much fervor. She did not kiss as he'd anticipated she would at all. Aspen had expected her kisses to be much like her exterior—proper, perfunctory, and tame. But instead, they were the opposite. When he licked, *she* licked. When he nibbled along her lower lip, she followed suit a heartbeat later. When he went deep, she answered, exploring his mouth with a passion to rival his own.

Suddenly a thought occurred to him, one he wasn't certain he enjoyed at all. He pulled away staring into her star-bright eyes. "Have you been kissed before?"

"Not like this," she admitted and blushed. "A peck or two, nothing more."

Gratification filled him even as possessiveness fired at the thought of any other gentlemen touching her lips, chastely or otherwise. "What made you choose to... broaden your horizons with me?"

Vesper lifted a finger to trace his brow and trail down the side of his cheek to his tingling mouth. Her fingertip outlined his swollen lips, lingering across the curve of the lower. The teasing pressure of her touch was maddening. "When I'm with you, it's different," she whispered. "You're safe, I suppose."

"Safe?" he asked frowning.

She lifted one shoulder into a shrug. "I knew you wouldn't

demand more from me than I was willing to give. With others, I have to be careful not to encourage their attentions so a perfunctory embrace was always the safest route." Her cheeks warmed with a blush. "You're not a prospective suitor in search of a fortune or a bride who could misread or misuse a fond or impulsive exchange. This was just a kiss between friends, a chance to indulge my curiosity without repercussions."

Well that seemed logical. He could not argue the sense of it, though the "between friends" part chafed slightly. Friends in his experience did not kiss as passionately as they had. Friends didn't threaten to incinerate entire buildings with the heat between them.

"And has your curiosity been satisfied?" Aspen asked huskily, despite his contrary feelings pulling him in different directions. His ego felt bruised at being used in such a puerile manner, but on the other hand, he wasn't about to complain about being a practice subject either.

Flushing, she licked her lips while staring at his beneath her fingertip. "I might require additional instruction."

"Will you now?" he murmured.

"I think so. Yes, definitely. For research."

He grinned. "I am a man of science."

Aspen eased the tip of his tongue between his lips, barely catching the pad of her finger. Her brilliant blue eyes flashed with fire, and he lifted a brow in challenge, half expecting her to retreat. But no—this was Vesper, after all—her finger dipped into his mouth. Her pupils blew wide when he drew the tip in between his teeth and flicked his tongue playfully against it. Watching her, he bit down on her fingertip just enough to make her gasp.

Drawing her closer, he sealed his lips to hers, capturing her finger between them. It was unbearably erotic to suck on both her finger and her tongue. She evidently thought so as well because she moaned into his mouth even as she angled her jaw for him to kiss her more deeply.

"Vesper," he whispered when she slid her hands around his nape and tugged on the ends of his hair. The slight pain edged into the pleasure dulling his senses, and he realized with a smile what it was—payback for his earlier bite. He liked it.

He especially liked that *she* had liked it.

Groaning, he tore his lips from hers and trailed a path of kisses down her neck. As lost as she was, Vesper obligingly threw her head back, exposing the rosy skin to him, daring him to take whatever he wanted. And he did. He sampled and sucked, nibbling along the pale column of her throat to her prominent collarbones and the rise of her bosom.

Pausing, he traced a fingertip along the edge of her bodice. "May I kiss you here, Vesper?"

She peered down at him, gaze hazy with lust. "Yes, everywhere. All of it."

Aspen smiled at her breathy command—she was as greedy and needy as he was—and closed his mouth over one silk-covered nipple while his hand palmed the other. She moaned and arched her spine, responding on pure instinct. It was glorious. *She* was glorious.

"So responsive," he muttered and nuzzled the damp fabric.

"Less talking, Your Grace," came the panted directive from above, and he grinned, biting down, not too hard, but enough to make her whimper and writhe. Perhaps this was the solution to their constant bickering—a battle that they both won.

His eyes flicked to the door, ears straining for the sound of footsteps.

Silence.

Christ, if they were caught, it would be disastrous…

"What are you doing?" she gasped, arching against him.

"Someone could come," he said.

"Yes. That."

His eyes went wide. Was she…? A spirited roll of her hips answered his unvoiced question. Well, then.

Aspen moved his right hand down to the hem of her skirts, bunching them to slide along a stockinged calf and then the soft bend of a knee. Flounces of her petticoats ruffled against his knuckles when he ventured higher, reaching a pair of silken ties, and then the embroidered edges of her drawers. His breath hitched as his hand climbed higher still to the slit in the fabric, and he reveled in what he found.

"Fuck, you're wet."

He didn't expect her laughter, husky and rich. "What did you think you'd find, Your Grace? Do you require instruction in the nature of female anatomy?" Aspen blinked at her teasing tone. She lifted a brow, a sultry smile curling her lips. "I am a grown woman, sir. While my precious virtue is quite intact, I am quite knowledgeable about my own body."

"Are you?" he asked in a choked voice.

"Would you like a demonstration, Your Grace?" she whispered, eyelashes dipping.

Fucking hell. The knowledge that she pleasured herself ignited a wildfire within him. A low growl of pure need ripped from his chest, but before he could do more, the sound of a large thud had them both startling upright. His hand dropped away from her as Vesper scooted from the table, her eyes wide as a white cat ambled into view to bunt her head against her mistress's arm.

"Shoo, Cat, off the table!"

So *this* was Cat. Aspen blinked. Obstructed by a feline… or rather saved by it.

"Heavens, what were we thinking?" Vesper muttered dully as if coming out of a trance, smoothing down her skirts and peering at the barely visible damp circle in the shape of his mouth on her breast. "What if it had been Lushing to find us? We shouldn't have...damn it. I can never think clearly when I'm around you." She shoved at his chest and glared at him. "Don't just stand there gawking at me like a creature in crosshairs. Move!"

She was having trouble meeting his eyes, he noticed, and in her attempt to avoid him she'd cast her gaze downward and he watched as horror and delayed alarm flashed across her face. "Goodness, my gown!" she groused as she began shaking out her rumpled skirts.

"Your gown is fine," he told her. "You look perfect."

It was a lie—she looked shockingly and deliciously mussed. He suddenly wanted to kiss her again, discovery be damned. But he knew nothing good would come of him succumbing to his desire and tempting fate any more than they already had. And so instead, he stepped away from her.

For both their foolhardy sakes.

Chapter Twelve

Vesper opened her eyes and stretched, rubbing her legs together and purring much like Cat, who was currently curled into a tight ball on the opposite pillow. She threw her arms over her head in contentment. Goodness, she'd just had the most delicious dream!

With a languid exhale she touched a finger to her lips, images bursting in her brain in rapid succession of a wickedly handsome dream lover. A lover who looked too much like the Duke of Greydon for comfort, though what harm was there in dreams? The memory of it was so real she could taste it—brandy and sin—his fingers on her breast and between her…

Oh, dear God.

It hadn't been a dream!

Vesper bolted upright in bed, making poor Cat fly off the pillow with an angry yowl. She slid a hurried hand to her breast beneath the thin night rail as the recollection coalesced and winced at the slight ache in her nipple. Oh, good heavens, he'd sucked and bitten her through her bodice. Her hand ventured lower over her fluttering abdomen to the warm juncture between her thighs. He'd touched her *there*, too.

She pressed down, imagining his big hand there instead, and bit back a moan. If the duke had continued his ministrations with those long fingers, she would have been lost to pleasure within heartbeats. Her cheeks flamed as she remembered her brazen boast about knowing her own body and its arousal. Goodness, what on earth would have made her expose such a private thing? She might have personal knowledge, but *nothing* had prepared her for how devastatingly erotic his touch would feel. There was no comparison!

She flung herself back to the pillows, frustration and embarrassment taking hold.

After Cat's timely interruption, Greydon had let her go without protest and she'd avoided him for the rest of the evening, though her body had remained dreadfully on edge… and deeply unsatisfied. No wonder she was forced to indulge in such scandalous dreams.

Gracious, what must he think of her!

A rap on the door had her fumbling to get her hands above the coverlet.

"Good morning, my lady," Lizzie said, bustling in with a breakfast tray that she set on the table near the window. "Here's your morning coffee and the newssheets. I've also brought a little treat for Cat." She placed a saucer of some kind of fish on the floor, and the kitten scampered over to launch headfirst into its breakfast.

With a sigh, Vesper stretched, and sat on the edge of the bed before rising to stroll over to the chair next to the window. She wrinkled her nose at the overcast sky. It looked like rain, which meant that it was going to be another dreary day…one that made the bed look like a wonderful place to spend the morning reading, but she had things to do. People were depending on her; contrary to what Greydon thought, she was needed.

"Oh, this is marvelous news," she said, scanning the headlines as she sipped the strong but heavily sweetened coffee. "Lizzie, come have a look."

The maid bustled over. "What is it, my lady?"

Vesper summarized a brief paragraph and pointed at the accompanying handbill. "I have no idea how Briar managed to get this announcement to the paper so quickly, but our charity ball for the Ragged School Union will have the best chance of success with this extra boost! Not to mention extra clothes and food for the orphans!"

"That is wonderful!" The maid patted her shoulder. "What you are doing, my lady, for those poor children is beyond anything they could hope for. To have hope of maybe making something of themselves one day... well, it's the greatest gift, you see."

Vesper bit her lip, warmed by the praise. "I wish I could do more."

"There should be more people like you." Lizzie frowned. "I don't understand why you do so much in secret though. The work you already do teaching those poor children every Sunday is honorable and decent."

Lizzie, as her lady's maid and constant companion, was one of the few who knew how Vesper spent most of her time—the hours that weren't spent dancing, simpering, and putting on a show for the ton anyway. After all, Lizzie was the one tending to Vesper and her clothing after she'd been sitting in dusty stables and under grimy railway arches in London's West End on Sundays, surrounded by earnest, hopeful children, greedy for instruction... and food.

"The ton prefers the illusion," she said. "That ladies are untouched by anything that could besmirch our lofty pedestals. As if sitting with the poor could lead to social contamination or such absurd notions. I fear half of the ton believes poverty is catching. They'll give their money but scorn a hungry child in the street." She let out a brittle laugh and shrugged. "So we must do the actual work in subversive ways. Educating those who do not have the means to better themselves is the first step."

Though her initial efforts had started out as a retaliation of sorts to the gossip that being shunned by Greydon had caused—*she'd show him!*—now they had become so much more. She was a woman of substance, not someone shallow. At first, she'd volunteered to fight the negative voices and the time spent with the orphans had had unexpected benefits. The activity had helped calm the continuous churning of her mind...and for the first time in her life, she had purpose.

Vesper felt a deep fulfillment from being able to make a difference, even in the life of one child. And if the offering of her time made that possible, then she'd spare as much of it as she could. This went beyond charitable duty...this felt like food to her soul.

Pleased, Vesper folded the newssheets. There was so much to do! She'd love to host the ball here at Harwick House, but the ballroom was not large enough. Nève had offered theirs, but the poor woman had just entered her confinement, and besides, her devoted husband had converted his immense ballroom into a ballet studio for his wife. A stroke of envy brushed over Vesper's heart...it had been such a romantic gesture, one that had made them all swoon on Nève's behalf.

Would a man ever care for her like that?

Suddenly her mind was brought back to last evening, when the duke had made his intentions of caring for her pleasure very clear. She shook her head. She shouldn't be thinking about Greydon. There was nothing so romantic between the two of them and attraction did not translate into grand gestures in enormous ballrooms.

But then, an idea occurred to Vesper and she exhaled a thoughtful breath. The duke would not like it, but if she had to choose between getting more money for her orphans or worrying about his feelings, it was no contest. She stuffed down the slight twinge in her breast. The Dowager Duchess of Greydon loved to entertain, and if Vesper could put the notion to her in such a way that it became the dowager's own idea, she could catch two fish with one worm.

One, the duchess had a large ballroom that could easily handle a sizable crowd. And two, she had many older friends with deep pockets who flocked to the extravagant gatherings she was known for. On top of that, being the benefactor of such a public charity effort would make the dowager—and her wealthy friends who would vie with each other over the size of their donations—look good in the eyes of society. Since the lady was rather influential with the denizens of the ton, including the parents and guardians of Vesper's peers who had yet to inherit their fortunes, she could provide access to a valuable, untapped source of funds.

That was settled. She would call in on the Duchess of Greydon this afternoon…and hope that her son wasn't at home.

"Lizzie, can you kindly run me a bath?" Vesper scowled at the cat valiantly attempting to scale the window curtains. Though it was soft and cute, the thing was truly a menace. Vesper could already feel her nose tickling. "And do have one of the footmen fetch that creature before it destroys the drapes and everything else in here."

The maid shot her a grin at her disgruntled expression, but disappeared into the bathing chamber to do as she was bidden. It wasn't long before Vesper was immersed in the tub, taking the time to consider when she should call upon the duchess and deciding that there was no time like the present.

After bathing and dressing, she made her way downstairs, popping into her father's study to let him know that she was on her way out.

"Papa," she said, without knocking. "I'm off to see a man about a dog." She broke off as two men turned toward her—one her father, and the second, the very gentleman she'd been hoping to avoid today. Her face warmed of its own volition, even as she schooled it into ferocious neutrality. "Oh, my apologies, I didn't know you were with anyone." She gave a demure curtsy. "Your Grace."

"Lady Vesper," Greydon's deep voice returned. "Seeking a new hound? A companion for Cat, perhaps?"

She cleared her throat, his voice doing things to her senses that shouldn't be legal, inciting memories of whispered promises over that pool table in full force. And curse him that he should be wearing those wretched gold spectacles. They suited him and yet looked so out of place... like seeing a wolf wearing a scarf and a quizzing glass.

Though why a man could not be virile *and* scholarly was beyond her. She'd always loved a clever gentleman as well as an athletic one. The fact that Greydon had both brain and brawn was a particularly heady combination to her.

Oh, enough about the sodding man, Vesper! That was the problem with her brain, it jumped from idea to idea and ran off on tangents if it wasn't kept busy. *Your mind was blank when you were bent over that pool table.*

She closed her eyes and counted to three.

"It's an expression," she explained politely. "I'm not actually looking for a dog."

Greydon smiled and her useless knees shuddered like twigs in a brisk breeze. "I know what it means. I was just being flippant." He pointed down toward his lap, and she hesitated, but looked anyway. "Besides, it looks like Cat is not in need of any companions, considering she seems to have claimed me."

Sure enough, the dratted scamp was curled up in his lap like the fluffy little hussy she was. Had Cat finished her climbing expedition and raced down here as soon as he'd arrived? The duke mustn't have been there long. Vesper could still smell the hint of a crisp, damp morning and the scent of horses on his person.

"That creature is a nuisance," she grumbled. "I'll have one of the servants remove her."

Greydon smiled and stroked the purring little monster along her spine. "No need. I like her."

A deep pulse hummed to life in the vicinity of Vesper's lower abdomen. She pinned her lips hard and met her father's gaze. "I'm off, Papa. Don't forget that tonight is the Franzberg musicale. You did say that you would attend with me."

"Is that tonight?" he asked with a frazzled expression. "Yes, very well. Where are you off to now?"

Vesper blinked, unable to come up with a quick enough reply other than the truth. "Ah, to call on the Duchess of Greydon, actually."

She felt the duke's stare pierce her like a lance. Her father exchanged a look with the younger man that she couldn't decipher. "What about?"

"About hosting a ball," she said brightly, ignoring the burst of incredulity coming her way. Greydon's issues with the dowager were not her concern. That was between the two of them. "The most fantastic ball in London, in fact. A ball to outshine all others."

"Vesper..." her father began with another concerned glance at Greydon.

Smiling, she blew him an airy kiss. "See you tonight, Papa."

She hurried out to the hallway but was clearly not fast enough to avoid Greydon because the gentleman himself followed in her wake, his heavy footsteps slapping against the marble. He cupped her elbow, turning her to face him. "What do you think you're doing?"

"Going about *my* business," she said and stared pointedly at his fingers. "Kindly release me, Your Grace."

He dropped her arm like a hot potato. "Why would you want to involve the duchess in this ball of yours?"

"Not that it's any of your business, but she's a denizen of society, and I need to take advantage of her social connections."

That golden-brown gaze turned contemptuous. "Take advantage?"

"Yes, to make use of, to benefit from, to *capitalize* on."

"I know what it means. I don't require a dictionary."

Greydon's eyes narrowed with ire, peering at her over those irritating spectacles. How did such a thing make him seem more attractive even as furious as he was? Vesper was ashamed that a shiver slid through her body right then at the thought of being scolded by him. Mortified laughter bubbled into her throat.

"You think this is amusing?" he demanded. "I've told you—"

"Yes, I know what you believe, Greydon, but even if she did not love him, that does not mean she intended to hurt you or your father by doing something inevitable for a man in need of help," Vesper interrupted. "And while I am sorry for all of it, that doesn't change the fact I require her guidance."

"For yet another of your insipid intrigues? The ball to end all others?"

Stung at his mocking tone, she nonetheless adopted a wide sugary smile. She'd be damned if she let him know he'd struck a nerve. "Call it what you want. You already assume the worst of me."

"Why?" he bit out.

"Why what?" she asked, determined to hold steady under his thunderous gaze.

"Why is it imperative that you involve the duchess in this frivolous eyewash of yours?" His words were so clipped, she was afraid he might chip a tooth.

It was pride that made her twist the truth. "Your mother is the most esteemed woman in London, Your Grace. And I desire what any female aristocrat desires. To see and to be seen. To form the most venerated attachment the marriage mart has to offer. And who better to help me achieve that goal than the duchess, whose many connections reach far beyond my own?"

Vesper didn't know why she didn't just tell him the truth—that she needed the duchess's help with her charity endeavors. But deep down, a perverse part of her wanted Greydon to find out for himself that she wasn't the haughty miss he'd always assumed she was and then drown in his own guilt. Why should she have to defend herself to him when he was the one with the gross misassumptions? Let him believe what he wanted and look the fool later.

He stared at her. "God, you haven't changed, have you? Still as selfish as ever."

It hurt—that predictably harsh summation of her character—but Vesper tossed her head. She had nothing to prove to him. Her smile was so sweet, it dripped honey. "Then it's a good thing that I'm no burden of yours, Your Grace. Good day."

Flummoxed and seething, Aspen stared after her, having heard only one thing in her explanation. Of course she would want to make an enviable match—she was the ton's precious diamond, after all. Just because she'd kissed him and let him touch her didn't mean he was a contender for her hand. He'd simply been . . . practice.

Aspen pressed a hand to his chest, a strange malcontent brewing there.

It felt too much like disappointment. Like *disloyalty.*

He frowned. Vesper hadn't done anything wrong. He'd given her a half confession of what his mother had done when she'd exiled his father to Camberwell. How could he expect her to understand the level of deception and the manipulation he'd endured as a boy? Or guess that the duke had been wrongfully committed by his self-serving wife? To the rest of the ton, including Vesper, the Duchess of Greydon was a paragon . . . not a liar and a charlatan.

Aspen raked a hand through his hair and removed his spectacles to clean them before setting the frame back in place. In truth, it was no business of his who Vesper chose to marry or whether she leveraged his mother's connections to make a good match. He had enough work of his own to worry about. His focus should be on what he'd come back to England for—seeing Judith settled, pushing his bill through Parliament with the Duke of Harwick's help, and finding the doctors who had committed fraud. Speaking of the last, perhaps he should take a page from Vesper's book and ask *her* father if he had any useful connections.

When he reentered the study, Harwick was observing him with a keen expression. "Something on your mind, Greydon?"

"I don't suppose you know a good investigator?" he asked. When the duke lifted his silver brows, he continued, "I'm searching for the men my mother coerced into incarcerating my father." Aspen shrugged. "I need to know if the diagnosis was real." And if his father's illness meant he might follow the same path.

"Sometimes the past should be left to the past," Harwick murmured.

Aspen's jaw firmed. "And other times, it needs a push to catch up with you."

"Very well then, I happen to know an excellent private detective. I'll have Cross get the contact details for you."

"Thank you." Aspen rolled his neck in a futile attempt to release the gathered tension and felt the duke's scrutiny again.

"What else troubles you?"

"She's so bloody headstrong," he muttered before retaking his seat with a grim smile. "Apologies."

There was evidently no need to identify the "she" as the old duke chuckled. "No apology needed. She's like her mother. Trust me, that apple did not fall far from the tree. I've learned over the years that it's simply better to let Vesper do what Vesper is going to do. When she sets her mind to something, she's almost impossible to thwart."

Aspen resisted the urge to rub at his chest again—if she planned to find a husband, she would. *Her future nuptials are none of your business.*

If that was true, then why did he feel so unhinged?

"That hasn't changed since we were children," he said in a strained voice. "She was mule-headed then, too."

Harwick nodded with a fond if sad laugh. "My daughter looks for happiness and validation in all the wrong places. I fear she will never find what she's actually seeking." He sighed. "A grand love."

Aspen let out a derisive huff. It earned him a piercing look from Harwick, one that slid beneath his skin like a thorn. He blinked at the duke in surprise. "Don't tell me you believe in such a thing?"

"Of course I do. I once had the grandest love known to man. The duchess was the love of my life." He smiled. "My Elspeth was overly affectionate. She hugged the servants—scared our butler silly the first time she did it." The duke started laughing, tears streaming from his eyes. "The poor man was certain he was going to be sacked or worse."

"She sounds like a mother should be," Aspen said, bitterness filling him.

Harwick wiped his eyes and sat back in his chair, his gaze still hazy with memories. Aspen wasn't sure if his tears were happy or sad ones, but he felt oddly moved. "I am sorry for your loss."

Harwick nodded. "Thank you. Her death hit Jasper the hardest." He let out a sigh. "I love my son, but his marauding ways will not do him any favors. My daughter searches for love in any place but a husband, and my son has walled himself away from anything remotely resembling affection."

"So what you're saying is that love is a dangerous trap."

Harwick graced him with a stare so intense it burned. "Nothing worth keeping isn't without hardship, otherwise every fool would have it, wouldn't they?"

Aspen held back a chuckle. It was a paradox, considering only the fools were the ones who fell hopelessly in love. He articulated as much and the duke eyed him again, only this time, it was with pity. "I know you've been hurt, boy, but one day, you will find that love—that great love that makes your heart roar, your blood thunder in your veins—and you will find the one who will be worth laying your soul bare for."

"But at what risk?" Aspen asked, a lump forming in his throat.

Harwick smiled. "The risk, my boy, well, that's the rub, isn't it? Without risk, we could only hope to achieve the mundane and what's the point of that? Why not strive for the extraordinary?"

Chapter Thirteen

Vesper sat primly on the edge of the seat cushion, sipping her second cup of tea. She'd arrived at Drake Manor and had expected to leave her card, but instead had been politely ushered into the beautifully appointed but spare salon, whereupon she'd been graced by the duchess's presence.

"Lady Vesper, this is a surprise," the Duchess of Greydon said in a cool voice, sweeping into the room in a swish of emerald and cream skirts, and making no excuses for keeping Vesper waiting, not that Vesper expected her to.

She smiled demurely and canted her head in a gracious nod. "Your Grace, thank you for seeing me. Apologies for calling upon you without an invitation, but I had hoped to leave my card. The short of it is that I need your help."

Vesper was a powerful woman in her own right as a duke's daughter, and she knew that such a practical plea would intrigue the duchess. Being owed a favor by anyone with influence would always be of interest—such was the nature of the ton—everyone coveted power.

The duchess lifted her brows. "Go on."

"I wish to throw a ball for charity to raise funds for underprivileged children," Vesper explained with quiet poise.

"With your mentorship, I think we will be able to exceed donations, particularly within your own impressive sphere of influence in the ton." Vesper knew she was laying it on thickly, but flattery was a tool that sometimes needed to be wielded like a blunt weapon. "With my peers in the younger set and yours, it would be the charity event of the season. With you as its shining patron, of course. I was even thinking you could be the host here, if that pleases you."

A calculated look passed over the duchess's face, and Vesper knew she had seized her attention. More prestige was a magnificent lure in their circles. She waited quietly, sensing that to push would not be the best course.

"If I were to agree to host your little ball, what would I get for my contribution?"

Vesper bristled at the condescension, but it wasn't unexpected. "Everyone will be moved by the depth of your altruism. In fact, I imagine guests will try to best each other in the amount of their donations, simply to impress you. You would be lauded as a shining example of the peerage and revered for your generosity and grace."

"I am esteemed already."

The duchess regarded her with a steady gaze, and for a moment, Vesper felt like she was the fly in the web instead of the spider. She kept her face neutral, despite the sudden nervous tension in her stomach. Aspen's worries drifted through her brain—that the duchess wasn't who everyone thought. What could she possibly want?

"Then, what is it that you desire in exchange, Your Grace?"

"I wish you to convince my son to marry," she said bluntly.

The brusque demand took Vesper by surprise, even as butterflies fluttered in her belly. Was the duchess insinuating the possibility of a match between *Vesper* and the duke?

She cleared her throat. "Yes, well, the duke plans to return to America, once Judith is engaged."

"I am aware," she said and signaled for a nearby servant to pour a steaming cup of tea. "But Greydon doesn't know what's best for him."

"And you do?" The scathing words emerged before she could curb her tongue, and she cursed internally as the duchess favored her with a glacial stare.

"A mother always knows what's best for her children," she said in frigid tones. "I intend for him to do his duty and wed Judith." The declaration struck Vesper like lead ballast to the chest, carving through sinew and bones like pebbles through parchment.

Aspen and *Judith*. Not Aspen and Vesper.

It was shocking how easily she could envision them together—both studious and serious, with their passions aligned and so much in common. A match between them made sense. Though that logic didn't help with the heartrending thought of Judith being on the receiving end of Greydon's passionate kisses. Not that she had any claim to those.

The billiards room was a mistake, she reminded herself harshly.

"I see," Vesper said with a false smile. "However, I'm not sure how you expect me to convince him."

The duchess peered at her over the rim of her teacup, eyes sharp and already gleaming with triumph. "Greydon is reluctant, you see, because he sees the girl as a sister, but there is no blood relation," the duchess said. "And I know he values your opinion."

That was surprising. "Does he?" Vesper murmured. "I did not think that I had that kind of influence over the duke."

A hint of displeasure passed over the woman's face. "Well, my son doesn't know what he wants, though what he wants hardly matters. He's getting on in age and he requires a ducal heir. Judith is a suitable bride. She is the granddaughter of an earl and her mother was a dear friend." She let out a sigh. "We'd always dreamed that our children would marry each other one day."

"How does His Grace feel about a union?" Vesper asked carefully.

The question made the duchess scowl, though her brow quickly smoothed. "How does any man feel about wedlock?"

"I suppose." Vesper gave a forced laugh and set down her teacup, even though her stomach soured with the weight of her decision. She was determined to move past whatever transient feelings she still held for the duke. "Very well, I will do what I can, Your Grace."

"And I would be delighted to host your ball," she said with a gratified expression.

Thanking the duchess for her time, Vesper took her leave.

In the barouche, she shook her head as the coach rolled forward. She'd gotten what she'd come for, which would help the children and that was all that mattered. The duchess was doing it for the glory, and as far as Vesper was concerned, she could have it. As long as the Ragged School Union received the funding for the opening of more schools, then the real winners would be the children.

"Where to, my lady?" the coachman asked.

Vesper thought about it. Between the duchess and her son, her emotions and thoughts were all over the place. Doubt, regret, and jealousy were a poisonous cocktail, and when her mind was especially restless, it never boded well. She needed to clear her head. And there was only ever one thing that truly allowed her to leave her worries behind.

"Head home, Laurence," she told the coachman. "I wish to ride."

Aspen sensed the minute that Vesper returned to Harwick House. The woman was like a hurricane on the horizon—he could taste her on the wind. But she hadn't yet ventured near the study, where he'd been with her father all afternoon, lost in thought over the articles for the proposal to Parliament following Harwick's impassioned discourse on love.

Aspen couldn't discount the duke's take, but a lifetime of painful experience had brought him to an entirely different conclusion. Love was a beautiful snare—one that had snatched his father and eaten him alive. And while he knew his view on the matter might be cynical, Aspen was in no hurry to fall into a similar trap.

"Shall we take a break for now, Harwick?" he asked, pocketing his spectacles and rubbing his gritty eyes. "I think I have everything I need for the next session."

"Oh yes," the duke said, looking up. "Deuce it, it's quite late, isn't it? Would you like to stay for a spot of luncheon? I suppose it was rather rude of me not to offer before."

The hurried tapping of boots echoed down the marble staircase, accompanied by the faintest scent of mayhem and wildflowers, and the old duke lifted a brow when a lilting voice called for one of the footmen to arrange for her horse.

Aspen stood abruptly. "Not at all, and I'm afraid I must decline anyway. I have a pressing engagement."

"Pressing, you say?" Harwick asked with a knowing smile as if he could see right through Aspen's lie and his haste to depart after overhearing Vesper's request. His neck heated and he tugged at his collar. Bloody hell, was he *that* transparent that even the old duke would know he meant to chase after his daughter?

Aspen felt a dull flush warm his face. "I just remembered," he said half-heartedly. "I must meet someone."

"Does that have to do with a certain headstrong blonde?" the duke teased.

Aspen opened his mouth and closed it. Good God, were his bloody cheeks warming?

"I am just ribbing you, lad. Go, enjoy what's left of the day. I'd go for a ride myself if my arthritic bones didn't plague me." He waved him off, but just when Aspen reached the door, the duke spoke again. "You know, on occasion, I do enjoy a good artichoke. It takes work to get through all the hard, wiry layers to the heart, but it's quite delicious when you do get there. Sometimes the roughest, thorniest of artichokes have the most succulent of hearts."

"Are we talking about vegetables, Your Grace?" Aspen asked with a frown.

Harwick shot him a wink. "A good lemon butter does the trick."

Aspen blinked in confusion before taking his leave. The man was a brilliant mentor, but by God, he loved to go off on metaphorical tangents. Only the Duke of Harwick would compare his prickly hard-nosed daughter to an artichoke, but Aspen couldn't fault him for the comparison. He was beginning to believe that Vesper was more than the facade she put out to the world.

He called for his horse, then nodded to the nearby groom. "Did Lady Vesper just depart?"

"Aye, Your Grace, just a few minutes before."

"In which direction did she go?" he asked.

"Hyde Park, Your Grace."

She couldn't have been that far ahead of him, but he took the quickest route to the park nonetheless. He'd bet his hat that she was likely heading for Rotten Row. It was much too early and well before the fashionable hour to be promenading, which meant that she was going to put her horse through its paces. Even as a girl, she'd always loved to race.

Like her brother, she'd been taught to ride as a child, and had grown into an excellent horsewoman. Though the last time Aspen had seen Vesper in action, she'd been thirteen and riding hell-for-leather without a saddle along the sea cliffs in Dorset. A faint memory of her that day—bright-eyed and red-cheeked with blond hair flying out like a silken sail behind her—danced across his thoughts. How fearless and carefree she'd been! Though her father and brother would more often than not deem her reckless with little sense of danger.

He caught up to her near the carriage road and took a beat to admire her graceful bearing. She wore a smart wine-colored riding habit that molded to her lithe curves. And even though she had a light touch on the reins, Aspen could see that she was in perfect control of the dappled gray stallion.

He cantered to her side. "Not quite like Dorset, is it?"

Diamond-hard eyes met his over her shoulder, her lips pulling tight with irritation. "Are you following me?"

"Turned out to be a beautiful day for a ride even with the clouds this morning."

She pointed at the other side of Rotten Row. "Then ride over there. The Row is a hundred feet wide. There's no need to crowd me."

"Am I?" he asked.

"Are you what?" she snapped, frowning as the huge horse stamped beneath her as if sensing her frustration.

He nudged his mount closer. "Crowding you?"

"You know very well that you are, Your Grace. Dimwittedness does not suit you." She eyed the satchel he had over his shoulder. "Have you finished with my father?"

"For now," he replied. "As I said, I wanted to enjoy some of the day. All work and no play makes Jack a dull boy, or so they say."

She let out a dismissive laugh. "You're not one to play, Greydon. You have always been work and more work. In fact, I'd wager the last time you had any fun at all, you were likely in swaddling cloths."

A slow smirk crested his lips. "And yet, I would counter that I have enough fun at the billiards table on occasion. Just recently, in fact." The emphasis on "fun" was not subtle, nor was his pointed stare.

The rejoinder was worth the violent blush that filled her cheeks, before a haughty eyebrow arched. "So you're *not* following me?"

Aspen almost laughed at her deliberate effort to ignore his comment. "Well, now you've caught me. I can't pretend to be dimwitted, nor can I invent that we've managed to cross paths in a way that was not contrived, so yes, very well, I did follow you." Before she could reply, he lifted a hand. "I wanted to apologize."

Her mouth parted in surprise. "I beg your pardon?"

"I'm here to apologize. To you. For earlier."

Frowning, Vesper shook her head. "I'm sorry, but a herd of tiny unicorns with shimmery wings just flew by and I didn't hear a word that you said over the thunderous drone of their flight. Can you repeat that please?"

"With that kind of talent, you really should consider a role in comedy on the stage someday," he said drolly, before going solemn. "I'm sorry for how I spoke to you earlier. I was out of line. My...personal feelings toward the dowager are mine alone, and I should not have put the burden of them on you."

Her expression softened. Marginally. She met his eyes. "Yes, well, it would be ungracious of me not to accept your apology, wouldn't it? Though I'm not quite sure I've forgiven you. That tongue of yours requires a lesson in manners." Her gaze dipped to his mouth and darted away.

He grinned. "Will you be my teacher then, my lady? Keep my philistine tendencies in line? I can assure you that I'm a quick study with careful instruction."

"You're being absurd." With an aggravated huff, Vesper closed her eyes and tightened her fingers on the reins. "Are you doing it on purpose?"

"Can you blame me?" he said with a straight face. "You are rather adorable when you're riled," he said.

Her eyes rounded in affront. "*Adorable* is how one would describe a pet, like Cat."

"Yes, I agree. She was cute and content in my lap, wasn't she?" He grinned. "In fact, you both have quite a lot in common. Independent. Beautiful. Partial to a good rub."

Her lips parted, even as a spark of lust ignited in that blue gaze. "I'm hardly a lap cat, Your Grace," she sputtered, that lovely blush spilling down her neck. "You're a rogue to speak about such things in broad daylight."

Aspen leaned close, his knee nearly touching the curve of her hip as he whispered in her ear, "I told you. I enjoy it."

"Then enjoy it somewhere else!" She jerked on the reins to move her horse away from him, giving him her back.

"You don't mean that," he said, undeterred. "I'll tell you what, if you can beat me to the end of this track, I will go away and leave you in peace."

She hesitated, but he could see the interested glint in her eyes. This wasn't like the billiards wager where he'd held the upper hand in skill. She'd always been the better equestrian, which meant she knew she could win. "And if I lose?"

"Then you put up with my presence for the afternoon without complaint." Aspen smirked, knowing he had her. She was much too competitive to not take him up on the offer. "And you have to be nice to me and allow me to escort you back to Harwick House."

"*Nice* to you? What are you, a child in short pants?" Then, with a bored nod to the groom who had accompanied her, she led her horse to the middle of the track. "Very well, I will agree to this asinine wager. But only because you have no chance of winning, Your Grace."

With that, she shot him a blazing grin.

And it was glorious.

Vesper was confident she would win with ease. Even on a sidesaddle, she was the better horsewoman by far. Giving Feral some encouragement though the horse did not need it, she watched as Greydon handed his satchel to the anxious groom and instructed the boy to count off the start.

At the word *go*, she was off in a flash.

Exhilaration pumped through her as the horse thundered down the path. She could sense the duke keeping pace with her at the beginning of the track, but he was no match for the Spanish racing bloodlines of the stallion she rode. It was almost unfair. She eased off Feral's pace, knowing there was no way he could catch up, and peered over her shoulder. Greydon was lengths behind her. Grinning to herself, she praised the horse and slowed even more.

She didn't want to rub it in too much.

Glancing behind her, Vesper frowned at the look on the duke's face. What on earth was he yelling about? Did he really think he could distract her enough to win? Shaking her head with a laugh, she set her sights on the finish line.

But it was she who was distracted, as she didn't notice the small girl who had wandered onto the bridle path until it was much too late. Keep going and jump? No, that was much too risky. Instead, she yanked on the reins, feeling the horse protest beneath her as he attempted to slow and veered wildly to the left.

The sudden sweeping motion threw her off-balance, but it was with gratitude that she registered they would not endanger the child. Unfortunately, the sharp turn also shifted her position in the ridiculous sidesaddle and sent her sliding backward. She could have pulled herself up but any movement on the reins might make the horse change direction.

The only thing she could do now was prepare for the fall.

Blue sky filled her vision when she released her grip on Feral's reins. Vesper could faintly hear the sounds of screaming and shouting in the background over the blood pounding in her ears as she kicked her feet free of the stirrups. There was nothing worse than being dragged behind a horse.

Hellfire. This was going to hurt.

She'd taught herself to fall as safely as possible over the years, but there was always a risk of injury. Exhaling, she forced herself to relax—tensing up was a surefire way to get hurt. Tucking her chin to her chest and rounding her back to prevent a neck injury, she allowed her body to tumble.

Vesper hit the dirt hard on the back of her shoulder, the wind whooshing completely out of her as she struggled to catch her breath. *Roll*, she growled to herself, keeping momentum to move away from the horse. Every muscle in her body groaned as she came to a hard stop. She blinked, exhaling and inhaling, checking each of her limbs for mobility. They ached like the devil, but nothing *felt* broken. Always a positive sign.

Greydon leaped off his horse, falling to his knees beside her. "Fuck, Vesper!"

She peered up at his panicked face and tried for a reassuring smile. She was certain it probably came out like a grimace, given her entire body felt like mash. "I think we can both agree that before the fall I was in the lead."

"Who cares about the race, you foolish woman? You could have been killed!"

She sat up gingerly and winced at the ache along her shoulder. She was going to have a beast of a bruise in the next few days, but that was better than the alternative. "Is the child all right? And my horse?"

"Yes, she's fine. Her governess is in a state, but she's fine. The groom has your horse. He's no worse for wear either." He exhaled and shook his head. "It's only you... so harebrained without a single thought for your own safety."

Relief flooded her. "That little girl was so fast. It's as if she appeared out of nowhere." She closed her eyes. "If I was only paying attention instead of gloating, perhaps I would have seen her sooner."

"No, Vesper," Greydon said. "She dashed out onto the track. It was only by luck that I saw her out of the corner of my eye and tried to warn you. What you did was... nothing short of miraculous." He peered down at her and smoothed the strands of hair that had fallen into her brow. "Honestly, I thought you might have to jump over her."

"The thought had crossed my mind, but I had no idea which way the girl would run. I didn't want to take the risk that she'd get clipped by Feral's hooves." She shrugged and groaned at the ache. "It was me, the child, or risk a broken leg for the horse."

"And you chose you," he whispered, a strange, haunted look in his eyes as if that choice had hurt him more than it had her. How odd.

"It was the only option."

A wave of dizziness hit, and Vesper felt herself crumple, only it wasn't the ground that caught her, it was the duke. His body was stable, and secure, and she felt herself melt into him.

"We should move before we're trampled," she murmured, watching the small crowd that had gathered.

He shook his head. "I've sent the groom to fetch a doctor."

"I'm fine, Greydon. And it's probably best to get out of the way before we cause more of an accident. I promise, I am unhurt." She glanced up at him, marveling at the perfect bow of his lips, even as they pulled with displeasure. It really was perfect, as if sketched by an artist. Any number of women would kill for such succulent lips.

Those brown eyes of his widened, and Vesper blinked. *Oh no*, she hadn't said that out loud, had she? She didn't think she'd hit her head, but maybe she had and some part of her brain had shaken loose. The impetuous part that didn't care what people thought of her.

"Would *you* kill for them?" A smirk tilted one side up, and she nearly died with mortification. *I'd kill to kiss them.*

The thought was fleeting, however, because in the next instant, to her profound and welcome relief, Vesper fainted.

Chapter Fourteen

Vesper's eyelids fluttered, images flickering to life. Images and memories. Horrid unspeakable memories that deserved to be forgotten forever. Oh, dear heaven above, please let her have not told the duke that he had succulent lips or that women would envy them.

Or that she wanted to *kiss* them!

She let out a groan. It had to be a dream. Her nighttime fantasies had been rather fixated on the duke of late, and while she would never act on any of those indecent urges, dreams were undisciplined things. They did what they wanted from the time her head hit the pillow to when she woke in a tangle of twisted, rumpled sheets.

The sheets beneath her now were not unkempt, however.

Nor was she in her nightclothes...though she was in her bedchamber.

She licked dry lips and encountered downy fuzz. Why was there *fur* in her mouth? She sputtered and the bundle attempting to squat on her head shifted. "Get *off*, Cat," she grumbled as a fluffy tail smacked her lips, setting off three sneezes in a row. The tiny beast gave a peeved meow and relocated an inch to the side. *Silly capricious thing*, thought Vesper, who would admit to no one that the soft little body purring against her was an unexpected source of comfort, despite her hyper-sensitive reaction to cat fur. Some pleasures were worth the price.

She blinked her eyelids open, wincing at the soreness she felt everywhere. Bloody hell, it felt like she'd been trampled by a herd of elephants. A small whimper escaped her lips when she attempted to turn her head.

"Oh, thank God, she's awake this time," a soft voice said. "I think. She could still be dreaming."

"Laila?" she groaned.

"Yes, dear," Laila said, stroking her arm. "It's me. Effie's here, too. Briar sent word that she's on her way."

"Hellfire Kitties unite!" Vesper exclaimed weakly.

Laila shook her head with a half sob, half snort. "Nice try. Just because we're worried about you doesn't mean we're calling us that. Ever."

"How are you feeling?" Effie asked from where she stood beside Laila.

Vesper's head throbbed as she focused on her body. "Like that time we went to Paris to visit Nève, drank two bottles of absinthe at that tavern on Rue de Constantine, and I cast up my accounts over the bridge into the Seine. A hundred times worse than that actually."

Laila gave a low laugh, wrinkling her nose and looking over her shoulder as if someone else was behind her. "You took quite a fall on Rotten Row to avoid a small child who had gotten away from her governess. Undoubtedly, you will be the romantic heroine of the hour in every single newspaper that will be printed tomorrow." She sat on the edge of the bed. "There have already been a dozen floral arrangements delivered and endless sonnets composed in your honor."

"Wonderful," Vesper said, attempting to sit up and groaning

at the sharp pain in her shoulder as Laila propped a pillow behind her. "I remember what happened, though some of it is a bit fuzzy."

"By all accounts, you were lucky you didn't break your neck or your spine."

Vesper winced as she shimmied herself slowly into an upright position and made herself comfortable, or at least somewhat comfortable. She wasn't about to admit that her behind was sore, too. Cat gave an annoyed mew but remained in place like a princess being inconvenienced by a peasant, and Vesper gathered her into her arms with a chuckle. "How did I get here?"

"Greydon brought you."

She stroked Cat's head and blinked, a foggy gap in her memory. "The *Duke* of Greydon?"

Effie cleared her throat, a blush stealing over her pale cheeks. "Do you not remember what happened after you fell?"

Clarity dawned much too slowly as her brain struggled to catch up. "Yes. I remember the race and the child, then the fall. The duke was with me." She breathed out, *that* particular recollection of lips and kisses hovering in her thoughts again. "Wait. Then Greydon was talking about lips." Vesper faltered, cheeks blasting with heat. "I mean *I* was talking about lips. *His* lips. Oh, dear God, no." She sank back into the pillows, burying her nose in the kitten's warm belly.

Not a dream at all.

"What is it?" Effie asked in a worried voice. "Do you feel faint? Does it hurt?"

"If I swoon, it will be from sheer stupidity." She sighed. "It's just . . . well, I might have told His Graceless he had nice lips . . . and . . . that I, er, wanted to kiss them."

At her bald admission, Vesper closed her eyes and then cracked an eyelid open moments later, when neither of her friends responded with their usual laughter. It was the very sort of confession that would send them into hysterics. At the very least she'd expected giggles at the nickname and some modicum of teasing. She stared at Laila, whose cheeks had gone an interesting hue.

"Nothing to say?" She glanced over at Effie, who looked like she was having trouble holding back a frightful storm of giggles, her own face nearly purple. "What is the matter with the two of you?"

Laila choked. "Greydon."

"Greydon *what*?" she demanded.

"Is here."

Oh.

"Welcome back, Viper," a husky baritone drawled from the vicinity of the door, and there he was, one shoulder propped up against it, a look of amusement in his eyes and the smirk curling those cursed lips. Heavens, they were not kissable in the least—they were damnable! Execrable! Repulsive, revolting, atrocious. All the awful things!

Vesper yanked the bedclothes up to her neck, making Cat howl and leap off the bed, even though she was still dressed in her soiled riding habit. She collected her scattered wits, watching as the wanton little traitor wandered over to wind herself about the duke's legs, purring loudly. "What are you doing here?"

Effie was the one to answer, a smile on her face at Cat's obvious adoration. "He brought you here, silly. The duke carried you from Hyde Park all the way here and made sure that you were snug in your own bed. He would not put you down for a second, not even when Stanley offered to help take you up the stairs. See? Even Cat knows he's a perfect gentleman."

Laila made a soft sighing noise, but Vesper was too busy gaping over the fact that Greydon had *carried* her. In his arms. She was not a small woman, not petite like Laila, willowy like Effie, or svelte like Nève. Carting her around would have been like hefting an entire sack of potatoes.

"Thank you," she grumbled in his direction.

Greydon cleared his throat, a palm going to the back of his nape. "You are welcome, but it was not so dramatic as all that. We took a hackney back to your residence, and I made sure you were comfortable before sending for your friends."

Vesper's chest tightened, an unfamiliar sensation filling it. Gratitude? Warmth? She didn't want to dwell on it, whatever it was, so she closed her eyes for a few breaths and then looked to Laila and Effie instead. She sensed when the duke moved away and tried not to feel disappointed. "How long have I been in bed?"

"Half a day at least," Laila said. "Your father's physician came as well and said that your body had gone through a trying experience and would require rest." She let out a soft sob and clutched at Vesper's hand. "I've never been so happy to see those blue eyes of yours in my life!"

"Yes, agreed," Effie added. "Never scare us like that again!"

Vesper smiled wanly at her best friends. "What would you have had me do? Trample the poor child?" She frowned. "How is she, by the way?"

"She's fine. Your horse is fine, too, feasting on a fresh bucket of oats like his life depends on it. He's been thoroughly checked from mane to hooves. It's only you who wouldn't wake. Oh God, Ves." A tear slid down her friend's cheek and Vesper reached up to swipe it away. "What on earth were you thinking?"

"I had to save her life," Vesper whispered. "Any of us would have done the same."

There was some commotion on the landing and her heart leaped, but it was only Briar bursting into the room with Lushing close behind. Vesper nearly laughed as Briar scowled and punched him in the arm. "You abominable liar, you told me she was at death's doorstep!"

The earl smirked. "I had to get you to comfort me somehow," he said and pretended to swoon. "Who knew that my perpetually petulant Sweetbriar had such a tender side?" He pretended to stroke his cheek. "Oh, Lushing, you poor baby…"

"You and I will have words, my lord." She poked at him before rushing over to the bedside. "Vesper, my darling, how are you feeling? Your cretin of a brother told me you'd been run over by a horse."

"*Fell* off a horse, Briar. You've seen me take many a fall before. I'm fine, I promise you." Vesper directed a glare at her brother. The impish rogue didn't look apologetic in the slightest. "And you, stop tormenting her."

Lushing winked. "Charming her, you mean."

All three of her friends stared at him with varying looks of incredulity. "Time to leave, brother, before you are set upon by a handful of very *uncharmed* women," Vesper said with a fond smile. Obligingly, he backed away, but not before blowing a kiss at a glowering Briar. She threw a pillow at him.

Vesper grinned. "Are you certain you're not fond of him?"

"I'd be fonder of burying him in the back gardens," she snarled, though there wasn't much heat in the threat.

Vesper snorted a laugh and then groaned at the piercing ache in her ribs. Despite the pain, there was nothing she would have done differently, given the dreadful circumstances.

A child's life was worth more than a few bumps and bruises.

Aspen paced a hole in the carpet in the study downstairs, nursing a full glass of whiskey in hopes of it calming his nerves. His heart had been firmly lodged in his throat ever since Vesper had taken her fall. The only time he'd felt such an intense emotion was when his father was dying and he hadn't been able to do a damned thing about it.

Aspen took another sip of whiskey, then let out a tight exhale. He did not think he, or anyone else, would have been capable of such a feat—Vesper had saved the child, her horse, and her own life. The doctor had said she was lucky to be alive, but luck had nothing to do with it.

His chest squeezed with familiar emotion—one he'd taken pains to ignore for as long as he could remember. He'd always felt conflicted around Vesper Lyndhurst. She was the balm that stung before it soothed. The tongue that cut before it caressed. How a man could go from wanting to tear his own hair out by the roots and wanting to kiss a woman senseless was beyond him, but she pushed him to the limits of patience... and provocation. Beyond self-preservation.

He had to stop lying to himself.

She was under his skin... and he fucking cared more than he should.

Lushing stalked into the study, a perverse look on his face, and poured himself a healthy glass of whiskey. Aspen racked his brain for a boring subject so he wouldn't have to think about what losing Vesper would have felt like or the hollow sensation in his chest. "Have you seen Stone's latest dividends on the railway numbers?"

The earl shot him a dry look. "You wish to talk about investments right now?"

With the Duke of Montcroix's direction, Aspen's estate ledgers had seen excellent growth, and numbers were always a safe subject. He sent Lushing a disgruntled glare. "Why shouldn't I? What else would I want to talk about?"

Lushing peered at him over the rim of his glass, a smirk appearing. "I don't know. How about the way you moon over my sister when you think no one is watching and ogle her every move?"

Aspen spluttered, feeling the whiskey going down the wrong way, and his eyes streamed when he set down the glass. The earl's obnoxious chortles filled the study. Aspen coughed and glared as best as he could. "I do not *moon* at her. You are misguided. Nor do I ogle—"

"Save your denials, my friend," Lushing interrupted with a wave that nearly sloshed his drink all over the carpet. "You forget that I live here, and we have been friends for a very long time. You have been enamored with my sister since we were in leading strings, and quite possibly she with you as well, even though neither of you will ever admit it, for reasons known to absolutely no one."

"I am not enamored of her." He blinked. "Nor is the reverse true."

"Just because you say so doesn't make it so," Lushing said with an arrogant smile that made Aspen want to punch him. "Even her murderous cat is infatuated with you." Aspen glanced down at the cat who had followed him downstairs and was now swiping at Lushing's boots with tiny claws. "Besides, what were the ladies saying about you not relinquishing my sister to Stanley? You had to see her all the way upstairs for yourself? What do you call that then?"

"Friendship."

The earl burst into laughter. "Good to know that you would carry me wrapped in your arms like the sweetest piece of muslin your eyes ever did see if I ever fell off a horse." He cackled. "In friendship."

"I am considering dissolving said friendship at the moment," Aspen muttered.

An arrival had them both turning toward the study door. "Got here as soon as I could," the Marquess of Marsden said, breathing hard as Stanley took his hat and cloak. "Received Laila's note about Vesper. What have I missed? Is she well? I assume my wife is here?"

"They're upstairs and Vesper's fine—you know nothing can damage that girl, even a fall during a race on Rotten Row with this scoundrel." Lushing grinned and lifted his tumbler in a silent toast. "Heard the poor bastard was eating her dust long before she was unseated."

"She's the best rider among us all, what do you expect?" Aspen returned drily. "I knew I was going to lose even before the groom said go."

"You see!" Lushing crowed in triumph and then glanced at Marsden who was watching in confusion. "He likes her."

"I said that she was competent at something, you simpleton," Aspen said. "That is not a devotion of undying love."

"What are you two quarreling about?" Marsden asked, settling into the seat opposite the earl.

"Greydon and Vesper."

Marsden grinned and peered over at Aspen with a knowing look. "Finally realized you were in love with her, have you?"

Oh, for the love of God.

"Not you as well." Aspen closed his eyes and pinched the bridge of his nose, striving for calm. "I might have cared for her when we were children, but I am *not* in love with her."

While it was true that there had been real affection between him and Vesper once upon a time, his friends of all people knew all that had changed after her coming out. He'd been barely able to speak to her without tripping over his own tongue that night. They'd grown apart during their adolescence, and he could no longer remember what he'd expected when he'd attended her come-out ball, but it certainly wasn't that she'd grown into the most stunning woman he'd ever seen. When they'd come face-to-face, instead of making a fool over himself, he'd clamped his lips shut, feigned indifference, and turned away.

Out of sheer, awkward embarrassment.

Vesper hadn't taken it that way, though, nor had anyone else.

The gossip mill had run rampant after the ball. Wagging tongues had spread the word that the very eligible Duke of Greydon wasn't interested in the supposed diamond of the season—which was the furthest thing from the truth. He'd been out of sorts and confused.

Naturally, she took it badly and the chasm between them widened even more. She treated him with haughty contempt whenever their paths had crossed, and he'd opted to keep his dignity intact rather than admit he'd been terrified to talk to her…terrified of sounding like a bumbling boor with nothing to say to the only girl who'd ever mattered.

In truth, pride had been his downfall.

Aspen often wondered if their story would have been different, had he not been so prideful, cowardly, and full of bitterness. After learning of his mother's perfidy, he'd lumped Vesper in with all those chaotic, ugly feelings, and things had gotten worse. But the past could not be changed.

Now, of course, Aspen was much more confident in matters of charm and seduction, but Vesper was no longer the young debutante she'd been then either. No, this woman was a warrior in disguise who saved small children with no thought to her own life. His mouth tightened, hands balling into fists as he recalled the terror he'd felt when he'd seen her fall.

Lushing tutted from where he sat, watching him. "What are you thinking now, I wonder?"

Aspen felt his cheeks flame and he cursed himself for blushing like a chit fresh out of the schoolroom. His brain spun with a dangerous mix of aggravation, panic, regret, and complete denial about the unwelcome deluge of feelings he had no wish to pick apart. "About a round in your ring with my fist on your face."

Lushing grinned. "Thou dost protest too much, Greydon. Admit it, you're besotted."

Aspen had had enough. "For the last time, I am not in goddamned love with your infuriating, hardheaded, irrepressible brat of a sister who doesn't give a thought to her own safety!" Lushing's eyes widened comically, and Aspen glowered at him. "What? Cat got your tongue now? Let me say it again for good measure: I will *never* be in love with her. We are like oil and water, and never the twain shall mix. Is that bloody clear enough for you?"

Both men stared at him like a pair of foxes caught in the light of a torch, but then a soft feminine throat cleared at the door. "I'd say your feelings are more than clear, Your Grace."

The heat that had flooded him moments before vanished and Aspen felt nothing but icy dread as he turned to look over his shoulder. A pale and weak Vesper stood in the doorway with her friends at her side glaring daggers at him, though her face was starkly unreadable. "You should not be out of bed," he managed gruffly.

"Don't tell me what to do," she replied, as she hobbled slowly into the study with the help of the Marchioness of Marsden on one side and a scowling Lady Briar on the other. "I came to retrieve some special willow bark sachets my father keeps for his migraines. Laudanum makes me ill."

Effie trailed behind them, looking at him as if he'd kicked her favorite dog. Guilt sluiced through him. "You could have sent a servant," he mumbled.

"Only I know where Papa keeps them," Vesper replied as she stopped to rest on the other side of the desk before fumbling in a drawer and removing a small reticule made of netting. "And since I haven't broken any bones, it's better to keep the blood flowing after a fall from a horse. If I had been in Dorset, I would have climbed back onto Feral after making sure he was well." Her face remained blank. "I am experiencing no dizziness, shivering, weak pulse, or anything resembling shock, so you can stop pretending to worry for my sake. No need to waste your air on a woman like me."

Aspen raked a hand through his hair. "That's not what I said or meant, and you know it."

Glacial blue eyes, ringed with bruising shadows, met his. "What *did* you mean then?"

Everyone was listening, though some were pretending to look elsewhere or busy themselves with books in the bookcase. At least the two men were. Three pairs of furious female eyes were fastened to him, promising retribution. "We can talk later."

"My brain is not broken, neither are my ears. Speak your piece now, Greydon, no one's stopping you."

Christ, why was she so *stubborn*? He really did not want to do this in front of an audience, more than half of whom looked like they wanted to dismember him. Except Effie, though knowing he'd put the heartbroken look on her face felt almost as bad as being eviscerated.

"We are friends," he began after inhaling a fortifying breath. "Your brother and Marsden seem to think we are more than that."

Those icy eyes narrowed. "You expect me to believe that *that's* what you were so furious about that you would bellow your disregard for me to the ends of Mayfair?"

Aspen frowned. "I didn't *bellow*." He cleared his throat and then said more calmly, "You don't wish for marriage, Vesper."

Her eyes rounded. "What does that have to do with anything?"

Hell, this wasn't going how he planned, especially not with their avid audience. He lowered his voice and parsed through his thoughts before speaking. "From me, I mean. We are on different paths. You have your life and I have mine." Wishing they were alone, he exhaled. "I'm sorry I hurt you. It was not my intention."

Vesper's jaw tightened. "You didn't hurt me. In fact, you opened my eyes, so thank you."

"Viper—" he whispered.

"Don't call me that," she said, voice cracking but she lifted her chin. "We are not friends. We are not anything. You've made that more than clear." And with that she turned and left the study.

Aspen let out a strangled breath. He should have felt relief, but he only felt like he'd lost her all over again.

Chapter Fifteen

"I want this to be the grandest ball this season and any season before it has ever seen," Vesper said to her father's man of affairs who was watching her with a wary expression that never boded well in her experience. She hadn't even asked the solicitor for funds yet and already he was shaking his head with a frown that was growing heavier by the second.

Vesper scowled back. Shouldn't he be deliriously in love with Mrs. Elway by now? Honestly, Mr. Cross should be much less cross if he was able to let go of some of his frustrations in the bedchamber. Vesper's nose wrinkled. She didn't want to think of her father's man of business *or* their housekeeper twined in the sheets, though indeed, that had been the goal.

Well, that and marriage, though neither of them seemed inclined to walk down the aisle. She frowned. Had she miscalculated somewhere? Should she have set the solicitor up with someone else? Lizzie, perhaps? No. Her lady's maid was much too young.

Uneasiness gripped her. Had she been wrong about this match? Perhaps her instincts were off. In fact, hadn't *everything* felt off since the unfortunate return of the Duke of Greydon?

She swallowed, remembering his awful words from her father's study. Despite her secret fantasies and dreams, she'd known that Greydon did not truly harbor a grand affection for her, but to hear him declare it out loud had stung more than she'd imagined.

You don't wish to marry, Vesper.

The plain, sad, pathetic truth was she didn't wish to marry anyone *else*.

Even when Lord Eldridge had approached her father with an offer her very first season, she hadn't felt a single urge to agree to his proposal. On the surface, Lord Eldridge was a good match—he was handsome, young, wealthy, and a favorite of the ton. But Vesper couldn't imagine being wedded to him, or worse, being taken to his bed. There was only one man she'd ever dreamed of in such a manner.

Not that Greydon truly wanted her. A recollection of her hips pressed into a billiard's table and a very eager hand caressing her intimate parts flitted across her brain. Well, his body might want more, but his heart and head did not. Clearly. She exhaled, banishing both the vision and the sudden ache behind her breastbone.

Mr. Cross cleared his throat and made to dismiss her with a noise of disapproval. "Lady Vesper, I will need to speak to His Grace about this."

Vesper held her temper. "Mr. Cross, the duke already knows and has given me permission to continue. I will require payment for the flowers, the food, and the orchestra. That means those funds need to be allocated and the accounts settled."

While the Dowager Duchess of Greydon had agreed to lend her influence and put her name to the charity ball, that didn't mean she was going to foot the entire bill. As it was, the duchess had already demanded that the Duke of Harwick's accounts be made available for her use. But while Vesper was generous at heart, she was not foolish. The duchess was not known for her frugality.

"Mr. Cross, I assure you that you will have final approval over all the expenses, and I shall personally give you guidance on what is required."

He shook his head, blinking rapidly. "I was not hired to mind you and your social intrigues, my lady."

Social *intrigues*?

"Are you saying that managing my father's accounts isn't your responsibility, Mr. Cross?" she asked so softly that a pair of beady green eyes met hers and narrowed. "I am his daughter, and this ball is more important than your miserly little mind can comprehend. So either you help me out or we do this the hard way."

Low laughter echoed behind them as her father walked into the library, interrupting them. "You won't win, Cross. When she puts her mind to something, she's as tenacious as a fox hound with its prey. Give her what she wants."

"But Your Grace, it's an extravagant sum for a *party*."

"Yes, I know." The Duke of Harwick nodded, sending a fond look her way.

Vesper felt the warmth of his affection sink into the marrow of her bones. He had always believed in her, even when some of her ideas had been outrageous...like the time she had brought in half a dozen hungry children from St. Giles to be fed in their kitchens, and he hadn't batted an eye. In fact, after that day her darling father had given Cook standing orders to pack up any leftovers from their formal functions and ferry them to a church in Seven Dials. That had happened nearly two years ago, and it was still a Lyndhurst tradition.

"Thank you, Papa," she said rising to fling her arms around him.

It was only then that she noticed the man who had arrived behind the duke. Her shoulders went tight before she forced herself to relax. It should not have surprised her that Greydon was there. He and her father had been working closely together over the past fortnight. In fact, it was rare that she didn't walk past her father's study and see their bent heads together as they pored over old parliamentary bills and documents.

The hurt from his words had faded enough for her to realize that it was better this way. She had plans to see through...including facilitating a match between him and Judith. She couldn't do that if her heart was involved. In a way, Greydon had saved her from losing everything she'd worked for.

On occasion, Greydon took dinner with them. Those evenings had been awkward at first but had become easier to bear after a while. Even Lushing had remarked about how congenial they all were the last time he'd joined them for dinner. Most evenings, her brother was at his club. Vesper often wondered whether her brother was envious of the close friendship Greydon enjoyed with their father, but Lushing didn't seem to mind. On the contrary, he seemed happy that *he* didn't have to spend time with the old man.

"He's not going to be around forever," Vesper had told her brother once when she'd scolded him for missing dinner yet again.

Her usually amiable brother had glared at her. "I have a business to run."

"Setting up boxing fights is not a business, it's a hobby," she'd shot back. "When Papa dies, you will inherit this dukedom and that will be your sole responsibility."

He had stared at her with an unfathomable expression. "Too bad you weren't born a boy. You would make a much better duke than I ever could."

Vesper hadn't disagreed. Lushing was a man who busied his many demons with a life of leisure. But women did not inherit dukedoms and girls did not become dukes. They became duchesses if and when they *married* a man with such a title. It dug at her from time to time. Her brain was just as capable, if not more so than her brother's, and obviously, they both knew it. That didn't buck the rules of primogeniture, however.

"How are you today, Lady Vesper?" the Duke of Greydon greeted her with a polite smile.

"Well, thank you, Your Grace. How are you?"

"Busy," he said.

It was always scrupulously civil between them, almost as if the two people who'd clawed at each other, grasping desperately at clothing and kissing like their lives depended on it, had never existed.

"Will you be joining us this evening for dinner, Your Grace?" she asked.

"I hope so," he said with another of those bland smiles.

Her father let out a loud sigh. "I'm afraid I cannot join you two, but please don't let my absence stop you. I promised the Earl of Lassiter that I would join him this evening."

The Earl of who? Vesper frowned. She didn't recall her father ever speaking of such a man or mentioning that he had plans, and she had inquired barely two days ago whether he was busy during the week. "Who is Lassiter?"

He waved an arm. "No one you know. Cross arranged it."

The solicitor looked taken aback for a scant second before he nodded when her father drilled him with a glare that did not go unnoticed by Vesper. Her frown deepened. That was peculiar. Was her father in his cups? He didn't seem foxed.

"I'm late aren't I, Cross?" he went on. "Must get a move on."

"Papa," Vesper said, watching him as he hurried past her,

dragging the bemused solicitor in his wake. "Are you well? You seem out of sorts."

He paused, but his eyes kept darting everywhere but toward her. "Oh yes, of course. Healthy as a horse. Didn't realize what time it was. Late, you see."

"I see." She *didn't* see. The duke could be odd at the best of times, but this was out of character even for him. Vesper didn't have the time to pursue it—she would take it up with him later in private. She did not, however, want to lose the opportunity to confirm her expenditure. "What about the funds for the ball?"

He nodded. "Yes, whatever you need. Cross will see to it." A small frown creased her father's brows. "Within reason, Vesper."

"Of course, Papa. No golden statues, exclusive Cyprians, or fountains of Spanish chocolate, I understand." She bit her lip to hold back her mirth as Mr. Cross goggled at her, his watchful eyes widening and his cheeks flushing. Her father, of course, did not notice or pretended not to hear her scandalous reply as he left the library with his man in tow.

The Duke of Greydon, though, had heard and was staring at her—or more precisely, staring at her *mouth*. A reluctant chuckle left him, and she felt that dark, delicious sound reverberate right between her thighs. *That* wasn't normal, was it? A gentleman's laughter didn't cause blood to surge and knees to weaken. It didn't make well-bred ladies turn into thirsty little creatures, their entire existences narrowing down to one urgent need. Desire.

Control, control, control.

"Exclusive Cyprians?" he asked, one brow raised.

"I like to keep the ton on their toes," she said. "Or perhaps the Cyprians would anyway. Or would it be off their feet completely? I suppose that's up to the participants, isn't it?"

His nostrils flared for a second at her hardly veiled innuendo, and then he blinked as though convincing himself that she couldn't possibly be talking about something so crass. Vesper grinned to herself. Of course she'd meant it. A perverse part of her *wanted* to torture him.

"What do you even know of such things, Lady Vesper?" he choked out.

Her eyelashes lowered. "You would be surprised."

"Would I?" His voice sounded unnaturally hoarse.

She nodded. "Like my brother, I have friends in many places, Your Grace, and some of them are not highborn lords and ladies. Some are from the demimonde. I am not a stranger to the courtesans at Lushing's tavern or what they do." With a dismissive huff, she exited the study, but Greydon was quick to close the distance between them.

A firm grip on her elbow held her in place. Vesper turned, expecting to see a bland or bored expression, but what she saw instead was sheer possessiveness. Hot bronze flames burned in his eyes, taking their tawny color to something predatory and formidable that made her insides quiver. Not with fear. With lust.

"You provoke me intentionally, Viper," he growled, and blast if the low raspy sound of his voice didn't make her knees and the rest of her turn to jelly.

"I speak the truth. It's not my fault if you cannot handle it." Feigning a confidence she did not possess, she jutted her chin and shook out of his grasp. "See you at dinner, Your Grace."

The brazen little minx.

Hours later, Aspen was still seething from a potent cocktail of anger, lust, and powerlessness. Anger at her hobnobbing in places a lady should not be, lust at her boast that she was not such an ingenue, and powerlessness that he had no control over her—or any of his fucking instincts—at all. He'd been the one to place the wedge between them, and it *galled* more than he cared to admit.

Once more, he was in a state of complete aggravation... and arousal.

He'd gone back to the duke's study to work but had written the same thing three times, spilled ink all over the desk, and managed to stab himself with the quill. Did her fool brother even know that she'd been frequenting his public house? The tavern that housed a clandestine boxing ring within its walls also housed all manner of bawdy happenings in its upper rooms as well. Things that no gently bred lady should ever lay eyes on.

By the time a footman had informed him that it was time for dinner, Aspen was in a fine froth. A froth usually reserved for husbands when it came to the safety of their wives. He, however, was not Vesper's husband, which did not give him any rights at all. Still, it was his duty as a friend to the family to steer her straight. To be an altruistic guardian.

Yes, that was it.

No, that's not it, you liar. No guardian has the untoward desires you do. Altruism is the last thing on your mind, admit it.

He would admit no such thing. Once he packed up his belongings, Aspen straightened his clothing and made his way into the dining room, where two footmen dressed in livery stood at attention, a few steaming dishes on the sideboard, ready to be served, but there was no Lady Vesper in sight.

After nearly a quarter of an hour, his irritation grew. When another fifteen minutes passed, Aspen was certain she was making him wait on purpose. Any attempt at maintaining a polite, benevolent demeanor had all but fled in the wake of his dark mood. Christ, why did he allow her to needle him so? He could have opened his bag and continued his work, but he preferred to stew.

When the lady of the house finally arrived in a flutter of sea-foam green skirts, with a white cat in her arms, he could feel the muscle keeping time in his jaw. Was she late because she'd been entertaining her pet?

"Apologies, Your Grace," she said sweetly. "I was detained."

His lips flattened. "Detained? By a cat?"

Cool blue eyes met his. "Not exactly, and not that it's any of your business, but I was on the other side of town for an important engagement, and yes, there was a small accident with Cat in the carriage, which forced me to have to change. I am sorry to have kept you waiting."

"Where were you?"

He could see her debating whether to tell him the truth as her fingers slid over the animal's white fur, but then she firmed her jaw and shrugged. "Seven Dials."

The West End of London was a cesspool of crime and vice. Alarm bells tolled in his head. "What were you doing there?"

"I told you, Greydon, it's none of your business what I do or where I go."

They stared at each other in silent standoff. Her color was higher than usual, but she did not look worse for wear. The truth was she was right. It *wasn't* his place to interrogate her on her whereabouts—he wasn't her father, brother, or husband—but if she was putting herself in harm's way, then he had a responsibility to take action. It was his bloody duty.

"What kind of accident?" he asked.

"A carriage accident." Taking her seat, she released the cat and signaled for the footmen to serve the food that had been removed from the room once before and reheated, given her delayed arrival. "I am famished. Honestly, you should have started without me."

Aspen could feel the blood thundering between his ears at the thought of her putting herself in danger. *Again.* She could have been hurt or worse. Clearly, like with the incident with the child on Rotten Row when she'd flung herself off the horse, she had no sense when it came to her own well-being!

"What kind of carriage accident?" he repeated.

She set down her soup spoon with a sniff. "Why does it matter to you? I am here, safe and sound. My belongings weren't stolen by cutpurses. My person wasn't pillaged by flashmen. I live to see another day. Rejoice and enjoy your fine soup, Your Grace!"

The words and her cavalier attitude were like tinder to flame. His temper erupted. "This is not a joke, Vesper. The area is dangerous, especially for a lady."

"I am well aware." She sent him a smile. "Don't worry about me, Your Grace. I am more than capable of taking care of myself. I've done it quite competently for many years."

"Do Harwick and Lushing know that you're gallivanting around Seven Dials?" he asked.

"I suspect they do. They are my *father* and *brother*, after all."

It rubbed—the emphasis that he was no one to her, and it was like poking an angry bear that was already caught in a trap of its own making. "And they allow it?"

Her brows shot high, a cool laugh leaving her lips. "*Allow* it? I hate to destroy your pretty illusions, but we are not in the Dark Ages, Your Grace," she said, lifting her wineglass and sipping. "You have to stop this, Greydon. This possessive, prevailing male performance when you have no right to be this way. I am *not* yours to command."

"You should be."

He had no idea where the growled words had come from—somewhere deep and raw and primal. *Fuck.* Aspen wanted so many things in that moment. He wanted to forbid her to put herself in peril. He wanted to chastise her for defying him.

Most of all, he wanted to silence that acerbic tongue that skewered him with every word. Even though any man with a lick of sense in his head wouldn't prevail to order a woman like Vesper about. Or any woman. But he was too far gone to be rational.

"Out," he snapped to the footmen.

Her eyes narrowed as the servants filed out after a firm look from him. As if she could sense what was to come, Cat scampered out of sight and made herself scarce beneath the table. Wariness flitted across Vesper's face when he pushed back his chair and prowled toward her. He relished the flash of surprise in her deep blue eyes before she tried to hide it with disinterest.

He turned her chair to face him, propping his hands on the armrests, effectively trapping her in place. He knew he was crowding her from the inaudible gasp that left her lips and the slight flaring of her pupils, but instead of cowering, she folded her napkin, set her hands in her lap, and arched a brow. "I assume there's a point behind this... territorial display," she said. "You might as well urinate around the chair at this juncture for good measure."

Even with him looming over her as he was, she glared him down like a queen on her throne. Aspen loosened his clenched jaw, one side of his lip kicking up. "Marking my territory in such a manner would mean I was worried about competition, Viper."

"There's that false modesty we all know and love. I was worried it had gone missing."

"There's nothing false about confidence."

"Are you certain you aren't mistaking arrogance for

confidence, Your Grace? It's a baffling thing for most gentlemen, I know." She made a sympathetic face and tapped one finger against her lips. "So easy to conflate the two."

He couldn't help his chuckle at her dry tone. "You are audacious."

Vesper pushed up in her seat and stood, forcing his hands to leave the armrests and his spine to straighten until she was situated scandalously close to him. "No need to enumerate my extraordinary qualities, Your Grace," she said huskily, walking two of her fingers up his waistcoat buttons. "I've not quite recovered from the last time."

Aspen could hardly formulate a thought with her standing so near. How quickly the tables had turned! A moment ago, he'd been the apex predator, and now, after a few diverting words and a hint of a luscious bosom teasing his chest, he'd become the prey. The all too *willing* prey.

He jolted out of his stupor, remembering what had started this argument in the first place, and tried to ignore her marauding fingers. "I don't like the idea of you going out on your own, Vesper. Even if Lushing and Harwick know, I won't stand for you putting yourself in harm's way."

A gentle smile graced her lips before she tapped his chin, curtsied, and strolled away from him. Was that just... agreement? He gaped, eyes narrowing as she bent to collect the cat that was winding its body about her ankles.

Still smiling sweetly, she paused at the door and peered at him over her shoulder. "You are truly quite adorable if you think you can control anything I do or don't do. Have a wonderful dinner, Your Grace."

Chapter Sixteen

The ballroom at Drake Manor looked like it had been lifted from a seventeenth-century French palace. With all the gold decor and the many mirrors, it could rival the Château de Versailles. Not to mention that all the guests were dressed in black and gold. That had been the dowager's idea: the *Touch of Midas* ball. The hint of decadence—gold ink on the jet cardstock invitations indicating dress requirements—had been hers as well, and the ton had gone nearly apoplectic with delight.

Vesper had to hand it to Greydon's mother. She was indeed a master of the game. They had sent out only a few dozen invitations at first, which they knew would whet the appetites of those who had yet to receive theirs. The pause had caused a fever, and when the second batch had been delivered, that fever had turned into a frenzy. *Everyone* who was *anyone* sought an invite, and by the time the last round had gone out, people had been teeming with excitement.

They were more than willing to give up their coin to see and be seen. Especially when it was rumored that the Duchess of Greydon had sent an invitation to the palace. Prince Albert would most likely make an appearance in that case, though Bertie would be sure to cause some kind of scene. His predilection for hedonism was infamous.

Vesper watched as the Duchess of Greydon simpered and fawned over the guests as they were announced, presiding like the high ranking, powerful aristocrat she was. Her son could say all he wanted about her, but her influence among the ton was legendary. And Vesper had desperately needed her support. The *children* needed her support. She would not apologize for that.

"Miss Angela Burdett-Coutts," the majordomo announced and Vesper whirled, her heart beginning to pound in her chest. She'd been a longtime admirer of the so-named Queen of the Poor, the famed philanthropist who had unknowingly changed the course of Vesper's life.

"Miss Coutts, what an honor," she said in a breathless rush after the woman had strangely swept past the duchess with a frigid nod that spoke of some salted history.

The somber dark-haired woman paused and smiled at her, however. "The honor is mine, Lady Vesper. I've heard quite a lot of you lately."

Vesper blinked. "You have?"

"Charles cannot go on enough about your efforts, and how much you remind him of me," the woman said, and Vesper blushed. To be a topic of conversation between the woman she emulated and the famous writer, Charles Dickens, was almost more than she could stand, but Vesper kept herself composed.

"I take that as the highest of compliments, Miss Coutts."

She smiled. "Oh, do call me Angela."

"I'm Vesper," she blurted and blushed. "I know we've only just met but I feel like we're dear friends already, so I'm just Vesper."

"So Just Vesper, tell me more about yourself," Angela said

with an affable smile, extending an elbow for her to take. "I've heard of your work in some of the poorer churches."

After sending a glance to the duchess, who was busy greeting their new guests, Vesper happily accompanied the woman down the stairs. This was beyond her wildest expectations. She'd been sent an invitation, but Vesper hadn't been sure she would come. Angela Burdett-Coutts, one of the richest women in England and a social activist with the biggest heart, was here at her ball!

"The generous donations we collect tonight are for the Ragged School Union," she blurted. "My father, the Duke of Harwick, and Lord Shaftesbury have been working to make changes in Parliament to support the education of children. I'm doing what I can to help gather information and support for this. These donations will also fund local initiatives with orphans in particular, which can then lead to bigger changes."

"That sounds marvelous," Angela said.

"It's not much, but it's something," Vesper said blushing. "I have to say that your work has been such an inspiration to me. What you've done to build housing and arrange fresh drinking water for our city's poor communities, help women who need a home and basic care, all your work with the ragged schools...I'm dumbfounded. You're a true humanitarian."

The woman gave a demure smile. "Thank you, dear. I only do what I can, which is really all we can ask of anyone." She waved an arm. "Even our friends here. Every little bit helps." Her humility was refreshing. "Keep doing what you are doing, young Vesper."

Vesper felt like a fuse had been lit in her spirit. A light that did not diminish when her nemesis approached, his handsome face brooding. The duke looked entirely too gorgeous, too, dressed in raven black with a deep golden waistcoat that gleamed in the candlelight. She tried not to appreciate how well it brought out the gold flecks in his eyes.

"Lady Vesper," Greydon greeted her with a bow, and bent to kiss Angela's cheek with a shocking familiarity. "Aunt."

"*Aunt?*" Vesper gasped.

"On my father's side by marriage." He thought for a moment. "Twice removed or is it thrice?"

"We are probably not even related by blood, but I claim you nonetheless, Nephew," Angela said fondly while Vesper gaped at the two of them. The woman she respected and practically venerated was the aunt of the man she wanted to bury six feet under? It boggled the mind. "Thank you for encouraging me to attend this evening, Greydon. I have met your young lady and have been most impressed."

Vesper felt her heart lurch. "You persuaded her to attend?"

"She's not my young lady," Greydon said at the same time. He eased out a breath and canted his head. "I remembered the pamphlet you had asked Lady Briar about and managed to put two and two together when you said you needed to ask for my mother's help to host a ball. A bit late on my part, but I got there in the end." His eyes canvassed his ballroom. "You've outdone yourself."

She blinked. She had to be in an alternate universe because the Duke of Greydon was complimenting her *and* meaning it. And he'd worked out for himself that she wasn't some rich, indolent heiress who demanded to be doted on. "Thank you, but I cannot take all the credit. The duchess did have a hand in it as well."

Angela lifted a brow, her mouth curling into a moue. "The very reason I had not replied in the affirmative until my nephew convinced me otherwise."

"They don't get along," Greydon said by way of explanation. "They're like cats and dogs."

"A flea-bitten mongrel draped in diamonds," Angela added with a fierce scowl to where Greydon's mother stood, and Vesper was taken aback by the vehemence in her voice. "One day that woman will get what is coming to her for what she did to my gentle second cousin, but that's a story for another time." Vesper blinked, wondering what on earth the lady meant by such a forceful accusation. Aspen's father had needed institutional help, hadn't he? Angela turned to Vesper with a warm smile. "You enjoy your evening, dear. You have earned it. Please feel free to call on me at Holly Lodge whenever you need."

"Thank you," she whispered as the woman wandered off to speak to someone she knew. Vesper turned to the duke. "I cannot believe you *know* her."

The corner of his lips tilted in a way that made her heart quicken. "If pinching my cheeks qualifies as an endorsement of a relationship, then yes."

"Somehow, Your Grace, I cannot fathom anyone having the boldness to pinch your cheeks." Said cheeks were lean and unyielding, and bracketed by sharp cheekbones and an even sharper jawline. Heavens, everything about him was *so* deeply forbidding.

And yet…her gaze drifted to his lips, the only hint of softness in his face.

Suddenly hot, Vesper shifted her gaze to look into his eyes, only to find herself pinned by a mercurial tawny stare. God, was nowhere safe? Discomfited, she focused on his diamond and sapphire stickpin instead. Upon more scrutiny, the blue gem was an unusual stone—a strange sort of blue.

"Is that a sapphire?" she asked, frowning.

"Lapis lazuli," he said, faint color cresting those high cheekbones. "I had it made. It reminds me of your eyes."

"Why would you—?" Heat sizzled through her. "Oh."

He likes your eyes.

No, no, no. This duke was meant for Judith—Vesper had given her word on the matter. He should be wearing an emerald stone to match *her* eyes. She'd promised the duchess to convince him of Judith's suitability, though for the life of her, everything inside stubbornly rebelled against the notion. It was the only reason she hadn't made any effort or headway into pushing the match since the agreement. She'd also been much too busy planning the ball and dealing with Cross and all his obstacles to handle matchmaking.

Because you have feelings for him and he rejected you.

Again.

First at her debutante ball and then in front of their friends. She could only ignore the reality for so long. Just because he fancied the color of her eyes enough to commission a piece of jewelry for himself didn't mean he was suddenly not a jackass. He was still controlling and autocratic. Arrogant and annoying to a fault.

Shifting away from his confusing orbit, Vesper shook her head. The more distance, the better, especially if she were to see this bloody bargain with the duchess through. Her attraction to the duke was an inconvenience that needed to be quashed. At once!

"Oh, there's Judith," she said, waving the girl over. "Doesn't she look lovely this evening?"

"I suppose so," the duke said, though a small crease appeared between his brows.

When a smiling and fresh-faced Judith approached, Vesper's heart rebelled. Dear God, she couldn't bear it. For once, she did not want to be successful. If a connection happened on its own, then who was she to argue? But to push them together thus felt wrong.

If she hadn't interfered with Laila and Marsden, would

they have married? What about Evans and her own cousin? Had she manipulated them into a match? Doubt and indecision gripped her, sending her thoughts into a violent, negative whirlwind. All along, had she been meddling as opposed to matchmaking? She could barely keep up with her thoughts.

Was she a *fraud*?

Vesper felt sick to her stomach. She backed away, almost tripping over her own feet, her voice emerging on a defeated whisper, "You two should dance. Excuse me."

Stupefied at Vesper's sudden flight, Aspen stared at the space where she'd stood, her sweet perfume tickling his nostrils as she disappeared into the sea of golden gowns.

Earlier, he'd had to catch his breath when he caught sight of her speaking to his aunt. Her hair had been swept to the side and cascaded over that deliciously exposed shoulder, offering tantalizing glimpses of luminous skin. She'd resembled a warrior goddess from some other fantastical realm. Unattainable. Sublimely beautiful.

All that had been missing was a gilded bow and arrow.

Though arming her would be a mistake.

He would most likely be her first target. Aspen frowned, knowing that it was his own fault for pushing her away, yet again, because of his complete inability to use words like a capable human being. He regretted what he'd said in such haste, but his logical brain defended that it wasn't unreasonable. He did not plan to stay in London... and to dally with Vesper would be unconscionable, especially if he had no intention to offer for her.

Would that be so bad?

"What on earth is making you glower so?" Judith asked,

peering up at him. She looked quite splendid in a pale gold gown as Vesper had remarked. "You're positively brooding."

He frowned. "I do not brood."

Judith pointed at his tight brow and wrinkled her nose. "Your forehead would disagree. You have a fierce line just there as though something on your mind was making you very displeased indeed. Might I fathom a guess?" She grinned and waggled her eyebrows. "Does it have to do with the sudden flight of our lovely hostess, perhaps?"

"I don't know what you're going on about," he said. "Lady Vesper and I are just friends. Enemies, most days, if you ask her."

She rose on tiptoe and lowered her voice so only he could hear. "Friends who stare at each other all the time whenever they think the other isn't looking? Enemies who squabble at every turn, only to capitulate a day later for no reason other than they are desperate to see their mortal foe? Yes, that makes a capital amount of sense."

"It sounds nonsensical when you say it like that," he said with a dismissive look.

Judith gave a sage nod. "It *is* nonsensical."

"The lady doesn't want to marry," he said quietly after a while as they stood there companionably, watching the guests milling about. That was the thing about Judith—she was easy to be around. Aspen glanced down at her. She was pleasant, amiable, and intelligent.

Why couldn't he have been interested in her? It would have solved so much, made things so much easier to fulfill his duty. Marriage could be a nice, agreeable arrangement. It need not be antagonistic, combative, and fraught, but instead a congenial understanding between like-minded individuals.

A pair of flashing blue eyes dared to disagree.

He was well aware that he was thinking of Vesper and not marriage at all, and that his frown had returned.

"You're brooding again," Judith murmured.

"You are not even looking at me," he retorted. "How do you know?"

Her laughter met his ears. "I can feel you vibrating like a tuning fork, Aspen, or like some kind of feral animal about to defend an encroachment on its lair."

"That's rather specific," he said, lips flattening.

"No less true." She peered up at him. "So, are we going to stand here and wither on the vine all evening, or shall we do as Lady Vesper suggested and dance?"

His heart leaped at the sound of her name, but Aspen groaned. "I like being a wallflower."

Judith laughed again, the sound attracting many curious stares, as well as an unreadable look from Vesper, who now stood in conversation with his mother. The dowager, however, couldn't hide her smug smile as Aspen escorted Judith to the ballroom floor.

"You, Aspen dear, could not be a wallflower if you tried," Judith told him when they took their positions. "You're much too...tall and stern looking to be any kind of flower. And you're a duke, which means that women would notice you even if you were a truculent weed."

He faked an affronted look. "A *weed*? By God, you don't hold back any punches, do you?"

"No, and speaking of punches, why doesn't the lady want to marry?"

Aspen's gaze drifted to his obsession again, noticing that she was being led to dance as well. Lord Eldridge, the gentleman who had offered for her once. He had a weak chin, Aspen noticed, and probably an equally weak disposition. His frown returned in full force along with a sour emotion in the pit of his stomach. They looked entirely too comfortable with each other for his liking.

"They make a beautiful couple," Judith said, following his stare.

"He's too passive for her," he bit out.

Judith shrugged as they moved into a turn. "Maybe that's what she needs. A man who won't cause a scene, will let her do what she wants, and they can live amicably together."

"Amicably?" he scoffed. "A life without passion?"

Judith looked surprised at his outburst. "What do you know of it? You're the least impassioned person I know unless you're talking about your work."

Aspen cringed at the blunt estimation. It was true. He'd learned early on to keep his emotions and passions buried, lest they be used against him like his father's had been. Being melancholy could be a deficiency. Being interested in something could easily be deemed too excitable. Speaking out of turn or arguing could be construed as moral insanity. Any state other than the most evenly benign was treated with suspicion.

It was supposedly in his genes, after all. But once Harwick's detective located the men his mother had hired, he would uncover the truth. According to the last report he'd received, both Dr. Parker and Mr. Rhodes were very much alive. Parker was in Bath and Rhodes in York. It wouldn't be long now.

Given the duke's incarceration and his mother's unsubtle threats of a hereditary disposition to madness, control had always been Aspen's refrain. From the time he'd become duke at twelve, he'd buried everything with his father. It had simply been easier not to feel. And a life of austerity and restraint had become palliative in its own way. Until *her*… the pebble in his shoe.

The extra-sharp bone splinter.

Aspen exhaled, the clawing sensation in his chest returning as Vesper laughed at something Eldridge said. It grew and grew until he could hear nothing else but a roaring between his ears. A need to conquer and claim as though he were some uncivilized, territorial creature.

Breathe.

It was all he could do to finish the dance, his body as tight as a drum, before delivering Judith to his mother and stalking out to the gardens. Air, he needed air. Or so help him, Eldridge would find himself in a heap of bloody bones in the middle of Mayfair.

Vesper felt the duke's departure, a tangible pressure lifting from her skin when he left the ballroom—as though a storm tide had suddenly eased in the eye of a thunderstorm. Such a false sense of calm did not sit well with her, not when *he* was the storm. The ache in her breast widened like an impossible crevasse and she felt…empty.

"Thank you for the dance, Lord Eldridge," she said politely, attempting to make a quick escape.

He bowed and kissed her gloved knuckles, holding her in place. "A pleasure, my lady. I have missed our precious interludes. You seem to grow more beautiful every time we meet."

"Thank you, my lord, that is sweet of you to say," she said, cheeks warming in slight discomfort.

With an earnest expression, he cleared his throat. "Dancing and conversing with you is something I treasure. I hope you know my offer of marriage still stands."

Vesper nodded with a cordial smile, though she didn't have the heart to tell him that she hadn't heard a single word he'd said during the dance. Her attention had been occupied elsewhere. As far as his offer, Eldridge was a perfectly nice man, but the idea of marriage to him had no appeal. He was adequate. Better than adequate, in truth. He possessed no dreadful vices that she knew of and he was kind, which was estimable. He was a perfectly suitable husband...for someone else.

"Thank you, my lord. I shall remember that if and when my father decides it's time for me to wed." *Which would be never.*

"Then I shall endure in everlasting hope," he replied in earnest.

"Please don't, Lord Eldridge. There could be a lovely young lady waiting for you to be her knight in splendid armor. I wouldn't want to deprive you of that."

"You are truly the most gracious lady in London, Lady Vesper. Please save me another dance." The look of adoration in his gaze made her stomach hurt. She tugged her hand away as civilly as she could and made her escape to where she knew he would not follow.

After hiding in the retiring room for a good few minutes, Vesper made her way to where her friends stood in hushed conversation. She was ready for a cold glass of champagne. Or three.

Only Laila and Effie were there tonight. Nève was at home and on the cusp of giving birth, and Briar was, miracles of miracles, dancing.

"Who is Briar dancing with?" Vesper asked, squinting to see the man's face.

Effie let out an uncharacteristic growl. "Lord Cuntington."

Both Vesper and Laila goggled. Surely she hadn't said what they thought she'd said. "Do you mean to say Lord *Huntington*, Effie dear?" Laila asked.

She sniffed, her fair cheeks the color of poppies. "That is what I said."

That was emphatically *not* what she'd said, but Vesper bit her lip in stunned glee. The ever-calm Evangeline Raine rarely swore. But it was no secret that Lord Huntington, the ton's leading bachelor, had treated her abominably during her first season, when she had disputed his archaic opinion on a woman's place in society. He'd been so insulted that he'd humiliated her in front of everyone, and Effie's marital prospects had never recovered. Not that she ever wanted to wed—she intended to remain a spinster for the rest of her days.

That reminded Vesper.

"Cat is a menace, Effie. You must take her back."

"No. She's yours to care for. And stop trying to pawn her off on everyone," she replied. "Laila told me that you tried to con her son into taking her."

"The little beast defecated in my shoes and left a squirrel tail in my bed!"

Effie's even stare held hers. "The squirrel is a sign of esteem. And the other thing is a silent protest. Maybe you should pet her once in a while. She just wants your attention."

"Why did you even give her to me, Effie? I'm hopeless with animals. The poor creature will become a defecating murderess under my watch and end up terrorizing the whole of London."

Effie shrugged. "Because you need to realize that you deserve to be loved fiercely and unconditionally, Vesper. Even if it's just by a cat. Don't think I haven't noticed how you hold yourself apart because you've convinced yourself you're not worthy of love as you are."

Vesper's breath caught, a heavy feeling crushing her chest at Effie's soft, far too insightful words. It wasn't that she didn't think herself worthy... she refused to let herself be hurt. And if that meant keeping the door to her heart firmly closed, then so be it. Seeing her friends fall in love was reward enough for her. She let out a light laugh. "So you gift me with a monster? That is the most twisted reasoning I've ever heard. I'll be lucky if I survive the week at this rate."

"You're so melodramatic," Effie said, but they were interrupted by a breathless Briar, who looked like a cat who had a mouthful of canary. Out of the corner of her eye, Vesper noticed Lord Huntington rushing up the stairs as Effie frowned warily at their friend. "What did you do?"

"Come now, Effie, you know a lady never kisses and tells," she said with a saucy wink.

Laila snorted. "Good thing you're under no such compunctions."

"Why is Cuntington running out of here with his tail between his legs?" Vesper demanded.

Briar burst into laughter, and her grin was so wide it almost split her face in two. "I found out a particularly juicy piece of gossip from one of the ladies who marches with our suffragette group. Apparently Lord Huntington's fiancée has eloped to America with his best mate." Three pairs of eyes rounded in unison, gasps escaping. "I wanted to be the one to see his face when I informed him of that fact after what he did to our Effie. It's too late for him to do anything anyway. She and her lover absconded on a liner tonight."

"That is...astounding," Effie whispered. "I mean, it's dreadful. Poor man."

"Poor nothing." Laila lifted her glass, an evil smile on her pretty face. "A toast then, to pigeon-livered cockwobbles, who get their just deserts."

"To pigeon-livered cockwobbles!" they chorused.

But even as she sipped the crisp champagne, Vesper felt a beat of envy for the eloping couple. She wondered what it would be like to leave the security and safety of the ton behind and follow a lover into the great unknown with no plan or purpose. Despite her earlier thoughts of shielding her heart from harm, she wondered what it would be like to give in to so great a passion that nothing else mattered.

Nève and Montcroix had that. The fractious duke with the heart of stone had gone to France to woo the love of his life. Laila and Marsden had it, too—a burning passion and enduring love that wound them inextricably together.

And she had…nothing.

A deep lonely throb echoed in her core. Sadly, the only prospective husband in her future seemed to be the saccharine-sweet, ever solicitous, gentle Lord Eldridge. On cue, he sent her a shy wave from across the ballroom. Her stomach roiled at what a possible future would look like as his wife, and everything inside her rebelled. The champagne, her bland future, her envy, all of it.

It was as if the floodgates had opened. Why shouldn't she have a shot at being impulsive? At going after what *she* wanted, duty and decorum be damned? What had being anyone's perfect darling gotten her all these years besides a heart full of envy and loneliness, and the attentions of London's kindliest gentleman who planned to suffocate her with sweetness.

"Lord Eldridge seems to be in good spirits this evening," Briar said. "He hasn't stopped smiling since his dance with you, Vesper."

That was the straw…and she was the camel's back.

Vesper exhaled, the weight of expectation and envy suddenly too much to bear. "Then why don't you marry him!" And then, immediately after, "I'm sorry, Briar. I don't know what came over me."

Briar, Effie, and Laila stared with varying degrees of

concern at the outburst, but Vesper couldn't bring herself to care. She was over the pretense. Over performing and being perfect. Over men like Eldridge who wanted her for what she symbolized and not who she truly was.

Only one man had ever been able to see her as she was.

And she wanted to be seen.

Chapter Seventeen

"I thought I would find you here."

Aspen swiveled toward the door and let the book he was flicking through fall to his lap. He wasn't surprised that Vesper had found him, only that she had felt compelled to follow him. The circular hedge maze was almost impossible to navigate, if one did not know its secrets. She was one of the few who did... who could find the hidden folly at its center.

When he didn't reply, she ventured up the single step that ran the circumference of the transformed dovecote and tugged on one of the flowering vines that covered the dome of its roof and climbed down the sides. "I always loved this place. It felt so magical and not really part of London."

He couldn't disagree. With its whimsical design, flowering rhododendrons, and thick rosebushes, the elegant folly with its narrow marble columns stamped with Greek gods and goddesses felt as though it belonged in another realm. Quotes from famous poets and writers were etched around the moldings at the top, including Jane Austen over the door.

There is no charm equal to tenderness of heart.

His father, fanciful and quixotic to the last. Who could

have known that those harmless qualities would get him committed to an insane asylum by his own wife?

The duke had designed the garden folly with the dovecote at the top as a reading nook and he used to escape there every day, satchels full of books in hand. On the inside of the folly, the shelves, once overflowing with volumes, were now sparse, having been stripped in cold rage by the duchess, though Aspen had replaced some of the lost books with a few of his own in memory. She had always suspected that his father esteemed his books more than he had her. Aspen couldn't fault him one bit.

Needing respite earlier from the ball and the presence of his mother, Aspen's feet had led him here, and he'd sat on the circular bench at the center of the folly, legs pushed out wide and cravat loosened, staring up at the dirty stained-glass windows for what seemed like hours before reaching for a thin book that sat on the side table. The volume of Percy Bysshe Shelley's poetry, one of the duke's favorites, that now sat in his lap.

A bird's soft coo from the level above made him look up. "He would have loved that the doves were still nesting here," he said. "That they, too, hadn't been chased away."

Vesper's eyes followed his as she entered. "You must miss him."

"I do."

Her stare snagged on the quote from *Emma* above the entryway on the inside and she smiled. "He loved Austen," she said.

"He did." Aspen gave a soft smile. "He wanted to name me after her, but my mother loathed the idea. She resented his love for Austen in particular. How could a woman feel threatened by a dead author?"

They fell into a heavy silence and he watched her in that

golden-bronze dress, her face giving away nothing as she ventured deeper into the dovecote. The door swung shut behind her, and Aspen's breath caught. What was she doing? She should be at her ball. He shifted, watching the emotions play across her face.

The tension swelled in the protracted silence until she exhaled and worried her lips between her teeth. A look of resolution overtook her features. It was the look she used to get as a girl when a harebrained scheme unfolded in that rather excellent brain of hers. More often than not, he'd go along with her capers.

She was the sun . . . and wherever she went, he followed.

Now, however, Aspen's eyes narrowed when she moved toward him, not stopping until she was standing in the space between his spread knees. She peered down at him, tucking that bottom lip in between her teeth in a way that always heated his blood. His cock, already at attention with her presence, swelled in his trousers.

He swallowed, well aware that his splayed position would hide nothing of his condition. "What are you doing here, Lady Vesper?"

"I wanted to find you." Her voice was soft and husky.

He swept an arm out. "A young unmarried lady in a deserted folly with a man is not ideal. If we are discovered, you'll be ruined."

"Ruined," she echoed with a small smile. "Such a catastrophic thing for any highborn lady. What does that mean anyway? That a woman is suddenly less than because she has been caught in a compromising state with a gentleman, even if she does nothing but stare at him from behind a door?"

"Yes, that's exactly what it means."

Vesper laughed, the airy sound echoing like bells in the small room. "By default, I would have already been ruined having spent a night with you in a dark attic as opposed to being here alone with a man *and* with my bodice untied."

His stare flicked to her chest—her dress was respectably intact—but then, he watched in stupefied disbelief as a gloved hand lifted to the ribbons above her décolletage. What was she *doing*? The answer to that became clear when she tugged on the laces, loosening the ties so that the neckline gaped and exposed a flushed expanse of rosy flesh that made his jaw drop. Oh, he looked. He couldn't *not* look. His fucking mouth watered.

Aspen's frown deepened as her intent became glaringly, heart-poundingly evident. "Vesper, what the devil are you doing?"

"I should think that was clear, Your Grace."

"It's not clear," he said.

"I wish to seduce you then." The grin curling her lips was pure sin. "If you require me to spell it out for you, I intend to disrobe. I intend to join you on that bench. And I intend for you to introduce me to the world of carnal pleasure."

At a complete loss for words, he blinked at her bluntness. "Not asking for much are you?"

"I know what I want."

His golden nymph watched him, a smile playing around those beautiful, provocative lips, and then sank to her knees right there between his legs. Aspen had been bemused before, but now, he sat up, his senses on high alert. Worry for her weighed upon him. "Vesper, this is not a game. This is your reputation."

She eyed him. "Do you know what the most important word you said in that sentence was?"

"Reputation?"

"Your," she countered softly. "It is *my* reputation to tarnish, *my* ruination to face, *my* virtue to lose. They are my choices to make, Your Grace."

Good God, did she just say *virtue*? It was a cold reminder that Vesper was a virgin, but Aspen couldn't seem to form a logical thought as she pressed closer, her scent engulfing him like incense meant to intoxicate. Unable to help himself, he breathed her in.

Silken gloved hands slid along the tops of his thighs, the firm pressure of her fingers sublime. Aspen nearly felt his eyes roll back in his head when they kneaded the taut muscle near his hip. She was so unbearably close to where it ached the most. One handspan and she would be upon him. The bulge of his arousal was painfully obvious, but he couldn't help his body's heated response to her presence or her touch. Would she be as wet as he was hard?

No, no, no. He should not be thinking of her in that way, wet or otherwise.

"Vesper, this isn't right," he gritted out through clenched teeth, fruitlessly willing his body to calm. An exercise in futility.

"Why?" she whispered.

He nearly groaned when her fingers crept an inch higher, those hooded blue eyes fixed upon him like she intended to do deliciously filthy things, and God help him, he wanted them all. "Because you will marry eventually and your husband will expect you to be a virgin."

The words were coarse but needed to be said.

Her fingers stilled. "I am three and twenty, Greydon. On the shelf and abandoned in the back of the pantry, by all accounts. If any husband I take expects me to be an innocent maiden, then that will be because of *his* naivete, not mine. I am a woman grown."

"This is a mistake," he whispered, body and mind at war.

"For whom?" she asked, and boldly moved her right hand to the distended protuberance between his legs. Aspen hissed out a breath as she stroked him. Her tongue snaked out to moisten her lips, her voice raspier than it'd been a moment ago, as she gripped him.

"For you?" *Stroke.* "For society?" *Stroke.* "Who decides that a woman's pleasure is not as important as a man's? We have the same needs that men do. Should we not indulge them, if we so choose? Or do I need a man's esteemed permission to experience pleasure? I think not." She rubbed her hand along his length as if she'd done this a dozen times before. "It's my body and I decide who I should share it with." *Squeeze.*

This time his eyes really did roll back in his head and he could barely formulate a coherent word. *Fuck.* Someone should have a working brain in this situation. Unfortunately, all his blood seemed to have descended to below his waist. Aspen shook himself out of his stupor, sitting up to face her and ignoring the fingers teasing his most intimate place. It was next to impossible, but this was important. *She* was important.

"It is your body, Vesper," he said. "But..."

She sealed his lips with a finger. "I want this, Aspen. I want *you.*" Color rushed into her cheeks as her bare, elegant shoulder rose. "For once, I want to choose something for myself, before you move on to do your ducal duty, and before I am forced to kneel to mine."

A smile kicked at his lips. "You're kneeling now."

"By choice," his nymph replied. "There is a difference."

Aspen couldn't help frowning, something wriggling beneath the fog of his lust. "Why now, Vesper? Why *me*?"

"What better time than now, and I trust you," she said slowly. "I trust that you won't hurt me."

His eyes met hers, so much burning in those banked blues. Desire, fear, nerves. She wasn't as confident as she was pretending to be, but there was determination there, too. Some kind of deep-seated yearning that he'd never seen before. Despite her resolute words, this—whatever she was about to do—meant something to her. It was the only reason he hesitated, when in any other situation his rigid nether regions would have rejoiced and risen happily to the occasion.

Aspen simply didn't want to cause her any harm.

She believed he wouldn't; he wasn't certain it was avoidable.

"Are you sure?" he said softly. "Once we do this, there's no going back."

A low laugh left her. "Yes, I'm aware that unlike the first time for a man, a female, once plowed, will suddenly become used goods in the eyes of the world, while the man is venerated for his everlasting virility. I am *well* aware, Duke, of the injustice my fragile sex affords me. Plow away, then, the honors are yours."

Fierce to the last, his beautiful viper.

"That's not what I meant," he said, though his lips twitched at her dry expression and his cock leaped at the lewd invitation. "And I'm not sure I'm comfortable with that plowing analogy. You're hardly a field."

"Does poking a hot pie suit His Grace's delicate sensibilities better, then?" Her lips tipped up in a wicked grin that *did* things to him.

He very nearly growled. *Yes!* "No."

Done with explanations, she rode his length hard with her hand, an unexpected pump from root to tip, causing a groan to detach from his chest. "I know what you meant. Now will you agree, or will you sit there coming up with every excuse under the sun for why you cannot accept what I am offering?"

"Vesper..."

She squeezed and met his eyes. "Yes, Aspen?"

Weak for her in every way, he gave in. "I hope you know what you're doing."

And then no other words were permitted to escape his mouth when she grinned and leaned upward, filling her palms with his coat, and dragged his mouth to hers.

The kiss was a collision of mouths, teeth, and tongues. Aspen hauled her into his lap, those strong arms banding about her waist, and Vesper gasped. She couldn't get enough of him as her lips parted over his. She wanted to drink him in. Take his scent and his taste deep into her where she could hoard the memories of them for the rest of her life. She wanted to paint herself with him. Mark her body as his. Mark him as hers.

It was primal and raw and animalistic.

And so very wrong…

No. It *wasn't* wrong. She was only thinking that because of centuries of indoctrination and societal dictates heaped upon the heads of women. She would bear the consequences if she had to. For now, all she wanted to do was dare to *live*.

Everything she had told him had been true. This had been her choice to make. She understood all too well that in the world of the aristocracy, a woman's virtue was prized…at least second to her dowry. But anyone she married in the future, if she married at all, would not dictate her actions now.

With a happy sigh, she let herself fall into the magic of his soft lips and the decadent stubble abrading her cheeks. The sensual scrape felt better than she had imagined. God, he was so delicious, like a bold, smooth whiskey that she wanted to gulp instead of savor. She refused to entertain an ounce of shame for her earlier boldness, for touching him as wickedly as she had. Gracious, he'd been so hot and hard, and shockingly thick in her palm.

Was that part supposed to be so heart-poundingly *thrilling*?

A beat of worry stirred in the mire of passion. A thought

occurred to her brought on by said part in question and its basic biological function and Vesper let out a gasping breath, dragging her lips from his. "We cannot conceive," she said to him. "I will not bring a child born on the other side of the blanket into this world. Do you have something? A French letter or some such?"

His eyes widened in astonishment, and she wanted to laugh. Surely he didn't think she was *that* much of an ingenue! A woman should look out for herself, after all.

"No, I do not," he choked out. "Not here."

Vesper bit her lip. "What about withdrawal, can you do that?"

"Vesper, please." The Duke of Greydon was actually blushing.

She reached up and removed his spectacles, now askew on his nose from their wild bout of kissing. "Have I told you how much I love these? They make you look so intense and studious. Every time I see you wearing them, my blood starts to simmer like a pot on the boil."

A chuckle rumbled out of him. "If only studiousness was a quality aristocratic women admired."

"I admire it." She blushed hot at the admission.

His fingertips feathered along her chin, making her curl into his touch, before they lifted to pull the pins from her hair. He watched as curl after silky curl tumbled to both shoulders. "You're *you*. An anomaly. Brave, beautiful, infuriating. Where did you come from?"

"I've always been here, waiting for you," she whispered. Truer words had never been spoken. Well, she was done waiting. "Kiss me, Aspen."

He obliged and those soft, full lips took hers again. His tongue slid into her mouth, his teeth nibbling her lips, and he explored every inch of her with a careful expertise that left her breathless. Learning as she went, Vesper did the same... discovering what made him jerk beneath her and what made him groan. It was heady having this much power. Though, in truth, he held the same sway over her.

When his hands drifted to her exposed bosom, her heart jackknifed in her chest. His fingers tugged on the delicate silk of the slackened bodice, loosening it more.

"Don't rip it, it's expensive," she muttered against his mouth. When he paused with a slight frown drawing his brows together, she leaned back. "I donate my dresses to women in need. They sell the trimmings and the fabric. If it's torn, it won't fetch as much."

"I always seem to underestimate you, don't I, Viper?" he said, staring at her with wonder, eyes dark and lips swollen. "All these years and it seems I never knew you at all."

Then he was kissing her again, and when his palm brushed against a taut, achingly sensitive nipple and rolled it between his thumb and forefinger, she almost fell off his lap. A moan tore from her lips as she arched back, and he pressed a trail of hot kisses down the column of her throat. When the duke closed his mouth where his hand had been, her vision went white at the raw sensation shooting right to her core.

She'd experienced female pleasure, of course, but nothing like *this*.

This feeling of heated need spreading through her like wildfire.

Vesper clutched at his broad shoulders, watching his dark curls against the rosy skin of her breasts when he switched his attentions to the other. His tongue curled around her nipple, drawing a whimper from her before he sucked hard.

"Aspen!" she cried.

In one swift move, he lifted her and turned her about with barely any effort so that her bottom rested on his knees, her spine facing him. Goodness, she was not a small woman, and yet, he maneuvered her as though she were a marionette.

She felt him tugging at the laces of her dress, removing the overlay, and then deftly unlacing her corset. This was it. This was the point of no return. Vesper huffed a laugh and rolled her lips between her teeth—that point had been passed the moment she'd crossed the threshold.

"What's so funny?" he asked, breath gusting against the shell of her ear.

"I can't believe this is happening," she said.

His hands halted in their work. "You want to stop?"

"Don't you dare try to wheedle your way out of this, Greydon. We're doing this. You're taking me and that is it."

"I'd forgotten how bossy you are," he said and bit her neck where it joined her shoulder.

Oh, that was nice. "You like it, and I know what I want, that's all. It's not my fault if people choose to follow." Her voice was so breathy, it emerged like a sigh. "More of that, Your Grace."

"Patience."

But Vesper couldn't help squirming and grinding into him, needed the friction wherever she could get it. He lifted her to stand, and the outer layers of her gown, petticoats, and corset slid to the floor until she was left in her sheer chemise, silk stockings, gloves, and shoes. Gripping her hip, slowly, he spun her around so she faced him once more. His eyes were hungry upon her, so dark that his pupils had swallowed up the brown of his irises. She fought the urge to cover herself with her arms, knowing he was getting an eyeful through the filmy fabric.

"By God, you're a vision," he murmured.

The duke reached for her, setting her gently down on the bench before removing her gloves, dancing slippers, and unrolling her stockings. His fingers traced patterns down her legs, tickling the back of her knee and the sharp bones of her ankle, before slipping back up to the hem of her chemise.

"May I, Vesper?" he whispered, clutching the fabric in his large fist. She nodded. Ever so slowly, he lifted the garment with torturous care. Warm breath shivered across her sensitive skin, and Vesper closed her eyes when she felt the evening air kiss the bare heart of her. She could feel him staring. Oh, heavens, she was going to die of mortification.

"Fuck." The oath was guttural and hoarse.

She propped herself up to one elbow. "What's wrong?"

His eyes were hooded with lust. "Nothing at all. You are simply... the most incredible thing I've ever seen."

"Oh." Vesper blushed at his intense scrutiny. "Better than discovering a rare fossil?"

"Better than a thousand rare fossils. Now be quiet and allow me to memorize and catalog the details of this very interesting specimen, in the interests of scientific study, of course."

"Of course." She grinned, but her amusement fled when his knuckles brushed over the maidenhair at her center. A full-body shiver ensued when he parted her swollen folds with one finger, a raw sound escaping him that was so possessive she felt it to her marrow.

"I have dreamed of touching you ever since that billiards game," he said.

"Have you?"

"Yes, you were slick for me then." He groaned. "And you're drenched now."

Vesper knew what that meant, having been quite intimate with her own body for an age, but she still burned with mortification at the idea of this man seeing her in such an ungoverned, aroused state. "I'm sorry."

A hiss of displeasure left him. "Never apologize for your desire or so help me..."

"So help you what?" she asked, teeth sinking into her lower lip.

His finger swiped up, touching a spot that made her gasp. "So help me I will punish you with my tongue until you see stars."

Vesper stilled. With his tongue? *There?*

She was not so innocent, but that seemed rather forward. "Why would you—? Oh *God.*"

The Duke of Greydon had licked up the length of her most intimate place with the flat of his tongue, answering her question most expediently. Vesper lost all powers of speech thereafter when he repeated the motion with a hungry rumble that made her toes curl. Conscious thought was quick to follow when he set his mouth to the neediest spot... and *sucked.*

She hadn't apologized aloud again, but heaven help her, if this was his idea of punishment, then she wanted more.

Much more.

"I'm sorry," she whimpered. *So not sorry.*

Her vision tunneled as her duke made good on his threat.

Chapter Eighteen

He could slake his thirst on her forever.

If Aspen had taken a minute to think, he could have talked himself out of the scandalous interlude in short order. But in all honesty, he wanted everything she was willing to give him, damn the consequences.

She's your mentor's only daughter, you bastard! He or his son will call you out and where will you be? Six feet under with a lead round in your ballocks.

It would be worth it to die with the taste of her on his tongue. Aspen filled his mouth with her anew and groaned. Damn, she was sweet and succulent, like the ripest of fruit on the vine. He couldn't get enough. Her hands fisted in his hair, those needy whimpers driving him to pleasure her more. He added a finger to her warm, slick channel and couldn't help his own moan at the snug feel of her. His cock jerked in his trousers, desperate for its turn.

But he wanted her to shatter first, for her first experience with a man to be everything she deserved. Aspen had known from kissing her in the billiards room that she was inexperienced, but Vesper had never been a woman to let such a paltry thing as ignorance deter her. Her enthusiasm more than made up for any lack of skill.

She yanked on his hair with a growl, and he bit back a grin at her impatience. He intended to soothe the way with careful, lengthy preparation even if it drove her mad. Doing so was no hardship to him, not when the feel and taste of her had him hovering precariously close to the edge. He was so deliciously aroused, he could feel his crown leaking into the fabric of his trousers. Doubling his efforts, he added a second finger, gratified when her inner muscles clenched on them.

"Aspen," she cried out, her hands yanking on the ends of his hair. He hooked his fingers slightly, and when Vesper's body tensed and went tight beneath him, she came beautifully undone like a shooting star. Fuck, she was glorious!

"What was that?" she asked limply when her shudders had lessened.

"An orgasm," he said with a chuckle, pressing a kiss to her belly.

Her laugh joined his. "No, silly. I meant...with your mouth. Is that a done thing?" When he nodded, she looked intrigued. "Could I do the same to you?"

Aspen felt his cheeks flush as he lifted himself to his feet, careful not to crush her. He'd just been buried between her legs, and her innocent words could still make him flush like a boy in leading strings. Of course, she wasn't one to miss it. "You're blushing again, Duke."

"You seem to have that effect on me," he murmured, fingers working to divest himself of his clothing, starting with his boots and then going to his coat and cravat. She stared avidly as each article joined hers on the floor, no shame upon her face, only a beautiful, languid glow in the aftermath of the pleasure she'd enjoyed. Those eyes of hers glittered, the flames in them banked for now, but he looked forward to making them burn again.

Making them *both* burn.

When she let out a choked sound after he yanked his shirt over his head, her greedy eyes taking in every inch of his bare upper body, he paused at the waistband of his trousers.

"More?" he asked.

She licked her lips and propped herself up, looking like a tousled sated goddess. "Get on with it, Greydon. I want to see what's been pressed against me all this time."

Hell, he loved her boldness—the fearless vixen hidden behind all that demure and feminine charm. He couldn't fathom another man pleasuring her, seeing her like this en déshabillé and so painfully gorgeous it hurt to look at her. Watching her so open and unguarded after a stunning climax that he'd delivered made a burst of possessiveness throb in his chest. Aspen wanted *all* her orgasms...every ounce of her pleasure for himself.

"What are you thinking?" she asked softly, a tiny pleat between her brows.

"That you're mine," he answered without thinking.

Some unreadable emotion bloomed in her eyes then quickly faded. "I'm yours, Your Grace, for now." She smiled, and though some part of it seemed forced, the fierce light that remained in her eyes was real. "Though if your plan is to torment me or make me beg, I warn you that I'm not known for my patience. Will you ever undo that button or will you stand there like a handsome statue?"

He actually preened, lowering his lashes like a jade strutting his fleshly wares. "You think me handsome? In my case, it's usually the title that makes ladies swoon."

"I don't care about your title and you've always been attractive to me. Now, unfasten that button, you dreadful tease, or I shall get up there and do it for you."

"This button?" he asked, flicking it open when she nodded, and moving to the next. "What about this one?"

"*All* your buttons," she crowed with a devilish grin and reached up and pulled her chemise over her head. "Join me, Your Grace, in being gloriously nude."

The sinful invitation hung in the air. For a moment, Aspen could only stare at the picture she made lying back on that cushioned bench—the epitome of eroticism—as he committed every glorious detail to memory. She was a William Etty painting in the flesh…all lush sinuous curves and long elegant lines.

When she crooked a finger and beckoned, he couldn't shuck his trousers quickly enough, nearly tripping over them in his haste to be rid of the damned things. When he was fully nude, Aspen was gratified to see that she was now the one blushing and gulping. He grasped his thick erection in one hand, seeing her eyes fasten to it. "Still want me to join you?"

She arched a cool brow. "Do you require additional instruction, Your Grace? Perhaps a spot of tea to calm your nerves?"

Hell, he was going to fuck the sass from her lips.

Prowling purposefully toward her, he watched for signs of nerves or trepidation, but she only looked excited. Placing his knee between her thighs, he lowered himself to the chaise, then crawled over her and took her mouth in a deep, soul-stirring kiss.

Aspen wanted to make the kiss last, but he couldn't wait to bury himself in her body. Everything about her excited him—her impatience, her ardor, the hooded melting look in those jewel-bright eyes. As it was, he wasn't even sure he could keep from spilling the second he breached her. But he wanted to make this good for her. He *had* to.

"Vesper, are you ready?" he asked, positioning the tip of his cock at her core.

"So ready," she replied in a breathless whisper, her hands moving to his shoulders to draw him down for another ravenous kiss as she writhed against him. "Show me the stars, Aspen."

She was his. She'd always been his.

Vesper's mind was clouded with emotion—lust, fear, joy, sorrow—all of them swirling within her. Lust for the lover about to take her to the heavens for the second time, fear of the unknown and the large organ about to breach her untried body, joy in the drumbeat of her heart that threatened to dance its way clear out of her chest, and dread that this was the only time she might have him like this. As unequivocally hers.

Eventually, reality would intrude...and passion would give way to pragmatism.

But that wasn't *now*.

Be in the moment, something inside her whispered. *You wanted this. Savor it.*

Savor it, she would. She would hoard every single piece of memory, from the mouthwatering smell of his skin to the taste of his lips to the wildness in his tawny, gold-flecked eyes. He was unhinged now, and she loved him like this. She traced a dark eyebrow with a finger and brushed a lock of hair away from his face, adoring the way it wound around her fingers as if staking its claim on her as well.

He was beautifully built—all muscles and rangy sinew. Broad at his shoulders and trim in his hips with lean strong legs dusted in crisp dark hair, he made her breath hitch with pure, undiluted want. And his staff—dear God—she could barely look at it without sending herself into conniptions. That part of him was as intimidating as it had felt beneath his trousers, jutting proudly from his body like a sword about to lay siege.

To her... the unconquered lands.

Vesper bit back a giggle at her absurd thought. It was true though. This was new territory for both of them. She'd lay her claim upon him as much as he'd stake his. Skilled fingers found her breast to toy with her nipple, and she forgot what she was thinking about. Goodness, who knew that breasts were so sensitive? When she bathed, she hardly took notice of them, but in the duke's clever hands, they stole every intelligent idea from her brain.

His head bent and her nipple ached as he scraped his teeth over it, sending another wash of heat due south. Vesper canted her hips upward in an impatient roll, and the duke smiled. The feel of him there, but not *there*, made her wild. Suddenly, voraciously, she wanted that sword inside her, sheathed to the hilt.

"Now, Aspen," she demanded, angling her heels over his calves and dragging him down into the soft cradle of her hips.

"Patience, little viper."

She rubbed her breasts against the hair on his chest, delighting in the friction and digging her nails into his shoulders. "I already warned you that I was lacking in such a virtue."

"Good things come to those who wait."

"I will cheerfully break your nose again right now."

Grinning at her empty threat, he breached her in torturously slow increments, but a gasp left her lips as she felt the first deeply uncomfortable stretch of him. Even as well prepared as she was to receive him, she cried out at the intrusion and it was only the tip of his shaft. He was big, and she had never done this before.

The duke stilled, his face taut with strain, those muscled arms and veined forearms holding his large body poised above her. "Is it too much?" he asked, concern in his eyes.

"No, but go slow. Don't you dare stop."

It was near impossible for him to go any slower than he already was, but he did, inching back slightly before pressing forward again, his gaze alert on hers for any sign of discomfort. Every motion was so full of care that tears inexplicably stung her eyes. It wasn't *painful*, but there was an awkward sensation of fullness. He pulled back and rocked into her again, each time carving room for himself inside her body. Making himself at home and she welcomed him.

"More, Aspen," she whispered.

He gave her what she wanted.

Eventually, when he was finally fully seated within her, the profound pressure started to ease and need started to take over. She squirmed beneath him, eliciting a groan from his lips.

"Are you well?" he ground out, his handsome face stark with the same blend of pleasure and pain that she felt, though she suspected that the pain part was because he did not want to hurt her.

Vesper reached up to caress his tense jaw. "Yes. What's next?"

With a low chuckle, he turned his head to kiss her fingers before starting to move, and then she was lost as the delicious friction of his sex sent ribbons of pleasure cascading through her. *Oh*. That was...astonishingly good. She wasn't prepared for when he pushed back in and felt her eyes go wide with the overwhelming sensation of his pelvis grinding into hers.

She felt that thrust *everywhere*! When he repeated the motion, teasing her sensitive insides on reentry, her pleasure spiked even higher. Good Lord. No wonder so many people did this out of wedlock behind closed doors. It was extraordinary. She bit back a giggle.

The duke lifted a brow though there was no rancor in his gaze, only a feral sort of strain. "I am going to start taking this personally, this inopportune tendency you have to laugh whenever we are in intimate positions, my lady."

Vesper dug her heels into him. "I was thinking of how much time I've wasted by not seducing you sooner."

His expressive eyes went wide and she laughed again. "Why on earth would you be thinking of such a thing?"

"If coitus was this good, I could understand the draw, but then I realized that not all men are *you*, Your Grace." She squeezed her inner muscles and heard him groan. "Now try not to let that go to your head."

"You're so good to me, Viper," he said with a smile.

"Remember that, Lord Ass."

And then there was no more cheeky banter as he took her lips in a hard, drugging kiss that made all amusement flee her brain. Greydon started to piston his hips faster and all she could do was hold on through each powerful stroke as his body claimed hers. And by God, she loved every gut-clenching, exquisite second of it.

"I'm sorry, I won't last," he ground out as his movements became more erratic.

"Never apologize," she told him.

His admission gratified her...that she could drive him to such lengths. His face was harsh with tension. Damp hair curled into his brow and his pupils were wide with excitement, the black nearly swallowing the brown. Vesper could feel her own pleasure start to build with each formidable thrust and she slid her hand down to where his body met hers.

He slowed and she felt her cheeks heat more than they already were. "Keep going," she commanded. "I want to get there when you do."

"Is this a race, Viper?" he teased with a swirl of his hips that made her vision wobble.

"Is it a race if we both win?" she tossed back.

Touching herself just as she liked and remembering the skill of his mouth there had her pleasure rising to meet his in seconds. They soared over the finish line together, the bliss cresting so strongly inside her that she yelped even as he pulled from the greedy clench of her body and groaned his release. She felt his warm spend on her belly and sighed. Thank goodness one of them had had the presence of mind to think clearly. As it was, her brain was on temporary, delightful hiatus.

"That was..." She trailed off, mind sublimely blank. There didn't seem to be any words that could describe what had passed between them. Amazing? Mind-blowing? Otherworldly?

"Come now, don't lose your tongue. Flatter me, Viper." Brows raised, he stared at her in smug silence.

She rolled her eyes and grinned. "I doubt you need *my* flattery to endorse your sexual prowess, Your Grace."

"Don't you know a gentleman's ego is ever so fragile in the aftermath?"

Shifting his sweaty body to the side so he wasn't crushing her, Greydon kissed her and then reached for his discarded cravat. He wiped the evidence of their coupling from her belly and then stroked the soft fabric gently between her thighs before attending to himself. Once more, his thoughtfulness struck her. Before he discarded the damp cloth, she noticed the pink streaks on it.

Farewell, virginity. May you oppress some other hapless girl.

"I did not know that," she said, stretching like a cat. "Very well, you are the epitome of virility, Your Ever-Endowed Grace." His brows rose at her sugary, high-pitched tone. "And, *oh*, how will this poor maiden ever find another virile stallion to ferry her to *such* heights of passion? Or perhaps I shall simply wither away in unfulfilled despair." She gave a feigned sob. "Woe is me to never hope to experience such divine pleasure—"

"Too much, too much," he interrupted, kissing her to silence her and then tickling her ribs. She regarded him with passive amusement, and he froze. "You are not ticklish?"

"No," she answered seriously.

His eyes widened in false horror. "You monster!"

"Now you know," she said with a low laugh. Her palm skipped down his ribs. "The question is, Your Grace, are *you* ticklish?"

"Don't you dare, Viper!"

But of course she dared; she always dared with him. He burst into chuckles when she dug her fingertips into his hard sides, and she exulted in the uninhibited sound of them, holding them close as a pang struck her. They would never again be like this...so unrestrained and unguarded, nothing between them but desire and ease.

Greydon caught her wrist. "Enough, enough," he gasped between laughs. "You absolute fiend, curse you and your wicked fingers."

With a dark grin, she kissed him and when he was sufficiently distracted, her now free hand wandered down his abdomen to the wicked appendage that hadn't seemed to deflate much. "*These* wicked fingers?"

The duke groaned at her bold caress. He felt silky and hot to the touch, and Vesper marveled at the fact that this part of him had been inside of her. She squeezed, and it swelled in her palm. His hand slid down to cover hers, stilling her exploration. "Stop, unless you wish for a repeat, and you are much too sensitive to take me again."

"Are you claiming to know my body better than me?"

"You're not sore?"

She was, in fact, terribly tender. A delicious kind of tender, but the notion of taking him in again *was* too much. Vesper glowered though there was no heat in it and a strange warmth filled her. "Why are you this thoughtful?"

"Am I?" He drew her palm up to kiss her knuckles.

"Outside of intercourse, I prefer you being abominably horrid to me," she said. "This version of you is simply too sweet."

He nibbled a finger and held it between his teeth. "Good thing you're salty enough for both of us."

With a laugh, she poked him and then cuddled into his embrace. The bench wasn't terribly comfortable, but she loved the feeling of his long warm body plastered to hers, and she intended to take every second she could get before reality intervened. And that wouldn't be long. She stared up at the wooden eaves of the dovecote. "Do you think anyone will come looking for us?"

"Not here," he said.

"Not even the duchess?"

He shook his head. "She hates this place. Threatened to burn it down, and it was only when I countered with a reduction in her allowance when I became duke that she relented."

Vesper bit her lip, considering the fact that she had no idea who the duchess was at all. How could she have been so mistaken? But then again, how well did anyone truly know their neighbor? She herself wore a charming mask with the rest of the ton. "Were they ever in love?"

"Maybe at the very start. But they were not compatible. My father was a dreamer and my mother was... the opposite." His chest rose with a deep breath. "She wanted to be revered and the center of attention, and he wanted to live a quiet life. The fact that my father did not bend to her manipulations and intrigues enraged her, but there wasn't much she could do. The pretense of the perfect marriage was all hers, but behind closed doors, she was dreadful to him." He ran his hand through his hair and sighed. "She got her way in the end, though, by committing him under false pretenses."

Her eyes rounded in complete shock. "What? He was ill, wasn't he?"

"I do not believe he was," he said bitterly. "He was an obstacle to her goals, you see. My father valued his books more than outings and balls. My mother wanted to be venerated by the ton and when she couldn't get that with an absent duke and rumors of possible estrangement, she went for their sympathy." Vesper could hear the dulled edge of his anger even as her own disbelief doubled. "And the ton obliged—that poor heartbroken duchess, what a tragedy to be married to such a feeble-minded man...and with a young son, too. The travesty of it!" He shrugged one shoulder. "She got what she wanted, only at the expense of a man she claimed to love."

Vesper let out a horrified breath, her heart breaking for him even as her brain struggled to reconcile his shocking words. But whether she believed him or not didn't matter. It was his truth. "I cannot fathom that anyone could be so cruel. I am so sorry, Aspen."

"You've nothing to be sorry for," he said in a brittle voice, reaching for his trousers and pulling them on. He slid her a sidelong glance, his face carefully neutral. "Do you need help with your corset?"

That was the unsubtle hint that the interlude was over. Her heart hurt for him, for what he'd endured. How closed off he was to everyone as a result.

"Aspen."

His mouth hardened as he yanked on his shirt. "Don't pity

me. Pity my father who died alone in that infernal madhouse. It was famed for its mildness and salubrity, when in reality he was tied to a chair and had cold water poured over his head daily to treat his nonexistent melancholic condition." Tears sprang to her eyes, but he didn't see her, so lost he was in the painful clench of memory. "She committed him on the grounds of moral insanity." He gestured to the empty shelves. "That he wanted to live in books instead of real life. That *books* perverted his natural feelings, affections, and moral disposition."

"That is...unconscionable," she whispered, reaching for him and trying not to react when he flinched away.

"Tell that to the Lunacy Court. My mother presented a compelling petition, one I am in the process of deconstructing so that it never happens again. That's the foundation of the bill I've been working on with your father for the House of Lords." His features hardened as he put himself to rights. "It sickens me when she speaks of him with so much love and sorrow when it was all a bald-faced lie."

Throat tight, Vesper began to dress to give herself something to do and because she did not wish to be unclothed when he was not. She needed all her armor in place when this cold, impenetrable version of the duke was present. After she stepped into the corset, he silently did up the laces at the back. He was a quicker hand at it than her own lady's maid.

Once all her layers were in place, she repinned her hair into place as best she could without a mirror, grateful that it was a simple sideways style she could manage without Lizzie.

Both finally dressed, they stood in awkward silence, the memories of the last hour heavy in the air between them. Everything inside of her ached.

Aspen cleared his throat. "Well, this was..."

"Don't ruin it with unnecessary platitudes." Vesper sniffed and tossed her head with feigned nonchalance.

He nodded. "You should go back first then. I'll follow after I find a new cravat. There's one in the main house somewhere."

Vesper moved toward him, and he tensed, but she only drew her palm down the side of his cheek. A muscle leaped to life under it when she stood on tiptoe to press a kiss where her hand had been. "If I could change any of it for you, I would."

He stared at her, a muscle in his jaw ticking, though his harsh expression softened. "I can't fix the past or control someone else's actions. All I can do is look to the future and try to stop this from ever happening again."

"I know you will," she said softly.

She stepped away and just as she reached the doorway, he spoke, "Vesper." She paused and looked around as he stood there, shoulders slightly hunched and face tight. "I'm sorry I can't give you what you deserve." Fists balling, he struggled with the words. "What my parents went through, what she did... it broke me irreparably." His voice cracked. "I'm not... fit for anyone."

God. Vesper wanted to hold him so badly, but she knew it would not be welcomed. He was much too proud. Too fractured. Too angry. Impotent rage and sorrow slid through her as her brain spun through the rush of feelings. "You're not broken, Aspen," she whispered. "Sometimes the people who are meant to love us, hurt us the most." She shrugged. "And we're all misfits in our own ways. What matters is whether we find a way to accept who we are, flaws and all."

It was ironic that she could give such sage advice and yet not take it.

Throat working, he stared in silence. "How did you get so wise?"

"I was always this way," she said, opting for levity in the face of such heavy truths. "All the frills and ruffles do an excellent job of concealing my genius."

"You are one of a kind, Viper," he said with a ghost of a smile.

She winked, though her chest felt ten sizes too small. "Never forget it, Lord Ass."

Chapter Nineteen

A fortnight later, and he had yet to navigate his complicated feelings. He should have known it would have been different with Vesper. They weren't strangers. They had a complex past. He was a fool to think coupling with her could be anything superficial. Or that emotions wouldn't be involved. It was *Vesper.* Of course he'd feel something.

He hated it. He hated feeling vulnerable.

Each time he saw her out, whether it was at the theater, a soiree, or in passing at her residence when he was meeting with her father, he vacillated quite fiercely between wanting to throw her over his shoulder like a caveman to have her again or fleeing her presence just so he could take a full breath.

She was under his skin. An exquisite obsession that he could not get out of his head.

The scent of her. The feel of her. Those soft moans and whispered sighs.

Her coming apart so splendidly in his arms.

Scowling, Aspen swore under his breath and tried to focus on the final proposal they were pulling together for the Lunacy Act amendment. At this rate of concentration, nothing would get done and his peers would laugh him out of the House. Between his chaotic feelings about Vesper, the intricacies of the bill, and Parker and Rhodes arriving within the week at Scotland Yard, he felt stretched thin.

"Something the matter?" the Duke of Harwick asked from the other side of the table.

He swallowed a curse at being so obvious and settled on the thing he could control at the moment. "No, the wording for this is eluding me and I still have to make sure we have everything in order for the new proposition."

"Ah, that reminds me," Harwick said. "I've enlisted some extra help."

Both Aspen and Mr. Cross, also seated at the far end of the table, looked up. "Help?" Aspen echoed.

But before the duke could explain, the object of his ungodly fixation appeared in the library. Delight at seeing her and bitterness at being so weak warred within, but Aspen managed mercifully to keep his face expressionless. Every nerve on alert, Aspen waited for her to speak.

An unreadable gaze met his as she stood there, hands clasped at her waist. Her mien wasn't cool, but it wasn't excessively warm either. Was she regretting what had passed between them? Did she still pity him? "Good afternoon, Your Grace."

"Lady Vesper," he said and cleared his tight throat.

"Vesper has agreed to go through the documents," the duke said. "That should give us some extra time."

"But she's a woman," the solicitor bit out.

Harwick's glance was glacial. "A woman who can read and has more intelligence than most *men* of my acquaintance. Is there a problem, Mr. Cross?"

The man shook his head but sent a disgruntled look toward the duke's daughter. Vesper did not seem bothered by his insult, her usual charming smile in place. She looked lovely, too, in a deep blue gown that did no justice to her stunning eyes.

Look away for the love of God, you fool.

The duke invited Vesper to sit at the table and Aspen slid a stack of papers in her direction. "Sort the supporters into this pile and the naysayers into another," he told her. "We need to know where to direct our efforts and which peers we have to convince. Is that something you think you can do?"

Her lips twitched. "Genius, remember?"

Aspen's entire body clenched. Of course he remembered. Every single word she'd spoken was etched in his memory. He'd picked them apart so many times, worrying that he'd said too much, shown too much. After so many years of being guarded, he wasn't used to being so exposed. To *her*, of all people.

The solicitor kept shooting surreptitious glares at Vesper as if her presence offended him, but if she noticed, she did not say anything. After a while, they fell into silence, only the flutter of paper and the scratch of quill on parchment breaking the hush. Her presence still scraped at his senses, but if he didn't look in her direction, he could pretend that she wasn't there. Until she moved and her fragrance wafted into his nostrils... making him think of other lush scents.

Pay attention, he growled inwardly.

He removed and cleaned his spectacles, then got to work. The bill wouldn't write itself. It was only when his neck started to ache that he looked up and realized he was alone in the room. He hadn't noticed when the others had left. Sometimes he got like that—so immersed in his work that everything else fell away. It was a good talent for a fossil lover. Uncovering bones took patience and focus.

Aspen was mostly grateful that *she* wasn't there. Stretching his arms above his head, he rolled his shoulders and groaned at the answering knot in his back. He glanced at his timepiece. Good God, had it been five hours already? A feminine throat clearing had him looking up. Vesper stood in the doorway, a plate and cup in hand.

"I brought you something to eat," she said, lifting the plate. "We stopped for a break, but Papa said that you weren't to be disturbed. I thought you might be hungry."

His stomach rumbled loudly in answer when she set the food and drink on the table beside him. "It's not much. I didn't know what you liked."

Aspen stared at the steaming cup of tea, along with buttered bread accompanied by a few slices of cold chicken, a handful of grapes, and a wedge of cheese. "Thank you and thank your cook for me."

"You're welcome on both accounts."

He frowned. "You prepared this?"

"You act like I'm incapable of arranging a simple meal, Greydon. I might be spoiled, but I am not an invalid."

When had he gone back to being *Greydon*? "I never said you were spoiled."

A blond brow lifted as a smile appeared. "Not to my face, you haven't, but I know you've thought it."

He didn't confirm nor deny, but instead began to eat, wolfing down her timely and considerate offering. Aspen was fully convinced that Vesper was far from the fickle heiress he'd always believed her to be. She threw balls to raise money for schools as well as underprivileged and destitute children. She doted on her father and it was clear he was as devoted to her. Her friends were her most loyal supporters. She was... extraordinary.

She took her seat and resumed her task in silence, continuing to sort the papers into the two piles as requested. Sipping his tea, he watched her over the rim, her rich wheat-colored hair escaping its ties to curl around her face. He couldn't help recalling how those silky lengths had felt in his palms or the moans that had left her lips when he'd wound his fist in them.

"It's hard to concentrate when you're staring at me, Your Grace," she said softly, a hint of amusement coloring her tone.

Aspen blinked. "Apologies, I was gazing into space rather." Her eyes met his, skepticism in them. He scowled. "Fine, I was looking at you. Are you satisfied?"

"Naturally." The smile she graced him with was dazzling.

He lowered his voice, looking to the door to see if anyone was there. "Are we going to pretend that nothing happened between us?"

"Are you willing to talk about why you think you're not enough?" she returned, not looking up.

He went silent, his chest squeezing like an elephant had trampled upon it. "No, that's neither here nor there."

She let out a huff. "Then what is there to talk about?"

"I don't know. Perhaps a ragingly successful ball, your phenomenal success, the covert loss of your virginity? Any one of those would do."

"Aspen!" she hissed, eyes darting to him and then the door.

"No one's here," he said, thrilled at finally getting a reaction out of her. And good riddance to *Greydon*, too. "I love it when you say my given name with such ferocity. Though I seem to have developed a partiality for when you whimper it."

Lips pressed thin, she glared daggers at him. "There are footmen standing right outside this door and maids constantly wandering the corridors," she snapped in a whisper. "I'd rather not be the subject of their gossip at supper. And if my father found out about our tryst, trust me, neither of us would like the outcome."

His lip curled. "Which would be?"

"You before a priest standing in front of an altar, leg-shackled before you could claim no culpability."

Aspen didn't know why he was pushing it...pushing *her.* Perhaps he wanted her to feel as disordered—as *untethered*—as he did. "Would that be so bad?"

An incredulous gaze met his. "A marriage between us would end in manslaughter."

"We didn't murder each other two weeks ago in bed."

Flashes of memory passed across her eyes before she firmed her lips and dragged in a ragged breath. "We *weren't* in bed."

Aspen leaned in. "Bedding doesn't always require a bed."

"You are veering beyond propriety, sir," she said, but hot spots of scarlet erupted in her cheeks. "Honestly, why do you *do* this?" she hissed. "You bed me as you so eloquently put it, and then shut me out, and now you want to cuddle, commiserate, and plait each other's hair. I never know which Aspen I'm going to get on any given day. It's positively infuriating!"

Lord but she was stunning even while stewing with frustration. "I'm sorry," he said and meant it. She stared at him as if she hadn't expected the apology. "And besides, my hair is much too short for plaiting," he added solemnly.

"Oh, argh! You are impossible!"

He exhaled. "I really am sorry, Vesper. I wasn't shutting you out. I thought you were staying away from me."

"I was!" she shot back under her breath. "To give you the space you needed. And also—"

Whatever else she'd been about to say was cut short by the arrival of the dour Mr. Cross who stalked over to where Vesper sat, fuming into her sorted piles, and scowled. He poked at several of the papers in the first stack, spreading them over the table and ignoring Vesper's groan of dismay when he ruined her work.

"Good God, girl, are you incompetent?" he ground out, and Aspen frowned, certain he'd misheard.

Vesper, however, glanced up. "I beg your pardon, Mr. Cross? And might I remind you that I am the mistress of this household."

"Look at what you've done," he said, flicking one of the neat piles into a mess. "These don't belong here! They're part of the Ragged School proposal, not part of the House records for the earlier lunacy bill. Now we will need to go through all of these again. An entire day wasted, thanks to you!"

She opened her mouth and closed it, staring at the pile, a confused expression crossing her face. "These are the papers Papa gave me to sort."

A frown appeared between her brows and then her eyes widened in dismay. Aspen stood and looked over the papers, noticing that the two proposals had indeed somehow gotten mixed up. It wasn't an insurmountable issue and he wasn't sure why Cross seemed to be on the verge of apoplexy. Yes, it would take time to fix, but the situation was not unsalvageable.

"Can't you read, girl? Or are you simply oblivious as well as useless?"

"Now, see here—" Aspen began, but the man wasn't finished with his rant or his insults, apparently.

The solicitor's face was the hue of a ripe tomato as he towered over Vesper. "Always meddling and sticking your nose where it doesn't belong. Don't think I don't know what you've done, *my lady*."

"What *I've* done?" she burst out. "It was an honest mistake."

"Writing notes that I would never send," he spat. "Quoting poetry that I don't even know. How dare you do such a thing? On *my* account?"

Aspen was about to intervene and put the man in his place when Vesper's face went ashen. "Mr. Cross—"

His eyes narrowed as he slammed a fist on the table, making Vesper jump and Aspen growl. "I know it was your doing. Mrs. Elway thanked me for the flowers and the poems, ones I never wrote. The maid had told her I'd left them for her, but the little liar confessed to the plot when I threatened to have her sacked." His voice broke on the last.

She held out a hand and the solicitor watched it as though it were a snake. "Mr. Cross, please, I can explain."

"Explain what? That you meddled in our lives, and now she's so embarrassed she can't even look at me! You're just a silly, spoiled girl with too much time on her hands."

Vesper let out a strangled breath. "Please, I can talk to her."

"You've done enough," he said, all fight leaving him as he collapsed into the seat beside her, put his head in his hands, and burst into tears.

Aspen blinked. What in the bloody hell was happening?

He stared as Vesper patted the man awkwardly on the back, her expression stricken and guilty. After a few tense minutes, an embarrassed Mr. Cross stood, sniffed, and excused himself from the room. Vesper sat there, staring at the wet splotch on the table with a sickened look.

"Will you kindly explain to me what just occurred?" Aspen asked.

Her throat worked. "I've ruined everything, haven't I? He's right—I'm just a silly, meddling girl." She let out a dejected sigh. "Laila knew this could happen. She *told* me that it could toy with their livelihoods, and all I did was dismiss her concerns. Even Effie and Briar agreed that I should keep my nose out of their business." She put her face in her hands. "Heavens, I'm such a fool. I have to fix this."

Before Aspen could caution her to wait, she stood abruptly and left.

This was dreadful. An absolute calamity.

Vesper deserved every curse Mr. Cross sent her way and more. Now because of her meddling, two people had broken hearts. Poor Mrs. Elway. What she must think! Vesper stood outside the kitchen, wringing her hands in distress at the sound of the housekeeper's muffled mortified words and Mr. Cross's quiet pleading. It wasn't in her to eavesdrop, but there was no other way she could find out how bad the situation was and what she could do to fix it.

"How could you deceive me like this?" the housekeeper said, voice wobbling.

Mr. Cross sighed. "You looked so happy and I wanted to be the one to put that smile on your face."

"By lying?"

"It looks worse than it is," he said desperately.

"It's exactly as it looks. You made a fool of me. You could have made a clean breast of it at any point, and yet you chose to continue this deception, making me believe this was real..."

"It was real! *Is* real. Please."

"I'm sorry. Stay out of my way, Mr. Cross, and I shall stay out of yours."

Clearly, it was nearly beyond salvaging. Vesper swallowed a gulp and rubbed at her chest. Just when she'd decided to approach the stricken housekeeper, a large hand closed around her upper arm. "No," the Duke of Greydon said.

"But—"

"Vesper, in no universe is going in there a good idea. Trust me, they will sort it out one way or another."

She peered up at him, guilt riding her. "But *I* did this."

Aspen drew her away from the kitchen toward a nearby salon and closed the door behind them. "What exactly is it you think you did?"

Vesper threw her hands up and marched toward the window. "I don't *think* I did something. I'm responsible. I knew Mrs. Elway liked Browning so I wrote a poem."

"I remember you reciting it at the ball months ago," he said. " 'How Do I Love Thee.' "

"That's the one. I wrote a note along with a posy of flowers and delivered both to her, and then made Lizzie, my lady's maid, infer that it might have come from Mr. Cross."

He frowned but shook his head. "Did you sign his name to the note?"

"No, of course not."

Greydon walked toward her. "Then I do not think it is as terrible as you are making it out to be. The two of them believed what they wanted to believe. All you did was make a suggestion. Yes, you crossed a line by sending the poem and the flowers, but I believe you meant well in your heart."

More guilt swamped her until it felt like she was choking on it. God, she had to get the confession out or she would die. "That's just it, it *wasn't* out of the goodness of my heart. I wanted Mr. Cross to be more receptive to my requests." She bit her lip hard. "I figured that if he was occupied with an affair of the heart, he would be." Vesper threw herself into an armchair. "The thing is it didn't even work, and now I've bungled two people's lives."

The duke crouched down in front of her. His warmth comforted her, the scent of him soothing. She wanted to climb into his lap and beg him to hold her, but that hadn't been their agreement. He'd consented to seduction and sexual congress, not to succor and solace.

"You're being rather hard on yourself," he said. "People make their own choices."

"But—"

A gentle finger pressed to her lips, silencing her. "But nothing. Mr. Cross could have easily confessed at the start that he hadn't sent the note or the bouquet. There was no name on it. *He* clearly decided to claim responsibility for the action, even though it wasn't his doing, and that's on him."

What he was saying was logical, but Vesper hated the idea that she had caused anyone such heartbreak. The man had been sobbing! She also knew that Greydon was trying to assuage her guilt, but she didn't know if she could accept his offer of absolution either. There was one thing she could accept from him, however, that even she couldn't deny herself.

Vesper let out a ragged breath. "Aspen?"

"Yes?"

She licked her lips and squashed down the doubt that instantly bubbled. "Would it be untoward if I asked you to hold me?"

"It would be untoward if you didn't." His brown eyes were warm.

With that, he gathered her into him and then lifted her, depositing them both into the armchair. Sighing, she curled into his lap and his chest as he stroked her back, resting his chin on the crown of her head. Vesper could feel the bulge of his sex under her skirts, but the embrace wasn't sexual. At least it wasn't until she shifted and pleasure streaked through her. When he let out a muffled groan, she flushed.

"I'm so sorry," Vesper mumbled, cheeks heating with chagrin.

He huffed. "What have I told you about unnecessary apologies? I'm attracted to you, it's as simple as that. I cannot control my body's reaction to you any more than I could say no to your request. You asked me to hold you and that's what I'm doing. No more, no less." She felt his lips against her hair. "You're safe with me, Vesper. Always."

It was true—she had never felt safer.

Chapter Twenty

Safety was transient.

It stood to reason that everything in Vesper's life that could go wrong *would* go wrong. Because that was the way the universe worked. Nothing was ever simple or easy.

On top of the epic botch of a match with Mr. Cross and Mrs. Elway, Aspen was back to his usual brooding, antagonistic, surly self. She knew that he was worried about the amendment being supported in the Lords, but honestly, he was unbearable. It was a toss-up which version of the duke she would get at any given hour. In a week, she'd crossed paths with three versions of him: the fastidious duke, the playful duke, and her least favorite, the bellicose duke.

She had little patience for *any* of them.

In all truth, she was sick of *all* gentlemen and their idiosyncrasies. Brooding dukes, nosy brothers, and over-the-top suitors.

Case in point was the extravagant bouquet of lilies currently being carried by the butler who was buckling under the weight of it. Sighing, Vesper glanced around at the already crowded foyer filled with every kind of flower known under the sun, thanks to one undeterred and overzealous Lord Eldridge.

"Put that in the morning room, please, Stanley," she told the butler, then gestured to the bouquets that had been delivered yesterday. "See that these are all delivered to local hospitals. At least they will bring some joy that way."

"As you wish, my lady."

She pinched the bridge of her nose with her thumb and forefinger, fighting the onset of a headache. "And have the maids open some windows. I'd rather smell the Thames at this point than this cloying mess."

Apparently, her words to Lord Eldridge about his offer of marriage—that she'd reconsider if and when her father decided it was time to wed—while meant as a discouragement, were taken as incentive to change her mind. As a result, she lived in a house that looked and smelled like a funeral parlor. What on earth had he been thinking? She liked a good arrangement as much as the next girl, but this was too much. There'd be no flowers left in London if he continued down this asinine path.

Pinching the bridge of her nose again, she sighed. Lord Eldridge was currently ensconced with her papa in his study, persuading him to reconsider his offer. Thankfully, she was secure in the knowledge that her father knew her thoughts on marriage and would let her make her own choice in the matter.

"My lady," Stanley said, making her jump. "Her Grace, the Duchess of Greydon, has just arrived. Are you at home to callers?"

Vesper blinked. She was hardly in any frame of mind to deal with the dowager, especially after the horrid particulars she'd learned from her son, but if this had to do with the charity and the mountain of generous donations they'd garnered from their guests—something to the tune of ten thousand pounds—that was obviously of unavoidable importance.

"Show her in"—she wrinkled her nose—"to a room that's as far away from all this as possible."

"The Rose Salon, my lady?"

"Yes, that will do. Thank you, Stanley. Please let Her Grace know that I'll be there presently."

As soon as Vesper dashed up the stairs to change—she had a reputation to uphold after all—Lizzie helped her into a pale green muslin gown with white trim and redid her coiffure into something less plain. Hurrying back downstairs, she entered the room to a very displeased duchess, who was pacing by the window.

"I dislike being kept waiting," she said without turning, not at all recalling that she'd had no problems keeping Vesper waiting when she'd called at Drake Manor.

Vesper bit her lip to hold back a sharp retort. "My apologies, Your Grace. May I interest you in some tea?"

"No. This won't take long." The Dowager turned and observed Vesper with hard eyes the color of her son's. "I shall get straight to the point. I have fulfilled my end of our understanding though I have yet to see any evidence of yours."

"Your Grace, one cannot expect an engagement to come about so swiftly." Especially when one of the parties in question was dallying with another woman, though she did not share that part. Heat, however, stole over her cheeks.

"Not if there are obstacles," the dowager said, eyes narrowing. "Your interest in my son specifically."

A mortified Vesper blushed harder at her scrutiny. "I've no interest in the duke." The lie tasted sour on her lips. Her feelings for Greydon were complicated, but certainly not gossip fodder or a bargaining chip for this woman.

"Then why did the two of you disappear from the ballroom only to return within a short time of each other?" Without waiting for a reply, the duchess returned to the window and tapped a gloved finger against the pane. "This room is rather quaint."

Vesper blinked at the about-turn in conversation, but she was sure the duchess did not want to talk about window glass or room decor. "I do not know what you wish me to say, Your Grace. I have no designs on your son beyond friendship. I have agreed to exert the little influence I have to persuade him to offer for Miss Thornton and I shall."

"Good," the duchess pronounced. "But to supply a little extra incentive, I will be keeping the moneys collected from the *Touch of Midas* ball until your part is done."

A gasp of pure outrage left Vesper's lips. "Your Grace, that money has been earmarked for the care and education of children. I worked for every penny of that, and my father paid for all of the expenses. You cannot do this."

"I can and I will," she said without a stitch of care.

Vesper shook her head in disbelief. "People are counting on that money."

"And I need Greydon to come to heel."

"He's not a dog," Vesper blurted in ire.

The duchess did not answer, instead thinning her lips further as she closed the distance between them. "The sooner you convince him, the quicker your pathetic schools and your grimy little urchins will get what they need."

Vesper sucked in a breath. "Are you threatening me?"

"Of course not," the duchess said and patted Vesper's cheek, making her flinch and recoil. "Threatening you would be telling you that I have written testaments from doctors attesting to my son showing the same biological predilection to madness as his father." In horror Vesper's stomach sank as the duchess's meaning hit. The woman's smile was a rictus. "I see we have an understanding. Trust me, girl, you don't want this on your hands."

"You're his mother," Vesper whispered. "How could you be so cruel?"

"I don't need to explain myself to you. I'll show myself out." There was a complete absence of empathy on the duchess's face. As much difficulty as Vesper had controlling her emotions and vacillations in mood, at least she was capable of *compassion.*

When the duchess left, Vesper sank into a nearby chair and buried her head between her knees. Goodness, how could one woman be so beastly? Putting a hand to her chest, Vesper rubbed at the dreadful ache between her ribs. If she didn't get Aspen to agree to marry Judith, he would be made to walk the same path as his father.

Exhaling, Vesper gritted her teeth. She knew what she had to do.

The children were depending on her and she would never let such an awful fate befall Aspen, even if it meant losing him for good.

Aspen stared at the two men sitting across the table from him at Scotland Yard headquarters at Whitehall Place. Despite their disheveled appearances, time—and presumably the obscene fortunes his mother had paid for their cooperation—had been kind to both of them. They had lived full, comfortable lives while his father had been deprived of his.

"Do you know who I am?" he asked. When they stared at him blankly, he continued, not wanting to waste time. "I am the Duke of Greydon. You may have known my father, the late duke. He was incarcerated at Camberwell some years ago."

Watching them like a hawk, Aspen saw the same flash of horror as the name sank in...along with a telling pallor on the apothecary's face. Rhodes would crack first; Parker's expression remained stoic.

"That was long ago," Dr. Parker said. "What exactly is this about?"

Aspen gritted his teeth, blood beginning to boil. "You both falsified records about the late duke's condition at the request of the duchess." Parker opened his mouth, and Aspen held up a hand. He was done with the games. "I have written proof of your communication with my mother as well as a full confession from her of your involvement." While the former was true, the latter was a lie, considering his mother would never confess any such thing, but they didn't know that.

Rhodes's face blanched even as Parker continued to stare stoically. "She forced me to do it," the apothecary finally burst out. "Threatened me! I'll swear a statement that the duke was of sound mind—that it was the extended doses of laudanum that made him confused," he added in desperation. "But Parker was just as complicit, more so than me. It was by his order that the duke was confined—" Dr. Parker bellowed in rage, but one of the officers restrained him.

"Please, I have a family," Rhodes begged.

And I had a family.

Aspen stood and met the gaze of the detective who had tracked down both men and brought the criminals to the attention of Scotland Yard. "I'm done here. You can decide the consequences of their actions." He glanced at Parker, whose face was blotchy with fear and fury. "You ruined a good man's life and betrayed the oaths you took, and before you cry your innocence, Dr. Parker, I know that my father was not your only case of malpractice." The good doctor's mouth snapped shut very quickly after that.

Aspen took his leave, despite the urge to pound his fists into the men's faces. He'd gotten what he'd come for. And now, his mother had nothing left to hold over him...no more threats of paternal afflictions. There was only one thing more to do. One more door to close on the past forever.

With a measured exhalation, he glanced at his timepiece after entering his carriage. Hell, he was late. He'd promised Harwick he'd be there that afternoon. Thankfully, the drive from Whitehall to Mayfair didn't take long, and in that time, he'd sufficiently composed himself.

Making his greetings and apologies to Harwick, he settled into the duke's study and pored over the remaining documents. The proposal was almost complete, and Aspen took solace in the fact that this was the real homage to his father—a way to curb wrongful confinement with legal documentation from a justice of the peace and providing the right to an appeal.

Aspen was so engrossed in the work that he didn't hear the Duke of Harwick until Vesper's name jolted his attention. He glanced up. "I beg your pardon?"

"Eldridge has offered again for Vesper," Harwick repeated.

Proposal forgotten, he stared at the duke in disbelief, a flood of emotions drowning him. "And you are actually considering it?"

"It's high time she marry," Harwick responded mildly.

Aspen narrowed his eyes, the suspicion that something else was afoot too great to ignore. Why was Harwick all of a sudden so interested in seeing Vesper wed? Or was this her idea? Aspen frowned. That didn't make sense either. "What does *she* have to say about this?" he asked in a controlled voice that did little to hide the antipathy boiling in his veins.

The duke sent him a questioning look but shrugged. "If this is what she truly desires, Eldridge will be a good match. He's a decent man and seems to genuinely care for her."

"By smothering her with roses and lilies?" Aspen retorted,

thinking of the overly crowded floral display in the foyer. He'd found the constant arrival of bouquets amusing until he'd learned from Lushing who had sent all of them. "He will bore her to tears."

Harwick studied him. "You seem unduly bothered by the notion."

"He's a bumbling fool who doesn't deserve her!"

"You're quite invested in the subject of my daughter's happiness for a man who doesn't believe in love," the duke said, his brows rising.

Well, then. That parry struck him right in the gut. Aspen removed his spectacles and pinched the bridge of his nose between his thumb and forefinger. "I mean no disrespect, sir, but Eldridge is—" he began.

"None of your business," a calm voice said at the door.

Aspen couldn't help the skip in his pulse at the sight of the woman who he was beginning to crave more than the air he breathed. He drank her in, willowy and elegant in a peach gown that made her look edible. And then he remembered Eldridge and scowled. "It is my business."

Her brows rose, the expression identical to her father's. "How so? I only have one sire in this room and he's sitting over there. Whatever influence you seem to think you have over me is misplaced and unwelcome, Your Grace." She turned to her father. "I have reconsidered Lord Eldridge's tender of marriage, Papa, and I shall accept."

The floor fell out from beneath his feet, and Aspen goggled at her. Perhaps he hadn't heard her correctly. "What? No, you cannot."

"I can and I will." A queer look of distress passed over her features as she uttered those words, and Aspen frowned at the resignation in her expression. "I must, you see."

He stood and moved toward her to gather her in his arms

and convince her that she was so very wrong, until he remembered that they weren't alone. He glanced back at the duke to see that he wore an intense expression on his face. Not of displeasure. One of curiosity and then of comprehension, but Aspen was too preoccupied to dwell on it. When Harwick exited the room without preamble, Aspen was only focused on one thing. *Her.*

"Vesper, please, reconsider," he said when the tense silence between them grew to be too much. "This is not what you want."

"How would you know what I want?" She backed away from him, and he stalled in his tracks at her resolute look. "No, Your Grace. I've made up my mind. And you should do what's required for your dukedom." He frowned as she pushed on. "Marry Judith. You have the same interests, and at least you'll get companionship out of the union. Your mother will leave you both alone, once you've done your duty."

His brain was spinning at the implications of her words. What did the *duchess* have to do with it? "Did she put you up to this?" he demanded.

"So what if she did?" Vesper shrugged. "It makes the most sense and you know it. Judith will be settled and content with you."

"I don't want...that," he bit out.

He was losing her, and he hadn't even had a chance to fight...to declare his intentions. Good God, what *were* his intentions? All he was certain of was that he wanted more of her, in his bed, in his arms, he wanted to be the one to comfort her when she was distressed and to make her come apart again and again. But no, that was wrong. He didn't just want her. He *needed* her like he needed oxygen to survive.

"I love you," he burst out.

Her eyes went wide and then filled with anguish. "No, Aspen. *No.* I..."

"Vesper, please, listen. Did you hear what I said?" He heard the break in his voice and he didn't care. He would grovel if he had to. "I love you. I was gone the moment I saw you at your come-out."

She gaped. "You spurned me. You made your feelings quite clear and they were the furthest thing from affection."

"I could barely speak!" he blurted, throwing his spectacles to the table and scrubbing a palm over his face. "It was all I could do to not swoon like a besotted fool at your feet so I did what I do best—I buried it all and ran, but that was because of me, not you. Never you." He let out a harsh breath, seeing her stark disbelief. "The truth is my heart has always been yours. I don't want Judith." Desperate, Aspen swallowed. "Marry me."

A tear crept from the corner of her eye, and she wrung her hands together, a stricken look on her beautiful face. Aspen kept his eyes fastened on her. More tears emerged, but they weren't tears of joy. No, she looked like her heart was fracturing right then and there.

She swayed on her feet, and for one elated moment it looked like she would run to him, but then her spine straightened and her face hardened into that cool, composed, aristocratic mask he loathed.

"I can't. I don't feel the same, Your Grace. I am sorry."

Chapter Twenty-One

Vesper stood on the side of the ballroom, that persistent ache behind her breastbone not dissipating in the least. When her brother had suggested a soiree to snap them all out of their doldrums, she had half-heartedly agreed, thinking it would be the thing to distract her from her shattered heart. Now she was regretting it with every part of her being. Mostly because watching the Duke of Greydon dancing with Judith was a special kind of torture.

God, he'd said that he *loved* her. That he'd always loved her, even when she'd thought the opposite. He'd asked her to marry him. Was that real? Considering his opinions on wedlock, the proposal had been a shock, but to declare his feelings so bluntly when he'd claimed not to believe in love? Had he only professed to love her because he hated that she'd accepted Eldridge's suit? Was that why he had been driven to propose? Was he jealous?

Stop, none of it matters!

Not with his mother's very real threats.

That didn't stop Vesper's bruised heart from feeling like it was withering inside of her with every affectionate, reluctant smile that Judith drew from Aspen's lips. Vesper had nothing against the girl, but she couldn't help the tumultuous envy filling her chest at the sight of her in the duke's arms. It had physically hurt to invite him, but never one to do things in half measures, Vesper had also seen it as an opportunity to placate the duchess.

To keep Aspen and Judith safe. To save the children.

It was the only way she'd get through the evening.

On top of everything, she had received the most dreadful news that a large church orphanage in St. Giles had been lost in a fire, though thankfully, everyone had been evacuated and apart from smoke inhalation, all lives had been accounted for. But with so many of the children in desperate need of somewhere to live, the money was needed more than ever.

And that devious witch was holding it over her head!

Vesper met the Duchess of Greydon's pleased gaze across the room and inclined her head, despite the deep-seated urge to throw the vile woman out on her cunning arse. Vesper had hoped that if the duchess saw her making an effort to do as bidden with Greydon and Judith, she might be convinced to give up the funds sooner.

No such luck yet, however.

Appealing to her better nature would be useless... as the woman had none. Vesper firmed her lips, burying her frustration as she saw her father approaching the alcove where she'd tucked herself. She stared at him with no small surprise, considering he was supposed to be in his rooms. But no, he was dressed in fine formalwear and looking rather dashing for it.

"Are you well, my dear?" he asked.

She lifted a brow. "I thought you were going to skip this one tonight."

"I couldn't let the dearest light of my life be alone when she was sad, could I?" he asked, offering her his arm with a smile that made her want to weep. Her pitiful heart trembled in her chest, tears pricking the backs of her eyes. No matter what awful pickle she found herself in, whenever she was hurting, he always knew.

"Oh, Papa," she whispered and flung herself into his arms, not even caring who was watching or who might be gossiping as to why the straitlaced Lady Vesper was hanging on to her composure by the skin of her teeth. The duke returned the embrace with no concern for their audience, either, holding her as though he had no intention of letting her go.

"Shall we dance, dear girl?" he whispered. "Banish some of this misery."

She bit her lip. "I don't think I can manage it."

"You can," he told her firmly. "Chin up, love," her father urged softly, and her frantic stare met his. He squeezed her hand. "Come on, my girl. Dance with your father."

She exhaled and gave a tiny nod. After a while, Vesper let the music and her father's efficient lead guide her. She counted each breath with every step. *One, two, three, inhale... one, two, three, exhale.*

Her gaze drifted to the wide expanse of Greydon's shoulders and the diminutive woman in his arms, and then darted away as pain coiled anew. As if he could sense the press of her eyes, on the next turn a shuttered brown gaze bored into hers, held it for an interminable handful of minutes, and then released her as if she were of zero consequence.

One, two, three, inhale... one, two, three, exhale.

Vesper could barely heave the air into her shriveling lungs. "Heavens, he hates me," she whispered.

"Hate and love are very close cousins, they say," her father said.

Stricken, Vesper peered up at him. "He doesn't... love me. And I don't love him either."

Her father huffed a laugh. "Come now, Vesper. You have

loved that boy from the moment you made him bleed in front of his entire household."

She cringed, recalling the unfortunate incident. "That wasn't love, Papa. It was infatuation." She fell into silence and then sighed. She had to get at least some of the burden off her chest. "I asked Greydon's mother for help with her set, and in exchange for her assistance, she asked for me to arrange a match with her son and Judith."

His brows rose. "Does *he* want that? Does Judith, for that matter?"

Vesper shrugged. "Betrothal agreements are common in the aristocracy, Papa."

His expression was troubled. "I've known Victoria a long time and she has never cared for her son's well-being or happiness. People are like pawns to her, disposable and replaceable. Her husband was and that boy will be, too."

Tears pricked her eyes. He'd never know how close he was to the truth. They spun together in another turn and fell into silence.

"Why Eldridge?" the duke asked after a few more beats.

She looked into her father's eyes and willed herself not to cry. "If I am attached, Greydon will see reason and his mother will be placated. If they don't wed, she'll punish them both, and I can't bear that. Trust me, Papa, this is best for everyone."

Liar.

The ball was endless.

Aspen was sick of dancing, sick of conversing, and sick of smiling. Most of all, he was sick of trying to ignore the woman who had cut his heart out, fed it through a meat grinder, and tossed it aside. In hindsight, he could have done a better job of not blurting his feelings out as he had, but he'd seen red when she said she would accept Eldridge.

Aspen clenched his jaw. He was glad that the pretty fop wasn't in attendance, not for any other reason than Lushing hadn't invited him, thank God.

Earlier that week, the earl had shot him a look when he'd asked about the guest list. "Why do you care? Eldridge is a decent sort."

"He's a totty-headed clunch."

Lushing had formed a mocking grin. "Are you insulting his intelligence because he has a hankering for my sister?"

"Your sister has accepted his suit."

His friend had gone quiet at that, amusement fading, but then he'd nodded. "Well then, he's definitely not invited."

Aspen had successfully avoided her all evening, but he couldn't help noticing when she'd taken the floor with her father. God, she was so beautiful, a bit wan in the cheeks, but as regal and elegant as ever. Bitterness filled him and he tore his stare away. She'd made her position clear—she had chosen Eldridge.

A part of him had wanted to quit London, go back to the United States, where he could get lost in the wilds of Wyoming or Colorado. Bones and fossils were uncomplicated things. Unlike women. Unlike *her*.

But he couldn't leave, not while the noose of duty hung around his neck. For everything that had happened between them, Vesper wasn't wrong about his obligation to the dukedom. He would have to marry eventually and who better to be an *uncomplicated* match than the woman currently waltzing with him.

He peered down at Judith and suddenly noticed the fierce expression she wore. "What is the matter?"

"This is our *third* dance, Aspen," she hissed. "People will notice and assume things. Betrothal things."

He hadn't even realized—he'd just wanted to pass the time as quickly as he could. Perhaps that was fate intervening on his behalf. "Perhaps we should let them."

She blinked, her gaze drifting over his shoulder. "Weren't you courting Lady—"

"No!" he ground out, cutting her off before she could say the name, and her eyes widened. Aspen let out a breath and forced a smile to his uncooperative lips. "No, I was not."

"I don't believe that for one bloody second," Judith said fervently. "A fool could tell that you're both head over—"

"Enough, Judith, please," he commanded. When she concurred with a mutinous look, Aspen exhaled and made a decision. It was time to see to his duty. "I was giving some further thought about what it is you want to do with your passion for lost relics, and I think we can capture two birds with one stone."

Her indignation was replaced with interest. "How so?"

"It's no secret that my mother wishes us to wed."

She shook her head. "Aspen, we've already discussed how I feel on the matter."

Bloody hell, this was a casual proposition of convenience and he didn't know if his heart could handle another rejection. "Yes, I know, but please hear me out," he said, bleakly aware that it was Vesper who had seeded the suggestion in the first place. "If we marry, one, it will get the duchess off my back. Two, you will be settled. Third, once I have hired a reputable steward, I will allow you to accompany me out of this infernal town and you can do what you like on the relic-hunting front."

"What's the catch?" Judith asked with narrowed eyes. "That sounds like you expect me to trail in your footsteps like a lost puppy."

"You will have your independence. If you agree, it will be a marriage of two friends and no more."

Judith pursed her lips and narrowed her eyes. "What about children? The ducal heirs you will be expected to have?"

Fuck. Aspen nearly lost his footing. He hadn't thought of that. A vision of a child with a cloud of gossamer golden hair and bright lapis lazuli eyes filled his head, and he shoved it away. "Let's cross that bridge when we come to it."

She scowled again and then wrinkled her nose. "I do not wish to *cross that bridge* at all, Aspen. The thought of, well, *that*, makes me cringe."

It made him as well, to be honest, but dozens of aristocrats had arranged marriages with no passion to recommend them, and they had survived. Marital congress was practical, a necessary conjugal act. Memories of Vesper's impassioned whimpers assaulted him, and he bit his lip so hard that he tasted blood.

That hadn't been *practical*...That had been something else, something beyond mere description. Beyond mortal explanation perhaps. Aspen shook his head hard. If he kept putting her on a pedestal, it would be his own fault that no one would ever measure up.

Vesper Lyndhurst was not for him.

"My mother will marry you off to the first man she wants if we don't do this. Or worse, she'll make you pay because I didn't bend to her wishes." He was being blunt, but the statements were no less true for it. "She'll make both our lives a living hell, and though I'm not concerned about me, I am worried about you."

"How does one woman have so much power?" Judith murmured.

Aspen barked a laugh. "Years of witchery, I suspect."

He grinned at Judith's alarmed expression as she punched his chest and giggled. It was a dismal, nervous kind of laughter, but it broke the tension between them. His mother wasn't a witch; she was clearly something much worse.

"I'll think about it, but you should, too, before you take a knee," Judith said.

"Hedging your bets?" he asked with a grin.

She laughed and shook her head. "Hardly. I'm hedging yours."

Hearty laughter drew Vesper's eye. Oh God, they were both laughing. Why were they laughing? What could possibly be so funny? Were they talking about her? She scowled at her own absurdity. *Why* would they even be thinking about *her*?

"You're glowering," her father said.

"I'm not," she said, forcing her brow to relax.

Smoothing her face into serene lines didn't mean that the heat in her body lessened. No, that beast inside her thundered its displeasure, a burst of jealousy rattling the bars of its cage.

"Tell me the truth, Vesper," her father asked. "Are you in love with the duke?"

"Which duke?" she replied.

He gave an exasperated snort. "The one you have been stealing glances at ever since he arrived. And honestly, if you dig your fingers into my arms any more in vexation because he's dancing with Miss Thornton, I'm certain there will be holes in my sleeves."

"Sorry!" she said and dropped her lashes. "And I'm not looking at him."

The duke hesitated like he had something to say but did not speak his mind as the music came to a close and he escorted her back to where she'd been standing. "Just because Victoria wishes him to marry her ward doesn't mean he should."

"What do you mean?" Vesper asked him.

"She is the last person on this earth who would know a single thing about her son's happiness." His gaze cut toward where the duchess was standing. "Or about love at all. It was no concern of hers that her son would grow up without a father. Or that he would have to watch his father wither away, alone and forgotten."

Vesper's gaze flicked over to where the duke stood, his dark head bent toward Judith. As if he could sense her yet again, Aspen looked up. Her breath caught. For a moment, it was as though everything around them ceased to exist. Time and distance fell away and it was only the two of them sharing the same air, mirroring the same heartbeat, experiencing the same soul-destroying heartbreak.

She was the first to break the connection, the agony too much to bear.

There was no way any of what he said was true. People always coveted what they couldn't have, and his hasty confessions were a matter of pride, not love.

"In this life, Vesper," her father said softly, "things are never certain. If we are given a chance at finding love, we should go after it with everything inside of us because life without love is no life at all. The time I had with your mother was precious and I am grateful that she gave me you and Jasper. I want that for you—a loving partner, children if you so desire, companionship, and most of all, passion."

She felt her cheeks heat at the last. "Papa!"

"I'm old, Daughter, not dead."

With a glint in his eye, he shot her a wink and turned to say hello to a gentleman who had stopped to greet him. Vesper leaned against a marble column, letting her hot cheek rest on the cool marble. She would have some of those things with Eldridge and perhaps love would come in time.

Just then, a terrible thought occurred. Would Eldridge even permit her to continue her work with the children? Dread struck her. What if he didn't?

Greydon would never seek to pigeonhole you.

She didn't care about Greydon.

Lightning did not strike at the lie, but the universe must have had a sick sense of humor because Cat chose that moment to streak across the ballroom with the aplomb of an invited guest and scale a potted fern. Vesper watched in horror as the furry little beast fixed her sights on a feathered plume waving in the Duchess of Greydon's coiffure.

No, Cat, no!

It was only when her father goggled at her, and Greydon's head swiveled in her direction that she realized she had shouted aloud. Cat being Cat paid her not one lick of attention, and struck, leaping like some kind of acrobat, paws outstretched toward her feathered prize, and collided with the duchess's hair. The lady shrieked bloody murder as the headpiece dangled drunkenly off the side of her head.

The fluffy culprit scampered away beneath some skirts, causing more high-pitched screams, and chaos abounded.

"What *is* that?"

"Is it a mouse?"

"No! A weasel!"

"Catch it, for God's sake before it spreads disease!"

Lushing, her scoundrel of a brother, bellowed with laughter on the ballroom floor when the mischievous feline scurried beneath his partner's skirts and made her squeal in fright. Her wicked brother bent to whisper something in his dance partner's ear that made her go scarlet and Vesper could already imagine what he'd said.

Pussy under your skirts?

She let out a giggle as her father's brows jumped to his hairline. "Isn't that your pet causing such a ruckus?"

Yes and it was a *cat*astrophe. It was *hiss*terical.

Vesper started cackling. And then she laughed—a full

belly laugh—that didn't stop until her eyes started to tear, not even when the dowager glared in her direction and people stared as though she were in the middle of a fit. Her father's eyes crinkled at the corners as he fought a grin himself when more tiny snorts escaped her nostrils.

Oh, good Lord, she hadn't laughed so hard in well... ever.

Wiping her eyes and composing herself as best she could, Vesper kissed her father's cheek. "I'll get the little monster and then I'm going to murder Effie."

Or send her the most extravagant gift she could find. Her gaze met the lady in question, who was also laughing so hard she was nearly doubled over. Effie was standing beside Laila and Briar, and the trio was clutching each other in complete mirth, not even bothering to hide their preposterous reactions.

Vesper walked over to them, biting back her own mirth. "Help me find Cat, you lot."

"Not me," Laila protested, fighting giggles and pointing to a table against a wall. "She makes me sneeze, but I think she went under that table just there."

Briar snickered. "Don't look at me! That fuzzy little turd hates me."

With a sigh, Vesper bent to peek under the tablecloth where Laila had indicated, and sure enough, the tiny little fiend was there calmly cleaning her paws as if she hadn't just been the instigator of feline bedlam. Vesper made a soft noise with her lips. "Come here, sweetheart."

Cat didn't deign to move and watched her with a smug expression, if cats could have smug expressions.

"Don't make me come under there, you naughty little scamp." How she planned to get under there with her mountain of skirts was anyone's guess, but damned if she would let herself get bested by a defiant cat who had more whiskers than sense.

"I can get her," Effie said, appearing beside her in a crouch, even as they were joined by Stanley and two footmen who offered the same. Vesper shook her head.

"No, she's my responsibility," she said. "I'll do it."

Effie sent her a blinding smile. "Look at you being such a splendid cat mama. I knew you would be!"

"Hardly. It's just she's given me no choice," Vesper said with a pointed glance at the poor butler who had received more than his fair share of scratches from the Horror of Harwick House. "Just ask Stanley."

With a sigh, Vesper got down on her knees, ignoring the looks of shock that were sent in her direction from the servants as well as the guests, though her father had signaled for the music to continue and they should have all been dancing instead of gawking at her. But aristocrats loved any whisper of scandal and the sight of a lady on her knees would have them tittering.

"Let one of the servants do it, Vesper," Laila said from behind her.

"No. If I don't get her, she will just cause more trouble. She runs from everyone, except me and—" She broke off, having been about to say Greydon, to whom the cat had taken a ridiculous fancy, much like everyone else. "She might even not like *me* much right now because I locked her in my bedchamber. I have no idea how she escaped." Vesper frowned as the kitten yowled and arched her spine as though she was about to scamper in the opposite direction. "Effie, go to the other side and catch her if she runs."

"Got it."

With determined force, Vesper wriggled partway under the table and then scowled when the cat seemed to realize her intentions and darted out of reach. "Quick, Effie, snatch her. Quick before the little miscreant escapes!"

But it wasn't Effie at the other end who blocked the little troublemaker; it was a duke. Cat's favorite duke, in fact.

"What are *you* doing?" Vesper blurted at him moments after he'd ducked beneath the table.

"Rescuing a damsel."

Bright blue eyes peered at him, and hell if Aspen didn't want to close the distance between them there under that table and kiss her senseless. "I am not in need of rescue, Your Grace."

"I was talking about the cat."

Her lips twitched and she pinned them together. Aspen was regretting his decision to squash his frame into this tiny little space. His shoulders could barely fit, and it was scandalous beyond belief that a *duke* would find himself in such a peculiar position. Cat purred between them, as though pleased to be between the two people she adored most in the world.

"I think she planned this," he said.

Vesper frowned and blew at a lock of hair that had tumbled into her face. "Planned what?"

"You look beautiful tonight," he whispered instead of answering her question.

"Don't do that," she whispered.

"Do what?"

She bit her lip. "Pretend what happened didn't happen."

"Don't marry him, Vesper," he said. "He can't..." *Love you like I do.* But the words failed him, just like his courage.

An anguished expression crossed her face. "You don't understand, I have to. And we both know your proposal was ill-conceived."

God, she was infuriatingly stubborn and so very wrong,

but he would do anything to convince her of his sincerity.
Aspen crept closer. "Then explain it to me."

"You have to marry Judith."

He blinked at the desolate thread in her tone, a suspicion creeping into his head. "You never answered me. Did my mother put you up to this, Vesper?"

But before she could reply, a solid thwack on the surface of the table made them both jump and glance up. "Oy! Any survivors under there?" Lushing drawled. "I'm going to start to take wagers if someone doesn't emerge, and please think of doing so soon, unless you both hope to march to the altar to quell the scandal currently brewing in this ballroom like a witch's cauldron."

"Give us a minute," Aspen said in a louder voice. "The cat is proving most difficult."

Lushing guffawed. "Isn't *that* the truth?"

Vesper's eyes widened at her brother's dreadful innuendo and she inched backward, only to stop with a dismayed look.

"What is it?" Aspen asked.

"I am . . . stuck," she said.

He crept forward, grabbing Cat in one hand by the scruff of her neck, who made no protest at all to being so manhandled, and grinned. "Good," he told her.

"Good why?" Vesper asked frowning.

"Good because I'm going to kiss you."

Her lips parted and desire flooded those blue eyes. He waited for her to rear back or tell him to stop . . . anything to indicate she didn't want this as much as he did. And then he crashed his lips to hers. It wasn't the lengthy kiss he craved, but it would do. He relished the sweetness of her mouth with a deep plunge of his tongue, driving in when her lips parted on a shocked gasp, and groaned at the taste. Damn, she was fucking delicious. He went deep, once, twice, and then drew away. Despite wanting so much more, Aspen ended the kiss. He couldn't very well ravish her under a table.

His kissing cohort wore a bemused expression that was soon eclipsed by pure alarm. "What the devil do you think you're doing?"

"Catching a dangerous kitty," he said with an innocent look.

"Cat isn't dangerous."

He smirked. "I wasn't talking about the cat."

Aspen smirked at her and shimmied his way out. He handed off the furry bundle to a waiting Effie, and then nodded to Lushing and the footmen. "Give us a hand will you?"

They each took an end of the massive, ornate table and lifted on Aspen's count. The thing weighed a bloody ton, but they were able to lift it just enough for Vesper to emerge, mussed but unharmed. It gratified Aspen to no end to see those swollen, red lips and know that he'd been the cause.

His gratification fled when she stomped toward him, a palm cracking into his face with no real force, though the sharp sound of it echoed in the ballroom. "How dare you, sir? No, I will never marry you. Not if you were the last man in creation!"

His hitherto very smug jaw dropped.

It was a performance, he belatedly realized, one she begged him to maintain with her eyes. But for whose benefit? His mother's? Judith's? He was determined to find out, but for the moment, Aspen stared down at her and lifted a brow.

His smile was slow and purposeful. "Challenge accepted, Viper."

Chapter Twenty-Two

"Are you following me, Your Grace?"

It was the same question she'd asked him on Rotten Row, only this time there was considerably more vexation in her voice. Aspen loved her waspishness because it meant that she *felt* something, and in his experience, any feeling from Vesper—even a bad one—was better than her dependably haughty sangfroid. That perfected poise he *knew* was fake.

It was in the slope of her chin, the set of her shoulders, and the smallest tension in her lips as though it fought against its natural uplift. He'd give his soul to see that smile... to see her eyes flash with anything but neutrality. He fortified himself—one thing at a time.

He shrugged once. "Define following."

"When you dog a person's footsteps all over town, especially when they do not want to be pursued. This is getting tiresome, Your Grace." She waved an arm at their location. "This is a modiste's shop."

"And clearly, I am in the market for a new waistcoat." He faked an earnest look. "And besides, seeing me at your home does not count, Lady Vesper. I am there at your father's bequest."

"Yet you always seem to take the air at the same time that I find myself in the garden or have dinner with us when you have a family and should have interests and marital obligations of your own."

Aspen didn't react, though the aghast expression on her face told him that she hadn't quite thought through the blunt barbs in her reply—it was unlikely he would ever dine *willingly* with his only remaining family, the Dowager Duchess of Greydon. "I don't make it a habit of dining with Satan's sister."

A smile tugged at those rigid lips before it was quashed, her cheeks flushed with deep color. "I meant a woman like Judith who won't mind if the eligible Duke of Greydon pursues her."

"Alas, I require a specific type of lure. Clever, witty, and brazen with the saltiest mouth this side of the Atlantic."

That salty mouth flattened further as she tossed her head. "You know very well that Judith is both clever and witty." She sniffed and pretended to be interested in a display of gloves. "As far as salt, I have a feeling, Your Grace, that you are more than capable of driving any woman to the depths of the ocean without much effort at all."

Aspen almost grinned at the backhanded insult. *There was his girl.* His smile was easy. "I am quite particular in my tastes, Lady Viper."

"My name is Lady *Ves*per, Your Grace." The look she shot in his direction would have incinerated a lesser man. Thankfully, with prolonged exposure, he'd become quite immune to her flames. In fact, he relished them—they felt like the hottest kind of sunlight.

"How is Cat?" he asked, keeping pace with her when she moved to inspect a particularly garish hat. "Recovered from her ballroom escapades?"

"Cat is fine, up to her usual tricks," she replied without thinking and then let out a huff when he followed her to yet another monstrosity of a hat. "Don't you have somewhere to be, Your Grace? Your club? Shopping for your soon-to-be betrothed?"

"No one has caught me yet, my lady," he drawled in a low rasp that drew a smothered gasp from her. "In fact, the one lady I can't seem to resist doesn't want a bar of me."

"Then take the obvious hint?" she shot back.

A chuckle burst from him, eliciting a furtive glance. God, he loved this. He'd *missed* this.

"I've made no vows, and neither have you," he said.

"I plan to," she replied.

His brows rose. "Then why *haven't* you?"

"Have you always been this exasperating?" she countered and her jaw tightened. "You danced with Judith three times. Everyone in the ton knows what that means."

He closed the distance between them. "Good thing I don't give a damn about the ton, and I, like anyone, can change my mind."

"Or is it a change of heart?" she said.

His eyes met hers and held them. "This heart hasn't diverted from its course in nearly three decades."

Those blue eyes dilated, a soft exhalation leaving her lips as her fingers fluttered up to her throat. Within a heartbeat, her face fell back to its usual blank mask. She hurried toward a table of delicate lace—it was obvious they were meant to be examples of fabric for women's unmentionables—and Aspen's mouth twitched at her transparent attempt to get rid of him.

Most men would have run for the hills. He, however, was not most men. He smirked and snatched up a lace edging that was trimmed in sapphire-blue roses. It wasn't quite the same brilliant hue, but it would do.

He signaled to a girl who stood near the counter. "I'll take a half-yard of this, please. This blue is nearly the most perfect shade to match my beloved's eyes, I think."

The shop girl goggled at him. "A half-yard, sir?" she squeaked.

"Make it a whole yard. I'm certain some of it might get ruined in the heat of passion. Charge it to my account."

When the poor blushing girl had wrapped up his purchase and batted her eyes at him enough for Aspen to wonder if she'd gotten something caught in them, Vesper turned on him with a hiss. "You are truly appalling."

"Why?" he asked, keeping to her heels as she stalked toward the exit.

"Your Grace, please stop following me. This is unseemly."

On the way out, he tucked the package of lace into his trouser pocket and clasped his hands behind his back. "Who says I am following you? We are simply walking in the same direction, one hundred percent completely by chance." He winked at her lady's maid—Lizzie or some such—who had an unabashed grin on her round face. She'd seen him more than once around the house and approved of him pursuing her mistress from the looks of her. Good, he needed someone on his side.

"Lizzie!" Vesper said sharply. "This way then. I have an interest in visiting the cobbler."

"But we saw the cobbler last week, my lady," Lizzie said with a frown.

"The jewelers then," she said quickly. "They're just across the street here."

Aspen grinned. "What a coincidence. That's where I was headed!"

His pretty little prey stopped so suddenly that Aspen nearly crashed into her and found himself with an armful of sweet-scented, furious female.

"Now see here!" she said and then trailed off when she realized how close he stood. All he had to do was bend forward and his lips would be on hers...in full daylight and in full view of any and all passersby. Those sweet pink arches parted in silent wrath and it was almost everything he could do *not* to kiss them.

Instead, he set her upright and stepped a safe distance away.

"That was rather close," he murmured.

She frowned. "What was?"

"We could have both landed in a heap and that would have been a travesty." He glanced down at his clothes and tapped the brim of his hat with a jaunty little motion. "This is a new suit of clothing. Don't I look dapper?"

"I hadn't noticed," she said with a sniff.

He smirked. "I think you *did* notice, my lady, and you are fibbing."

The spots in her cheeks darkened, and Aspen couldn't help the satisfaction pouring through him at the fact that she wasn't as immune to him as she pretended.

"What do you want from me, Your Grace?" she asked.

"An afternoon of your time," he said. "That's all I ask. Your lady's maid can accompany us as a chaperone, or Lady Marsden has kindly volunteered."

"You talked to Laila?" she burst out.

"Marsden will come, too," he said. "Do this one thing and I promise I will make every attempt to stop being in the same places as you are, even though it's quite the coincidence, I say. I mean, it's obvious that the universe must favor our paths to intersect, but I will honor your wishes."

Her jaw went tight, and Aspen saw the very moment she considered refusing and then capitulated when the fight drained out of her. That lush mouth went flat. "One afternoon and you promise you'll leave me alone?"

"One afternoon," he said with a nod, though his words were slightly different. "And I will not follow you."

"Very well then."

The surrender was hard-won, but it was still a win.

Vesper hadn't quite thought through her agreement. The only way she could stick to her guns was to stay away from the aggravating, handsome vexation that was this duke. Spending an entire afternoon with him doing God knew what, even with her dearest friend in attendance, would be the worst kind of enticement, one she could *not* act upon. Earlier, when they had collided, it had taken all her wherewithal not to throw herself into his arms and demand he kiss her at once.

She blamed Lizzie's gothic romances—one of which included a sultry, very virile Viking hero whose libido was legendary. Said hero was described as being dark-haired and well-muscled. The thought of Greydon in a shoulder cape made of fur, tight leather lace-up breeches over those already muscular thighs, a shield and an ax, and well, her fantasies had taken on a life of their own.

He'd replaced the Viking hero in her dreams almost every night. With his unruly hair as long as it was, traces of dark stubble, and ridged stomach, it wasn't hard to indulge her fantasies.

Greydon would have made a fantastic Viking.

With spectacles.

By God, she couldn't leave those out. Just the idea of the man wielding a deadly weapon with his muscles *and* wearing those tiny gold-framed eyeglasses made her weak in the knees. It was an incongruous fantasy, but then again, so was Greydon.

He didn't fit any mold. Strong, smart, sinful. How could

such a learned, erudite man of the books who studied *fossils* be so damned attractive? So damned commanding? Was it normal to secretly pine for a man who could engage her in talk of parliamentary bills *and* toss her over his shoulder in the same breath?

Something was wrong with her.

But she couldn't refuse... she was too weak to do so.

Which was why she found herself in the Duke of Greydon's carriage with said irresistible, bone-hunting duke in the flesh and the Marquess of Marsden sitting opposite her and Laila with all of her well-laid plans askew. He should be with *Judith*. She should be with *Eldridge*... though the thought of him made her stomach twist in discomfort.

Just get through today and you will be fine.

Think of the children.

Ignore the scholarly Viking.

But by God, that latter half of that advice was a spark to dry, desperate, needy tinder. She couldn't stop slanting glances at Greydon, noting that deliciously stubbled jawline as if he hadn't shaved in days, and the glint in those brown eyes that caught the sunlight in just... that... way. Vesper couldn't help envisioning him in fitted trews and a leather harness, and she squirmed in her seat.

"What's the matter?" Laila whispered, noticing the slight movement.

"Nothing. Stiff petticoats." She leaned over, her voice just as low. "Do you know where we are going?"

"Marsden said it was a surprise."

Vesper scowled. "I don't like surprises."

"Fibber," her best friend retorted, poking her in the side with an elbow. "You love surprises."

Well, as it turned out, she liked surprises from everyone *but* Greydon.

What on earth was the wicked man planning?

As if he could sense her curiosity, their eyes met, his intense browns drilling into her blues. She held his gaze, mesmerized for a moment, before she realized that she wasn't breathing and sucked a gulp of air into her lungs. Scolding her body for acting like an imbecile around him, Vesper focused on what Laila was saying about the good spell of weather they were having.

It wasn't long before they arrived at their destination and as they peered through the carriage windows, Vesper's eyes widened.

"The Crystal Palace?" she asked in a voice full of wonder that she made no attempt to hide. Laila looked awed as well.

The Crystal Palace was a place where stunning, extraordinary exhibitions were held, and though Vesper had heard of it, she'd never visited. She gaped, eyes drinking in the lofty glass structure that resembled an enormous conservatory in the distance. It was massive, with two huge towers. She'd read that the palace and the grounds showcased entertainment, education, and even cricket matches.

"We're visiting the grounds today," Greydon explained as the carriage came to a stop, then offered her his arm when they'd descended. She knew it would be churlish to refuse, so she clasped her hand inside his elbow.

They strolled behind the marquess and marchioness, and Vesper felt an unexpected sense of contentment. And, despite the duchess's threat, a sly voice inside her whispered, *Neither of you are betrothed... yet.*

Bloody hell, she had to stay strong. She could not cave to the desire humming in her blood as if her body had been away from its other half much too long.

Feigning interest in a nearby ornamental garden that could rival those at Harwick House, she pulled away from him and wandered down to the edge of a beautiful fountain. "This is lovely."

"Come, I want you to see something," the duke said.

Vesper turned, looking for Laila, but she and her husband had disappeared. Her brows drew together—so much for her being a *responsible* married chaperone—but then she felt her face warm. It wasn't like she and Greydon needed chaperoning...

She hurried after Greydon who was strolling down one of the garden paths. She was determined to stay away from the man, but she didn't want to get lost in a strange place either. "Where are we going?"

"Not far."

He lied; it *was* far. Vesper's legs were aching by the time they had traversed a few winding paths, but she didn't want to complain and have the duke think her helpless or feeble. So she kept her gaze down so as not to stumble and plodded on.

The shriek that escaped her lips was inhuman when she came upon the first massive sculpture of some kind of lizard monster that stood in front of her. Upon a second glance, she knew it wasn't real, but she hadn't been expecting it to be so close, so huge, or so terrifying.

"Welcome to the prehistoric swamp." Greydon was grinning, one hand waving wide. "This is *Iguanodon*."

Her mouth fell open as she took in the detail of the neat scales, the thick head, and the fearsome teeth of the monster. "Did creatures like these really exist?"

"Yes. A man called Hawkins was commissioned to design and build the sculptures, based on the specimens of bones that had been discovered by Richard Owen."

Vesper caught on to his slight derision of the man's name. "You don't care for the gentleman?"

"Owen claimed many ideas were his own when they

weren't, but he's Prince Bertie's man so he gets what he wants." He gestured to a creature that had spines along its back. "You'll be happy to know that some of the statues, like the Ichthyosaurs and the *Plesiosaurus*, were born out of specimens discovered by Mary Anning, an avid fossil collector who often went unrecognized because she was female."

"Why does that not surprise me?" she said. "Our brains are so pitiably minuscule, after all. How dare a woman trespass upon male science?"

"Put your claws away," he told her with a laugh. "Mary Anning was brilliant in my book even if she went unrecognized for her contributions."

Vesper pointed at two creatures that lay half submerged in the water with elongated snouts. "Those look like giant crocodiles."

"You have a good eye. Yes, they were thought to be similar, only these were much larger. Evolution is an interesting phenomenon." He paused. "What we learn from the past can impact both the present and the future, if we choose to listen and change."

Her eyebrows rose. "Are we still talking about prehistoric creatures, Your Grace?"

"Yes, of course," he replied with an innocence that made her eyes narrow. "What did you think I was talking about?"

"It sounded personal."

"This is a passionate subject for me," he said.

They continued walking along the trail, and he pointed out the model cliffs and bedrock, explaining that everything had been constructed to match the geological rock the specimens had been found in. There was even a cave with stalagmites and stalactites.

"How did you get into this field?" she asked when they stopped to rest near one creature's hindquarters. The gigantic monster was facing away from the trail, its back covered by a row of vicious looking spines, and Vesper couldn't help but shudder at the sight.

"I found a book in my father's library by Gideon Mantell and would spend hours reading the notes my father had written in the margins." He patted the monster they stood beside. "This is *Hylaeosaurus*, which appears in that book, and my favorite of all the statues. I suppose in addition to Austen, Shelley, and Brontë, my father loved science, too. After he died, it was a way for me to be close to him. Like the same things he liked, I suppose."

Her eyes met his, and Vesper almost staggered at the emotion in them. Greydon never usually allowed himself to be this vulnerable. Vesper realized that he might have brought her here for a much deeper reason—he was giving her a glimpse into who he was—a boy who had lost his father and found a way to connect with him beyond his death.

Despite her desire to keep herself aloof, her heart swelled with sympathy and warmth. "I'm sorry you didn't get more time to spend with him."

"As am I. He was a brilliant man."

So are you.

Vesper nearly choked on the words that rested on the tip of her tongue. Instead of being bored, she found herself fascinated by his depth of knowledge. There was nothing to say for it—a smart man wielded a deadly kind of seduction.

Wait, no. She did not want to be more attracted to him because of his very capable brain! On the contrary, she needed him to be dull and uninteresting. She needed to salvage her rapidly fraying willpower.

Vesper frowned when he ducked under the dinosaur. "Why are you doing this, Aspen?"

Out of sight, his disembodied voice drifted back to her.

"Because I wanted you to see something I love." He reappeared behind her, grabbing her about the waist and making her squeal. A long arm snaked around her middle and Vesper forgot to breathe. "Besides fighting for change in the Lords, digging up old bone beds, and anything drearier you might assume of me."

"I don't think you're dreary," she admitted, his warm frame doing things to her that made it difficult to form a coherent thought. She craned her neck to glance at him. "I think you're very clever and that your father would have been very proud of your publication on one of his favorite subjects."

His brown eyes glinted, lips curling upward. "You've read my work?"

"Effie provided me with a copy."

"I am shocked," he said, but she could hear the smile in his voice.

Vesper's eyes narrowed. "Because I can read?"

"Because you care," he said in a low, husky voice.

She blinked. "No, that's not—"

Hard hips pressed into hers from behind, making her lose focus for a moment. God, he was so big. She loved when he surrounded her like this, all long limbs and broad shoulders, his bigger body commanding and so deliciously protective.

No, no, no. No commanding, nothing of the sort!

But pulling away would be rude and hurtful. He'd just bared his heart. He deserved a tiny bit of physical comfort, and besides, they were quite alone for the moment. She could endure his embrace for a minute or two...for *his* sake, of course. She wasn't soulless!

It was the right thing—the pious thing to do. A very wicked voice in her head pointed out that what she was feeling wasn't pious in the least. Her nipples were peaked, her stomach felt weak, and her breaths were so shallow it was a wonder she hadn't swooned from a significant lack of air.

Hot breath gusted against her ear as he lowered his lips to graze them. "Admit it, Viper, you *like* me."

"I do like you, as a friend." Heavens, did her voice normally sound so throaty?

The duke bit the upper shell of her ear, and she let out a ragged exhale. "Don't lie to me. You like me more than a friend. Ask me how I know?"

"How do you know?"

His fingers traced her rib cage beneath the muslin of her dress, grazing tantalizingly close to the mounds of her breasts. Vesper never imagined she could feel anything through the constricting corset, but the man's touch was a brand, incinerating fabric and whalebone like he was some preternatural god of fire. "Your heart races whenever I touch you. Your body has its own conversation with mine, letting me know what it wants."

"What does it want?" she whispered.

"You already know."

She *did*. Heaven help her, she did. It craved his with a fierce yearning that left her boneless. She could feel the hot press of him against her back, and all she could think about was how he'd felt inside her. Liquid heat pooled between her legs, dampening her at the juncture of her thighs. Her skin burned, her muscles quivered. Oh *yes*. Her body was desperate for his.

"Tell me what you need, Vesper," he whispered, licking the lobe of her ear and making her whimper.

"You."

It was a shameless sound, but so was the primal satisfaction in his guttural, growled reply. "Good. Remember that."

Vesper frowned. Remember that when? But then his

teeth were scraping against the lobe of her ear, his hips were pressing into hers, and he was sucking her flesh into the hot depths of his mouth, and she couldn't think. Not even when he walked them forward until they were pressed up against part of the enormous stone carvings. His huge body crowded hers, and she gasped into the stone, half from surprise and half from excitement. Desire soared up her spine.

"Greydon, what are you doing? There are people about. We are out in the *open*!"

Though they had passed a few visitors to the gardens earlier, Vesper hadn't seen a soul in a long while, but that didn't mean more wouldn't come. This was a public park—they could be discovered at any moment. For some reason, that only seemed to increase the illicit thrill of his embrace. Or the fact that she desired him more than she'd ever desired anything or anyone in her life. Was it so wrong to take this moment for herself? To have this *one* thing before she had to give him up forever?

"There's nobody here." He breathed her in, his nose going to her nape, trim hips deliberately rolling into her arse. She gulped when she felt her own spine bow in vulgar, delicious response. "Tell me to stop," he whispered. "Tell me you don't want me."

She ground back against him, making them both gasp. "I believe, Your Grace, you told me not to lie to you."

Chapter Twenty-Three

They didn't have much time and Aspen didn't intend to waste a single second of it. He wedged a knee in between her legs, pressing them apart. He relished in the moan that tore from her lips. Pulling her a fraction back toward him, he delved his left hand into her bodice, finding one nipple taught and tight, and so aroused it made his groin swell even more. Hell he was fit to bursting already.

"You have magnificent breasts," he said, filling his palm with her flesh. With a growl of need and wishing his mouth were where his hand was, Aspen licked and bit into the muscle at the juncture of her neck and shoulder.

Then he pinched her nipple gently, soliciting another sultry moan, and rolled the tip between his thumb and forefinger. His other hand went south, sliding over the curve of her hip and yanking up the fabric of her dress until his fingers met warm silk stockings. He didn't linger, climbing toward hot bare skin and cupping the round cheek above her thigh. Aspen squeezed, his mouth watering.

Fuck it, he had to taste her.

"Hold the stone," he ordered in a gravelly, guttural voice he barely recognized.

Vesper peered over her shoulder at him, blue eyes glazed with lust. "Why?"

But Aspen didn't answer in words, instead dropping to his knees and wedging himself under her skirts and petticoats. The scent of her arousal drove him mad, but he found what he was looking for and bit her right on the fleshy part of her lush behind. The muffled noise she made was indecent.

Aspen grinned when her hips canted back, telling him without words what she wanted. Sliding his fingers between her parted thighs, he found her drenched. He slid a finger into her tight passage, even as he pressed kisses to her hot skin. He teased her mercilessly, enticing her to jut her hips out with each plunge.

Emboldened by her whimpers, he coaxed her legs even wider and bent his head to the saturated length of her sex. She was a summer ocean and sunshine. Butterscotch drizzled with sea salt. Fuck, he'd never get enough of her but every second they spent tempting fate was a risk.

After one last sweet indulgence, he rose, but kept her skirts tangled in his fist and her plump arse exposed. Goddamn but her beauty was a sight to behold. All flushed rosy skin and lush curves, those bare cheeks on full display, skirts hitched over her hips, hands grasping the stone like a voracious sybarite.

"You're so fucking gorgeous like this," he said. "And you taste even better." Vesper turned her head toward him, lips parted and face crimson. He loved her like this, bold and wanting. "I could dine on you forever," he said, licking his lips.

Her blush intensified as she visibly fought for control, eyes sliding shut as if she couldn't bear a single second more of seeing his glistening mouth. "You are very blunt, Your Grace."

"Oh, is it Your Grace now?" He undid his trousers with one hand, freeing his aching cock. He pressed himself between the crease of her thighs, using one hand to angle her hips up. "Say my name, Vesper."

"Greydon," the minx said in a teasing lilt.

He rolled his pelvis, letting the crown of his staff notch against her soaked entrance and then stopped. "You were saying?"

She ground herself backward, her spine bowing even more. "Aspen, please."

"That's better." He rewarded her with one firm push, making them both moan in unison. He wasn't that far off shattering, and from the sound of her and the *feel* of her, neither was she. This wouldn't be slow and gentle. No, Aspen took her hard, their coupling animalistic and raw, but she wasn't complaining.

Voices drifted toward them in the distance, but he only quickened his strokes.

"Aspen," she panted. "I hear people."

"I know," he said.

"They'll see us."

He ground into her. "They won't."

Vesper chanted his name, meeting him thrust for impassioned thrust, and then he felt her body tighten on his, her inner muscles almost shoving him out as she flew over the edge into bliss. The sensual waves undid him, and he groaned his own release, pulling out to spend on the ground.

Breathing hard, Aspen exhaled with pleasure into her damp nape. Once he'd caught his breath, he reached into his pocket for a handkerchief, patting her dry between her thighs before dropping her skirts back into place and putting himself to rights. He kicked some dirt over the damp earth at his feet.

Red-cheeked, Vesper turned to face him, just as the approaching voices grew louder. "That was too close," she muttered. "What were we thinking?"

He winked, making her scowl at him, and cleared his throat, pointing toward one of the spines and adopting a scholarly expression as if he hadn't just fucked her right into the creature's front leg. "As you can see, my lady, the *Hylaeosaurus*'s back is heavily armored. The dorsal spines are the largest and longest up top."

Catching on, Vesper smoothed her hair and strolled idly around to the opposite side where a small group of well-dressed visitors had congregated. "What does *Hylaeosaurus* mean and would it eat people, do you think?"

"It means forest lizard, and no, it is a plant eater."

She nodded thoughtfully. "And how does one determine whether one of these creatures is an eater of meat or plants?"

Arching a brow, Aspen licked his own lips, making her blush. "By their teeth. They're either pointy to tear through meat or flat to grind vegetation."

"Fascinating."

Nodding to the newcomers, they wandered away from the beast, only to be met by the marquess and marchioness, who had arrived on the heels of the group.

"We lost you," Lady Marsden exclaimed, a perceptive gaze darting between them. "What have you two been up to and why on earth are you so flushed, Vesper dear?"

Vesper's face felt as though it had been on fire for a decade. She was blushing at every little bloody thing and her stampeding heart had yet to settle in her breast. She pressed her fists to her cheeks, willing them to cool.

Never one to miss anything out of the ordinary, Laila

sent her another pointed look, which Vesper tried valiantly to ignore. It prompted her friend to sidle over, take her arm, and pretend to want to show her something at the edge of the lake. The minute they were far enough away from the men, she pounced.

"You have a look about you," Laila whispered with narrowed eyes. "Out with it, wench."

"What kind of look? I do not have a look. You're imagining things." Vesper felt her stupid face heat and ground her teeth. Dear God, her nipples were still budded and a pulse still throbbed between her damp thighs. No wonder she had a *look*. It was that of a woman pleasured until she'd nearly fainted.

Laila's eyes went to slits at the protests that sounded thin even to Vesper's own ears. Her stupid cheeks heated more and she cursed her fair skin to high heavens. "I can see right through you, Vesper Lyndhurst, and I know you did something untoward with Greydon. Did he kiss you? Take liberties?"

"Define liberties," Vesper asked weakly.

Laila's eyes went so round, they almost popped from her face. "Oh, you cheeky little heathen, what did you do?"

Vesper didn't even want to think about what she and the duke had done because every second of the too-scandalous interlude would be written all over her face. The way he'd taken her had been so deliciously wicked, so primal as if his animal instincts—and hers—had emerged like the prehistoric beast they'd been hidden behind.

Forcing herself to remain calm, Vesper regarded her friend and decided to turn the tables—the best defense was a better offense. "What did *you* and Marsden do? Some chaperone you turned out to be."

Now it was Laila's turn to blush, her brown cheeks going a

deep ruddy color. "We are married. Suffice it to say that there was a tree, a very large tree. Now you."

"There was a large dinosaur leg."

Laila's mouth fell open as she burst into laughter, drawing the attention of the two men who were talking about one of the sculptures. Vesper didn't dare meet the duke's eyes for fear of what she'd see there. She kept her gaze on the waterline.

"So," the marchioness prodded. "He had you up against its leg and...?"

"Honestly, Laila, do you require me to spell it out for you?" Her best friend gaped as Vesper's unspoken meaning sank in, shock flitting across her expressive features. Dark eyes widened and her jaw hung slack. "You're going to catch flies if you leave your mouth open like that."

"Vesper, you didn't," Laila whispered. "You're not wed."

"So?"

The worry on Laila's face was real. "So if this gets out, you'll be ruined."

Vesper caught Laila's hand and squeezed. "That was my choice. I wanted it to happen. And please tell me you don't believe in any of that archaic hogwash, Laila. You and Marsden copulated before the wedding."

"We were engaged!"

Vesper shrugged. "And he could have cried off at any time. If you believed in such an antiquated thing as ruination, you would not have done it. Our bodies belong to us, Laila. We should choose what we get to do with them and with whom." She bit her lip. "Also, this wasn't the first time."

Laila seemed to be frozen in shock, then she blinked rapidly. "You've lain with him before? *When?*" The last word emerged like a whisper screech.

"The *Touch of Midas* ball," she replied. "It just happened. Neither Aspen nor I planned it."

"*Aspen*, is it?" With a sound of exasperation, Laila shook her head. "I always miss all the fun. Effie and Briar had mentioned something about you disappearing, but none of us would have ever guessed it was with Greydon!" She blinked. "I thought you two were merely friends? At least when it suited you."

"We were—*are*—friends," she said slowly. "But I've begun to think the infatuation I had with him when we were children never truly went away."

Still bemused, Laila turned back the way they'd come, her eyes widening in sudden understanding when they locked onto the *Hylaeosaurus*. "Wait, was that the *one*? Oh my God, of course it was." Laughter erupted from her in gasps and wheezes as she doubled over, holding her sides and practically convulsing with mirth.

"Why is that so funny?"

Wiping her streaming eyes, Laila snorted. "That poor creature might never recover. Good Lord, you made the beast with *three* backs!"

Her bloody cheeks didn't even have a chance against the crude sexual innuendo, and Vesper went crimson. "Hush! Greydon and Marsden will hear you."

Laila nodded, her expression sobering as she leaned in. "Did you take precautions with your two lovers?"

"Yes, Mother," Vesper replied and rolled her eyes. "I do not intend to birth a child out of wedlock. Of the human or stone variety."

"You are absurd."

"You started it."

They burst into laughter, clutching each other to keep from toppling over. "Do you not plan to marry him?" Laila asked with a frown when she'd calmed again.

"I cannot."

"Why? It's obvious that you fancy him, and he hasn't stopped glancing over since you've been here with me. He looks at you like Marsden looks at me, like you're his sun, moon, and stars, the breath in his lungs, and all the beautiful things the poets say."

"He told me he loved me," Vesper admitted softly.

Laila brightened. "That's even better. He's your match in every way, Ves. In fact, I've never seen a pair so perfect for each other." She smiled, dark eyes gleaming. "He's the only man who can stand up to a woman as stubborn as you and adore you for the capricious creature you are. He's a friend of Lushing's, Marsden's, *and* your father's. That's a ringing endorsement of a gentleman's character if I've ever heard one."

Vesper inhaled and her lungs burned, or perhaps that was her heart withering. "I can't marry him, Laila."

"That's ballocks. Why not?"

In a quiet rush of words, Vesper explained the situation with Greydon's mother, the threat the duchess had made, and the fact that the odious woman was holding the funds from the charity ball over Vesper's head.

"That is despicable!" Laila exclaimed. "How dare she? She can't do that to her own son, and that's not *her* money. Doesn't she have a soul? They're children, for God's sake."

"What's despicable?" her husband asked since she'd shouted it to all and sundry and he strode toward them, the sharp-eyed Duke of Greydon not too far in his wake.

Vesper was shaking her head, trying to meet Laila's eyes to tell her not to say anything more, but Laila was too outraged to notice. "The dowager duchess is blackmailing Vesper to stay away from Greydon by threatening to commit him. *And* she's holding back the funds meant for the Ragged School Union."

"She's *what*?" The words were soft and menacing, and the question was directed toward her, Vesper knew.

She let out a breath, upset that it had to come out in such a manner but relieved nonetheless. "It's worse than it sounds, I assure you. She told me she had everything she needed to get rid of you just as she'd done with your father, unless I was able to convince you to marry Judith."

"And just how did she imagine she'd pull off this scheme?" he asked in a quiet, dangerous voice.

Vesper's throat worked. "Records from doctors, claiming a biological affliction."

Marsden swore aloud. "That bitch."

A muscle flexing in his cheek, Aspen stared at Vesper, rage tightening his features. "And you agreed?" he asked softly.

"I couldn't let her do that to you," Vesper whispered, her voice clogged with tears. "That's why I accepted Eldridge." She eyed him in silence, noticing that Marsden had dragged a reluctant Laila away. "And the children need that money we raised at the ball. More than ever now that dozens have been displaced by that fire. Money that your mother is holding ransom. I didn't know what else to do, Aspen."

"You could have come to me! Told me the truth," he said and raked a hand through his hair. "I've had a private detective working with Scotland Yard to track down those responsible for months. They confessed to what they'd done. My mother has no leg to stand on, and any supposed documentation from her crooked doctor or apothecary are fraudulent."

Vesper blinked in surprise. "Well, I didn't know that."

The duke sighed, those brown eyes fairly simmering with hurt. "I wish you trusted me, Vesper. We could have faced it together."

"I'm sorry. I thought I could get you back to the United

States…that this was what you wanted. You were always going to leave. Don't you understand? It made sense. You and Judith would both be safe, and everyone would get what they wanted."

But not her.

Vesper shoved a curl that had come loose behind her ear and struggled not to give in to the burn of tears behind her eyelids. It was obvious he'd proposed only out of male pride or perhaps even some misguided notion of honor that she deserved more than Eldridge. "You don't truly want to be here, I know you don't." She waved an arm gesturing between their bodies. "This was simply a passing diversion."

"What the devil are you saying?" he bit out. "I'm not a man led around by his cock, Vesper. I thought you…*fuck*! You're bloody impossible and oblivious to what's right in front of you." He looked at her then, his eyes wide and glistening. "I am in love with you. I want you…today and every bloody day ahead. Not Judith. Not anyone else. You."

Emotions roiling, she could only stare at him. There was no artifice in his expression. No games. No lies. "Aspen…"

Instead of words, he responded with his lips, and for a heartbeat, Vesper didn't care that the Marquess of Marsden was a stone's throw away or that her best friend was probably throwing her fist into the air in glee…or even that other passersby would be ogling a man's very possessive, territorial display in the middle of the prehistoric swamp. All she could feel was the demanding press of his mouth, his tongue sweeping inside to punish hers for keeping secrets he'd deemed she shouldn't have. She fought back, stroke for stroke, unwilling to give in to the pleasure cresting up her spine and over her skin.

"Enough," she gasped when she couldn't breathe. "I will not cede to your…tongue tyranny!"

He arched a brow, amusement curling his reddened mouth. "Tongue tyranny? I seem to recall you enjoying my brand of tyranny between your thighs well enough, Viper."

"Do *not* bring that up," she said with a ferocious blush that she felt from the roots of her hairline to the tips of her toes.

"Why?"

"Because we are in public." She wanted to kick her own arse at her faulty reasoning—they'd been *in public* when he was doing unspeakably wicked things to her body—and the duke's answering smirk confirmed he was thinking the same thing.

"I told you, my heart has been yours for a long time, and I don't care who knows it," he said. "Whether you choose to believe that doesn't make it any less true." He punctuated that as well as the next three words with kisses. "I. Am. Yours."

Vesper's head was shaking before she could stop it and she parted her lips to protest. Once more, she was stalled by the unsubtle stamp of his mouth upon hers. He kissed her so soundly that her entire world drilled down to the existence of her senses—sight, taste, touch, sound, and scent—in a matter of seconds, all possessed by him.

"Every time you try to protest, I will kiss you."

"Kissing is no—" He promptly silenced her with his mouth again.

"We will fix this together, Viper," he said, giving her a moment to catch the breaths he'd stolen.

"But—"

"No buts." The devil had the audacity to smirk. "Unless it's the one I've had the delectable pleasure of sinking my teeth into."

The double meaning registered, and she went hot. Blast her infernal blushes! "Is sexual intercourse the only thing you think about?"

"On occasion, I think about other things." His eyes glinted wickedly. "Though, for the record, I'm not a lover who likes to share...I am a two-back kind of man."

Two-back? What in the world?

She was going to die of complete and utter mortification. "You dreadful wretch! Were you eavesdropping on our private conversation?"

"It was difficult not to. I had to stop Marsden from rushing over here when it looked like his wife was going to suffocate from laughing so hard." The duke took her hand, his face earnest. "I am here with you, Vesper. Trust me, please, even though I might have given you ample course not to in the past, but trust me now to catch you when you're falling. I'm not going anywhere." When she hesitated, he grinned. "Besides, you owe me."

She blinked. "I owe you?"

"You broke my nose."

"This again?" She shook her head, eyes darting to that strong slope with the slightest of bumps near the bridge. "I didn't break it. I only bent it a little."

"And you locked us in the attic," he added.

Vesper stuttered. "I didn't know the bloody lock was broken!"

"I seem to only be hearing excuses, Lady Viper."

"Fine, Lord Ass. Have it your way, and when the dowager brings hell down on your head, remember that you begged for this."

"I'd face hell for you any day," he said softly.

Chapter Twenty-Four

"The Duke and Duchess of Greydon," the Marquess of Marsden's majordomo announced.

"I like the sound of that," Aspen whispered to the statuesque, elegant woman at his side.

"We are not actually married you know," Vesper reminded him, keeping her practiced, perfect smile in place. "This is all for show."

He chuckled under his breath. But that didn't stop him from wishing it were true.

The strains of music died and the entire ballroom went so quiet, a cleared throat would sound like an explosion. Aspen had flawlessly timed their arrival right between dancing sets, and under direction from the marquess, the majordomo had performed as requested. Chatter screamed its way to the ceiling in a rising crescendo as faces spun toward them with varying expressions—from shock to disbelief to glee at the slightest whisper of scandal, but there was one face in particular that he was looking for.

He found it.

His mother was predictably livid. The dowager made sure everyone knew it when she was displeased and displeased didn't even begin to cover the storm brewing on her pinched face. Aspen fought to stifle his gratification. If anything, the chatter making its way through the crowd would be enough to rattle her. He needed her to feel that she was one step behind.

"Mother," he greeted her when they descended the stairs after exchanging pleasantries with their hosts for the evening. "May I present my wife, Her Grace, Lady Vesper Drake, the Duchess of Greydon."

Vesper, for her part, looked as serenely beautiful as ever, blond hair curled in fetching golden ringlets against her temples, face aglow, and posture flawless. She made the perfect duchess—no surprise there considering she was born for the role. Despite her initial reluctance to go along with his brilliant plan of a fabricated marriage to unsettle the dowager, Vesper had eventually capitulated to his logic—it was the only way his mother could be beaten at her own game. Aspen absolutely intended to convince the love of his life of his devotion, but one hurdle at a time.

"Your Grace," Vesper said with her usual elegance. "Or should I say Mother."

Aspen nearly cackled at the audacious delivery. Thin nostrils flaring, the dowager's mouth pinched further. "A word, Greydon."

"Say your piece here, *Mother.* We have nothing to hide from anyone. We wed in secret via special license for many reasons, and no, before you can accuse either one of us of something untoward, she is not with child." He reached for Vesper's hand and she took his without hesitation. "Not yet, though we cannot actually be sure."

He felt the sharp scrape of nails against the inside of his palm and nearly grinned. She might be calm on the inside, but his little viper was anything but.

"In *private*," the dowager hissed. "I insist."

"It's all right, Aspen," Vesper said in a soft voice, peering up at him with a smile, and he couldn't help letting his affection show with a kiss to her brow. His mother soured even more at their casual intimacy. "These matters are of a personal nature, after all, and we are in a public ballroom. Shall we?" She glanced over her shoulder to her friend and hostess, who was standing nearby. "Laila, is there somewhere we can adjourn?"

"You can use the library," the Marchioness of Marsden said and nodded to a nearby footman to escort them. The anticipation in the ballroom as they left was thick, chatter rising and falling in excited waves. Everyone wanted to be a part of what was certain to become the next scandalous on-dit. Speculative whispers were already hitting the rafters.

Had they been courting?

Why all the secrecy?

Was the lady with child?

When they were shown to the library, his mother and his wife had barely taken places at opposite ends of the room before the door was pushed open and his ward entered.

"Is it true?" Judith asked, her eyes wide with unhidden delight. "People are saying you've married."

Aspen nodded. "We have."

"Come in, Judith," the dowager said with a pointed look toward Vesper. "She has a right to be here as well."

Vesper only canted her head with gracious elegance. "Good, because we are expecting my family as well."

The door opened again and the Duke of Harwick and the Earl of Lushing appeared. His new brother-in-law wasted no time in slapping him on the back with a wide grin. "So we're brothers for real now!"

"It appears congratulations are in order, I am told," the duke said, offering a gentle, fatherly smile.

"Harwick, you knew of this?" his mother demanded.

Vesper's father didn't know all the details, but he was smart enough to figure out that something was afoot. "No, but anyone coming within two feet of the two of them was at risk of getting singed. Their connection is undeniable. It was only a matter of time before they realized it themselves."

"This is preposterous," the dowager exclaimed. "Greydon is promised to Judith."

"I do not recall agreeing to such an arrangement," Aspen said and glanced to where Judith was sitting beside his mother. "Do you, Judith?"

Her gaze darted to the expectant stare of the dowager and quailed at the frost gathering there. "I...er...maybe?"

His mother scowled but sat straighter. "You see! This is ludicrous. This vulgar excuse of a marriage must be annulled at once...and any bastard born on the wrong side of the blanket is not in line to inherit."

Vesper stiffened in affront, though she kept her lips pressed together, eyes on him. Aspen studied the woman who had given birth to him, but who remained a veritable stranger. She was selfish to the core, only concerned with her own welfare. "Why do you wish me to marry Judith so desperately, Mother? A highborn wife is a highborn wife, and Lady Vesper is of exceptional pedigree."

"Judith has an excellent dowry."

Both he and Judith blinked, though she was the first to speak. "I do?"

"The inheritance was put in trust from your mother to me when she became ill. Forty thousand pounds. If you made an advantageous match, the funds would go to your husband."

"To Greydon," Judith said slowly.

Aspen let out a breath. "Not exactly. If I hadn't returned and she had been successful in declaring me dead, she would have married you off to Eustace. With the help of her trusty steward, who would drain the accounts at her request, your money would have been hers." He tutted in deep thought. "It's too bad then that I've told Vesper she can keep her rather obscene dowry. It's only right, considering what you, and consequently I, owe her."

"What *I* owe her?" the dowager spat. "I owe her nothing."

He lifted a brow, keeping his temper under tight rein. Losing it would be exactly what she wanted as it would allow her to play the role of victim yet again. "I'm speaking of the money from the charity ball. I told her that she must have been mistaken in what she heard. No one would be so cold-hearted as to withhold money from destitute orphans on purpose, would they? However, seeing that those funds were urgently required because of the church fire, I encouraged Vesper to use her dowry to get the money to where it was needed."

"That is not what happened," his mother said quickly. "The money was mistakenly placed into my accounts and would have taken time to resolve. That was all."

Vesper bristled beside him at the lies, but he gave her a reassuring glance before waving his arm. "Regardless, it's of no import. Thanks to recent lucrative investments, the ducal estates are whole and functional. As duke and Judith's guardian, I declare that Judith can keep her dowry and use it however she pleases."

Delight lit Judith's eyes, and Aspen fought his smile. He knew exactly what she was going to do with her forty-thousand-pound fortune—travel to her heart's content. As long as she was safe and happy, he did not care what she did with her inheritance. It was hers, after all.

The dowager let out a snarl of rage. "You cannot do that."

"Actually, I am the duke and I can."

"How dare you?" she seethed.

"I dare nothing, Mother. You are the one who depends on unscrupulous schemes to get what you want. You and I both know you falsified that doctor's statement about Father's condition. Moral insanity? All because he did not want to be your social puppet?"

"You do not know that of which you speak," she said, hand flying to her chest. "He was a danger to you."

"I have found Dr. Parker and Mr. Rhodes," he said quietly. "The doctors who supported your insanity case were apprehended by Scotland Yard and confessed everything."

At that, she paled, her countenance going ashen before her stare darted around the room. If she was looking for clemency, there was none to be had.

"Shall I tell you what those two men imparted, Mother? Though I am sure you already know, considering you paid them both significant sums to lie. Dr. Parker maintained, on your order, that the duke suffered from congenital mental deficiency. I also found it quite odd that Father had no memory of entering Camberwell." He stood and walked to the window. "Dr. Parker had interesting things to say about that—specifically a significant and sustained dosage of laudanum he'd prescribed Father."

She swallowed, her throat working. "Greydon, your father was in excellent hands at Camberwell. He played chess and cards, could play tennis and badminton, and even had his own private library. Any medicine was administered for his own good and your safety."

Aspen ignored her lies. "What's even more interesting is what the attendant, the fine and upstanding Mr. Rhodes, had to say about being encouraged in his use of punishment, including restraints, cold baths, and seclusion in a padded cell." Aspen paused, bile filling his throat at what his father had endured on *her* directive. "All arranged by you to ensure he'd never leave."

"The duke was violent!" she bit out. "Melancholy one moment and manic the next."

"I would be, too, if I was isolated for days on end with nothing but memories of the life that had been stolen from me to keep me company."

She reached for him. "You don't understand, Greydon. I was protecting you."

"Enough, Mother. *Enough.*" Aspen was sick of the charade. "After I made it clear that they would be charged and shipped off to a penal colony, both men signed sworn statements, which I have in my possession. You, on the other hand, are a different matter." He bared his teeth. "And to think you planned to do the same to me... your own flesh and blood."

For the first time since she'd entered the room on the highest of horses, the dowager looked afraid of how far she might fall. "What will you do?"

"You can either go to court and face your crimes or you will retire quietly to the country and stay there. Live out the rest of your days in solitude and peace in Dorset. It's more than you deserve."

She gasped, a hand flying to her throat. "You cannot be serious! I have connections and influence! No one will stand for this. I will not be banished like some mouse."

"As you wish," he said mildly. "I will make arrangements with my solicitor to prepare the evidence for court. You will be taken into police custody. I give my word that you will be treated with respect."

Aspen turned and gestured to Vesper as if he intended them to take their leave. It was a gamble, of course, but he was banking on the fact that his dear mother would do anything to avoid jail. Such a scandal would destroy her reputation and tarnish her beyond repair. At least in Dorset, she could maintain the illusion of her influence however she wished as long as she stayed there.

"No, Greydon, wait. Please." Her voice was weak. "I agree to the country."

He glanced at her, expression cold. "You violate this agreement in any way, shape, or form, Mother, and you will be held responsible for your actions, do you understand?"

With a contrite nod, the dowager looked so small and defeated, but Aspen knew it was a performance. It was clear in the way that she glared at Vesper out of the corner of her eye and made even clearer when she let out a low snarl as if unable to contain herself.

"I mean it," he said. "And this is nothing to do with Vesper. It has to do with me. With the rot that has plagued our family."

Her mouth peeled away from her teeth as she glared at his wife. "You'll never be a fit duchess for him. I will see that you never get another invitation, even if I'm locked away in the country."

Vesper lifted a haughty brow and laughed. "That might concern me if I was actually Greydon's duchess."

The bombshell fell and detonated...making them the focus of four pairs of astounded stares.

His mother gaped. "You're *not* married?"

"No. It was all part of his plan to rattle you a bit, nudge you off that golden perch you've made your home upon." She gave a graceful shrug. "In fact, I suspect that you might be the one in need of *my* support in the days to come, so make your choices wisely."

With her head high, Vesper walked from the room, and for a moment, Aspen wished again that they had truly been married. He would never be prouder to call anyone *wife* than her.

Leaning against the balustrade of the terrace, Vesper felt drained to the bone.

She gulped in mouthfuls of cool air into her tight lungs. The confrontation had been more intense than she'd anticipated. She felt for Aspen, most of all. No child should ever have to hear how much their mother didn't love them. His internal struggle had been obvious, at least to her, in the brace of his shoulders, the stiff hands, and the deep lines bracketing his lips. She'd wanted to hold him, comfort him, but had held her place as the performance had required.

She'd been his pretend duchess for the better part of an hour and nothing had ever felt so right.

Her Grace, Lady Vesper Drake, the Duchess of Greydon.

"I thought I'd find you out here," a voice said, and she turned to see a tentative Judith, who hovered near the balcony doors. "I hope you don't mind."

Vesper shook her head. "I just needed some air. That was . . . rather arduous."

"Very much so." Judith joined her and sighed. "So no wedding bells between you and Greydon, then? I have to admit, I had hoped it was real."

Me, too, Vesper wanted to say, but she shrugged weakly instead. "I don't want to stand in the way of his dreams. He intends to go back to the United States, and my place is here with my father. I could never leave him."

Judith shot her a sidelong glance. "People's dreams change, Lady Vesper, and I'm quite certain that Greydon intends to stay in London."

She swallowed. "He does? How do you know this?"

"You know for a purportedly very clever woman, you can be quite dense," Judith teased. "In case you haven't noticed, the duke has a new passion now." Vesper didn't want to hope what that could mean, but hope was an unruly thing. It spread like flames, and burned like them, too. They didn't speak for a few moments, but then Judith reached out to squeeze her hand. "I came out here because I also wanted to thank you."

"For what?"

"For your kindness. I always felt I didn't really have a place in London, and even though I know it can't have been easy for you to support a match for me with the duke, you were never cruel to me."

"I've always believed we women need to lift each other up."

Judith worried her lip. "I never loved him like that, you know. I care for him as a brother." Judith swallowed, drawing Vesper's attention. "But I don't have feelings for any... gentlemen."

Vesper's eyes widened when the young woman's clear gaze met hers. *Oh.*

Judith smiled. "Marriage to Greydon would have been nothing more than a pretense. But now he has given me my freedom and I intend to use it to live the way I want. Perhaps even love who I want as well."

She exhaled a sigh, and for a second, Vesper wondered at what the girl must have borne under the tutelage of Greydon's mother, hiding so much of herself away. "You should," Vesper murmured. "Love has a way of making space for us all."

"Not enough of us lift each other up in this world, and I am glad to know you."

"And I you, Judith."

After the younger girl took her leave, Vesper was alone once more with her churning thoughts. Not for long, however, as a bevy of footsteps clacked on the stone. "Greydon's on the hunt for you," Laila said, accompanied by Briar and Effie, who surrounded her like protective mother hens or protective

Hellfire Kitties, rather, with their claws on display. Only Nève, who'd recently given birth to a beautiful, healthy baby boy, was missing. "I've sent him on a wild goose chase, but sooner or later, he'll figure out where you are."

Vesper's heart both hammered and balked at that. She was much too agitated. She had no excuses to lean on now that the threat of the duchess had been eliminated... She had to face her own feelings for Aspen. Even though they were too loud, too chaotic. Too *intense.*

"How are you?" Effie asked, always in tune with anyone else's distress.

"A bit all over the place," she admitted. "I didn't expect Greydon's victory over the duchess to feel as good as it did."

"When you care for someone," Effie said, stroking a curl away from Vesper's cheek, "it's natural to feel their emotions as if they're your own. You do feel something for Greydon, don't you?"

Vesper nodded. "I think I love him."

Briar frowned, the most logical and pragmatic of them all. "Then what's the problem? Laila said he told you he loved you." Vesper wasn't even upset that Laila had told them—they had no secrets from each other.

"I don't know. I'm scared, I suppose." She pinned her lips, searching for the right words. "I always thought love was simple—a stare, a touch, a sonnet—but it can be much darker. It can consume. The way I feel around the duke overwhelms me. Like I'm being towed out to sea by a wave and I can barely keep my head above water, and yet there's nowhere else I'd rather be, nowhere else I feel so alive."

"Love *is* scary," Laila said. "But sometimes you have to trust your heart, trust that it will take you to where you need to be. What does it tell you?"

"Not to trust myself with anyone."

Her friends both scowled in unison. "That's your brain talking, not your heart," Laila said, while Effie nodded. "Choose what *you* want for once, Ves."

Maybe Aspen had been right. Matchmaking had always been safe because it involved other people. Putting herself into the equation and opening herself up to heartache was too much to bear. How did people do this? How did they make such chaos bearable? She sucked in a breath, reaching for the poise and sangfroid that had always served her well in the past.

"Do any of you have a carriage to loan me?" she asked them. "I think my father has left, and I have no idea where Lushing has disappeared to."

"Use mine, but you should talk to Greydon, not run away," Briar said with a frown, as if she knew that Vesper was going to do exactly that last part.

"Maybe later. I simply can't right now."

Her friends looked at her with varying expressions, but she knew they would always support her, just like she would always support them.

"I'll be fine, I promise," she whispered and tapped her temple. "There's too much noise in here and I need quiet."

"Send a footman if you need anything at all," Laila said.

"I will."

Thankfully, Vesper was able to slip out of the ball without anyone noticing her departure or her escape in the borrowed carriage. By the time she arrived home, she was a mess. Her eyes burned with the sting of unshed tears, and it felt like she had a gaping hole in her chest where her heart should be. And to top it off, it had begun to drizzle. All she wanted to do was get undressed, curl into bed with Cat, and sleep for a million years.

However, when she entered the house, it was to complete pandemonium. Lizzie looked frazzled, the maids were scurrying about, and even Stanley was wearing a disgruntled expression. Her father, who had returned home not long before she had, stomped into the foyer wearing a hat, cloak, and carrying an umbrella. "What's going on?" Vesper asked him.

"The bloody cat ran out when I got home. Streaked right past me."

Normally, Vesper wouldn't worry. Cats were resilient things, but the rain was coming down hard, and the truth was, she needed her furry friend more than anything.

Vesper walked over to the duke and put a hand out for the umbrella. "I'm still dressed as I've just come home. I'll go look for her. You stay here in case she comes back."

"It's pouring," her father said, frowning as if expecting to see someone else behind her. Vesper had a good idea who he expected, but she pretended not to notice his gaze or the fleeting look of disappointment when he realized there was no one there. Greydon wasn't her actual husband—there was no real reason for him to be there. "Let me go," he insisted.

"No, you stay. You know how that menace of a beast is. She'll only run from anyone else."

Before he could argue, Vesper left the house, hurrying down the steps and into the street. Hopefully the silly creature wouldn't have gone far. Briar's carriage had already left, and it was early enough that the square wasn't crowded. People were still out on the town, so the streets were empty of traffic. Rain cascaded down her head and into her face. She'd forgotten the dratted umbrella.

Whirling around to run back inside to retrieve it, she crashed into a broad, solid male chest, the air whooshing out of her as she grabbed hold of the only thing around her to steady herself—the owner of said chest.

"We have to stop meeting like this," Greydon said, his

voice rumbling through her like the sweetest sound. "Though I can't find it in myself to complain when you end up in my arms." He frowned down at her, the brim of his top hat blocking the rain from drenching his face. "What are you doing out here in this deluge?"

She squinted at him, but only got rain in her eyes for her efforts. "Cat ran away."

"Go inside," he said. "I'll find her."

"No, I'll come with you." His brows drew together, but before he could comment, she lifted a palm. "I'm already soaked, and I'm not being difficult. It will be quick if we divide and conquer. You take that way, and I will go this way."

Those brown eyes searching her face, he nodded, but then unfastened his coat. "Take this for warmth."

"What about you?" Vesper tried not to stare at the sleeves of his white shirt that were becoming increasingly transparent with each raindrop, outlining the sculpted, bulging muscles of his arms, but it was a losing battle.

"Keep looking at me like that," he said. "And Cat will have to wait."

Flushing, she tore her eyes away and pulled his coat tighter about her. It smelled like him, but she had no time to savor the scent as she headed away from the house, peering into nooks and crannies, and calling for Cat. Vesper had walked past three houses and there was no sign of the dratted feline. It was so wet and cold that she was beginning to shiver, even with Aspen's coat. Her heart sank as she turned and made her way back home, only to hear a victorious shout from the other end of the street.

"I've found her!"

With no small amount of relief, she ran toward the duke, who held a squirming, sad, bedraggled white bundle in his arms. “Oh, you silly thing!” Vesper cooed, taking her from him and cradling her to her soaked front. “Kittens and rain don’t mix.”

Within moments, they were all three inside the warm house, where Cat was swaddled up in a warm drying cloth and taken to the kitchen for a saucer of cream. Even her father looked happy to see that she was unharmed. The aggravating little brat had wormed her way into everyone’s hearts.

After Vesper and the duke were bundled in blankets to ward off the chill and she reassured her father that she was also well, he took his leave and went to bed. A roaring fire had been built in the grate and the room was blessedly warm. Vesper hung Aspen’s coat to dry and stood as close to the fire as she dared. “Thank you for saving Cat.”

“You’re welcome,” he replied. When she felt hands in her hair, she tensed, but it was only the duke releasing the pins. “It will dry faster,” he said in an oddly hoarse voice as he finger-combed through the long blond strands.

“Thank you.”

“Why did you leave?” he asked eventually.

“I was tired.”

He exhaled and turned to face her, the firelight flickering over his handsome features. “Why did you *really* leave?”

“I don’t know,” she whispered. “I suppose I was overwhelmed. All these opposing feelings barreling into me and it felt like I was spiraling out of control. I wanted to rail and scream at your mother for what she’d put you through. For how much she wronged you.” She rubbed a hand against her chest and remembered what Judith had said on the balcony. “I don’t want to be another woman who takes you away from your dreams, from what you love.”

A gentle palm curved around her nape, his voice raw and soft. “You’re my dream, Vesper. *You.* The only one I love.”

At his tender words, she couldn't speak past the lump that swelled in her throat. "Tell me, what do you feel now?"

"Safe. Happy. Quiet." Vesper angled her body sideways to the fire and swallowed, her eyes tracing the features that had become so beloved. Her voice was a whisper. "In love."

His eyes flared. "Love?"

"I don't know when it happened or how, but I've fallen for you, Aspen." Her gaze dropped, and only lifted when she felt his finger under her chin.

"Let me see those eyes when you say it," he said gruffly.

She let him see everything—her fears, her hopes, all her scattered and windblown emotions. "I love you."

"Finally!" He laughed, his fingers threading into the dried curls at her nape as he drew her toward him. Just before he kissed her, he paused, hovering over her lips. "Now will you agree to become my duchess?"

She pushed up to her tiptoes. "Kiss me first."

"I know your tricks. Agreement then kisses," he countered.

"Yes! I'm yours." Vesper wrapped her arms around his neck and draped herself against his hard body, her soft curves fitting perfectly to his. It felt like coming home. She arched a brow, leaned up, and bit his bottom lip. "Now kiss me like you mean it, Lord Ass."

Her duke grinned. "Don't I always, Lady Viper?"

It was true...he absolutely did.

Epilogue

Aspen's heart filled with pride as he watched his duchess being swarmed by a bunch of ragtag children in the schoolroom adjacent to the church. She had brought them baked treats today. Her patience astounded him, even as she kindly told them if they weren't polite, they would have to go to the back of the line. They calmed instantly.

With the money from her devoted charity efforts, the Ragged School Union was able to fund more toward the education of England's poor. Together with his aunt Angela, with whom Vesper had formed a tight bond, they didn't only work with children and the less fortunate but also with downtrodden women who needed refuge, care, and lodging. It was a wonder that she continued her philanthropic efforts in her condition, but as his intrepid, energetic bride said, troubles didn't stop simply because one was with child.

When she was finished, she walked over to bring him a tea cake, her rounded abdomen *just* beginning to show beneath the lines of her dress. They had talked about children early on and had hoped for them much later, but to their surprise, a few months after their very intimate wedding—close friends and family only—Vesper's courses disappeared.

Even though he was a scientist at heart, it amazed him to think that there was a small life growing inside her body. Women's bodies were truly miraculous.

"I brought you this cake," she told him. "But I've decided I want it for myself."

He smiled, pulling her toward him. Aspen liked having her close, the scent of her in his nostrils and her soft velvet skin under his fingertips. "Then you eat it, and I shall kiss you. You will taste like lemon cakes and we will both be satisfied."

Holding a half-eaten tea cake, she stared at him in revulsion. "That is disgusting."

"I have my tongue in your mouth all the time," he whispered.

She shook her head and made a nauseated face. "But not when I've just eaten. Ugh, take this." She thrust the remnants of the tea cake at him. "I've completely lost my appetite."

Aspen wanted to laugh, but he took the offering and popped it into his mouth.

Little things like this set her off all the time now. Certain scents had her rushing to the water closet or the nearest receptacle, and it wasn't the odors one would expect. At a musical, the soothing smell of cedar had made her eyes water, and then at the opera, she insisted there was a cloying smell of lavender, even though Aspen could detect nothing of the sort.

Half the time, he remained on edge wondering whether she would declare him and *his* scent untenable. Not wanting to sleep without her in his arms, he took great care to wash himself with the mildest of soaps, had given up kippers, and made sure never to get anywhere near anything that smelled like lilies, or God help everyone, lavender.

Once she'd finished saying her goodbyes to the vicar,

he escorted her to their waiting carriage. Normally, Vesper would go to her classes on her own with a footman in tow, but lately, he'd felt extra protective, mostly because she was running herself ragged. In the carriage, her face was pale, and her blue eyes didn't have their usual sparkle.

"I received a letter from Judith," she said before he could worry over her.

"Oh?"

His wife gave a tired nod. "She's met someone in Cairo. An archaeologist. Her name is Salma. They've been excavating together in Nineveh near the Tigris River and discovered the remains of an old palace and some fascinating art. She's happy."

Judith had confided in Aspen before she'd left London, and he was glad that she'd found someone to share her life with. "She's well then?"

"Sounds like it. They're hoping to visit when the baby is born."

Just then Vesper gave a loud groan and settled herself against the squabs, her face pinching in exhaustion. Aspen felt his worry expand. Tiny lines bracketed her eyes and mouth, hinting that she'd been working herself much harder in the last few weeks. He knew she loved to keep busy, but sometimes she pushed herself to unhealthy levels. He wanted her happy... but he also wanted her safe.

"Viper, I know we've talked about this, but you can't keep doing this at the expense of your health," he said gently. A flash of annoyance crossed her features, but then it disappeared as an expression of disgust replaced it. Aspen was across the coach to her side in a flash. "What is it? Do you feel unwell?"

She held her nose, face averted and breaths coming in shallow pants. "Goodness, I think that smell might be *you*."

"What...are you certain?"

"Heavens, yes. Don't come any closer or I shall cast up my accounts all over the floor of this coach!"

Aspen went still...his biggest nightmare come to life. How on earth was he supposed to stay away from his *wife* for months? He moved back to his side of the carriage and tried not to breathe or shift, or do anything that might cause her to retch. When she let out a stifled snort, his gaze flew up.

"Oh, good gracious, you should have seen your face!" She convulsed into peals of wicked laughter.

He stared. "Are you jesting right now?"

"Of course I am, you daft man." She hiccuped. "I'm not and will never be averse to your scent, though it has been quite entertaining watching you scrub yourself from head to toe every single day."

"You know you will pay for that, don't you?" His lips curled in a very wicked grin.

Those wan blue eyes of hers lit with a hint of flames. "That's been my nefarious plan all along. Distract me with orgasms."

It was a marvel they even made it back to their bedchamber at all. Once they arrived at home, her husband scooped her up into his arms and ferried her up the steps so quickly Vesper barely had time to blush. Thank God, too, because if she'd made eye contact with any of their servants, she would have been mortified. Not that those who ran the household didn't know what went on in the house at all hours.

Her very virile duke loved bedding her. And she loved it even more.

She loved his hands on her body, the noises he made when he touched her, the appreciation in his eyes whenever he looked at her—like she was something precious beyond belief. Vesper had no doubts that Aspen would make a wonderful father when their child was born. He was one of those men who had been built to love...even someone like her who drove him to distraction.

Her duke never made her feel as though she were a burden. Or her emotions too tumultuous. He accepted her wholly just as she was, quirks and all.

After shooing a disgruntled Cat away, who disappeared under the bed, Aspen set her gently down on the mattress, so much adoration in his eyes that she felt it like a tangible caress. He kissed her, his tongue stroking over her lips in the way that she loved. Quickly and carefully, he undressed her—outer layers, then inner ones—until she was naked before him.

"God, you're beautiful," he whispered. His hand drifted over her rounded abdomen. "Gorgeous and glowing."

"I think you have calf eyes, Your Grace," she said.

"My eyesight is perfect, as are you, my perfect match."

She exhaled. "I'm not perfect and you know it."

"Perfect for *me*." He bent to kiss the spot right below her navel. The touch was chaste, but that didn't stop a throb from pulsing lewdly in her core or the breathiest moan from escaping her lips. The duke's gorgeous tawny eyes met hers. "What does my duchess desire?"

"You without a stitch before nausea takes me."

Vesper had to bite back a giggle at how quickly he moved. She really was awful, provoking him like this. Some scents were terrible, but they were already getting better as the weeks passed, which the doctor had said would happen. Her nausea would lessen with time as the baby grew inside her.

Aspen hopped on one foot, tugging off his boot and removing a stocking, then nearly fell over getting rid of the second. Vesper appreciated the sculpted appearance of his arm and thigh muscles, the sight of that ridged abdomen never failing to arouse her. But when he turned, giving her a view of his broad back, followed by the firm globes of his arse and thick, hair-dusted thighs when he lost the trousers, she couldn't get enough air.

Vesper barely recognized her own voice. "Now, Aspen."

"As my lady wishes."

With that, he positioned himself and slid into her, the stretch excruciatingly delicious. Being with child seemed to heighten every sensation, and she felt every inch of him filling her to capacity. A gentle palm grazed over the curve of her belly before drifting lower to the apex of her pleasure. She let out an unseemly moan as he gave her what she wanted, stroke after stroke, not stopping when she screamed her first release and tumbled into her second. Only then did he allow himself to empty inside her, saying her name like a benediction as he came.

She barely felt it, moments or hours later, when he shifted them, lifting her up to the pillows and pulling the covers over her. "What are you doing?" she asked sleepily when he moved off the bed.

"Letting Cat out before she shreds the door in a fit."

"She hates us," Vesper said with a yawn.

"She doesn't," he replied, after climbing back into bed. "She's just a jealous beast who wants each of us for herself. We shall have to find her a companion."

"I'll ask Effie," Vesper said. It became so quiet in the room that she thought he'd fallen asleep. "You won't mind another cat, would you? My sneezing seems to have improved, though that could be because of the pregnancy."

He pulled her close. "Cats, dogs, hedgehogs, children, whatever you want. I just want you to be happy." Aspen kissed the top of her head. "You are, aren't you?"

Vesper considered her answer, her hand gliding over her tiny bump and giving it a fond pat. She did what she loved every single day, fulfilling her purpose and her dreams with Aspen's stalwart presence at her side. She had her family, her friends, and her health. She was married to a man who made her feel cherished every single day, a man who fought for care for the mentally unsound in Parliament, a man who accepted her with all of her idiosyncrasies and jagged edges, and never expected her to change. A man who *loved* her fully and unreservedly.

Who would always love her. Exactly *imperfectly* as she was.

She pressed a kiss to her husband's lips. "Happier than I ever could have dreamed."

"Excellent. My plan to keep you barefoot and pregnant is working."

Vesper snorted and poked him in the arm. "Do I have to remind you that we're not stuck in the Middle Ages? I have plans, Your Grace, to open a few more schools, now that Shaftesbury's amendment has been passed. I have no intention of sitting here on my laurels with child or without shoes." She glanced fondly at him, knowing he would never hold her back from doing anything she truly wanted to do. "And besides, you're going to be much too busy preparing for the new exhibition at the Crystal Palace to bother with me."

He kissed her. "Bite your tongue or I shall do it for you. I will never be too busy for my wife."

She succumbed to his kisses with a soft sigh. "I'm very proud of you."

"The feeling is very mutual, my love."

It was true: their lives were so full. Aspen was working on the extinction exhibit with two American paleontologists—Mr. Othniel Charles Marsh and Mr. Edward Drinker Cope. He'd met them in Berlin and was often a mediator between the two quarrelsome and very competitive professors. In addition, he was also hoping to recognize and showcase the findings of Mary Anning, including the *Plesiosaurus* she discovered in 1823. It was an ambitious project, but if anyone could do it, Aspen could.

Vesper loved hearing him talk about his passion for fossils...especially when he was wearing his spectacles. With his sleeves rolled up, of course. She suspected that was how they got with child in the first place. Who knew a pair of spectacles could enhance one's passions?

With a grin, she rolled to her back, her brain whirring to life once more.

Apart from the slight tarnish on her record—Mr. Cross had moved on to new employment and Mrs. Elway had ended up rekindling an old relationship—Vesper wasn't convinced she'd lost her knack for matchmaking. Evans and Georgina were thriving, despite the hard challenges of being new parents, and Judith had gone on to find the love she deserved.

Vesper let out a pleased sigh. "Now that I know what true happiness is, I want for all my friends to be this blissful. Briar and Effie deserve partners who will love them for who they are."

Briar was busy with her suffragette causes and Vesper didn't even want to think about the capricious relationship she had with Lushing. Her brother had almost had apoplexy at having to retrieve Briar from jail after she'd been arrested at a protest. Vesper had her suspicions that they'd worked out their issues in a more carnal way, but Briar was close-lipped about the whole thing. Those two would be a work in process.

Perhaps Effie would be the better choice. One couldn't surround oneself with animals and avoid people forever. How else would she meet her perfectly imperfect match? Effie was kind, clever, and rather eccentric, but she had a big heart. She would need someone who appreciated all her special qualities...and loved animals as much as she did. A smile spread across Vesper's lips...she had *so* many wonderful ideas!

Her duke propped himself to one elbow with an exasperated, if fond, expression. "Vesper, no."

She wore the most innocent look she could manage. "My matchmaking days are over, I promise." Then she grinned. "Then again, a little nudge or two won't hurt, will it?"

Acknowledgments

It takes a village to bring a book to life so the whole village must be thanked!

To the reigning queen of this particular village, my incredibly awesome editor, Amy Pierpont, thank you for making *Never Met a Duke Like You* into the best version it could be. Once more, you have pushed me out of my comfort zone, allowed me to improve and hone my craft, and made this story shine. I appreciate you so much!

To Thao Le, who is literally a diamond of the first water, I feel like I need to bellow my gratitude and adoration from the highest rooftops. Sincerely, you are absolutely brilliant and I'm beyond thankful that you're my agent. Thank you for everything!

Big thanks to Sam Brody, who is a legit rock star. Thanks for doing all you do, for being so supportive and awesome, and for getting me through these last rounds of edits. PB&J forever. Thank you to the production, editing, design, sales, and publicity teams at Forever for all your efforts behind the scenes, especially my PR maven, Dana Cuadrado.

A heartfelt thank-you to the amazing ladies in my writing circles who read my first drafts, listen to my histrionics, flail over book covers, commiserate over publishing, and send me kitty videos. I have all the love for you. Thank you for your friendship through thick and thin.

To all the readers, reviewers, influencers, booksellers,

librarians, educators, close family and extended family, as well as friends who support me and spread the word about my books, my very sincere thanks. I wouldn't be here without you.

Finally, to my beloved family, Cameron, Connor, Noah, and Olivia, thanks for being my biggest cheerleaders and making me so lucky to be a wife and mother. Team Howard forever!

Bridgerton meets *10 Things I Hate About You* in this spicy enemies-to-lovers Regency romance in the Taming of the Dukes series!

Available Fall 2024

About the Author

Amalie Howard is the *USA Today* and *Publishers Weekly* bestselling author of *The Beast of Beswick*, "a smart, sexy, deliciously feminist romance," and one of *Oprah Daily*'s "Top 24 Best Historical Romance Novels to Read" list. She is also the author of several critically acclaimed, award-winning young adult novels. An AAPI, Caribbean-born writer, she has written articles and interviews on multicultural fiction that have appeared in *Portland Book Review*, *Entertainment Weekly*, *Ravishly* magazine, and Diversity in YA.

When she's not writing, she can usually be found reading, being the president of her one-woman Harley-Davidson motorcycle club #WriteOrDie, or power-napping. She currently lives in Colorado with her husband and three children.

You can learn more at:

AmalieHoward.com
X @AmalieHoward
Facebook.com/AmalieHowardAuthor
Instagram @AmalieHoward
Pinterest.com/AmalieHoward
TikTok @AmalieHowardAuthor

Get swept off your feet by charming dukes and sharp-witted ladies in Forever's historical romances!

A SPINSTER'S GUIDE TO DANGER AND DUKES
by Manda Collins

Miss Poppy Delamare left her family to escape an odious betrothal, but when her sister is accused of murder, she cannot stay away. Even if she must travel with the arrogant Duke of Langham. To her surprise, he offers a mutually beneficial arrangement: a fake betrothal will both protect Poppy and her sister and deter Society misses from Langham. But as real feelings begin to grow, can they find truth and turn their engagement into reality—before Poppy becomes the next victim?

ALWAYS BE MY DUCHESS
by Amalie Howard

Because ballerina Geneviève Valery refused a patron's advances, she is hopelessly out of work. But then Lord Lysander Blackstone, the heartless Duke of Montcroix, makes Nève an offer she would be a fool to refuse. Montcroix's ruthlessness has jeopardized a new business deal, so if Nève acts as his fake fiancée and salvages his reputation, he'll give her fortune enough to start over. Only neither is prepared when very *real* feelings begin to grow between them...

Connect with us at Facebook.com/ReadForeverPub

Discover bonus content and more on read-forever.com

THE DUKE'S ALL THAT
by Christina Britton

Miss Seraphina Athwart never wanted to abandon her husband, but she did what was necessary to keep herself and her sisters safe. And while she's missed Iain, she's made a happy life without him. But all that is put at risk when Iain arrives on the Isle of Synne, demanding a divorce. Despite their long separation, the affection and attraction between them still burn strong. But with so much hurt and betrayal simmering as well, can they possibly find their way back to each other?

Meet your next favorite book with @ReadForeverPub on TikTok

Find more great reads on Instagram with @ReadForeverPub

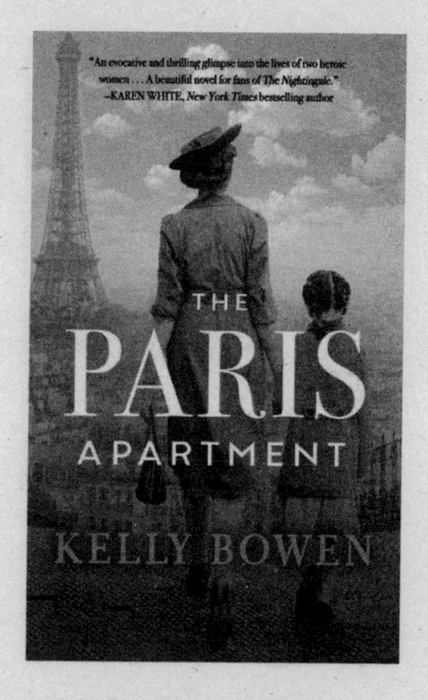

THE PARIS APARTMENT
by Kelly Bowen

2017, London: When Aurelia Leclaire inherits an opulent Paris apartment, she is shocked to discover her grandmother's secrets—including a treasure trove of famous art and couture gowns.

Paris, 1942: Glamorous Estelle Allard flourishes in a world separate from the hardships of war. But when the Nazis come for her friends, Estelle doesn't hesitate to help those she holds dear, no matter the cost.

Both Estelle and Lia must summon hidden courage as they alter history—and the future of their families—forever.

Follow @ReadForeverPub on X and join the conversation using #ReadForeverPub

WAKE ME MOST WICKEDLY
by Felicia Grossman

To repay his half-brother, Solomon Weiss gladly pursues money and influence—until outcast Hannah Moses saves his life. He's irresistibly drawn to her beauty and wit, but Hannah tells him she's no savior. To care for her sister, she heartlessly hunts criminals for London's underbelly. Which makes Sol far too respectable for her. Only neither can resist their desires—until Hannah discovers a betrayal that will break Sol's heart. Can she convince Sol to trust her? Or will fear and doubt poison their love?